THE TARGETED PAWN

SOME GAMES ARE PLAYED TO A DEADLY END

LOVE THRIVES IN EMMA SPRINGS
BOOK THREE

SALLY BRANDLE

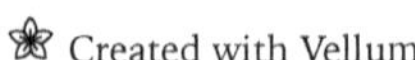 Created with Vellum

To rescue animals waiting patiently for a forever home, offering endless love and devotion. Thank you, Tallulah, Lance, Spock, Maggie, Cheeto and Nacho for being my faithful companions.

ACKNOWLEDGMENTS

Many deserve recognition for their help in creating this book. Michelle McDowell Photography captured the cover shot, with hair and makeup by Sharon Parker.

Beta readers Nada Hughes, Kent and Lynette Allen, Christine of Christine Lamb Studios, and authors Jodi Ashland, Susan McDonough Wachtman, Bethany Douglass, and Genie McFate all offered essential feedback. Neil McDonough provided weapon options. Cultural insight came from sensitivity reader, Thomas Smittle, an Oglala Lakota horseman and spiritual leader who operates a horsemanship/horse training business, Native Horseman. Marie Adamek provided medical tips. My sincere thanks to them all.

Special gratitude to Soul Mate Publishing staff and especially to Sharon Murray Roe, the talented and gifted editor I was privileged to work with on the first edition.

CHAPTER 1

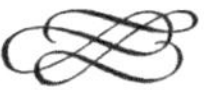

Elon's fingers clenched and unclenched the steering wheel while she waited for the 'all clear.'

Tim should've left for the clinic by now.

She rubbed her arms, staring out the windshield into early dawn. A streetlight shut off. Shadows recessed in the blocks of homes once tied to her life with Tim.

Her palm sought the comfort of the gold locket resting above her thumping heart. Pictures inside showed her pink-cheeked twin toddlers wearing matching sailor suits. Now eighteen, had they grown independent and responsible enough to step out on their own? At thirty-nine, had she?

Her cell dinged, and a stream of incoming messages loaded onto the screen from her observant friend living next door. *Dr. Deceitful just exited your house.*

Not her house anymore, but Tim more than deserved the Dr. Deceitful moniker. She grimaced and continued reading. *His car headed for the gym, same as every Thursday morning. Skinny girlfriend didn't stay overnight. Gotta leave for work.*

Elon let out the breath she'd been holding. *Thanks,* she typed. *We'll talk soon.* She sent the reply and pocketed her cell, waiting another moment to be certain he'd be well on his way to the thoroughfare in the opposite direction. Keeping in first gear, she crept around the corner—just in case. No way she'd chance running into her almost ex or his girlfriend du jour when she collected the divorce paperwork he said he'd left for her in the kitchen yesterday—the price she paid for not providing him with any forwarding address after vacating on her own terms.

She parked in the driveway of the brick rambler she naïvely thought she'd co-owned for nearly twenty years, all the while lovingly tending the miniature roses and lilacs lining the walkway. She sighed. Another wrong assumption to add to Tim's growing list of deceit.

"It's only a house," she reminded herself, and took deep breaths while she walked to the covered entry. She peered at the new rounded doorbell. Her stomach lurched. Legally, Tim couldn't change the locks yet. Legally, she could still be living here. And he'd told her to drop by. Her hand trembled until her fingers swiveled the key and pushed the door open. No familiar artwork or photos hung in the front hall.

On the floor, facing the wall, sat an ornate carved frame she recognized as holding the beaded angel on black velvet stitched by her grandmother. Stacked alongside it were the recent high school graduation pictures of the twins. After Tim dropped the divorce bomb, he'd softened the blow by giving her carte blanche on removing anything sentimental, and she'd missed important pieces.

She lifted the precious links to her past into her arms, stalked out to the car, and secured them behind her seat. Tim's twenty-something mistress probably preferred framed emojis hanging in the entry. Her steps slowed as she headed back inside, realizing she had one more chance to remove her possessions from Tim's damn house before she vanished from Seattle.

Tears formed in her eyes when she entered the kitchen. She brushed them aside and leaned over the sink to look out the window that provided the best view of the backyard garden. Her carefully tended herbs and medicinal flowers from her parents' nursery blended with shrubs and stalks bearing fall blooming perennials. If she had a place to plant them, she'd dig a slip of bleeding heart and a few iris rhizomes—Mom had loved the un-bearded, dark purple ones. She squeezed back tears. Nothing except frozen ground in her future.

A manila envelope bearing her name on the label lay on the counter. An attached sticky note in Tim's handwriting gave his blessing to use any luggage she wanted. How generous of him, after she'd packed most of her clothes in apple boxes the prior week. She jammed Tim's envelope into her shoulder bag.

Her puffy winter coat, an essential for Montana, hung on a hook beside the door to the basement. She grabbed it and the old leather jacket she'd used for welding in high school, then pressed her palm into her forehead. *Criminy*. The torch and tools hung on the pegboard over the workbench below.

Not a good idea to appear at a new job ill equipped. Holding the coats against her chest, she stepped onto the first wooden stair. What else had slipped her mind?

The board under her left foot cracked and broke.

"Whoa!" She pitched forward, flailing her arm toward the handrail.

Her right heel barely landed on the following step.

Splintering wood poked into her ankle as another board broke.

Her knees buckled and down she went, bumping and slamming into stairs and handrail posts while careening toward a cement floor with a washer and dryer at the bottom.

Metal banged as her forearm slammed into the edge of

the washer. She landed on her stomach, the jackets cushioning her fall.

She wheezed to catch her breath, pushed a hank of her wavy auburn hair from her eyes, and glanced up at the broken steps near the top of the steep stairs. A minor miracle she'd survived an eight-foot tumble.

Assess the injuries, she remembered from basic medical training.

Both legs and arms moved as she tentatively tested each appendage. She rolled over and pressed tender skin above her wrist.

"Ow." Bruised, not broken—hopefully.

"Stinkin' old house. Tim deserves you." She pushed off the floor and brushed splinters from her tight pants. Maybe they'd busted due to the pounds she'd gained since the divorce bomb dropped.

Not likely. These stairs never groaned or sank under the countless loads of laundry she'd toted over the years. With luck, termites infested the place.

She shook each shoe and scanned the area. On the luggage rack beside the dryer sat several old, hard-sided suitcases and a set of pristine Louis Vuitton bags, monogrammed *TKH*. The arrogant jerk never expected she'd take one of his precious suitcases. His Vuitton duffel bag looked perfectly sized to hold her jackets, dusty helmet, and tools. She loaded them in, left through the outside basement door, and climbed the cement stairs.

The gold-embossed status bag filled the last space in the trunk. After sliding onto the seat, she reset her odometer to zero.

This trip would end when her mileage hit 747—a number she'd previously associated with the namesake airplane of her home turf in Seattle. Today, it denoted the exact miles to

Emma Springs, Montana, and a welding job. Whatever had possessed her to answer the rancher's letter?

Because once upon a time the metal sculptures she'd welded in high school sold well in her parents' garden store, she reminded herself. Her knee-high leaping frogs and flop-eared bunnies had welcomed children to step inside Tim's pediatric clinic. He'd removed them after her parents purchased the last exam table he'd needed.

She should've signed off on Tim's rotten divorce settlement and given him the clinic building. Nope. Her parents would reel in their graves if she did that. Or would they? She glanced at the diamond she wore on her right hand: the beloved heirloom she'd received prematurely due to her parents' deadly boating accident. If she'd only seen the plug in the bottom of their boat was loose, she could've saved them.

But she hadn't. So many ifs in life without the possibility of do-overs. Her fingers tightened on the steering wheel, rehashing the impulsive decision to relocate out of state, ripe for disaster in so many ways. No one should take a job so quickly without meeting their new employer.

Too late now. She took a deep breath. Better to appreciate the fact that Corrin, a legal counselor and concerned new friend, had solved immediate dilemmas by suggesting the welding and cooking job. Regardless, was it ludicrous to think she'd manage the boys' mounting college expenses by herself if the divorce deliberations took more than a couple months?

Damn if she wouldn't try. Pressing the gas pedal, she coaxed the old Mercedes sedan onto the I-90 floating bridge to head east. Lake Washington waves slapped against the cement pilings. In the distance, the Cascade Mountains took shape bit by bit, aided by the late-October sun rising above them.

She glanced at the speedometer and settled into the beige bucket seat, as she'd done since she'd turned sixteen.

Seemed only yesterday her dad tossed her the keys and commanded, "Keep your eyes front and center." He'd been her idol and Mom her cheerleader. What she'd give to ask their advice. Just once more.

They'd approve of an early start and allowing two days to drive to the remote ranch. Not her making the drive alone. But she had no choice. And Corrin had made the same trip to move to Emma Springs a week or so ago, so why was she so tense? She straightened her sunglasses.

A kaleidoscope of colored light flashed in her rearview mirror. Her heart thumped. Must be an accident ahead.

Hopefully no injuries, and thankfully it couldn't be one of her sons. They'd still be asleep in the condo, conked out as only college students manage after late-night studying.

She slowed and hugged the edge of the right lane. The white Washington State Patrol car moved in behind her. Sirens blasted the ugly high-pitched warning tone. The sound reverberated in her brain.

Pulling her over? What'd she done wrong now? She steered onto the first Mercer Island exit, barely a mile from Seattle. Pulsing lights flashed into her car's interior, putting her jitters into hyperdrive as the color intensified the closer they came. Her stomach churned as she parked on the shoulder.

The police car stopped a few yards from her back bumper. The officer remained inside and cut the siren, leaving the lights on the top panel jumping between blue and red.

Her shoulders rounded. Great start to a new life—her first traffic ticket ever. She fished out her license and insurance card, pulled the registration from the glove box, and rolled down the window.

Gravel crunched and another white cruiser with flashing

lights jolted to a stop behind the first one. The pair of officers in blue uniforms got out and approached her door. Two policemen seemed excessive for a traffic violation. Did the second man have his hand resting on his gun?

"Driver's license and registration please, ma'am," the closest one requested.

Her fingers wobbled as she handed them to him. "I thought I signaled when I pulled onto the freeway. I don't speed, my hood shimmies above sixty-two," she squeaked.

"Please remove your glasses." He leaned toward her. "This vehicle was reported stolen this morning."

"Stolen?" Must've been Tim's work. Her heart thudded against her rib cage while she lifted off her sunglasses.

"Yes, ma'am." The officer scanned her face, then returned to his car clutching her documents.

She glanced at the packet on her passenger seat and let out a relieved breath. At their last meeting, Corrin had provided a list of paperwork to amass before she drove to Montana, including the car's title in her name only.

The second officer stepped to the window, his hand resting on his gun holster. "Please keep your hands on the wheel, ma'am," he instructed.

Right. They'd stopped a potential car thief. Keeping her white-knuckled fingers in view, she peered at him. "The envelope on the passenger seat contains the original bill of sale to this Mercedes and the title. Are you okay if I provide proof of ownership? It's my car." Bile rose in her throat. "I'm going through a divorce. My ex is aware Old Gold was a present from my folks, long before we married."

The larger, heavily muscled man leaned closer to the window. "Grab those, and we'll straighten this out." He twisted his lips in a grimace. "Went through an ugly split myself."

Judging by his size and attitude, he'd not been kicked out

of the family house or tolerated a cheating spouse since day two of his marriage. She pushed aside her maps and extracted the documents. "Here you are." She placed them in his outstretched hand. "Thank you for understanding."

He nodded and walked to the first car. Minutes seemed like hours while she waited.

The younger man reappeared. "The vehicle clearly belongs to you. Sorry for any inconvenience." He handed over her paperwork, then surveyed the roadmaps and boxes on the back seat. "You moving?"

"Yes, temporarily." She'd attempted cheerful and failed.

"Good luck and safe travels," he offered.

A barn full of luck wasn't enough unless a miracle happened. "Thank you," she called to his back. A tremor shook her body. *Get a grip. Tim's playing dirty.* She tipped her water bottle and took a long swig. No surprise there.

He'd never change, but her life was about to in a big way.

Both patrol cars drove past her.

A bad omen about her commitment to the rancher Corrin had encountered on a trip to Emma Springs? Accepting his job offer through written correspondence seemed outright crazy. Her two-hour refresher welding practice didn't count for squat when she hadn't lifted a torch in twenty years.

Yup, she'd need a miracle or two. She glanced in her side mirror. Somewhere out there, Seattle's iconic Space Needle rose between buildings on the west side of Lake Washington. She'd fallen for Tim when he'd taken her to the revolving Eye of the Needle Restaurant before his high school prom, using money he'd bummed from her dad—the first hint of things to come.

Leaving all the Dr. Deceitful memories in Seattle seemed wise. She'd make a fresh start while she and Corrin learned Emma Springs' customs together, fighting Tim from a distance for a fair settlement. She sat straighter. And him reporting her car stolen should be considered harassment.

She frowned at the map and the dot denoting her destination. The small town held some sort of appeal, she reminded herself. Corrin's friend, Miranda, also loved the community enough to want to live there after her recent marriage. Elon pushed the clutch, shifted, and smoothly accelerated onto the freeway.

On a bright note, her new boss didn't use email. Probably some old codger with bad eyesight, which would be a welcome break after Tim's microscopic scrutiny. This good-paying job offering free room and board solved two immediate problems.

If she got canned, Tim would tighten the purse strings enough to choke her into submission. Legally. Failing her parents and her boys this time? Not an option.

Tim glanced at quiet neighboring houses, confirming no one remained home at this hour of the afternoon, per usual. The phone app connected to the new doorbell security system proved invaluable to his plan.

Unfortunately, it had shown Elon leaving in her car, proving his strategy hadn't waylaid her. He pulled the trash bin from the curb onto his driveway, rolled it to the side of his garage, and lifted the top. *Empty.* His shoulders relaxed. A landfill now held the foxglove plant and busted stair risers he'd disposed of earlier.

He grabbed supplies from the new BMW he'd just bought for Jasmine. After setting the blooming chrysanthemum plant in the back yard, he took the outside steps to the basement and stuck the key in the lock. "Old piece of crap," he muttered, and jimmied it while keeping the hardware store sack tucked under his arm. If he'd measured correctly, the replacements would fit.

His fingers found the switch for the overhead light. A suitcase stuck out from a row of assorted travel gear. He kicked it backward and stopped in front of his new leather luggage.

No Vuitton duffel? Skin under his eye twitched. The nerve of tubby, disheveled Elon taking that piece. The camera showed her jogging with a bag to her car, not even limping after falling through the boards. Her paunch must've cushioned her. He turned and grimaced at the staircase, then walked past a shelf holding old yearbooks.

One of them featured photos of him as high school valedictorian and captain of the football team. The poor kid who'd surprised them all. He squared his shoulders. Hard work accounted for everything: extra hours on the gridiron, and endless studying.

The payoffs from his adult efforts in medicine brightened his future. Hospital bed shortages plagued Seattle, and he'd be the latest hero when his plans for the enlarged medical facility hit the news. If conflicts surrounding his clinic ownership arose in the divorce, he'd take any action against Elon to gain control.

He unclenched his fist and removed a cordless drill from the pegboard above the workbench. Empty hooks and an open space to the left caught his eye. He cocked his head and pictured a missing curve-handled wire brush, pliers, and an odd shaped black wrench.

Elon's old crap. There'd been something else, something large.

The timer on his phone sounded. Forty minutes until Jasmine stopped by after her Pilates class, wearing only leggings and a sports bra. Nothing jiggled on her body. She'd flip when she saw her four-wheeled present—motivation for her to move the remainder of her belongings into the house. She'd look stellar driving the crystal white BMW—the yin to the yang of his sleek black Porsche.

His fingers tightened on the handful of screws he'd scooped up. Planning ensured they'd have the perfect life together. He knelt below the lowest broken stair and removed all traces of the altered boards, then fitted on the new risers. After adjusting the safety glasses over his eyes, he screwed the new ones in place.

The lenses fogged up. He turned his head to the pegboard and wiped the clear plastic. *Of course.* Elon must've taken her old helmet and antiquated welding tools.

And he knew where she'd headed. The Mercedes mechanic he'd questioned regarding her car's repair charge provided a full accounting of how he'd gotten her old jalopy ready for a seven-hundred-forty-seven-mile road trip to Montana. Nothing beat German accuracy.

If she'd taken the tools, she must plan to support herself by welding. *Another glitch.* The letter of reference he'd offered on the medical employment site's 'people you should hire' section needed to be removed. After she'd spent ten years pretending to help in his clinic, logically she'd apply in that field, not shop her outdated skills. He clenched his jaw. Elon didn't have the brains to make logical decisions.

His fingers steadied the next screw in place. The drill bit missed its head and hit the wood. He tried again. *Damn blind spot.* If his vision continued deteriorating, he'd lose the chance to oversee surgeons in the new hospital.

No, he'd worked too hard. He swung his head from side to side, relieving tight neck muscles. Fact was, Elon's rusty, welded garden art from high school looked juvenile at best. She'd crash and burn the first day on a job requiring stamina.

The drill motor echoed in the empty basement until the last screw disappeared into wood. He switched to work boots and scuffed wear marks on the new stairs, then collected each tiny splinter scattered on the basement floor and swept the cement clean.

Things didn't always play out as expected. The creaky door banged shut behind him. There were ways to find out precisely where she'd run to, possibly from the police, he concluded, and climbed the steps leading into the back yard. He threw the wood scraps into the empty space created by the toxic foxglove he'd removed, then stuck in the chrysanthemum, and patted dirt around the base.

Not a leaf out of place. He rocked back on his heels. Nothing beat nature's poison. A smile came to his lips as he recalled how many times he'd smelled her herbal concoction in her stinky commuter mug.

Too bad if she lost control of her precious car and the police found her dead.

Four hundred miles and twenty-four hours between her and Tim wasn't enough. Elon checked her rearview mirror. Not good she'd overslept at the motel in Eastern Idaho, but she'd be safely in Montana for a late breakfast.

She lifted the travel mug of tea she'd brewed in the motel room, inhaling the scent from her stash of Mom's recipe for a mind-clearing herbal remedy. Eighty-mile gusts couldn't blow through her brain and dispel today's double shot of doubt.

The spicy aroma intensified while her mouth drew in the warm liquid, then bitterness assaulted her taste buds. Her eyes shot around the interior of the old car, not locating a place to spit. She forced a swallow and returned the mug to the cup holder. One of the kids must've used it for chocolate milk or a smoothie and put it away dirty. Cleanliness wasn't imperative to nineteen-year-old boys. The foul aftertaste coated her tongue. Breath mints, next stop, she decided, and drove another half hour through farmland backed by stands of trees.

A tricycle bell dinged from her phone in the dash holder. She grinned. Jeremy's tone, technically her first born. "Hey kiddo, what's up?"

"Wanted to see how you're doing. Hope Old Gold's not tarnished," he teased.

"Car's running great, thanks to Hans and Mastercard. Anything else?"

"Yeah. I need to buy another textbook. As of an hour ago, Dr. Deceitful cut off our credit card."

The jerk. Tim deserved the neighbor's nickname, but she shouldn't have told the kids. "Did you speak to your father directly?"

"He didn't answer his phone, so I biked to our house. I mean his house. A new Beemer sat in the drive. His latest ho answered the door with a smirk on her scrawny face and a key fob in her hands. She looks like the poster child for a feed the starving children campaign."

Elon squeezed the worn shifter knob. The ink hadn't dried on the petition for divorce papers and the latest fling occupied the only home her boys ever lived in. "Jeremy, don't call her names."

"Call 'em as I see 'em," he snapped. "You should be driving the Beemer."

Tim's newest toothpick could have him, the car, and the house. If her kids had chosen to live at home and not in her folks' old condo, she would be their new roommate. Thank the stars the condo was located closer to the University of Washington campus. Her arms felt like lead weights. "We don't know what your father told the young woman, so don't judge her."

"Regardless of Scrawny's possible, ah, profession, you

need to quit overlooking our paternal unit's dark side. Brandon told me you fell. We're betting he messed up the basement stairs, that's why you crash-landed. You could've broken your neck. The last few months, he's grown colder, if that's possible. Did he know you planned to grab stuff at the house before you left town yesterday?"

Her pulse spiked. *Tim weakened the boards. No. Jeremy was the dramatic twin.* "He'd left paperwork for me." She took deep breaths. "I'm not going to jump to conclusions. You shouldn't either, he's your father. Doctors swear an oath to save people, not commit murder."

"Wake up, Mom. He must've figured you'd go downstairs."

Not the time to mention Tim's note inviting her to grab a suitcase in the basement. In an emergency, they might need to contact him. "It's an old house with rotted stairs. I should've noticed them." She grabbed the tea and took a slug without thinking, winced at the flavor, and wedged the mug out of sight between two bags on the floorboard. "Brandon and I took those stairs multiple times before we moved out to start at the UW. No creaks or issues. We think he'll track you to your new job out of spite. Try to hamstring you."

What a screwed-up life: when her own children thought their father capable of harming her, no matter how crappy a parent he'd been. Besides, greed seemed a more plausible reason for Tim to want her to remain in Seattle, broken limbs or not. She'd tell Corrin, to add potential ammo to her lawyer arsenal. *Wait, what had Jeremy just said? Tim might track her?* "I didn't leave a forwarding address, so he can't find me."

"Your cell can. Soon as you're able, stick a paperclip in the little drawer on the side of your phone to remove the SIM card holding your contacts, then smash it. Promise?"

Of course, she hadn't thought of a tracking app. She slumped into the seat. "I promise. He'll drop us from his calling plan anyway. If you need me, check the emergency list on the refrigerator door. I left the ranch's phone number. Should arrive there this afternoon. Wish me luck."

"You'll do fine melting iron. When we've screwed up, your mom-glower burned us a few times," Jeremy joked. "Seriously. You can do anything you put your mind to. Words you taught us. And we'll work part-time."

Warmth filled her. Confident young men had replaced her dyslexic and bullied little boys. "Taking a job on campus may be in your future. Not yet though. You guys are my pride and joy. Don't ever forget."

"We won't. I better finish the paper for my three o'clock freshman English torture session. Jeeze, I hate that class."

Damn Tim for dragging the twins into his ugly exodus from their marriage when they needed to concentrate on college. "You're a born storyteller. Now you'll learn how to craft your tales into print. Don't worry about me. Love—" The cell signal died. "You both," she whispered, and pressed her fingers onto the etched grooves in the locket.

The challenges of raising children flowed in and out like tides. How much did Jeremy's book cost? Regardless, she needed the job to pay these kinds of expenses and bank money for their winter quarter. Just in case.

Her jaw clenched. A new BMW costs as much as two years expenses at the UW. If Tim really bought the car for his latest mistress, she'd love to roll it over his feet. The pounding in her chest intensified. Boxes in the back seat rattled when the tires hit the centerline rumble strip.

She corrected the steering and slowed the car, preparing to pull over. *Don't let anger at Tim cause an accident.* Deep breaths cleared her head and steadied her hands again. Her brain kept mulling over Jeremy's assumptions about his dad's capabilities.

History didn't lie. Twenty years ago, Tim persuaded her

father into purchasing the house as a surprise to her to celebrate their engagement, then duped the closing agent to list only his name on the title. And she'd been clueless until last week.

The bad taste from the tea lingered in her mouth, intensifying the urge to vomit. Or Tim's deceit made her physically sick. How naïve she'd been—letting her high school's prom king trick her from the start. He'd preyed on an insecure sophomore, and she'd fallen for his fake lines as he weaseled his way into her life.

Her spine stiffened. No more lying down for Dr. Tim Hardy to stomp on her in his custom-made Italian loafers, on his way out the door to a hotel rendezvous. She'd shielded young Jeremy and Brandon from Tim's indifference to them, now she'd fight him for every nickel.

But first, she needed gas. Thank goodness Corrin had also suggested carrying cash.

She filled the tank, bought munchies, and walked out into sunny fall weather, biting into a sweet snack cake. Eggs and bacon took too long, and fake frosting and the orange juice diminished the icky feeling of sandpaper in her throat.

Her eyes dropped to her worn tires—even after the scolding by her mechanic, buying replacements came after Jeremy's book and a burner phone.

Getting a job in order to hold out for half the value of Tim's medical practice in the divorce had seemed a great idea a few days ago, before the stairs mishap and the ticket. How dirty would Tim play?

Give it a rest. Jeremy's worries equaled nothing more than teenage dramatics. Tim possessed no interest in tracking her, she reasoned, and got in her car. She adjusted the rearview mirror, and her sleeve fell to her elbow, exposing the ugly bruise from the fall.

~

Fractured plans grated on Tim worse than an office full of babies needing surgery with no available hospital space. He stuck his phone in his pocket, locked his clinic office, and left through the back door.

Elon's spotty cell signal hadn't returned for an hour since she'd driven farther east this morning, and now he'd delayed two scheduled patient checks. No leisurely lunch today.

Only a stupid, stubborn, lard brain would've fled the state.

Getting rid of her should've been easy. He walked to his parking space. Sliding into his Porsche, he drove the familiar route to Tacoma Children's Hospital.

The faint scent of Jasmine's flowery perfume on the scarf she'd left on the seat made him smile. He'd soon spend his life with the right woman by his side. Years of sacrifice wouldn't be derailed by an old car piloted by a worthless haus frau.

He patted his blazer's chest pocket holding the Hawaiian vacation brochure, picturing in his mind the lithe figure of a bikini-clad Jasmine. They'd be celebrating by this time next month.

Tapping the gas pedal, he flew through a yellow light and turned into the familiar lot. The hospital cast a shadow onto parking spaces reserved for doctors. He wheeled into the last empty one and climbed out.

Thoughts of desperate mothers expecting immediate help increased his steps. Once his new building went up, he'd oversee a team of surgeons ready to help kids in a state-of-the-art facility. After clipping on his hospital ID badge, he refreshed his phone screen.

No blasted tracer signal meant the time had arrived to initiate procedure mode. He clicked on his phone's note app and quickly tapped a plan. *Check if the stolen car report went out of state. Reschedule appointments for potential Montana trip.* He stopped when the screen became blurry and closed his eyes, anticipating his impaired retinas to flash the awful shimmering lights.

The kaleidoscope began. *Fate be damned.* He'd worked hard to provide for Elon and the offspring she'd wanted— and he'd sure as hell earned his dream life without her dead weight dragging him under.

E lon's Mercedes crested another rise in Lord-only-knew where Montana. She adjusted the sun visor to view the first sign of human existence in over an hour. The cherry red pickup ahead slowed to a crawl in the valley below.

A silver silhouette of a reclining nude woman decorated one black mud flap; the other side advertised BABE TRADER written in shiny chrome. The truck's passenger door opened. A bald guy leaned out and tossed a live animal as if it were trash.

Elon gasped. A dog with its legs braced for impact landed on scraggly tufts of grass.

Tires squealed, and the truck sped off.

"Scumbags!" Her pulse spiked, every impulse screaming to give chase and ram decency into the creeps. Instead, she stomped on the clutch and brake while her hand shifted.

Her focus moved to the poor dog. The hollow place in her heart knew exactly how the animal felt—chucked out after tolerating disrespect for too long.

The black and white ball of matted fur hunkered near the ragged edge of the road.

Border collie? She steered to the shoulder and parked. Her fingers shook while she shifted her suitcase in the trunk to locate the emergency blanket and a granola bar. Sweet aromas wafted in the clean air from the unwrapped peanut butter snack.

The cringing dog raised its nose. A silver choke chain jingled on its shaking body.

"It's going to be all right," Elon whispered. "I got thrown out, too." She scowled, picturing Tim waving his single owner deed to the house in her face. "Come on, pup."

The dog took a tentative step, stopped, and tucked her tail, as if expecting a kick.

"You're safe with me." She pitched the snack bar between the dog's front paws. "The way you flew out of that truck brought to mind a furry, fallen angel."

The dog's chocolatey brown eyes studied Elon's face before it snatched the granola bar and swallowed it in a single gulp.

She took slow steps to within a couple feet of the quivering animal. "If you're hurt, I'll find a vet." Beyond the dog stretched a horizon dotted by pine trees and sloping foothills shaded by fluffy, cotton shaped clouds. Brown fall grassland stretched endlessly ahead, blemished only by snaking blacktop. Too bad life's circumstances wouldn't allow pooch or savior to enjoy the beauty right now.

"I'm going to carry you to the car and pray you're not injured." Elon gradually approached the dog, draped the blanket over its back, and lifted. "Easy now, little angel." The animal quieted in her arms. "You don't weigh much for your size. Didn't those thugs feed you?"

Inside the car, the dog slunk against the bucket seat, one speckled paw gripping the leather cushion.

"May I call you Angel?" she asked quietly and patted the seat. "You can lie down, Angel."

The dog dropped to a tense crouch.

Curses on the men who'd do this to an innocent animal,

and curses on Tim! She grabbed her phone from the console, bent a paperclip, and removed the tiny SIM card, as Jeremy had instructed. Her pulse quickened as she gently shut the door and stepped to the back bumper. She raised her hand over her head and chucked the cell to the ground.

The case crashed against gravel. Field crickets stopped chirping.

"Trace that, Tim Hardy," she announced, and stomped her heel onto the screen, cracking the glass. Sun glared off the shiny pieces. She pulled a tissue from her pocket, collected the shards, and dropped it in the corner of the trunk. Her eyes caught sight of her wedding band. Should she pitch the meaningless symbol?

She slid the plain silver ring to her knuckle, then stopped and moved it back in place. As much as she despised Tim, she'd decided to keep it on to prove to the boys she took vows seriously, even though his view of marriage equaled access to her parents' money. Also, wearing it might continue to ward off unwanted advances. Once burned, twice wary.

Angel raised her head when she climbed inside. "Probably should've waited until we found the ranch. Ah well, service is spotty here, and severing another connection to Tim felt great. Not like he'd ever care where I went." A niggling suspicion told her he did.

She placed her hand next to the dog's grubby outstretched foot and stroked until no toenails dug into the seat. "We'll be at our new home soon."

Angel's warm doggy tongue licked the top of Elon's hand, easing nerves rattled to brittle by events of the last weeks. Her teary eyes met the pup's timid dark ones, and a bond of undeserved humiliation passed between them.

"We're both due for a fresh start on a farm." The Mercedes' engine hummed to life after she twisted her key.

Not a pickup or hay-hauler appeared on the two-lane highway.

Quick glances in the rearview mirror helped her fight the creepy sensation that she wasn't alone while the car covered the last fifty miles. Still, fine hair rose on her forearms.

"I see our landmark," her hand trembled, downshifting.

Angel tilted her head, one black ear cocked and the other flopped at an angle.

"It's an old stove my employer described in his letter. Those two 'C's welded side by side on the warming shelf stand for Calderon Cattle."

The skills she'd learned to create metal sculptures in high school were rusty at best. And basic. And lifting broken machinery took strength. "Saints preserve us."

Her hands stuck to the wheel as she turned onto the dusty lane, passing a mailbox welded to one end of the boxy cast iron antique.

Baking and cooking might save her. Years ago, her grandma used a similar wood burning stove at their cabin to bake the best bread on earth. Elon had first learned cooking secrets at her side. Memories of her loving parents and grandparents had forged to steel in her brain. Thoughts of their harmonious marriages had kept her trying to please Tim after she'd discovered his infidelity.

Nothing had dazzled him, but fresh makeup never hurt during a first impression. Throwing the car in neutral, and stepping on the brake, she fished out blush and lipstick and applied a liberal dose.

Her hand hesitated before she shifted into first. Quit stalling, she scolded herself and stepped on the gas. At a curve, she veered left in time to dodge a branch hanging from the last tree on the hill.

Below sat a rambling log house, a sizable barn, and a square building attached to a carport capable of holding a couple of tall RVs. The structures sat adjacent to an open field. Cattle grazed in the background.

Her decades-old car, engineered for the autobahn, bumped on rutted gravel leading down a gentle slope. She parked at the edge of a large corral, beside a mud-splattered white truck. *Edward Bell, DVM* stood out in black letters on the cab door. Her fingers relaxed.

"Stay here, Angel." She patted the dog and lowered the windows. Dust surrounded her feet as she approached an assortment of men outside a wooden corral, standing with their backs to her. Not a Stetson or baseball cap swiveled her way. All heads faced the activity in the corral.

She stood on tiptoes. On the other side of the split rail fence, a mountain-sized bull lay flopped on the ground, a wide canvas sling around his belly. Its dusty head was cradled by a broad-shouldered man. His cowboy hat topped jet-black hair and a rugged, handsome face, right down to the square jaw and chiseled cheeks.

It was a scene straight out of a Levi's ad—the boot cut style. She blinked and noticed a gray-haired man wearing a dark blue jumpsuit crouched over the animal's hind leg. A stethoscope dangled from his chest pocket. He held a needled syringe in one hand, balanced a probe in the other, and used his pinky to adjust settings on a portable machine sitting near his feet.

Elon glanced at the blurry screen image, wiped her palms on her jeans, and stepped closer to the onlookers. "I may be able to help adjust the image for clarity," she offered quietly.

The guy ahead of her flinched and turned to face her. "Hey, there's a gal here who says she can help," he shouted.

Grubby male faces jerked around. A ruddy-faced younger man looked owl-eyed surprised.

"Might be able to help," she corrected in a shaky voice. "I've only assisted with ultrasound images of babies."

The man in the jumpsuit raised his head. "Bones are bones, Miss. To a doctor or a veterinarian." He waved the probe and threw her a relieved smile. "Come on in. I'd appreciate an extra pair of experienced hands."

Pungent diesel and manure scents radiated from nearby blue jeans and Carhartts.

"Excuse me," she said, then turned sideways and shuffled between two men.

A stocky guy in greasy, blue-striped bib overalls swiveled his barrel chest and gave her the once over. A low wolf-whistle pierced the air. "Nice ass . . . istant, Doc."

Snickers came from the group until the cowboy holding the bull's head shot them a glare fierce enough to send a sane person running for cover.

The foul-mouthed brute in bibs kept staring. Heat rose to her face. She'd had it up to her hairline with men—doctors, lawyers, and creeps in red pickups.

"Clear a path, boys." Beads of perspiration lined the vet's wrinkled brow. "A doctor's office you say?"

"Correct. I know an ultrasound from ultra-crude." She tugged the back of her wrinkled, crimson-colored blouse over her butt and wiggled through the gap in the wooden fence rails. Barely.

"I appreciate you already." The vet raised the syringe. "Serum I'm injecting needs to flow precisely into the fracture above the bull's fetlock."

"Not familiar with a fetlock. Let's see if we can clarify the picture." She bent over the machine and adjusted two dials until a clear image appeared.

"Yes, that's it. Perfect." The vet nodded. His eyes remained on the monitor while he moved the probe. "Now, I can administer the BoneGlu." He poked into the cow's hide and pushed the plunger of the fist-sized syringe. The screen displayed liquid oozing into a bone break.

The doctor removed the long needle and wiped the patch of shaved hide. "You had excellent timing, Miss. Next, I'll splint and wrap the area." He threw a two-fingered salute to the cowboy kneeling at the front end of the animal. "Rane, you can relax."

Rane, as in Rane Calderon? No way! Elon swallowed a groan. Tall, dark, and deadly described her new boss. And he had to be within a couple years of her age.

Rane gently patted the sleeping bull's head. "Thanks, Ed. Tomo deserves a fighting chance. Glad the BoneGlu inventor sourced and overnighted enough. I'll tell him how it works on a two thousand-pound patient."

The veterinarian tipped the control pad of the machine and snapped it shut. "Good idea. And a huge thanks to your guest. Watch for signs Tomo's waking from the sedative in thirty minutes."

"Got it." Rane's attention shifted to Elon. "To whom do I owe gratitude?" Narrowed eyes pierced into her—cold, confident, and demanding an answer.

She'd saved the day, so why'd his glare mimic Tim's perennial disdain? "I'm Elon, the welder and cook you hired last week."

A chorus of chuckles and guffaws erupted from the men. "And I bet she isn't kidding, boss," one of them spouted.

Not hardly. Elon wiggled back between the boards and spanked dust from her new pair of stretchy jeans, doing their best to chafe her legs.

Rane stood up, towering at least six foot three. He pressed his lips into a sour line and let his gaze rest momentarily on her bust. "Elon isn't a woman's name," he stated.

Murmurs stopped. Men leaning on the fence backed away, creating clouds of sifted earth.

Elon brushed off the front of her loose shirt. Not enough miles on the map to drive away from nasty confrontations.

Wasn't the first time she'd defended her name, wouldn't be the last. "I guess my great-grandmother didn't abide by that rule." She met his dark, russet-colored eyes. "This Elon isn't related to any muskrats or electric cars."

Rane issued a snort, put his hands on the top rail, and vaulted to her side. He threw off an intimidating shadow. "I'm Rane Calderon, owner of this spread," he announced, as if she hadn't realized that disturbing fact. "We'll settle this in the kitchen." He stood straight backed: the teacher pointing to the dunce chair, and indicated the house with his thumb. "Thanks for assisting Ed," he murmured.

How gracious of him. Well, Angel rated higher than an irritated bull coddler. "You're welcome." She flashed her brightest smile. "I'd appreciate a moment with the veterinarian before we meet, Mr. Calderon."

"Make it quick." Rane's stomping broke the pin-drop quiet as he headed toward a wraparound porch.

In the movies, cattle ranches always kept dogs. No wagging tails or doghouse caught her eye. She approached the vet, who'd begun stashing his medical equipment in the bed of his truck. "If you have time, Dr. Bell, I need a tiny favor."

The vet turned. "Please, call me Ed." Smile lines etched his cheeks. "For all the mechanical expertise around here, you're a lifesaver. In this instance, a prized Wagyu bull saver."

"Wagyu? That beef costs mega bucks in Seattle. Glad I could assist."

The doctor's grin welcomed her. "Rane's intent on getting his beef into some fancy restaurant chain. Might not be obvious, but we're both mighty pleased you arrived. How can an old country vet help?"

"Elon Hardy, mail-order welder and rescuer of a dog thrown out of a truck." She stuck out her hand and matched

Ed's firm handshake. "I hope the pup didn't break any bones."

"Let's have a look." He pulled a supply box to the tailgate and laid out a disposable mat.

"Thank you for taking the time to check." Elon led him to her formerly champagne-colored Mercedes, now dusty brown.

"Of course." He slowed by her bumper. "Washington plates. I don't imagine Rane placed an ad in a Seattle newspaper."

"He approached a friend of mine, Corrin, while she attended a wedding in Emma Springs. She recently moved here."

"Ah, charming Corrin, the lawyer Doc Kyle's dating and rescuer of my grandson. We felt so blessed she fit into the old mineshaft hole and could pull little Bobby to safety. She's one brave lady."

Elon nodded. "I'll ask Corrin to tell me the rescue story. When she alerted me to this job opening, she mentioned Mr. Calderon appeared desperate for help." Elon pulled her passenger door open.

"Rane's currently lacking more than a welder, but he's clueless as to what his life's missing." Ed stepped around her.

Manners topped the bull handler's list of inadequacies in her book. She patted the dog and stepped back.

Angel spotted Ed and cowered in the seat.

"It's okay, he won't hurt you," Elon used her special tone for calming her own boys and many a tearful child in Tim's waiting room.

"Good dog," Ed cooed.

Angel inched her black nose to his hand.

"The doctors here sound casual in respect to professional titles. My almost ex-husband corrected patients who called him Doctor Tim and not Doctor Hardy."

"I prefer Ed." He straightened. "My clients are my friends. When you do your best, the accolades aren't necessary."

Tim could benefit from a ten-gallon dose of Ed's philosophy. "I hope they appreciate your knowledge. I've never heard of glue for bone fractures."

"Sharing cutting-edge techniques keeps our little community functioning smoothly. Doc Kyle noticed the rollout of the glue in an AMA piece, heard about Tomo, and enlisted the inventor to help wrangle a vial of the animal version. Lucky break, so to speak."

"Networking at its finest," she said.

"It takes a village to mend a bull." He chuckled and lifted Angel off the seat. "Here we go, little cast off." Angel whimpered as the vet carried her to his truck.

"I'm not leaving you." Elon stroked the dog's head. "Is she a Border collie?"

Ed unwrapped the blanket and moved each limb. "I'd guess a young, female Australian shepherd and collie mix." His fingers gently probed her ribs. "Likely bruised, probably didn't break anything."

"Thank you for examining her. It removes one worry from my plate." Elon eased a bramble from long strands of white hair on Angel's hind leg.

"Glad you found her before nightfall when predators hunt. If you're looking to turn her in, the nearest animal shelter's in Three Falls." Ed snapped his medical case shut. "Adoptions are less likely on full grown dogs."

"Angel and I will stick together, no matter what." She fingered the choke chain. "Oh criminy. The guys who tossed her out might have stolen her, and a family may be frantic."

"I'll check for a chip." He took out a handheld scanner and ran it over her neck. "Not finding one. I'll post a sign at my office and inform the shelter. Call me immediately if she seems lethargic or limps."

"Of course."

He placed a business card in her hand. "Bring her in next week and we'll do a workup and shots. It'll be my payment for your skills on the ultrasound." He leaned in close to her ear. "Don't be afraid of Rane, he's under a lot of pressure from his ranch and should've been over the Shelly incident years ago."

Shelly? A bit more than she needed to know concerning her employer. "Thanks for your insight."

"Give Rane a chance and you'll see his big heart. It's a burned and broken one, but big just the same."

"I'll remember that. I'd better hustle inside," she said, and tucked his card in her pocket.

Ed moved the dog back to her car seat and closed the door. "You'll do fine, Elon." He tapped a finger on his temple. "You're smart. Don't be afraid to ask for help if you're questioning something."

The understatement of the decade. "Will do. Thanks." She waved goodbye.

Even taking calculated steps, her feet lost the battle of retaining any white on the only tennis shoes she'd brought. Her glance flicked to the carport holding a welder. Beside it sat a six-foot by ten-foot trailer. One of the support pieces attaching the box to the hitch lay on the ground.

At the steps to the porch, she grasped a solid handrail, willing her body to climb four stairs. Her eyes darted to where the vet's truck left a dusty trail heading out.

Starting fresh meant no more intimidation. She squared her shoulders and rapped on the sturdy doorframe. The partially open door provided a view into a large living room bathed in sunlight. A fireplace dominated one wall. Yellow stones flecked by reddish veins surrounded a huge hearth. A golden-colored oak desk sat in a far corner and assorted over-stuffed chairs, an ugly seat made partially of antlers, and a well-worn brown leather couch filled in some of the remaining space.

"I'm in the kitchen," Rane's deep voice announced.

She walked inside. To the right of the entry lay a dining area holding a roughhewn wooden trestle table capable of seating at least twelve. Rane sat in the next room, his long legs stretched under a battered, pale green Formica table.

Her eyes adjusted to the dim interior. She entered the kitchen and sidestepped his cowboy boots. "May I turn on a light?"

"Switch to your left."

Elon flicked on an overhead fixture. The bulb struggled to illuminate the room.

His hands lay folded on a stack of paperwork, topped by her typed reply letter. No weak light or broad chest could hide dirty dishes stacked precariously on the counter behind him, even while he projected the image of a proud conqueror guarding a pillage pile.

No one would fight him for his plunder.

"Have a seat. Coffee?" His forced attempt at civility broke the silence.

"Please." Elon lifted a stack of dog-eared John Deere manuals from the chair opposite him and slid onto cold green vinyl that pierced through her thin jeans.

Rane pulled a full mug from the counter and shoved it to her side of the table. The only warmth in the room flowed to her fingers when she clutched the sturdy cup.

"I employ seven men on my ranch and in my farm equipment repair shop. Women and machinery don't mix." His scowl implied he'd presented ample reason to send her packing. She wasn't a bull he could boss. Play on his weakness, she told herself and sunk against the padded vinyl back on the '50s-style chrome chair. A sharp-edged crack pierced into her spine. "I saw a boxy trailer with a broken hitch."

"That's a manure spreader."

Bad start at farm jargon, hopefully the spreader arrived empty. "You need a welder to make it functional."

"A male welder."

What she'd give to pound her fist into a mound of bread dough to dissipate growing irritation.

He stretched his broad chest as if he'd won the battle. *Not with her kids' future at risk.* She forced a businesslike demeanor. "I included contact numbers on the application letter for questions concerning my credentials." She'd provided the condo's landline and her cell number.

"Our phones work half the time, and I don't chitchat." He raised an eyebrow and glared at her, expecting a retort.

She who says the least, wins. Especially when annoyed.

They remained in a polite version of a stare down until Rane's eyes traced a slow path from her top button to the one at her waist, then back to meet her gaze. "I've purposely never employed females on this spread," he said, in a low, husky tone.

Thought his charming manner too irresistible to the weaker sex? The guy possessed unlimited nerve. Resolve grew from deep in her chest. "Mr. Calderon, I have two sons in college. I'm not interested in anything but employment to support us." She crossed her arms. "I can assure you of that."

"Do you need . . .?" His voice turned leather smooth, like he planned to retract the job offer.

"Due to your location," she interrupted him, "I'll need the on-site lodging you mentioned in your correspondence and access to a bathroom." She stared straight into his hooded eyes.

"Do you need sugar or cream?" He placed his hands on either side of his stacked papers and tilted forward. His eyes bored into her as if determining how hard he'd have to blow to send her tumbling out the door.

Not today. No sending her off bearing a few token dollars for her trouble. She raised her chin. "I take my coffee black. I choose a simple life, Mr. Calderon. Work, payment, repeat."

He glanced at her wedding band. "Your husband's unemployed?"

She snorted. "No, a pediatric surgeon in high demand. I'm in the process of settling my divorce. In the legal sense, I'm still married, but not for long."

His hand shot up, palm facing her. "Don't need details." His voice held a cold edge.

Too much information. Crap. Act nonchalant, she coached herself and put the mug of burnt smelling coffee to her lips, anticipating thick liquid coating her throat and pushing tiny particles of Montana grit into her queasy stomach.

The loose sleeve fell to her elbow, his eyes immediately zeroing in on the exposed purplish lump on her pale skin. She gulped a quick swig, lowered the mug, and dropped her hands to her lap.

"That's an ugly bruise," he said.

She looked away. He'd croak if he saw her hip and ribs. "I misjudged a step. When can I start working?"

"Yeah. About that," he shifted in his chair. His lips became a tight line.

Every muscle in Elon's body froze.

CHAPTER 2

Fired before she started? No, the Bull Boss couldn't do that to her. Elon gripped the underside of the table edge, willing him to give her a trial run. One stinking opportunity to prove she wasn't as worthless as Tim maintained. She bit her lip. There wasn't enough cash to return to Seattle. "I drove here in good faith. Give me a chance, Mr. Calderon."

Rane took a deep breath, then let it out slowly. "You did me a favor helping my bull, so I'll do the same." He folded her letter and rested his fist on it. "Wasn't expecting to accommodate a woman." His glance flicked outside and back to her. "There's an unused bedroom and attached bath down that hall." His face softened for a split second before he flipped his thumb over his shoulder. "You may bunk in my grandma's room. She didn't handle stairs either."

She'd handle him all right. Her fingers relaxed. "Sounds ideal. You have a MIG welder?"

He glanced around the kitchen, as if noticing the mess for the first time. "Yup. Welding can wait until tomorrow. Start by feeding the men at five o'clock. Plenty of grub in the storeroom through the door by the sink."

"I'll fix a hearty meal." She palmed her locket. "I don't have a cell phone. May I call my sons to tell them I arrived?"

"House phone's on my desk in the far corner of the living room. No incoming calls after ten at night, Montana time. Anything else?"

"When do you cut checks?"

"On the fourth and the twenty-eighth." He rifled through the stack and pulled out a photocopied timesheet. "Normally the men hand in hours three days earlier. I can take yours that morning."

"Thank you. I can work through the weekend, if that helps you catch up."

"Good. Other questions?"

Angel needed an advocate. "Just tell me where to park my car and oh . . . I, ah, have a dog."

"Your car's ok where it's parked. Didn't realize you brought a guest," he said, in a voice turned soft as suede.

The calm before the storm? "Hadn't planned to adopt a pet. A jerk tossed her from a truck on the highway an hour ago." She clenched her fist. "I won't abandon Angel. That's what I named her."

His boots scraped the floor as he pulled them in. He rose to his full height. "Angel can bunk inside, or I'll find her a temporary doghouse."

"I won't let her bother you."

"Dogs never do. If she needs kibbles, ask for Fred. He'll find someone headed to town."

The man did have a heart. For the first time today, she smiled. "Thank you. I'll find something to feed her tonight," Elon said.

Rane leaned over her, close enough to show dark stubble on his perfectly sculpted jaw. The guy's black lashes appeared thick as paint brushes. His eyes glowed a deep shade of russet.

Flutters swirled in her belly. She blinked several times and leaned back.

With one fist braced on the papers, his chest stiffened into a shield. "Animals I trust, Ms. Hardy. Women are another story. A month's trial, then we'll talk." He straightened and walked out, leaving a trail of spice-scented annoyance.

The front door slammed shut. Elon flinched.

So much for the misconception of a kindly old rancher. Nope. Her fortyish boss possessed the ability to morph into a hardened commander with one scowl from his squint-eyed, condemning looks.

She fingered the buttons on her blouse. How gracious of him to give her a month's trial run. The divorce might take a year.

Rescuing Angel had helped win him over. They both needed a home until she got the settlement check, and she'd use the pup's plight again if necessary. She removed a crusty saucepot from the sink. Stacking dirty fry pans cleared a space under the faucet to scour a water bowl for her dog.

Stagnant air surrounded her. "Uggh." The place needed an open window and a stiff breeze. A metal ring hung from the middle of the lowered roller shade. Tugging it sent the blind snapping upward. She shoved open the pane of grimy glass on a window that faced her car. Dust particles danced in the filtered sunlight. Outside, the men gathered in the corral around the bull.

She collected Rane's papers, crossed into the living room, and dropped them onto a desk capable of seating six. Angel would think she'd been abandoned again, but first she'd phone her boys.

Brandon didn't have late classes. She punched in his number and smiled to hear his voice. "Hi. Hoped to catch you. Made it to the beautiful ranch. Cowboys and cattle."

"Glad to hear, Mom. Beats deadbeat dads."

She couldn't agree more but wasn't going to bad-mouth Tim. "Did Jeremy tell you the cost of his book?"

"I think he said two-fifty for a stupid, newly minted, print-only book. I'll look for a part time job online tonight."

The shameful practice of overcharging for a college book hadn't ceased. "I'll send him the money next week. I'd prefer you concentrate fully on schoolwork."

"Okay. I'll tell him. Thanks for leaving the freezer full."

"You're welcome. Tuesday's my first payday. It won't be a windfall, but we'll manage. I'm sorry about the divorce drama."

"We're all better off without Dr. Deceitful judging our every move. We think he's gone off the deep end."

"Let's not jump to conclusions. I'll open a bank account tomorrow so I can transfer money to you, okay?"

"Yeah." He cleared his throat. "Please be careful. Did you smash your phone?"

Her eyes teared from pride of their protective instincts and sadness at the reason. "I did. You boys mean the world to me. I'll be back in Seattle soon. Love you."

"Back at you."

Her stalwart Brandon sounded worried. The handset wobbled into the cradle. "Damn you, Tim," she whispered.

Her eyes dropped to her letter. Next to it sat a Montana tax assessor statement. She did a double take on the huge payment. Tim regularly carped about rising property taxes in Seattle. They seemed less exorbitant after viewing Rane's bill for his spread.

Her hand flew to her throat. She'd need an additional eight or nine hundred dollars by October 31st to pay the taxes on the condo her kids occupied. No way Tim would continue footing bills on a unit the boys legally owned, but they couldn't sell until they turned twenty-five.

Brandon and Jeremy living there cost less than the dorms, she reminded herself, and wound her way out of the house. She'd weld till she dropped. Her pace slowed at the corral occupied by her temporary Bull Boss.

"Tomo's half-opened his eyes." Rane rubbed the head of the injured bull. "We need to start," he said to a stoop-shouldered cowboy with hands gnarled like bird claws.

"Sure thing, son." The older man signaled the driver of a boxy tractor carrying a waist high bucket on the front. He drove the rig in and positioned it over the prone bull.

Rane hooked the sling to the underside of the bucket. He tenderly stroked the curled ruff between the animal's short horns and gave a thumbs up sign to the driver. The tractor's arms wobbled, and the heavy bundle rose slowly.

Tomo wiggled his hooves when his body left the ground, then went limp, same as her feet did when she rode the Ferris wheel. If a giant stork flew over, it could swoop in and carry Tomo away.

They moved the swinging animal to a makeshift stall on the outside wall of the barn. "Hold it." Rane raised his hand, and the tractor stopped. "I'll keep him quiet. Fred, hook the sling to the rafter."

The old cowboy grabbed a thick line draped over a roof beam. He snapped its fastener onto the sling. After taking the slack out, he tied the support rope off on a clamp mounted on the barn wall. "Never seen this set up in near sixty years ranching."

The bull's hooves barely touched the pile of straw under its dangling feet.

"My old buddy deserves a chance." Rane signaled the tractor to back out.

Elon stepped closer to a young, ginger-haired cowpoke who was propping one of his dusty boots on the front bumper of her car. Stamped into his tooled leather belt was an E. "How'd the bull break its leg?" Elon asked.

His gray eyes met hers. "Not sure. We found him limping in a field."

"Oh, my. I hope he pulls through."

"Rane will do whatever it takes to save Tomo," he said.

Bulls equaled money. "Of course. I'm Elon. Is the 'E' on your belt for Eric or Edward or Eve?"

He dropped his foot to the ground. "Stands for Emmett. Got work to do, ma'am." He stuck his hands in his pockets and ambled off toward the machine shop. Grinding noises boomed from the opened door.

Elon shook her head. Angel possessed better social skills than this bunch of dirt-encrusted, bull-enamored cowboys now expecting a champagne dinner from a six pack of beer.

She walked to her car and opened the trunk, moved the broken cell pieces into a nearby garbage barrel, then lifted out her suitcase. One chapter of her life ended, and another began.

Hopefully, a short one where Tim became a footnote.

What the hell had he gotten himself into? Near as Rane could tell, about one hundred-fifty pounds of the prettiest, most stubborn, worst kind of female trouble stood beside her dusty car aiming to coax out a frightened dog.

He turned around, aimed a stream of water from the spigot into Tomo's bucket, and forced his eyes out to the rusted body of his first pickup. He'd left it out back to remind him of the ride he'd given Shelly years ago and the ensuing tailspin of his life. Women shouldn't be trusted. He'd learned that lesson after she'd left town. Future messes had been prevented by staying uninvolved.

Until now. His damned thoughts kept returning to Elon. Her cornflower blue eyes, heart-shaped face, and sable brown hair shining like a mink's coat. Nope. None of those would dazzle him and ruin years of hard work—even paired with a body whose sexy-as-hell hourglass figure barely squeezed through fence rails.

Quit dreaming. Circumstances forced her into this job. Her creamy skin had paled further while he'd deliberated in the kitchen on immediately cutting her loose.

The hired men didn't need any distractions. Overflowing water drenched his thigh. "Oh, hell," he muttered. He dumped out a couple inches and hung the water bucket on the wall close to Tomo's head.

Giving Elon a trial run equaled weakness. If he'd been smart, she'd be wheeling her fancy car off his spread. A car that needed a new set of tires. Didn't take a mechanic to see that the worn-down tread needed to be replaced two thousand miles ago.

The sound of metal grinding metal broke the silence.

A few weeks from now, he'd sell the steers and offer higher pay on the welding postings in Three Falls. This time he'd personally interview all candidates. If she could weld, Elon would get a bonus before he sent her home, enough to buy a decent set of snow tires. Meantime, it didn't matter if the boys thought he'd gone soft. She needed money, and he never explained decisions.

Had she called out to him? He pivoted. Nope, but his focus had shot to her like bees spotting fireweed in full bloom.

Elon stood beside her car and scratched the pup between its black ears and spoke softly. She'd probably perfected the soothing voice persuading unknowing men to do her bidding.

The dog stuck to the side of the car.

She planted one hand on her hip and looked from Angel to the house. A bright, beautiful smile came to her ample lips. She pulled the purse from her shoulder and made a leash out of the strap.

He'd give her gumption points for not giving up. Not on the dog or employment. She clearly took the job for the money. Blast, he'd have given her two weeks' pay simply to get her to leave. But for the dog—the pitiful scrap of a dog she'd saved and her helping Tomo.

Damned weakness for strays got him every time. A month's wages might make her solvent enough to weather her problems at home. His fist clenched. The purple lumps on her arm posed ugly questions.

Emmett approached. "I'm heading into town, Rane. Need supplies?"

Rane glanced at Elon. Time to learn if his new hire possessed all sizzle and no steak. "Nope, not a thing."

"Thanks for prodding me to attend vocational college instead of shooting off to backpack in Europe," Emmett said. "I've used a couple techniques from the engine repair class. Maybe I won't be poor forever."

"Even decent mechanics earn mega bucks. I'll continue to cover tuition. Glad you took a beginning welding class. Is it going well?"

"Harder than I thought, but I'm catching on."

"Keep practicing and add as many welding classes as you can to next semester." He removed his hat and ran his fingers through his hair. "You may have started along the wrong path, but you changed direction in time."

"Because you offered me a second chance." Emmett headed to his motorcycle and buckled on a helmet.

His cousin's kid possessed a good heart, and he'd need Emmett's help welding if Elon possessed anything short of a golden arm: excellent techniques and end results. "You've earned your place in my shop. Ride safe." He walked toward the machine shop and glanced into the burn barrel.

Broken pieces of a cell phone lay on top of ashes. Had to be hers. What caused an urbanite to smash a revered gadget? Rane shifted his eyes to the only bump in his smoothly graded road.

The pup stayed plastered against her ankle, tail tucked between her legs. Damned if he hadn't felt the same scared vibe from Elon during parts of their talk in the kitchen.

She led the dog to the lower step leading to the back door and began wrestling her suitcase—a bulging one with the zipper straining to keep the sides shut.

A raincoat hung out a side pocket. Sloppy or she'd packed fast? He'd learn soon enough. A scuffle might've caused her bruise. His eyes flicked to the burn barrel, then back to her.

Abusers of any type topped his lowlife list. Crooks came next. His head swung to face the west gates where they'd tried to steal Tomo. The toe of his boot produced a dusty cloud as he sent a rock flying out of the driveway and onto the grassy field.

The vet's plastic baggie containing shreds of rope removed from Tomo's leg provided positive evidence of rustlers. He'd take them to town first thing tomorrow morning.

Sheriff Riley better find the bastards before he did.

His stomach growled. Considering all the crap on his plate, if Elon failed to cook a decent dinner, he'd pay her two weeks wages and send her packing.

~

Angry, strange men expecting dinner on short notice induced Elon to increase her pace. The heavy suitcase bumped one ankle, while Angel's damp doggy nose bumped the other.

Her stomach churned. Rane stood scowling at the edge of the corral, watching her move with the grace of a drunken elephant. She'd chosen the worst day to wear her only red shirt. If he sprouted hooves and horns, her Bull Boss would be pawing the dirt.

Failure wasn't an option. She tugged the suitcase up the final step and onto the back porch. "Appears to be the servant's entrance."

Hinges on the storage room door squeaked the only greeting she'd hear from this household. She flipped the light switch, and a yellow bulb came to life. Angel scooted inside.

An enormous chest freezer hummed softly on linoleum flooring. Next to it sat an upright freezer. Wooden shelves held a motley assortment of canned tomatoes, bags of rice, and boxes of elbow macaroni—possibly from this century. Tim would die before he'd eat those carbs.

She rubbed her brow, trying to wipe out the vision of another demanding man. This one wore Armani suits and had occupied too much real estate in her brain for the last twenty years. He'd transposed her life from the Le Creuset frying pan into the campfire. At least the rancher gave her an opportunity to succeed. "This storeroom must hold something to feed him and his minions," she whispered.

Angel rested a paw on her shoe.

"Don't worry. My welding skills are questionable, but picky Tim never refused my cooking on the few occasions he made it home for dinner." The empty room swallowed her wavering voice. A battered wall clock showed under three hours to get a praiseworthy meal on the table.

The top shelf held an array of antique Pepsi and Canada Dry wooden crates. No canned meat, and she could trace her initials into the layer of dust on a few tins of pork and beans. She studied the dented lid of the chest freezer. "We'll need pieces of meat thin enough to thaw quickly in water, pup. No microwave in the kitchen." She dug her way to the bottom, shoving aside bulky packages in white butcher paper stamped 'roasts.'

Her fingertips turned white. "Eureka. This one says individually wrapped steaks, and I spotted a giant bag of diced potatoes. Please, oh please, let them be edible."

She yanked the meat free. Her back strained at the weight of the frozen beef—a lot less malleable than the babies she'd cuddled when Tim's nurses relied on her to soothe crying infants. Past tense, past life, she chided herself.

The jagged bone from a steak protruded through paper and poked her forearm. "You and I will share the freezer burned one." She huffed on her fingers. "Should have time to thaw the meat in cold water."

Angel wasn't paying attention. She'd stuck her nose under a bottom shelf holding giant cans of peaches, her tail wagging an alert.

"Hold on." Elon toed out a shriveled mystery lump and a pile of dirt. "Ugh. This place gets doused in cleaner tomorrow." She stomped off her foot. "In the kitchen, Angel. No icky snacks. I'll boil you some rice."

An hour later, the industrial-sized dishwasher began its second cycle after giving up a half pound of dark gunk from its drain. Clean bowls and Montana-sized white ironstone plates sat in neat piles on the counter.

Angel polished off the rice and sat in the corner. Her eyes followed Elon, who hummed and envisioned platters loaded for her first meal. Broiled steaks, fresh rolls, and seasoned roasted potatoes should bring a smile or two. Thanks to Angel, they'd have peach cobbler for dessert.

She lifted the last stack of heavy dinner plates and carried them to the plank table, straight out of a pioneer novel. The tabletop shone. She reached for the ceiling to stretch, mentally giving herself a pat on the back for cleaning the kitchen and dining room.

How many previous generations had sat in this room and rested their feet under the beautifully grained wood? The original occupants might've owned the worn 1914 edition of *Aunt Babette's Cookbook* she'd found in a kitchen drawer, holding handwritten recipes. If the grandmother Rane mentioned had left instructions for sweetening ill-mannered ranchers, she'd follow them step-by-step.

No such luck. The mantle clock struck four. She fingered the dog-eared recipe she'd pulled from the book. Nothing beat fresh-baked, flaky biscuits drizzled in honey, and there'd been a quart jar of the amber nectar in a cabinet. Honey didn't spoil, and she'd had the foresight to bring fresh baking powder, yeast, soda, and a few spices.

She moved to the kitchen, mixed the dough, and cranked the oven knob to four hundred degrees. Her thigh bumped the end of a makeshift grill section wedged between the stove and counter.

Lumps of burnt food clung to greasy iron. She bent her knees and hefted the massive amount of metal onto the commercial six-burner gas stove. If it fit, grilled beef would taste and look better than broiled. The top slid into place. Her muscles strained to leverage the grate into the deep aluminum sink to soak and soften remnants of former meals.

Softening Rane Calderon was another story—one that would contain short chapters and an unhappy ending. Her nervous fingers slid the biscuits into the oven. Tim had been right on one call: she'd gotten out of shape. Her body ached from the tips of her wrinkled fingers to her sore arches.

But she'd prepared a decent meal. Hints of garlic and pepper perfumed the air from the meat's seasoning. All men appreciated a good T-bone.

Loud mooing came from outside. *Criminy*. They probably got a daily ration of steak and eggs for breakfast, judging by the two freezers full of beef. Her head dropped to her chest.

The clock struck five. Elon watched Rane's seven employees jostle for seats at the plank table. Intent faces snuffed the air, resembling hungry coyotes out hunting. Some cast curious glances her way. Four of the men bore coal black hair and bronze-toned skin. Emmett and the burly creep who'd wolf whistled stood out with their stubbled jaws and pale arms. The stoop shouldered man, with a face wrinkled by years in the sun, hung his hat on the coatrack and sat at the far end.

She'd planted herself in an arched opening between the dining room and hall, holding an empty platter against her chest. Family style or buffet? By the clenched forks in boulder-sized fists, the idea of throwing the food on the table and running seemed smartest.

The only chair with arm rests remained vacant, at the end of the table closest to the kitchen. Rane sauntered in and took the empty seat, never glancing her way. His attempt at face washing had missed one streak, slanted across his cheek. He lifted his nose in the air and did an exaggerated sniff. "Seared beef, I think I recognize the scent."

The men guffawed. Her throat went dry. The clumps of burned meat on the grill should've clued her in. Another inept decision.

Might as well hand off the food and roll her suitcase back to the car. She slunk out and spread unfolded napkins inside a rectangular, blue-and-red-painted leather basket she'd rescued from the back of the cupboard. The perfect holder for hot, fluffy biscuits.

Eight pairs of eyes stared at the steam rolling off the heavenly scented rolls she carried. She walked to the closest end of the table and lowered the basket.

Before it landed on the table, Rane grabbed one side of the container, and the black-haired man to his right grabbed the other side.

Elon released her grip and stepped back as they began a tug of war.

"Hey. Easy." Rane grimaced. "That basket was sacred to my grandma," he scolded.

The other man dropped his hand, his eyes wide. "Oh, ah . . . sorry."

Elon froze. *How dumb, of course it was an antique.*

"Ah, just kidding." Rane tipped his chin up and laughed.

The group of men chuckled. The chastised guy grabbed two biscuits and held one to his nose. "Smells delicious." He turned his head and grinned at Elon. "This old hide cleaned up purty good." He passed the container to the man next to him.

Any humor beat no humor. She smiled and then rested her arm on the sideboard. "I admire the painted diamond pattern on the leather. Deerskin?"

"No. Parfleche." Rane quit buttering his biscuit and watched her. "My great-great-grandmother made it from buffalo hide. There are larger ones up in the attic."

"How wonderful to have special heirlooms." she said. "Someone had untied the lid. If I always line it carefully, may I use it occasionally for rolls?"

"Yes." He scanned the dining room. "When you're done, place it on top of the sideboard."

"A treasured keepsake deserves to be seen. I cherish a beaded angel wall hanging my grandmother created."

"Nice." Rane said and chatted with the men while she carried in the bowl of roasted potatoes and the platters of meat. He sat back, one elbow on the armrest, his focus centered on the food.

Her knees quavered. "Red toothpicks denote rare meat, blue for medium." No one acknowledged her comment. "If you need one cooked longer, I can flip it back on the grill." She centered the tray of glistening steaks on the table in front of Rane.

He speared a medium one and sliced into it, rosy pink showing between knife cuts. "This is very well done in these parts. I need a Montana rare one." He thrust his plate toward Elon, the cuts showing a perfectly cooked medium-rare steak.

She rotated the platter and pointed to red toothpicks. Her heart pounded. "The red indicates rare, Mr. Calderon. They're red in the middle."

"Montana rare, Ms. Hardy." Predator eyes, recognizing the smell of fear, leveled at hers. "If you please." His challenge arced in the air—a whiplash just before it snapped flesh from its victim's bones.

This time he wasn't kidding. Bull Boss figured she'd cooked them all. Elon grabbed his plate. "One Montana rare coming up." She vaulted back to the kitchen. Something snapped inside—unleashing frustration of wasted years spent placating Tim and tolerating his disturbing behavior. To get the ingrate through med school, she'd shelved her own ambitions to be a pastry chef.

A potholder cushioned the plate she slammed on the counter. Angel squeaked out a frightened yip.

The frostbitten steak for her and the dog remained

uncooked. Elon twisted the gas knob under the grill to high. She bent, whispering in Angel's ear. "My culinary instructors didn't serve free-range cowboys." She forked the gray, splotched steak onto the sizzling metal, rotated it to char perfect diamond hash marks, flipped it over, repeated the process, and placed it on a clean plate. Chin raised, she carried it to the dining room.

Rane jerked his elbow off the table to avoid the plate she slid in front of him. His eyes rolled to the side—his thick brows etched in surprise.

No wonder. Not even two minutes had passed. He wanted uncooked, seared meat, he'd get it. "Should be Montana rare, Mr. Calderon."

He grunted something unintelligible and sliced into the bloody hunk of beef. Her toe swiveled in the direction of the storeroom holding the luggage she'd never unpack.

Bull Boss got credit for cutting off a large bite. "Plenty rare." He raised a lump on his fork and aimed it at his open mouth. A drop of crimson fell to the white plate.

His workers shoveled in food. Two argued over the last of the twenty-four biscuits.

She averted her eyes from Rane and shuffled back to her sanctuary. "I blew it, Angel. Probably our first and last meal here, hope you enjoy it." She motioned for the dog to sit by her foot.

Angel licked her chops at mouthwatering scents of grilled beef and garlic. Not a word came from the men, only random clinking of forks on plates.

Keeping her back to the doorway, Elon sliced into the tender, rejected steak mottled with white threads. She piled smaller chunks into a chipped, flat bowl. "Good girl, Angel, enjoy your share of the unfit meat."

She rested her hand on the counter, faced the window, and placed a juicy bite in her mouth. The best she'd ever tasted by far. In Seattle this dinner would be paired with a hundred dollar bottle of cabernet.

Scraping chairs and the sound of shuffling feet came from the dining room. The first meal over without a complaint? She chewed slowly and closed her eyes, savoring the rich flavor—a welcome departure from her last meal, the convenience store brunch.

"The food impressed the boys." Rane's voice filled the compact kitchen.

She nearly choked. "I'm glad you approved." Her hip brushed against the sink as she turned to face him.

"I said the boys."

The tender beef she'd swallowed hit the bottom of her stomach.

Rane's eyes dropped to the plate in her hand. "Are you eating my first steak?"

"You ate mine," she replied.

"The next time you decide to serve me a steak just a little south of mooing, remember who signs the checks." He took a step closer.

"I'll do that." Her butt pressed into the counter.

Dried blood stained the corner of his mouth. "Or single paycheck in your case."

Cold metal from the sink edge cut through Elon's thin jeans. She shivered. Three ten-hour days of pay would barely cover taxes and Jeremy's book. "I'll confirm your precise doneness preference from now on."

His stare shifted to the overflowing trashcan and the crumpled freezer paper. He jerked out the top sheet and flattened it on the table. "You used steaks from the chest freezer," he growled.

"Yes. I needed to thaw—"

"These T-bones might make or break my restaurant

contract." He yanked out the other two wrappers. "Damn it to hell. You used them all." His face turned dark red.

He'd fire her for certain. "I'm sorry," she swallowed hard. "I didn't realize how important they were."

The oldest cowboy stepped in and put his hand on Rane's shoulder. "Ease up, son. The rib eyes and tenderloins passed the test. The meat distributor hasn't contacted you in a month. I'd bet a dollar to a hole in a donut that the mucky mucks from the restaurant don't need more beef testing."

Rane let out a low, painful groan. "What if they do, Fred? She used the only T-bones cut to their spec'd size." The wrappers dropped to the floor.

Panic ripped through her. By not checking, she'd jeopardized his cattle business. She opened her mouth to apologize again.

Fred caught her eye and shook his head. "We'll figure out something, Rane." He spoke in the same tone she'd use to calm a terrified child.

"I won't sell Tomo," Rane blurted, and stormed out. The front door slammed shut.

Elon slumped against the counter and let out a breath. She'd blown it.

"Miss Hardy. Don't you fret none. I'm Fred." He tapped his old cowboy hat against his leg. "Welcome to the Calderon Cattle Ranch, known hereabouts as the Double C. You served the best meal since Rane's Grandma Bia cooked for us. Those biscuits of hers are somethin' special." He offered his weathered hand.

"Thank you, that's nice to hear." Elon shook his gently. "Anyone can make baking powder biscuits using a good recipe."

"I disagree. Pappy always said you can throw a pair o' boots in the oven and they don't bake up as biscuits." He chuckled, then his pale eyes met hers. "Rane's a bit wound up, is all. He's got a lot riding on the next two generations of his herd making the cut to bring top dollar for their meat."

"Financial pressure's ugly." She rubbed the dull ache on her lower spine.

"Yes, ma'am. Been through my share of money droughts." He pulled out a bandana and rubbed it across his forehead. "Overheard the boys. They're wonderin' if you'd sell 'em some of your biscuits to take home on the weekend. Many of them have wives and families livin' out of town. 'Cept Emmett and me. We're the resident bachelors. Oh, the boss, too."

No surprise at Rane's marital status. The local women probably galloped away on their ponies when he appeared. Elon smiled and looked into the first friendly face since the veterinarian.

Fred's kindness soothed her frayed nerves. "Wait until you taste my cinnamon rolls. I enjoy baking and could use extra cash, so I'll make a list of baked goods to sell."

"Count me in as your taste tester and messenger." Fred rotated the hat in his hands. "Saw your reaction to Rane's basket joke. If the guys tease you that way, it means they like you. And don't ever think Rane doesn't need you here. He got caught in the crossfire of a misunderstanding between a little gal and her family a long time ago. Too young and too stubborn to see it for what it was and move on." He scratched his nails across his gray chin stubble.

"Oh, that's a shame." Elon waited for him to say more, without luck. "I'll bake on my own time and check first to see if Mr. Calderon minds."

"Good idea, but he shouldn't care. Let me know if you need supplies from town. Anytime." Fred put on his sweat stained cowboy hat and pulled the front door shut behind him.

Allegations confirmed. She'd managed to be hired by a

female-phobic Bull Boss. And she'd put his future income at risk. She counted her blessings he hadn't fired her. Yet.

Rumbles sounded from her empty stomach. She speared a chunk of steak and chewed slowly. Even cold Wagyu melted in your mouth. Literally. Between bites, she removed empty plates and serving platters from the dining room and loaded them into the dishwasher. She cleaned the basket and placed it on top of the sideboard.

The Double C of her new world no longer stood for crusty cooking. A clean, organized kitchen waited for another meal preparation. Without a week's dirty dishes, counter space seemed adequate. An oversized antique platter air-dried on a rack. Flour in the tip-out bin smelled fresh enough for frustration baking until the cows came home. Unfortunately, not improving her welding skills.

An owl let out a low hoot. "Think that's funny, do ya?" she muttered.

Filtered evening light came through the open window above the sink. The sun set in a pink and purple hued sky behind foothills.

No wavy Lake Washington water off a deck, the view in Seattle from the old condominium her sons enjoyed. She placed her palm on the gold, heart-shaped locket holding their precious photos. Thoughts of them kept her going. Her eyes scanned the barns and shop.

Low voices drifted on breezes ruffling through trees. Fred and Emmett sat outside the bunkhouse. Rane Calderon didn't appear, completing a serene setting.

Corrin rated a call. She grabbed her tiny address book from her purse, hustled to the desk, and turned on the crook necked lamp. An elk head mounted above the stone fireplace cast a shadow on the phone while she dialed.

"Hi, Corrin. I made it to Rane's ranch. Thanks again for the job tip."

"I hoped you'd be ready for a challenge. I'm due to meet Kyle in a couple minutes to assemble Halloween decorations. But I need to caution you."

"About Rane? That horse busted out of the starting gate," she forced a cheerful voice.

"No. Kyle noticed your name on a job site for health care workers in Montana when he searched for office temps yesterday. Your ex-husband appeared willing to give you a reference. Kyle wanted to show me the posting this morning and it's gone. The deletion struck both of us as odd."

She bit her lip. "Actually, giving me a recommendation seems disturbingly far from Tim's self-absorbed character. He wants me poor, so I'll beg to settle the divorce. And I didn't tell him my out-of-state travel plans."

"He found out, and he's searching for you. Be on alert and call me if anything odd happens. Okay?"

"Sure." She cleared her throat. "Might've been a suspicious incident at the house before I left."

"You're going through an acrimonious divorce. What happened?"

"I broke through boards on the basement stairway. The boys think Tim planned the accident. In addition, the Washington State Patrol detained me on the way out of town. They said my car had been reported as stolen. Thanks to you, I had proof I've owned it since before we married."

"I'm relieved you left town. Tim sounds dangerous. Tomorrow, I'll take detailed notes. In the meantime, you need to be careful."

"I will, and my kids made me destroy my cell in case it had a tracer app."

"Smart sons. That's why I couldn't reach you."

"Where can I buy a burner phone in town?" Elon asked.

"Kyle bought a new phone. I'd bet you can have the old one and join us on the family plan."

"Thank you. If Kyle's amenable, I'll grab the phone after breakfast and pay my share. I'm surrounded by Rane's posse here but appreciate the Tim warning."

"I'll ask Kyle tonight if the cell's available. He's a great guy."

"I'm excited to meet your kindly doctor."

"Gotta run. 'Night."

The world needed more great guys.

A warm, furry head pressed against her shin. "Come on Angel," coaxing the dog to follow her took little effort. "Time to brew a cup of soothing tea and move into our quarters." She ran water into a blue enameled teakettle and cranked on the burner.

The dog fell into position while she trudged to the storeroom to retrieve her suitcase. She unzipped the top and parted layers of clothes to retrieve a mesh tea ball and glass canning jar filled with carefully selected dried leaves and flowers.

Memories flooded her of being taught the proportions by her loving mom who could grow anything. She looked at her hands, which bore a few age spots from working out in her backyard garden and the courtyard space at the clinic. Tim resented her plants, too.

She rotated the jar in her hands. Had she added additional dried lemon verbena leaves before she left? Her mind was frazzled these days.

Angel's flicking tail brushed her ankle.

Extra lemon flavor didn't matter, and the water should be hot. She propped her suitcase against the stove, packed herbs into the infuser, set it in a mug, and poured on steaming water. Her tired hands strained to hang clean cooking pots on the metal rack above the sink.

Curses on Tim for forcing her to abandon her former life.

She stirred her tea. Scents of lavender blossoms culled from the shrub in the old backyard perfumed the air.

The boys helped her cut the purple stems each fall. She'd be a failure in their eyes if Rane fired her.

$\sim$

Rane rested his cheek against Tomo's neck. The quiet of the stall helped him think. The Wagyu contract ensured enough money to buy the adjoining property and guaranteed a stream of income. If he lost out, there'd be layoffs. The thought of pink-slipping newer employees raising kids would suck.

He scratched under Tomo's neck, and the bull placed his nose on Rane's shoulder. "You're going to pull through, old buddy." At least the sling worked out. He fed Tomo a pain pill and left. A light shone from the kitchen.

Elon's food deserved top billing in a restaurant. But he needed a welder, not a chef who'd cooked meat that could make or break the future of the ranch. He eased open the front door and crept to his desk.

Banging from metal pans rattled through the empty house.

He sat in the old leather desk chair and turned on the crook neck lamp. Light shone on the growing stack of invoices. Elon's welding would complete jobs and pay a few bills. He grimaced at the increased property taxes due late in November, shoved the notice aside, and skimmed the contract for purchasing his neighbor's parcel.

They'd stapled the yellow receipt for his earnest money on top—more than he'd anticipated spending. Safeguarding the Blackfeet burial ground adjoining that tract provided ample reason to empty his savings account. Maybe he should've talked to Chayton, seen if his little brother had extra cash. *No, he'd have wanted to contact the tribe to get involved.* He sat back until the chair groaned in protest. Grandma Bia entrusted this section of mainly grassland to him because she'd encouraged him to work cattle. She'd given Chayton other land and her father's ceremonial regalia, knowing he'd participate in Blackfeet dances.

He flicked off the light and remembered her insistence they attend powwows and learn the songs and the language. Chayton absorbed the teachings like rain on a dry creek, and now showed passion coaching the reservation kids to dance—all his spare money bought their feathered regalia.

The nearby painting of a Blackfoot hunter overlooking a buffalo herd caught his eye. Raising Wagyu cattle fit his own role of caretaker to the ancestral land of Bia's father, his great-grandfather. Calderons took responsibilities to their family seriously. Four of the local Blackfeet men hustled to learn skills in his machine shop. For now, fixing farm equipment provided steady income while he solidified his reputation for raising premium beef. He'd hire more people from the reservation as the herd grew, they were the best horsemen on the Plains.

Suitcase wheels rattling across the wooden floor sounded from the kitchen. Slumped shouldered, Elon passed through the doorway into the back hall. The silhouette was that of a beaten, tired soul.

Her ex-husband must be an idiot not to appreciate a spunky, smart woman, let alone one whose tight jeans produced interest he hadn't felt in a long, long time. He fidgeted on the seat.

Trudging footsteps and clacking noises grew faint. She'd headed in the right direction to sleep in Bia's room.

Hell. That door hadn't been cracked in years. Probably an inch of dust on everything. He pushed the chair out from the desk. *Not the time to go soft.* She ought to be thanking her lucky stars she wasn't sleeping in the bunkhouse beside the boys.

Grit's commenting on her butt at the corral popped into his brain. Tomorrow he'd end their thoughts about potential hookups. She didn't need more complications in her life and he didn't need drama. He moved to the kitchen. Better check if she'd turned off the gas range, then see if the plumbing still worked in Grandma's bathroom good enough to last a month.

He looked through the kitchen window toward his pole barn and the welder. Who was he kidding? She brought a new energy to the old house. If only she wielded a torch as well as a frypan. He'd hate to cut her loose.

Juggling the mug while rolling the heavy bag down the hallway sapped what little energy Elon had left after cleaning the kitchen, cooking the meal, and then making it through Rane's steak confrontation.

A bed never sounded so good. The first door beside the stairwell opened into a washroom. The next door pushed against a stacked washer and dryer. Little space lay between the tiny laundry room's sink and counter.

The dim corridor contained another door, at its far end. No photos lined the walls. No sweatshirts or coats hung from protruding hooks to diminish eerie echoes of her footsteps and the clacking wheels. Nothing indicated a family had ever lived here.

The cool glass knob gave no comfort while she pushed the final door inward. Stale air assaulted her nostrils. Her suitcase flopped against the wall as she rested it to flip on a light.

Angel backed up.

"It's okay. The place just hasn't seen the light of day in

this decade." Her gaze took in a lavender gingham bedspread, inlaid rosewood dresser, and a roll top desk. She swung her suitcase onto a trunk at the foot of the bed and watched a hazy white poof dissipate.

She took a long drink of lukewarm tea and swallowed. An acrid taste hit her mouth. *Metallic?* "Gack. I should've scoured the tea kettle." She pushed open the bathroom door and dumped the liquid into a white porcelain sink resting atop a matching pedestal.

Angel followed, her toenails clacking against green and white floor tiles. Dark wainscoting ran waist high on each wall, including behind the claw-foot bathtub.

With a worn hand towel, she wiped the sink and faucet, then stepped back into the lavender-colored bedroom and dusted the wooden surfaces. A wave of dizziness hit. She grabbed the bed post, rubbed the pain in her chest, and coughed.

"Must be the dust. We're sleeping in a room from yesteryear, let's give it some air." She pulled lacy curtains aside and unlocked a window.

"If it doesn't meet your standards, there's a top bed in the bunkhouse," Rane's deep, smooth voice challenged.

Her heart pounded an irregular beat. Elon forced a smile before turning to acknowledge the form leaning against the doorframe. For his size, Rane tread lightly, akin to a large, prowling cat. "The room's perfect, simply needs airing out." She pushed the window frame, not budging it a fraction.

He crossed the room and reached his tanned hand above her shoulder. Flicking once, he popped it free. The earthy smells of cows, hay, and Old Spice aftershave wafted from his body.

Male heat warmed her back, creating a thrumming sensation buried for decades. "Thanks." Cool, fresh air filled her lungs. When she turned around, he'd left, yet his scent filled the room. She slid open an empty bureau drawer and then stepped back to her suitcase. Her touch lingered on floral embroidery decorating a nightgown lying on top.

Mom's handiwork.

A tear fell to her cheek. They'd begun planning her divorce from Tim two weeks before she'd died in the boat. *No sense dwelling on the past tonight.*

She removed an old novel and her clip-on reading light from the side pocket of her suitcase and placed both on the nightstand. Tonight, she'd need an hour of reading. *Dream on.* Four or five hours wouldn't suffice.

Inhaling brought the lingering essence of Rane, who determined the fate of her and the boys. Another scent caught her attention. She bent and sniffed Angel. "You need a bath."

In a few minutes, a clean, fluffy dog turned trusting eyes to her. "You're easier to wash than twin toddlers." Elon smiled and removed her soggy clothes. "Pajamas, here I come."

The flannel nightgown brushed against her skin; the material soft to her touch. Emptying her suitcase tonight meant one less chore for tomorrow, she thought, and tugged on the lowest drawer pulls.

Her heart thumped against her ribs. She rubbed her chest. Rane encounters racked her nerves worse than Tim. But for good reason, this job set the stage for how the rest of her life played out—beholden to her awful ex or becoming an independent woman. Welding skills determined her fate.

She panted for breath. What was happening to her? Had she inherited her dad's heart problems? Did panic attacks start this way? *No.* Quit worrying and regroup, she chided herself. *If Kyle's phone isn't available, buy one and watch a YouTube video on fixing a trailer hitch. Repeat for other projects. Rane won't catch on.*

Yeah, right. He could work for the FBI. She shoved the empty dresser door shut. Unpacking meant commitment.

She opened her purse and removed the business card from Corrin. *Calderon Cattle* stood out on the front in block letters. The back held the farmer's hand-written number and name done in friendly blue ink.

If the other man Corrin met at the wedding, the farmer, still needed a nanny for his little girls, he might consider her and Angel as a package deal. No welding for a Bull Boss involved.

The interior of the rented SUV appeared large enough to hold the new bike. Tim wiped his brow and positioned the backpack behind the driver seat, aiming the short-barreled rifle he'd stowed in it at the floorboard. He checked the zipper lock again and yawned. Meeting the seller in an alley in Tacoma at 3:00 a.m. had disturbed his sleep cycle. Elon's life deserved to be disrupted, not his.

He rolled his mountain bike out of the garage, removed its front tire, and lifted it into the cargo area. Plenty of space left for Jasmine's suitcases. He glanced at their bedroom window and pictured her sculpted butt bent over the bed, packing lingerie. Later tonight, they'd stay in a luxurious suite at the restored Davenport Hotel in Spokane, then travel on to a hick town.

Best of all, no one suspected a thing, including Jasmine. The mention of taking a fall color vacation to process the impending divorce garnered plenty of sympathy. One way or another, he'd find Elon. An old Mercedes driven by a woman welder would be an anomaly in the outback of Montana. He'd marked the last phone ping—shouldn't be too hard to find her precise location.

If she balked at his offer, he'd act. Doing the right thing wasn't always easy, or painless. He shut the hatch and placed his hands on the rear window, straightened his arms, and stepped to a modified plank position which stretched his posterior deltoids. The back muscles flexed on cue until a text dinged on his phone.

It was Jasmine. *Ready when you are, baby.* A total understatement. He'd begun strategizing his future the day he met malleable Elon driving her Mercedes twenty years ago. Thanks to her father's real estate investments, he'd soon be escorting a size 0 wife to the groundbreaking of a hospital honoring Dr. Timothy Karl Hardy.

He'd strategized each play and won. Every game produced a loser. If Elon wasn't willing to concede to his rules, she'd become the targeted pawn in a game with a deadly end.

CHAPTER 3

The first rays of sunlight glowed through the clean kitchen window. Rane slid his finger across the dust-free sill. A city girl probably slept in after driving, cooking, and scrubbing. Elon hadn't asked about their breakfast routine.

A late meal provided a reason for a demerit, if he needed one. Rane hit the brew button on the coffee maker and shoved Tomo's bottle of pain pills into his pocket. Damn rustlers, picking on innocent animals.

He jumped at the sound of footsteps. "What the—"

Elon stood in the opening from the hallway, holding a brown wooden rolling pin and bulging cloth satchel. "Sorry, I didn't mean to startle you," she stuttered.

For a moment, he'd forgotten the appealing woman who'd already complicated his carefully hammered out life. If she intended to hide her curves in loose shirts, she'd failed. Today's campaign lost the battle in a shade of blue, making her eyes the color of a spring sky. "No one's bunked with me for a long time." Warmth crept from under his collar.

"Oh." She raised perfectly arched eyebrows. "No visiting . . . family?"

"Nope." He threw back his shoulders. "You always travel toting a rolling pin?"

"Keeps the men in line."

Rane fought a grin. "Duly noted." He leaned forward. "Your pin's honed from one chunk of wood. Nice workmanship."

"It belonged to my grandma." Sadness rimmed her eyes. "As did some of the baking tools I treasure." She clutched the bulky cloth pouch to her chest.

Her past would become his problem if he wasn't careful. "I need to roll outta here. Got the coffee started. At seven, the men take a twenty-minute break for grub."

"I'll make things they can eat quickly or take with them."

"My grandma made Indian fry bread. The guys loved it. She was sturdy built, too, and took on a variety of tasks." He glanced her way, anticipating a smart retort.

She'd wrapped her arms around her chest, her head lowered.

He'd scored a demerit, judging by her deflated stance. *Duh.* City women thought skinny ruled, contrary to the opinion of most men. "Ah, lemme know if you need anything." His feet didn't move him out of the house fast enough. A hawk squawked overhead as he stepped off the porch. Intelligent conversation this early was for the birds.

He glanced out to the ridge. A long ride to check the herd might clear her from his thoughts. He shifted focus to the barn. Tomo stood quietly in the sling amongst the straw bedding, same as when he'd checked on him during the night. The bull needed grain and a once-over before he ate any food prepared by his other challenge.

The memory of Elon's generous profile as she stretched to open the window last night shot through his brain. Again. He ran his fingers around the brim of his hat, then put it firmly on his head. First, though, he needed to clarify some things to the boys.

The door to the machine shop opened on well-oiled hinges. His crew surrounded a chalkboard printed with the day's work. Rane found a hammer and tapped metallic pings on a lathe. "I need everyone's attention. You saw our new cook."

"Couldn't miss her."

Rane's jaw clenched at the smart-ass reply from Grit, his lead machinist. The smirking clown hooked his thumbs under the buckles of his bib overalls, feet wide apart.

"She's off limits. Any questions?" Rane looked from man to man, seeing challenge in Grit's eyes alone. He'd seen the same look when he'd caught him gutting an elk that he'd shot out of season. "You have a problem, Grit?"

"My free time's my own." He puffed out his chest, resembling a strutting sage grouse.

Rane's knuckles turned white as he gripped the smooth wooden hammer handle. Grit wasn't a harmless bird. "If any of you hit on her while you work for me, you'll be fired."

Grit's eyes narrowed, and he let out a throaty chuckle. "Got it, boss."

Arrogant ass. If it weren't for his lathe skills . . . Rane unclenched his hand, allowing the steel head of the tool to bang onto the workbench. "Breakfast's at the usual time."

Two of the men elbowed each other. Both were unmarried, younger, and bragged about dating conquests. Hushed voices followed him out the door. Rane stopped on the landing and shook his head. The attractive package of female trouble needed to leave his ranch—the sooner the better. Several vocational colleges in the area graduated welders. He'd double the hourly pay on the job he'd posted and buy Pop-Tarts and Spam on the next trip to town.

He strode past the barn. The newest rescue horse, Possum, nickered to him from his turnout beside Tomo. Rane let out a deep breath. Scratching the thickening coat on the horse's neck soothed him. Winter wasn't far off.

He grabbed a halter from outside his stall. "Thought I forgot our exercise date, didn't you?" The horse stuck his nose into the band and kept his neck low for Rane to fasten the buckle. "Your tendon damage must've been minor. Those former owners were blockheads to take you to the kill pen. Ed thinks you'll be fine in no time."

Tomo bellowed on the last round they made to strengthen Possum's leg. "Twenty minute is up." Rane led the patient gelding back to his stall. Possum gently took the carrot Rane offered before he headed to Tomo's shelter.

The bull's brown, sad eyes swung to greet him. "Sorry. You'll have to tolerate this contraption for a few weeks or become steaks and burgers." He rubbed the soft nap on the bull's head. "Don't worry, I'll find the bandits. They won't try to steal you again."

Tomo swiveled his nose to Rane. His scratchy tongue curved upwards.

"Doc gave me plenty of pain pills so we can keep you comfortable." Rane pulled the bottle from his pocket and offered Tomo a lump of shredded carrots hiding a pill.

He balled and flexed his fists returning to his house. Someone would pay in broken bones for Tomo's misery.

Elon turned away from the kitchen window. Rane had morphed from calmly walking the horse to a glowering tower quicker than a toddler given the bedtime warning.

Tires scrunched on the gravel outside. Another welding job equaled job security, she concluded, and looked out hopefully. A blond-haired man emerged from a Jeep. Rane smiled and slapped the newcomer on the shoulder and ushered him to the front door.

Making points with the stranger served her best interests. She plated the remaining fruit and savory pie pockets. If her never-fail crust didn't score, she'd be surprised. She slid the recipe for it back in the end slot of the unrolled tool satchel lying on the counter.

The men stepped from the dining room into the kitchen. "Doc, this is Ms. Hardy, my cook and welder," Rane said. "Ms. Hardy, this here's Doc Kyle, the man who recommended BoneGlu for Tomo."

Gads, when Rane threw a happy look her way, she felt fifteen again. "Pleased to meet you. Corrin's sure thrilled you welcomed her to Emma Springs." Nerves raised her voice a notch. "How about an egg- and cheese-filled breakfast hand pie? Or a peach one?"

Kyle's bright blue eyes held warmth and kindness. "I'd take a fruit one. And we're always glad to welcome newcomers to town." He pulled a cell out of his pocket. "I loaded and charged my retired Samsung for you. Called our carrier and they're more than happy to add another customer. Corrin gave me your old number."

A cell phone! And she'd smashed a Samsung. "Wow. Nice it's a similar model to my old one. The SIM card might fit. How much do I owe you?" She held her breath; her wallet held a couple twenties.

"Roy, my dad, routinely complains the town lacks a bakery. He'll want to meet you soon," Kyle said. "You provide a few pastries when you hit town, and we'll call it good."

She'd brandish every lattice cutter and wire whisk in her satchel to please them. "That's very generous. I'll pay my share of the monthly charges and bring you and your father some pastries."

"Deal." Kyle bit into the warm, flaky pie pocket. "These are fabulous. Don't bring cash, bring a pie." He took another bite, removed his own phone from a belt clip, and scrolled his thumb over the screen. "Sorry. Gotta run. Hey, nice to meet you, Elon. Rane's a lucky guy."

Warmth crept up her neck. "Nice meeting you. Tell Corrin thanks."

"You bet." He waved the pastry and left.

The crucial question came next. "Any chance you have Wi-Fi, Rane?"

"I added it to my DSL. You're not totally in the boonies. Password's Calderon Cattle."

"Easy to remember," she said, and waved the phone. Thankfully, Rane headed outside. She laid out breakfast, grabbed a pastry for herself, and padded to her bedroom to regroup. Her tiny SIM card slid into the new phone. One problem solved. YouTube videos provided a smidgeon of confidence to tackle the first job. Satisfied at what she'd seen, she returned to the dining room.

Emmett and Fred filed out patting their bellies. "Now that's a breakfast," one said.

She passed under the archway and nearly bumped into Rane.

"I'm sure you can keep yourself occupied for a couple hours," he said. "Meet me in the open-sided pole barn at nine-thirty to begin welding."

"Sure," she agreed. "Um, I saw you walking the chestnut horse you keep near the barn. If it's therapy and he's gentle, I'll lead him around in a halter."

"Maybe tonight. Possum's the sweetest gelding I've ever met. He went lame and nearly became horse meat due to a rich snob who wanted his daughter to barrel race on the best mount money could buy. I think his leg's sound again. When he's ready, your small size can get him used to a rider."

Small for Montana. She'd take the complement. "Okay." Elon smiled, and he beamed back like a proud schoolkid.

"Glad to assist."

"Missed you at breakfast. Boys left happy," he stated.

"If I bake on my own time and buy supplies, do you mind if I sell the men pastries for the weekend?"

"Anything to keep them happy." He turned on his heel and headed out.

Elon lifted Angel's paw. "A shake celebrating success."

She washed her hands and tucked cleaned knives and fluted pastry cutters into the hand-stitched slots in the canvas satchel. Mom had measured each knife, cutter, and whisk to create pockets and flaps ensuring the tools wouldn't fall out. Elon's fingers lovingly rolled and tied the treasured bundle, a sad reminder of the last remnants of her first broken dream—to become a professional baker. It had been so long since Mom encouraged her to attend culinary night school, happily offering to babysit.

Tim's controlled hostility had surfaced each time her parents tried to bolster her confidence. How spineless she'd been in placating the calculating bastard.

Angel's nose bumped her leg, her brown eyes soft and curious. She patted her head. Regrets produced nothing. "We've got two hours until the welding showdown."

The dog's ears perked. She wagged her tail and tipped her nose toward the back door, as if she knew the drill.

Angel had acclimated. If they didn't have to move, it would be best for the pup.

She flipped the bulk pack of chicken thawing in the sink for tonight's pot pies. A giant roast sat in the refrigerator. Both cleared by Rane.

She'd prepare Grandma's sauerbraten beef recipe in the instant cooker for tomorrow's dinner. Thank goodness she'd brought the handy appliance along. She set a baking sheet in the other side of the sink, filled with sudsy water. Tender pot roast and gingersnap gravy should have Rane eating out of the palm of her hand.

No need to go that far. Soap bubbles and water jettisoned to the back splash as she plunged her hands in and scrubbed them together. Men demanded a price. She toweled dry and dialed Corrin. "Thanks for the phone. I see who's keeping you in Emma Springs," she teased.

Corrin coughed. "Kyle's dad, Roy, keeps me busy in his law practice. We're currently discussing a project. I'm available tomorrow to record detailed notes on Tim's harassment prior to your leaving Seattle. Can you meet at my office?"

"I'll work out a trip to Emma Springs. Everyone thinks Tim's a pillar of the community. The boys and I know otherwise. Talk to you later."

She collected last night's pile of used cleaning cloths and wandered into the laundry room. An overflowing basket of Rane-sized jeans and denim shirts blocked the washing machine.

Angel put her nose into the pile. She rooted around and lifted her head. A crumpled red bandana now hung over one ear.

"Give me that." Elon removed the cloth. She rubbed crescent-shaped white patches above Angel's eyes, hidden yesterday by a sooty mask. "We got our bedroom dusted and you bathed last night, maybe we can brighten our fearless leader's outlook with clean duds. If I can make myself indispensable, he's less likely to fire me after my first mistake."

The dog tilted her head, as if questioning her logic. Maybe for good reason. Taking on all the responsibilities of home, office management, and their boys hadn't satisfied Tim. Well, in this relationship, she didn't need to give the pretense of matrimonial harmony in public to save face. Do the job and collect the pay. No one should fault her for cleaning the laundry room.

Two loads later, a pyramid of his folded laundry teetered in front of the wheezing dryer. She balanced the basket against her hip.

The stack swayed precariously as she tromped up steep, half-log steps suspended by side rails. Glancing through open stairs made her feet tingle. She focused on the upper hallway. The thought of careening downstairs gave her the willies.

At the top, she leaned against the wall and studied several doors. Heavy footsteps overhead at night indicated Rane's bedroom sat above hers, the last on the left.

Dust bunnies lined the hallway to the door. She wedged the pile against the door and sneezed into her arm. Her elbow pushed in the door. At eye level sat a framed photo of a young Rane Calderon. Smiling, happy, and victorious, he stroked the nose of a russet horse with a purple ribbon attached to its bridle. A beaming man with a shock of Rane's dark hair stood on his left, a woman with Rane's russet eyes grinned from his right.

"Don't take another step," Rane boomed the warning.

Elon froze. "I planned to set the basket outside. Bumped the—" The laundry teetered.

His hands, one on top and one on the bottom, secured the mass of clothes. "No one goes in my room. Understood?"

"Yes. My kids appreciated laundry help."

"No kids live here." He dropped the stack onto the dirty floor and pivoted toward the stairs. "Didn't hire you as a housekeeper," he barked. "Welding starts in five minutes."

"Yes, sir." Elon slunk against the wall. Mental note, cancel the idea of doing any additional work to earn praise.

Angel bumped her shaking knee.

"Come on, time to exit the man-zone and face the fire, in a literal sense," she whispered.

From the laundry room she grabbed the length of clothes-line she'd spotted and led the dog to her car's trunk. Out of the Vuitton duffel bag came the requisite thin goatskin and thick cowhide leather gloves, lace-less engineer boots, a pock marked leather jacket, and her tools. "Please let them do me proud today," she whispered under her breath.

Rane exited the machine shop and walked into the adjoining metal-roofed structure, open-sided except for the wall attached to his shop. Against that wall stood racks of equipment and tools hanging from metal hooks. He glanced at the red manure spreader parked on the opposite side, rubbed his neck, then paced the twelve feet from its broken trailer hitch to the tailgate.

Her son, Brandon, paced when nervous. What would it take to alleviate Rane's doubt in her skills? She shut the trunk and marched into the space, the dog by her side. A breeze hit her face, carrying the ripe manure stench from her first project. *Baby pooh had competition.* She walked to the corner that opened to the meadow and tied Angel to a support pole. "You sit here," She took a last breath of fresh air and turned to face Rane. "I'm ready to melt metal," she declared, and smiled.

When he smiled back, she did a double take. If his lips weren't curved in a snarl, the man rated drop-dead gorgeous. She realized too late her hand now preened flyaway strands of her shoulder-length hair.

By the spark in those fiery eyes, he'd noticed. One of his inky brows raised a fraction, then he turned and pointed to the thin metal beam that had come unattached from the hitch. "This broken tongue and a bent haybine jack both need repairs ASAP. My MIG welder with a 250-amp outlet's new, unlike your headgear. See if the helmet on the rack fits. I bought a half mask respirator, too."

Strikes one and two on her involuntary response and

outdated equipment. "Thank you, I'll try your newer head gear." She adjusted the straps on his Vader-like helmet, reviewing in her brain the YouTube videos she'd watched. If only there'd been more time than one afternoon to practice in front of the welding instructor she'd met while volunteering at the kids' high school. He'd praised her time-lapsed skills. Too bad his faith hadn't rubbed off.

Rane narrowed his eyes. "Helmet seems to fit. I've got a neighbor needing this spreader last week."

The haybine jack must be the thing resembling a pull behind mower on steroids. Every section looked bent.

She was so screwed. "Dung disperser's my first victim."

"Hope your torch is as good as your wisecracks," he chuckled.

"I'll grab the handheld grinder to clean the surface." She swung around and did her best to strut to the rack holding supplies.

"Later," he said, and left.

Two hours of welding, and she'd finished the row of tiny, melted metal circles on her last pass. She let go of the trigger and turned off the welder. The man-sized helmet slid off her damp head. The simple weld looked perfect. Both sides of the V-shaped tongue met again at the hitch. She took off her gloves, removed the respirator, and stretched out her cramped fingers.

A bleachy, burnt metal odor hung in the air. Multiple shampoos might remove the stench from her hair. She shucked out of her hip-length leather coat. There'd be plenty of spark holes in the faithful garment by the time she finished this gig.

Rane strode into the shed and tipped back his hat. He stopped and stood, arms crossed, his legs apart. His head slowly turned while he scanned the repair and the surrounding floor area. One brow arched, then he nodded. "I guess that passes as a seam. Not much bird poop."

The seam was perfect. "Excuse me? No ropey blobs of metal have fallen from my work since I first raised a torch." She put her hands on her hips.

He flashed another disarming grin. "Ahh, just kidding. Wondered if you knew the term."

Only because of websites listing slang. "I'm no rookie, don't worry," she countered.

"Nice work, by the way." He threw her a thumbs up. "Next project's a rush job. Let's see how you do welding a dozer's push frame holding the blade. A guy's dropping it off in an hour. You can work on the haybine later, it's more complicated."

So, he'd tested her on the simple job. A good sign, but she wasn't out of the woods yet. "Okay. In the meantime, I'll cut meat for dinner. It's the approved chicken, for the record."

"Good choice. Keep an eye out for a truck and trailer."

"I'll reappear when I see the ridges on its treads." She threw a mock salute—glad Jeremy's toddler fascination with bulldozers taught her about their rolling parts.

He nodded and headed into his shop.

Behind his back she did an in-place happy dance, swinging her hips. Angel spun in a circle. She leaned over and patted the dog's head, then whispered, "We succeeded, and got a complement. Can't beat that."

She strode to her car and lifted out the framed, beadwork angel and photos of the twins. Entering the quiet house, she padded down the hall and into her room, followed by her pup. The best place to hang them would be on the wall opposite her bed.

Several nails stuck out of the lavender plaster. She hung the boys' photos on either end, placing the angel near the middle. She ran her fingers over the smooth glass beads. Her sons and two angels would be the first things she saw each morning, all providing courage to fight Tim.

She perched on the end of the bed and stared at the golden wings. Her grandma would be proud of how she'd taken on a new challenge. Or several, like the next job—welding a load-bearing section on a massive dozer blade involved structural integrity. Please, oh please let there be a video showing the technique, she silently prayed, as she pulled out her phone.

Tim admired Jasmine's trim derriere while she pushed open the women's bathroom door of the Montana restaurant. She'd return to him soon, unlike his ex, who'd religiously plastered on too much makeup. He drained the last of his orange juice and thumb-scrolled down a new email forwarded to his phone.

The Hospital Expansion Committee supported his brilliant suggestion to convert the old building currently housing his medical practice into a ten-story or more medical facility to satisfy growing needs for beds in Seattle.

From the wording of the letter, talking dollars came next. Twelve million or so if he'd estimated the approximate value of a block zoned commercial in the center of the city.

He squeezed the edge of the tabletop. Damn if he'd share a penny with Elon. He'd put in the hours to build his reputation through successful surgeries and researching the latest techniques. He'd more than earned the title to the property her parents bought for peanuts during the '70s recession.

Their pampered daughter deserved to fade into the sunset in this godforsaken state, for whatever stupid reasoning she'd used to come to Montana. Her last location, and the precise mileage from Seattle narrowed the search.

He located the map app on his cell and arced a circle from the old condo in Seattle to seven-hundred-forty-seven miles out. Nothing but open land, and one, tiny town. *Couldn't be many women welders new in the area.* His vision blurred. He held the phone to the side. Emma something. Every blip on the map would have a tavern and a know-everything bartender.

Flashing lights subsided, and the screen came into focus again. Three Falls appeared the only decent-sized burg for miles. Tonight, he'd find a hotel for him and Jasmine, then tomorrow pay Elon a personal visit.

Bills and a warning should encourage her to relinquish the property. He looked out at the SUV holding his Yeti mountain bike and the backpack.

If she didn't comply, he'd use his marksman skills from childhood rabbit hunting.

The repaired bulldozer sat on its trailer, parked in front of the machine shop. The owner patted the blade, then slapped Rane on the back. Both smiled, infusing relief into Elon's weary bones. She'd used contortionist positions to lay a straight seam.

She surveyed her clean work area. Stringer beads in a simple weld without whip action mimicked decorating a cake. In this instance, a mammoth yellow cake in the form of a vintage Caterpillar D7 dozer. Happy customer equaled a happy boss, equaled job security. She hummed while walking to the house.

After throwing vegetables into the slow cooking chicken, she gathered a manila envelope from her bedroom dresser. By not taking lunch, she'd earned free time before dinner. She snapped her fingers and Angel trotted to her car.

Rane stood in her pole barn workspace, his head stuck under a tractor hood, butt angled out.

The man did slim-cut Levi's proud. She fanned her face using the envelope and called to him. "If it's okay, I'm taking break time for quick appointments with Ed and my lawyer. Dinner's cooking."

Rane waved a wrench, the rest of his body staying in repair position. "Sounds good. Noticed you worked through lunch."

He noticed everything. "Bye." She opened her car's door. "Hop in, Angel." She steered around dips in the gravel leading to the highway and turned right at the mailbox welded to the rusty stove.

Flat, empty pavement took her past a combined fire station and Hanlen County Sheriff's Office. A few buildings sat low on the horizon.

She turned left at Sam's Gas Station as the vet had instructed. In a quarter mile, the cow-shaped sign advertising Bell's Veterinary Clinic swung in front of a red brick building. Nearby sat a low outer barn and fenced paddock holding several goats.

A chime sounded a greeting as she opened the door. Ed emerged from a side room, drying his hands. "Hi, Elon. I'm glad Rane hasn't scared you off."

"I'm grateful for a paycheck and a place for us to live." She patted Angel. "Not certain of Rane's opinion."

"Probably nervous as a calf at branding time." He bent to scratch Angel's back. "You, my little fluff ball, he'd give an open arm welcome to."

"I weld whatever broken equipment rolls in the driveway and feed Rane and the crew. He leaves my domains alone. Working so far."

"Glad to hear. Your pastries caused a buzz in town. You should open a bakery."

"Yup. That was once my dream in a former life." Elon reached in her bag. "I brought a few cookies and a cinnamon roll for you."

"That former life must've included baking training," his kind voice replied.

"Baking's my relaxation technique. I enjoyed two years of culinary school, then dropped out to work in my husband's medical practice. Free labor at its finest." She rubbed her brow. "I appreciate you looking Angel over. She's been eating less than when I found her."

"We're glad you both found your way to Emma Springs. Come on back." He walked them to the exam room, lifted the dog onto the metal table, and listened through his stethoscope. He took her temperature and examined her tummy. "I think we might find a little surprise or two if we give her an ultrasound."

Elon ran her fingers through Angel's silky fur. "She's okay, isn't she?"

"Oh, I think she's more than okay, maybe going to be a mom. Some dogs experience morning sickness."

She bounced lightly in place and patted Angel's belly. "I'm delighted at the wry twist of fate—my almost ex is a pediatrician. I've lived and breathed babies for years, but he'd never allow a puppy to invade his domain."

"You're in for a treat. No diapers. Let's confirm it." He rolled in equipment and got the picture focused. "She's only got two puppies, a small litter for her breed."

Elon scratched under Angel's chin. "You'll receive wonderful prenatal care. Promise." She turned to Ed. "Any idea how long before her birth?"

"I'd say three weeks, give or take. Being malnourished and not knowing the sire, I'm only estimating." He reached into a wall holder. "Here's a pamphlet on good care for Angel. Add weight on her slowly and call me if you're concerned."

"Thanks, Ed, I appreciate your help."

"I hope you stick it out. Rane needs a woman with your mettle. What happened between him and Shelly's folks entailed bad communication affecting good folks." He held open the door.

"Thank you again." Elon patted the car seat and Angel bounded in. Always more questions than answers relating to Rane's past, she conceded. Her focus shifted to the directions Corrin had supplied to her office, a block from Main Street in Emma Springs.

The Craftsman-style home she'd described, sitting atop a slight hill, took advantage of a picturesque view of Sunrise Lake. She pulled into the driveway and opened the car's windows for Angel. "Have a nice nap, mommy."

She opened her door and lifted her purse. Angel looked at her with nervous puppy dog eyes. A short visit seemed a perfect time to show her this human wouldn't abandon her. "You found a forever home." She stroked her ear. "I'll be back."

Behind a large pane of glass, Corrin sat at a desk, studying a monitor. She glanced up and pointed to the front porch.

Elon's feet touched the landing, and the door opened.

"It's nice to have another friendly and female face in town." Corrin ushered her to a room holding an antique desk, an overstuffed chair, and a wooden rocker. "Rane treating you well?"

"The job's a life saver. And working there's certainly interesting." Elon handed her the papers she'd received from Tim's lawyer prior to leaving Seattle.

"Nice side-step from discussing your boss. We'll revisit him later. Precisely describe the incidents in Seattle."

Corrin pulled out a notepad. "Please take a seat in either chair."

Elon chose the rocker and described the stolen car scenario.

"The police try to keep us safe." Corrin scanned the pages from Tim's lawyer. "Your ex may slither on the other end of the spectrum."

Her feet increased the heel-to-toe tempo to propel the chair forward and back. "Thank you again for suggesting Kyle's old cell. The model's close to my old one."

"Your chair's rocking enough to power a city. Tim messed with stairs?"

"The boys think he booby-trapped the basement stairs I fell through." She peeled back her sleeve. "Whacked my arm, hips, and ribs in my tumble. My bum and a pile of coats stopped me from cracking my head open."

Corrin's eyes widened. "Your twin sons moved out prior to you and used the same stairs?"

"Repeatedly. It might've been my weight." She sucked in her stomach. "Tim bugged me to diet."

"You're not overweight, you're a curvy girl, same as me. He's a narcissistic, philandering jerk from what you've described. Consider the source and remove his warped comments from your brain."

Elon rifled through her purse. "Except one. Tim left this note encouraging me to grab a suitcase from the basement." She handed it off to Corrin.

"Bloody hell," Corrin said. "I want photos of your bruises." She aimed her cell and took several shots. "Not my idea of a coincidence. What else?"

"He cancelled the credit card, the only source of money for the three of us. I should've withdrawn more cash. My first paycheck's spoken for."

"I'll check into the legalities of him denying you funds

during the divorce." She flipped another sheet. "The medical practice appears to be solely in Tim's name." Corrin's finger paused on the page. "Did you build the clinic after you married?"

"Not exactly. That end of my parents' building held their garden store until they financed the remodel shortly after we tied the knot." She held her hand to her throat.

"Saved Tim finding a space."

"And clients. Prior to our marriage, Tim struck a deal to buy his mentor's practice to gain access to the existing patients."

Corrin took notes. "Washington is a community property state. If you didn't receive money or property as a verified inheritance, this could be sticky."

"Sticky's my middle name these days." She handed Corrin a wrapped cinnamon roll. "The copy I'd kept of my parents will disappeared from its file at home, I mean Tim's house. Mom didn't keep a lockbox, so the original's sure to be in their storage room. Couldn't search all the old boxes before I left."

"We'll assume Tim destroyed the copy of the will. Who prepared it?"

"No idea." Elon swallowed. "I hadn't reviewed it in years, but they left me their commercial property. When they moved to the condo, they willed it to the twins, hoping they'd attend the UW someday." Elon glanced at a foot-high stack of legal papers next to the computer. "You're busy."

"Always. We'll stay in a holding pattern on your divorce until we find the will."

"I'll ask the boys to search for it immediately."

"Next order of business. Tim cheated on you, and we'll use that. You weathered twenty years in an unhappy marriage. Any relationship of yours I should consider?"

"No. Several offers, but I kept busy running his clinic, the household, and raising our sons. I'm not the undercover type, so to speak. My sons deserved one example of fidelity."

"Good to know." Corrin patted her pile of papers. "I'm assisting Roy on a critical case, and we've hit a turning point. Stop by this weekend if you need a break from testosterone hills."

"I will if no overtime's available."

"I understand." Corrin pointed out the window to a cabin across the street. "That's my new abode on the lake edge, perfect for chats, or venting. Rane seemed mighty uncomfortable talking to me, so I'm itching for an update on your relationship."

"Nothing to tell. He doesn't appear to trust females unless they have four legs." Elon smiled and grasped Corrin's hands, "I want to hear every detail about you and handsome Doc Kyle."

Corrin let out a long breath. "Nothing too exciting. We're taking things really slow."

"Smart move."

"I have a bit of my own baggage." She walked Elon outside, waved, and went back in the house.

Elon made it to the car before disgust permeated every pore. If Mom and Dad were alive, they'd seethe at Tim cheating her out of the house they'd purchased for her bridal gift. She slouched in the seat. Her parents paid for every upgrade to open Tim's clinic and also for his expensive medical equipment. She'd spent hours doing the bookkeeping and cleaning to stretch money in the early years, all for nothing. Her keys slid from her grip and fell onto the passenger seat.

Angel's nose bumped her wrist. She licked Elon's hand.

Elon grasped her ears and kissed the top of her head, then ruffled through soft fur. No hesitation or shudders from the pup. Angel was healing.

"I've got you, and I've got two fabulous sons. The rest will fall into place."

Fall into place. A memory flashed into her brain of her mom showing her the great spot in the condo to stash emergency money under the kitchen counter. *This constituted one heck of an emergency.* One of the kids should be home to check this evening.

Gravel crunched. A Mustang swung into the driveway beside her, and a tall, russet-haired woman approached her car.

"Hi, I'm Miranda. You must be Elon," she said, and gave her a warm smile.

"I am and nice to meet you. Corrin's told me part of your story." She stuck her hand out the window.

Miranda offered a firm shake. "From what we've all been through, the three of us deserve a support group." Her focus flicked to Angel. "Oh, what a darling dog. I told Grant a pup's the only thing missing at our ranch."

Finding Angel's offspring good homes might not be so difficult. "Angel came into my life unexpectedly. Ed just alerted me she's carrying two puppies. Want pick of the litter?"

"Absolutely."

"Okay. Better run. I've got a hungry crew at the ranch, and I need to hit the grocery store."

Shopping complete, she wheeled her car onto the ranch driveway fifty minutes before dinnertime. Scents of chicken and thyme wafted from the instant pot.

The pie dough she'd made and refrigerated rolled out perfectly. Root vegetables she'd bought at a roadside stand and then roasted completed the loaded pot pies, decorated by fork pricks in the shape of a chicken. Fresh, local apples went into a crisp topped by oatmeal crumbles.

After she'd stuck them in the oven, she pulled out her phone and dialed the condo.

"Hello," Brandon responded.

Just the voice she needed to hear. "Hi Brandon. Glad I caught you."

"Mom. How's it going?"

"Met with my lawyer. This weekend I need you guys to check the stack of boxes against the far wall of the storage unit. Look for an envelope marked *Last Will and Testament*. Call me immediately if you find it."

"We'll make it a priority."

"Meantime, Grandma had a hidey hole. To the right of the refrigerator, under the pots and pans cupboard, sits a kick plate made from wood. Pry out the left side." Elon rubbed her diamond ring.

"Sure." Scraping sounded from his end. "Hey, there's an envelope holding old passports and cash." Brandon whistled. "There's four hundred in here."

Facing the window, she let her head fall back and looked skyward. "Thank you, Mom." Her fingers clenched the edge of the sink. "That covers Jeremy's book. Can you manage other expenses until I'm paid?"

"We'll be fine."

A warm hand tapped her shoulder. Elon twisted, her arm grazing Rane. He threw her the time-out sign.

"Hold on, Brandon."

"Didn't mean to eavesdrop," he said. "Do you need an advance?"

Warmth crept into her cheeks. "No, Mr. Calderon, but thank you."

His chin jutted up as if she'd struck him. He spun on his heel and left.

"Gotta go," she whispered. "Love you."

"Wait! Your boss tried to help, Mom. Can't wait to tell

Jeremy. Makes me feel better you took the job."

And by refusing Rane's offer, she felt much worse.

Standing on a platform inside the haybarn, Rane tilted his head so the brim of his Stetson allowed a concealed view of the woman sitting on the porch. She'd proven efficient at cleaning up after suppers and occupied Grandma Bia's wooden porch swing early tonight, rocking with purpose.

Money worries weren't alarming her, maybe she doubted her skills. Much as he hated to admit it, she'd proved to be a damn good welder. Her work on the dozer satisfied his crankiest customer. If only he could quit eyeballing her.

She tapped her fingers on her jeans and checked her watch again. Her brows drew together.

Bored or bothered about something? Oh hell, not his problem. He needed to pitch a few more bales onto the front of the flatbed trailer that he'd backed inside, readying it for Fred to feed the cattle. He took off his jacket, feeling crisp air on his bare arms.

Clanking chains signaled Elon's rise from the seat, but somehow, he also knew the precise moment she'd entered the open barn.

"Mr. Calderon? Can I bother you a second?" She stood beside the trailer hitch.

A jolt hit his body as if he'd touched an electric fence. He was way past bothered when a simple question put every nerve ending on alert. Every damn one.

"Angel scampered off over twenty minutes ago."

The worry in her voice tamped him down a notch.

"There's a lot of smellograms out there."

"She's usually not gone this long. Could Possum and I

walk through the pasture to look for her?"

He cleared his throat. "Cows and calves in my fields make it dangerous. Our old dog responded to a whistle. Angel would hear if you stood by the fence."

"Okay." She walked to the fence and managed a couple weak tweets, then poked her hands in her pockets "Angel," she called.

"Do you ride?" The spankin' new tight jeans she'd arrived in now hung loose. But those curves, they still tortured him. "Horses?"

"I loved horseback riding as a kid." She approached the platform and stood close enough for him to see childlike anticipation brightening her pretty face. Close enough to catch a lingering scent of vanilla and cinnamon in her tangle of hair.

He'd been cornered like a greased pig in an alley. A greased pig who'd gorged on seconds of apple crisp and ice cream. The guys raved about her cooking, maybe she deserved a reward. And the need to supply one wouldn't quit percolating in his brain. "If you take it easy, you can ride Possum while we search for Angel. I've been checking his left hind leg, and there's no swelling. He hasn't limped for a week."

Elon tucked an auburn curl behind her ear. "Thank you. Possum's friendly. I offer him carrots when I pass his paddock. What a thrill to ride him . . . if it isn't a bother."

Widened, sky blue eyes melted something deep in his gut. "Give me a couple minutes to finish here." The next three-strand bale he pitched felt lighter than goose down.

"Possum's an odd name. Did you raise him?" Her glance flicked to his upper arms and stayed there for a long moment.

Ranchers didn't need health club memberships to shape their muscles. He'd never considered the advantage until today. "Nope." He stuck the hay hooks into each end of a bale. "Thirstys Possum is on his pedigree. He's from a long line of cow ponies bred to boss cattle. They voice their opinions. Similar to women."

Elon pursed her lips, as if fighting back a wise crack.

He pulled his eyes away from admiring their pouty plumpness. The last bale nearly flew over the wagon. He flexed his back and jumped off the platform, landing a couple feet from her.

She wrung her hands and stepped back until her thighs hit the trailer tongue. Her cheeks grew pink.

Trying to ignore attraction or scared of it? He grabbed his jacket and stepped closer. "Do you still want to ride?" he'd managed a calm voice.

"More than ever."

His pulse spiked. "You wait here, and I'll bring him out." He owned manuals for every engine in his shop. Someone needed to write one on women.

R ane Calderon took in strays. A fact she could handle. Not how she gawked at his powerful biceps in action when he tossed hay bales. The man threw her off balance. Worse, her composure wobbled too easily while she struggled to survive this thirty-day trial and unwanted cravings to touch every inch of his rock-solid physique.

Clip clops alerted her to the approach of her tormenter. He led out a bridled but unsaddled Possum and a caramel-colored, larger horse. She rubbed her hands down the thighs of her jeans.

Possum whinnied to her. Rane scratched the horse's nose. "He likes you. Let's check his leg with a rider aboard. Hop on bareback."

Exactly how she'd ridden as a kid. She grinned, until

noticing that Possum's withers stood above her shoulder. No way she'd leap onto him. "I'm happy to saddle him."

"Not necessary. Watch me mount," Rane instructed. "Stand by his side, facing his hind end. Next, grab hold of his mane, take two steps, and swing your leg over." In one fluid movement, Rane sat comfortably on the other horse's back.

"There's a substantial difference between the length of my legs versus yours," she commented.

Rane slid off. "Hadn't noticed."

Oh, he'd noticed all right. She moved close enough to scratch the gelding's coppery-colored shoulder. "Hi Possum, double carrots and apples if you hold still." She stood on tiptoes near his ear. "Sugar cubes if you bend low." Rane chuckled.

She grabbed a handful of flaxen mane, took two bouncy steps, and swung her leg. One calf landed in the middle of the horse's back, while her other leg dangled a foot off the ground. "Yikes!" She scrambled to heft her butt onto his back, inching her leg over his spine. "Guess I'm not twelve anymore."

"None of us are." Rane's warm hands cupped her knee and nudged her up. "Let me help you aboard. My dad coached me to try anything until I succeeded, before deciding whether I liked it or not. Try to hop on again."

Third strike, coming up. She patted the calm horse on the neck before sliding off. "Good boy, Possum." This time, she crouched before she leapt, got some height, and sprung aboard to the center of his back. "Score."

Possum lowered his head while she scratched both sides of his shoulders.

Rane tipped his hat. "We're both impressed."

"I remembered a basketball coach teaching my sons how to do layup shots."

"Whatever gets the job done. Move him a couple steps

forward, then backward."

She'd barely leaned forward when Possum began to slowly walk. Sitting back caused him to stop. Slight leg pressure and a couple taps on the reins moved him backward.

"Everything checks out." Rane's sharp eyes remained squarely on her. "Now, we'll throw on his saddle," he announced.

Next he'd tell her he'd been kidding. He didn't. She put her hands on her hips. "I can't ride bareback?"

"Too dangerous on the range for a beginning rider."

Maybe a Montana beginner. She flipped her right leg across Possum's neck and slid off his left side. "Why didn't we start using a saddle?"

Rane gathered his horse's reins and headed for the barn. "I needed to verify you'd listen to my instructions."

Or he wanted to see her attempt to sling her rear end five feet off the ground. Elon compressed the soft, worn leather in her fist. "Possum, you need to teach me some of your patience."

The gelding's whiskers tickled her ear.

He'd mentioned his dad coaching him. She mustered her courage to learn more. "Are your parents alive?"

"Yup, I believe they are."

Goosebumps rose on her forearms. "They sure looked proud of you in the photo on your dresser."

"Probably the last time they felt pride, I reckon. Subject closed." Rane led his horse into the barn.

Elon felt a tug at her heart. Something had turned him off women and split his family for the past twenty years. Nothing could separate her from her boys.

Angel bounded around the side of the barn and stopped at her feet.

"Where have you been?" The dog cowered, and she softened her voice. "You had me worried. There are coyotes out there." She scratched Angel's head. "You've been digging. Hopefully not a flower bed. The dog dropped a smooth, indented rock into her hand. She cupped the smallish, egg-sized stone in her palm, pocketed it, and brushed dirt off the black nose. "Thanks for the gift. Time for you to meet Possum. We'll explore together."

The horse bent his neck and sniffed the dog. Angel bowed on both front paws, spun around, and plopped onto her back. Possum snuffed her tummy until Angel bumped his nose.

"Good. You're furry friends. Let's see if a ride's still possible." She led the dog and horse through the wide doors into a cool, dim sanctuary. *Life broken down to simple elements.* She sighed and listened to horses shuffling in stalls on the far end. To her left, Rane lifted a saddle onto his gelding in a tack up area outfitted with cross ties hung from an overhead beam.

"Angel returned. Can we still ride?"

"Sure." He looked at the pup. "You need to know the area."

That sounded as if he intended to keep them around. "Agreed."

"Tack room's on your right. Possum's saddle and pad are marked. Clean them after each use." He pointed to cloths and leather polish in a wire basket hanging outside the tack room door. "I brushed and hoof-picked earlier, so you can skip those today. I brought out the saddle pad."

Combing the twin's hair used to soothe her nerves. She'd need to groom a wooly mammoth at this point. "Thanks. I'll gather his tack." She gave him a bright smile and stepped inside the spotless room.

Scents of leather and wool pads worn by warm horses took her back to childhood. Those naïve, carefree summer days ended when her girlfriend and her horses moved to Denver.

She let out a slow, cleansing breath. Shiny patches implied years of wear on the western style saddles. Elon hefted the correct one, walked out, and placed it onto Possum's back, which now held a black and white woven pad. Bringing the cinch under his belly, her brain struggled to remember the knot at the cinch ring. She pushed the strap under and around. "It doesn't look right."

Rane stepped beside her. His calloused hand undid her effort. "It's close. Wrap it through the girth ring twice and tighten it to two fingers between Possum's belly and the tie straps. Try again." His hip brushed her waist as he undid the knot.

They shot apart faster than opposing magnets.

Flutters radiating through her body did not come from saddling angst. Ignoring his appeal proved substantially more difficult than mastering welding seams and cinches. She fumbled wrapping the strap behind, around, and under the cinch ring. Rane had either jumped from irritation, or Lord forbid, the same attraction she'd felt. He'd moved to Keeper and pulled his hat low on his brow. Well, he couldn't hide his face forever.

A hesitant shade of quiet surrounded them in the tack up area. No munching or tail swishing or hooves shuffling. Whickering from the end stall finally broke the strained silence between them. Possum whinnied an answer and shook his head. Familiar smells of hay and manure usually grounded him. Not today, not with her in his barn.

Rane blinked, but his focus remained on her. He needed a swift kick in the keister to end the misery. Inhaling sweet scents wafting from her hair further clouded his brain.

He scratched Keeper's cheek and followed Elon's long

fingers snugging the leather strap into place. When she concentrated on a task, her shapely lips repeatedly opened and closed. Keeper bumped his shoulder in a 'ha, ha dude, you're screwed' kinda way. And he was, in a way he'd never felt before.

His gelding pawed the floor, letting him know his impatience to get moving.

"Chill out." Rane straightened the bridle's brow band. "You're worse than a kid." And if he were thinking straight, he'd realize that with her being the kind of mother who cared, Elon's home wasn't in Montana. She'd taken a temporary job until the damn divorce finalized or whatever else had disrupted her life smoothed out. And once it did, she'd go back.

The less he interacted with her the better. She'd saddle her own horse from now on. "Check the girth one more time before you mount. There's a stump out back you can use as a mounting block." He moved his horse through the open rear door. "We'll head west where there's a good area to ride. I'll bet Angel sticks close."

"I'm training her to stay by my side." Elon followed him and snapped her fingers.

The dog trotted beside her to the stump.

He knew exactly why the smart pup followed Elon—she'd gotten the entire crew to eat out of her hands by great meals and her torch work. And him, he couldn't stop watching her shapely hips swing onto Possum again. She settled gently into the saddle with the expertise of a caring cowgirl. Looked like he'd estimated the stirrup length correctly.

His eyes moved to her wavy, thick hair hanging to her shoulders. The evening sun burnished copper into the strands, perfectly matched to Possum's coloring. Probably not a complement to a city girl. "Your horse is trained to leg pressure. Stay off his mouth."

She kept the reins loose beside Possum's withers. "I used to picture being at the dentist when I rode. I won't pull on him, promise."

Her imploring voice tugged his gut. Either her wish to please him or his own excitement. Damn distractions. He swung into his saddle, then exerted slight pressure from his lower legs, signaling Keeper to walk. "Don't ride when it's windy, makes the horses nervous when they can't hear. Possum doesn't spook easy, but if he takes off, pull one rein to your knee." He grabbed his rein closer to the bridle and nodded approval as she followed suit. "You force him to circle. We call it a one-handed stop."

"I appreciate the tips. As a kid I epitomized a classic pony girl, in the innocent, old-fashioned sense. My best friend lived on a farm. Her patient horses babysat us for hours."

He nodded. "The best kind for kids."

Serenity took ten years off Elon's face, like a brush stroke covering her worries with fresh paint. Her eyes met his gaze. "So, who are you riding, Mr. Calderon?"

"I'm aboard Keeper. Maybe it's time you called me Rane."

"Sure. If you'll call me Elon." She urged Possum to walk abreast of Keeper. "Odd name for your horse, I bet there's a story."

He leaned back comfortably in the saddle. He hadn't talked this much to a female since his parents vacated. "City folks have the habit of buying spreads, collecting animals, getting bored, and leaving. They don't take horses on return flights to LA."

"How terrible. An animal is not a bicycle. It makes me furious how people think pets are disposable."

"Before one particularly entitled group cleared out, one of their horses kept appearing in my pasture. I'd return him.

The owner pegged him to be an ornery gelding. Said he kicked, bit, and bucked. He threatened he'd take him to the kill pen where a knacker buys them by weight and the horses are sent to slaughter in Canada or Mexico. Turned my stomach."

"People are barbaric."

"Tell me about it. I paid the jerk three hundred bucks for him." He stroked the gelding's neck. "He's the friendliest, most patient pony I've ever ridden. A real keeper."

"Very appropriate name. His coat color reminds me of the sauce I make for my sons' favorite double caramel birthday cake." A wistful look crossed her face. "He's lucky you found him."

No sense encouraging her to miss her kids. "Keeper deserved a better ending to his story. He's a helluva cattle horse." Rane moved his big horse through a gate. "Speaking of which, don't ride the other horses on the far end of the barn. Those are my ranch hands' cow ponies."

"I'd never ride a horse without permission."

"Good. Stick to Possum. Let's head up the draw, and I'll show you a safe area to explore on your own." He rode toward a shallow ravine between two hills.

"Head up the draw. I never thought I'd be experiencing that term." The low sun cast purple shadows into the swales created by grassy mounds.

"You can use gully if it suits you better." Rane shrugged. "Guess cowboys have their own dictionary."

"Not too many cowboys in Seattle. I rode with my friend a few summers on Vashon Island, where her family owned horses."

"I see." Rane crested the top of the hill first, and Keeper came to an abrupt stop. "Damn rustlers! Stay back, Elon. Trouble!"

CHAPTER 4

R ane pivoted Keeper, feeling the horse's muscles bunch in anticipation for the signal to bolt.

A truck and trailer created a brown cloud while barreling away from them on the easement road from the highway.

His heart pumped double time. Fury burned in his chest.

Cows stood in a bunch forty feet away, mooing distressingly. Keeper danced in place: head up and ears alert as if he sensed the danger.

"What happened?" Elon kept her distance.

"Damn scumbags stole calves from their mothers! Unweaned babies." He thumped his saddle horn. "Five minutes earlier and we would've caught the bastards."

"How horrible, "Elon gasped. "I brought my cell phone. I'll call for help." She slid it from her back pocket. "I've got a signal."

Keeper snorted while Rane held him in check. "Tell 911 we need Sheriff Riley."

"It's ringing." Elon moved Possum to Keeper's side. "Here, you talk to the dispatcher." She passed the phone between the horses.

Rane growled out the situation and handed back her phone. "Sheriff Riley's on his way. I need to close the gate. Go on ahead and I'll catch up."

Elon stowed her phone and pointed Possum downhill.

His heart sank while he wove Keeper through the plaintively mooing cows and turned a few away from the open gate. "Hey bossie, easy there now." He pulled his horse alongside the fence and dismounted, away from the tracks. With careful steps he swung the old stock gate shut and anchored the cut chain to an exposed nail on the fencepost. *Bastards would be halfway to a slaughterhouse before the sheriff arrived.* He remounted Keeper, and the gelding willingly galloped toward the distant rider.

When they pulled alongside, Elon asked, "Is this the first time cattle thieves struck?"

"Last week they tried to take Tomo. Bad aim and they roped his leg, breaking it."

"Unbelievable they'd act during daylight."

A soft glow lingered in the western horizon. "If I'd thought to bring my rifle, they'd have been sorry." He slapped the reins on his thigh. "Must've seen us from the ridge. I need to take photos of any prints or tire tracks before dark."

"I can canter on this flat area." Her voice held concern as she continued, "If Possum's leg is okay."

"Should be. If his head bobs, it indicates lameness and the need to walk."

"Got it." She urged Possum into a lope. Her body matched the tempo of the rocking horse.

Ahead, the outside ranch lights flickered in the dusky glow. The bulbs cast an eerie blue beam, further chilling the unsettling in the pit of his stomach. He galloped past her, reached the barn first, and jumped off Keeper.

Elon shot around the paddock fence and slowed Possum to a trot. "I'll put the horses away."

"The sheriff and I will need them. Please loosen their girths and walk them." Rane tossed his reins to her and headed inside for his camera. He grabbed his old Nikon and his rifle before closing the door.

Elon held a pair of reins in each hand while circling the two lathered up geldings around the house. As he reached her, the patrol car sped into the driveway, kicking up a dust bowl.

"Thanks, Elon. We'll talk in the morning." Rane walked to the parked squad car.

Sheriff Riley emerged, carrying his hat and wearing a grimace on his thirty-year-old angular face. His eyes were pinched to slits. "We'll catch the damn cattle thieves, Rane." He ran his hands through his reddish hair and shoved on the hat. "You have my word."

"Glad you were on duty. There's a chance they'll pack weight on the calves for more money."

Riley bent his muscular frame to unlock an AR-15 from inside his car. "I'd like to collar these creeps. Guess they're thinking about building a private prison nearby. That may be a good idea—as long as it's not in our county."

Rane flinched. Prison? They needed manufacturing plants, not jail cells. Later, he'd ask more details. Right now, stolen calves took priority. "Hadn't heard about a prison. Sure as hell hope it's not close." He stepped inside the barn, grabbed two rifle scabbards, and threw one out to the sheriff.

"I assume you'll ride Possum." Elon tightened the cinch and handed off the reins to Riley.

"Yes, ma'am. Thanks." He buckled on the scabbard and slid in his gun. "You must be the new hire I've heard mentioned." He mounted Possum and leaned toward her. "Cattle rustling isn't normal in Emma Springs."

Ditto for attractive female welders, Rane realized, and he threw the unmarried, securely-employed officer a side eye. Elon looked nothing short of sexy with her windblown hair and big eyes, and the way Riley leaned over the saddle horn, he'd noticed. "Disaster could've struck if we'd surprised armed thugs. I'm responsible for protecting everyone on my ranch." He pushed his rifle into place and touched Elon's shoulder. "Glad you brought your phone. I need to get one someday."

"When you have kids, keeping a phone welded to your hip is a necessary habit. Please be careful," she said. "In the movies rustlers ambush their adversaries."

Her strained voice and pale skin told him she cared. He gave her a cocky grin. "Don't worry. Those vermin won't come back tonight." He watched her nod in response, but then she stumbled on the porch stairs.

Elon was shaken. No one had shown him that kind of concern in twenty years. It felt good to have a woman care what happened to him, and it unnerved him as much as the damn rustlers. They'd hauled away expensive cattle. No doubt, they'd strike again.

Elon flipped up the visor on her welding helmet and fought to keep her eyes open in the bright morning sunshine. She'd listened for Rane's footsteps until well after midnight, praying the cattle thieves wouldn't return. Thank goodness, they hadn't.

She removed the heavy head gear and shook out her damp hair. The previously bent haybine jack occupying her work-space held the battle scars of a seasoned warrior. Her fresh welds added to other repair ridges on the frame. She cleaned and stowed her equipment and pulled a carrot from the pocket of her old winter coat.

"Hey, Possum," she called from beside his paddock.

The gelding raised his head and nickered a greeting.

"You must be a little lonely here by yourself. Keeper gets to graze with friends in the pasture. Let's do a couple of exercise rounds, then I'll take you to munch beside them."

She slipped a rope halter over Possum's nose and knotted it snugly near his ears. "I found this in the tack room. Let's show Rane how much better it looks than the gaudy pink leather one hanging outside your stall." She led Possum out onto the gravel driveway, checking his leg for hesitance. "I can't see any effect from your loping yesterday."

A pearly white Cadillac Escalade kicking up gravel passed her and parked in front of the machine shop. "Hmm," she said to Possum. "It's not dirty enough for a ranch vehicle and neither the driver or kid inside are smart enough to realize they startled you."

Possum danced at the end of the lead rope, and Elon went into calming mode. "Easy there, just some dumb city people." She stroked his neck, and the jittery horse moved behind her.

A man in his early thirties, dressed in a sweater and cords, and a blonde girl of about ten got out of the flashy vehicle.

Possum backed up, pulling against the halter. "Hey, it's okay." She touched his cheek.

"Daddy, he's not wearing my custom halter. She probably sold it." A diminutive finger wagged in Elon's direction.

He went to his daughter, putting his arm around her while they walked forward. "We're not certain, honey."

The girl exhibited more wasp than honey. Possum shied when the kid stepped forward, her face scrunched in a scowl.

Elon thrust her hand out. "Stop. You're scaring the horse. Not another step."

The man grabbed the kid's hand. "We owned Thirstys Possum before Rane. My daughter forgot to retrieve her new halter before I retired him."

"You mean when you dumped him off at the auction, figuring he'd be sold for slaughter, don't you?" Elon kept her voice controlled to calm the panicked horse.

Rane stepped out from behind a tractor parked in her work area. He wiped his greasy hands on a towel and approached the group. "Hello, Curt. I thought I recognized your voice. Didn't notice on his paperwork that you'd owned Possum."

"Yeah. For a while. We just found out you bought him." Curt's nonchalance at taking the horse for slaughter made Elon's skin crawl.

"Did I hear someone's missing a halter?" Rane glanced at the kid and veered to the barn.

Elon noted his smile didn't reach his eyes. "Must be the halter hanging in front of Possum's stall. You can't miss its pink glitz," she yelled

The little girl pulled a sparkly pink crop from her boot.

"Still limping?" She waved it at the horse.

Possum's nostrils flared.

Brat! Elon stroked Possum's neck. "Don't come any closer," she managed in a controlled growl.

The girl pirouetted and patted her father's arm. "Daddy did the right thing, as always. Too bad we spent so much money on the cripple." She held her nose aloft, as if smelling something disdainful.

"Here's the only tack he came with." Rane faked another smile.

"Thanks, Calderon." The father handed it to his daughter's outstretched hands.

Rhinestones sparkled in afternoon sunlight. The girl flipped it over. "It doesn't look too dirty." She raised the whip to the halter. "I knew they matched perfectly!"

Possum issued a shrill whinny, the whites of his eyes showing. Elon glared at her and bunched her fist. "Put that—"

"Come on kiddo, you've got a cutting lesson." Her dad opened the passenger door. "We'll be on our way now."

Elon led Possum toward the barn. "Easy fella," she whispered. "The evil princess is leaving the premises."

"See you later, Curt." Rane threw them a cursory wave while they drove past. He jogged to her side and patted Possum's shoulder. "Sorry 'bout that. Must say, your scowl could've wilted June corn."

"Wilting is too good for that brat. My Dad called her type a dime store kid," Elon said. "Plenty of change, buy something, break it, and discard it."

"Well, dime store kid's father owns the largest farm equipment dealership in Montana and sends me repair business. I appreciate you not thrashing her."

"Fortunate she didn't take one more step waving the bedazzled whip."

His deep chuckle took away some of the edge. "Funny thing," Rane said. "I've heard the few townsfolk you've met describe you as a sweet city girl. If they saw your battle-ready side, they'd change their tune."

Possum's coppery nose stayed glued to her shoulder as she opened the gate to his turn out. "Kids and animals—I'll protect either with my life."

"Admirable and formidable." He saluted her and headed to the shop.

She wouldn't disagree. "You're safe now," she promised Possum before giving his neck a final scratch. "See you tomorrow. Gotta fix grub."

Confrontation sucked out more energy than she could spare. Her shoes scuffed into the house and onto the kitchen linoleum. Pulling the old refrigerator door open and grabbing containers of veggies and meats took effort. Once she got dinner served, she'd call it a night and take a long, hot, muscle-soothing bath. She sighed and finished scattering toppings on homemade pizza crust.

Fred stepped into the kitchen and handed her a list. "Here's what the boys want baked for the weekend. Price doesn't seem to be an issue."

She blinked at the large quantities and forced a cheerful smile. "Wow. Nice. If I make them affordable, it'll ensure repeat business."

"Smart business sense." Fred grinned, showing a couple gold-capped teeth. He tipped his hat and left.

Thirty minutes later, she pulled out of the oven fresh baked cheese, pepperoni, and combination pizzas. At home they'd be called extra large, in Montana they were probably mediums.

The men filed in for dinner, some giving their boots a cursory rub on the porcupine boot scraper she'd found in the storeroom and placed outside the door. She centered the pizza trays on the long wooden table and began cutting the nearest one into slices. Her arms ached with each stroke. *Take heart,* she told herself. *With minimum cleanup you'll clock out in thirty minutes.*

Grit moved to her side. He adjusted the strap on his blue striped overalls. By his size and at times his smell, he reminded her of a shaggy black bear. She took two steps away from him.

"We're watchin' a new horror movie tonight, ma'am. Thought you might want to join us for our pre-Halloween tradition." Two days of splotchy growth on his jowls bobbed at each word.

Rane hung his hat on the hall tree, stopped, and stared. If he'd been a bug with antennas, they'd be pointed at her. His clenched jaw made it clear she and the hired help shouldn't fraternize.

Elon moved to the end of the table. Feeding them quickly occupied her only interest. "Sorry, I hired on as the welder and cook, not to socialize." She sliced through pepperoni using her wheel cutter.

Grit pulled out a knife and hacked the combo pizza nearest him into four pieces.

Elon pictured the blade being used on a hunting trip. She looked away.

"We'd enjoy something to munch tonight, Ms. Hardy." Rane walked to his usual chair, his back to Grit. "Maybe a little snack buffet of meatballs, chicken wings, and Indian tacos. Can you whip those up and join us? Say seven o'clock?" The tone fell somewhere between a request and a command.

Indian tacos? Her jaw dropped. And they were back on last name only terms. "Sure," she muttered. Was he trying to prove he could boss her around in front of the men?

"Ahh, just kidding," Rane said, and grabbed a slice of pepperoni pizza. All the men laughed, except Grit.

She rolled her eyes and squeezed the potholder. "I'll find something to serve, don't worry."

"Unfriendly for you to feed us and not watch the show, right boys?" Rane continued jokingly. "The leftover potato chips from lunch will work fine. You'll like the movie."

Several men grunted their agreement between bites, unaware of her annoyance at being the butt of another joke.

"Hey, Ms. Hardy," one of the machinists said. "Spoke to my wife. Please double my order for cinnamon rolls to take home this weekend."

She'd welcomed Fred's willingness to compile orders,

allowing her to keep a low profile. That cow had left the pasture, and this could be the test of Rane's friendliness. "Not a problem. They'll be ready Saturday," Elon replied.

Two other men raised their hands and put in larger orders. She grabbed a pad and took notes, then collected the empty trays and salad bowl. *Nothing like creating a pastry monster.* She deposited the dishes on the counter and rubbed her tired eyes.

"Could I see you for a minute in the storeroom?" Rane's voice held the smooth tone that set her teeth on edge.

Elon wiped sweaty palms on her apron and adjusted the neck strap before following him through the kitchen. Her new cottage industry might fail before it began.

He leaned against the freezer. "If money's tight, it'll make you nervous on the job. The torch requires your full attention."

"I'm fine until payday. I don't want to be treated any differently than your men."

He stood to his full height and squinted down at her. "You don't think much of me if you believe I wouldn't do the same for any of them." His sleeve brushed her arm when he passed her.

Believing in a man—a novel concept. "I enjoy baking," she called to his backside. She retreated to the kitchen, filled a pitcher to overflowing, and let cool water spill onto her fingers. He'd can her if she irritated him further. Her chin dropped. The connection he made between nerves and welding didn't make sense. Ed, the vet, inferred a heart did beat under Rane's steel exterior. If she considered the facts, Rane's offer showed kindness. Regardless, she'd agreed to make snacks.

She managed to clean up dinner debris in time to change before movie night at the cowpoke frat house. Her quiet bedroom offered a respite while she flicked through the few hangers holding tops in the closet. She scanned a drab gray one, then a pale blue, silky blouse trimmed in white lace at the boat necked collar—her last birthday present from mom. It always made her feel special. She slipped into it and headed to the living room.

Heeled boots scuffled on clean floors, signaling the gang's arrival. Elon silently counted participants. Full house. Men in chairs and couches faced a five-foot wide television.

"Popcorn tonight, fellows?" she asked.

"Sounds good," said the young guy they called Lefty.

"Sure, Ms. Hardy," Emmett chimed in while she made her way to the kitchen.

An old kettle took up one end of the overhead pot rack. The corn rattled and pinged as it fell to the bottom. Shaking it on the stovetop gave her time to dissect the first invite to a social interaction. At Grit's insistence she attend, Rane had acted irritated, given her grief over preparing snacks, and finally suggested she'd like the movie. Gads, he had more mood flashes than a hormonal teenager.

White corn popped the lid off the kettle, ready to be drenched by a golden stream of melted butter. The previews flashed as she scooped popcorn into bowls and handed them out. Her eyes adjusted to the dimness in time to spot the only empty space in the crowded room.

The two-person monstrosity, shadowed by a huge rack of moose horns forming the back and arms, stood sentry behind the men. Narrow, polished planks of wood constituted an unpadded seat.

Tired bones didn't deserve to be plopped on the floor. She perched on the edge of its burled seat, rubbing her finger across the morbid ode to antlers, which needed dusting. After the action began, she'd head for the hallway.

Rane's warm breath whispered near her ear. "Excuse me, miss, is this seat taken?"

Adrenaline spiked in her veins, starting at her neck and working to her toes. Her eyes traveled from Rane's broad frame to the scant foot remaining on the seat. "It's vacant, sir."

Keeping a friendly distance, she wedged her hip into the space on her side under the bony armrest. Waves of sheer male radiated from Rane's solid thigh as he pushed her further into the antler. The wood creaked under his weight, issuing a not-so-silent protest.

Her idea of friendly fell to the wayside while her entire body shot to alert, some parts more than others. She jumped when the opening creepy doll sequence illuminated the room for a flash. The scenery changed to a darkened haunted house. Minutes droned on like hours.

Rane casually draped his arm over the back of the settee, his brushed cotton shirt tickling a patch of bare skin on her shoulder.

Her body stiffened into perfect posture while he squeezed his bicep between the knobby antlers.

Flashing knives and screaming teenagers kept the men's focus on the TV. One of the actors resembled Jeremy. A zombie jumped out from a stairwell and bit him. Her hands flew to her face to stifle a scream. Rane's arm provided a strange sense of security while the body count grew, and her sense of foreboding rose in her chest.

A loud CRACK sounded from Rane's side. Elon slid down the seat to the right. Her side of the seat remained anchored to the frame, while his had busted out and dropped. He'd landed on the floor and she'd flopped onto him.

Heads whipped toward them. "Should I stop the movie?" Emmett asked.

"Everything's fine. Keep it rolling," Rane's voice boomed authority.

Nothing was fine! She wiggled her rear, vised between the

broken boards and his thigh. And if that wasn't bad enough, her legs were flung across his lap. "I'm stuck," she hissed into his chest, which put out the heat of a convection oven.

"Shhh, it's the big ending. You're not bothering me."

Smart ass. Smoldering retorts froze on her tongue. Her first paycheck came Tuesday, and she needed every penny.

Taking her cue from this morning's refresher session on mounting bareback, she grabbed a fistful of material just below the V-neck of his shirt and thrust her hip up and out of the broken trap. If she grabbed a little chest hair, too, it served him right.

Rane Calderon might give her the feelings of a schoolgirl concealing a crush at times, but she didn't have to like it.

Rane dusted splinters off his jeans. Knees bent, he heaved forward and pulled himself out of the broken relic. He patted one of the antler arms and scanned the room. No shapely, irritated brunette in sight. He couldn't help grinning.

Emmett shut off the TV. "Quite an ending to the movie. Judging by her scowl, I don't think Ms. Hardy likes so much action in a flick." The crew sniggered agreement.

"You have no idea." Rane rubbed his chest. He'd have paid good money to see Elon's face when she plopped onto his lap. The memory of her sexy butt planted on his thigh would warm him on more than a few cold nights. Only a fool divorced a woman like her.

A low whine came from the front porch. Cool night air breezed across his face as he held the door for Angel. Her clean fur felt soft as he scratched her head and rubbed her sides. Packing a little meat on her bones had relieved the scrawniness he'd noticed on her arrival.

Anxious brown eyes peered back at him. The pup either worried about her own hide or her owner's. "Everything's okay," he assured her.

The men filed out past him through the open door, praising the evening as one of the best so far.

"Angel!" Elon called from her room, the tone a pitch higher than normal. The dog jetted into the hall.

Oh, to be a fly on their bedroom wall. He'd heard her commiserating to the dog often while she cooked. Rane walked to the master suite he occupied. He'd waited ten years after his folks cleared out to replace the furniture, remodel the bathroom, and inhabit the prime space.

Elon had been the first woman to walk these floors since Mom. He chuckled again at the thought of her flying onto his lap. Hell, she acted skittish as a colt when their knees barely bumped under the dinner table. He pulled on pajama bottoms and crawled into bed, recalling Emmett's assessment.

The crash certainly provided his most entertaining evening in a long time. He laced his fingers behind his head and closed his eyes. The image of Elon's bruised arm and smashed phone when she first arrived overshadowed tonight's fun. If he ever found out her jerk of a husband had hurt her . . .

A lone coyote howled in the distance. Tonight, the cry wasn't calling the pack, it begged for companionship for the cold winter ahead.

He could relate. Whether to act remained the question. He lifted the comforter off his chest.

~

Tim glanced at Jasmine, who lay peacefully asleep in the dismal excuse of a bed offered by the only Three Falls hotel that rated higher than two stars. She'd sleep soundly—thanks to the pill he'd dropped in her drink at dinner.

The outline of the neon chopping tomahawk hanging from the corner of the building blinked on and off through thin curtains. Adjusting the light-blocking blind took care of one problem.

He pulled horn-rimmed glasses and a ball cap from his backpack. The reflection he saw in the bathroom mirror screamed clean-cut out-of-towner.

Jasmine's brown mascara stuck out of her cosmetic bag on the counter. He smudged some between his fingers and rubbed it onto his cheeks and chin to darken his pale complexion.

He exited the room and made his way to the tavern two doors down. From under the brim of the low-slung cap he scanned the cowboy types, two men in cheap sport coats, and a few couples occupying tables.

His sliding onto a barstool caught the attention of the gray-haired man drawing a beer from a Bud Light tap. Behind him a dismal variety of liquor sat on a shelf. "I'll take a scotch on the rocks," he stated quietly. No single malt offered in this joint. "So what's the latest news in Three Falls?" he asked casually.

Getting the guy to spill how a local yokel recently employed a female welder hadn't taken two pours of their foul scotch. He'd no more than mentioned a buddy looking for a welding gig, and the guy willingly offered the rancher's name.

He sat back and sipped the remaining swill. A pinball machine dinged in the corner.

The barmaid sidled up to the bartender. "Feel this." She

thrust out her bare forearm. "The mud wraps at Beverly's Spa made my skin touchably soft," she purred.

He smiled into his drink. Jasmine loved spas. She'd willingly spend tomorrow being pampered while he gathered facts on a bike ride to the Calderon Cattle Ranch.

E lon paced in her bedroom until she heard footsteps overhead, then quiet. Rane thought the little episode tonight was funny. Maybe to some of them.

Every taut nerve shouted for a dough ball to pound into submission. Why not, she fumed, and entered the sanctuary of a quiet kitchen. Kneading bread at midnight still soothed her.

By the time she'd replayed the broken chair incident in her head a dozen times, the loaf of baked bread she thumped for doneness produced the perfect hollow sound. She lined four golden brown loaves on a rack to cool. Two would be sold.

Composed steps took her back to her bedroom. She pulled out her phone and found a YouTube video about reattaching a front-end loader bucket, the project for tomorrow. After watching it twice, she slipped on her nightgown and slid between cool sheets.

Damn her body for responding to Rane when she'd landed in his lap. Her thoughts kept returning to his muscled arm resting on her skin. She yawned and closed her eyes. How comforting his strength felt, how warm it made her . . .

Something nudged her hand. She glanced at her clock. "Criminy." She'd forgotten to set the alarm.

Angel tugged her sleeve.

"Good girl. Only a few minutes late. A sponge bath, and we'll be out of here." Blush, lipstick, and eye shadow went on without a thought. She threw on the jeans she'd ridden in yesterday, feeling the rock from Angel. On closer inspection, the smooth stone bore a man-made depression, and colored stains marred its surface cracks. She'd show it to Rane. Maybe.

Peaceful silence greeted her in the hallway and kitchen—empty bowls and the popcorn kettle were the sole remnants of last night's finale. Lingering scents of fresh bread perfumed the air. She placed a loaf atop a cutting board, added a serrated knife, and set it on the dining table.

Machinists ought to be able to slice bread, she determined and grabbed two boxes of cereal and jam from the cupboard. After placing a pitcher of milk in a bowl of ice, she checked the coffee pot and whistled for Angel.

"Almost forgot," she whispered, and set Angel's little indented stone at Rane's place. By avoiding the men this morning, they'd have forgotten the incident by lunch. The door eased shut behind her without a sound.

Scents of cut carrots produced Possum's familiar whinny as she entered the barn. "Slept inside last night, did you?" Gentle lips took the orange pieces from her flattened hand.

Soft rays of gold lit the pasture as she loosened Possum's reins and encouraged him to canter away from Rane's house. *This was her first time to be the first one up, and it felt like the freedom she'd had riding on Vashon Island as a kid.*

Possum cantered through grass and slowed to a trot when they reached the draw. From a ridge above, a cloud of dust rose. Low mooing sounds broke the still air. Lack of sleep didn't help the tingliness in her fingers as she gripped the saddle horn. She topped the rise and stood in the stirrups.

Two men herded a group of Rane's cattle onto a ramp leading into a trailer. Their hooves banged against metal as they jostled to the front of the empty, covered trailer. One stuck his nose out a side slat.

"Hey! What are you doing?" she yelled, and pressed Possum's sides.

One of the men, his face covered by a red bandana, jerked his head around. "Get loaded," he yelled in a shrill voice. His eyes narrowed to slits, then he pivoted his horse to face downhill and whipped the reins side-to-side across its shoulders.

Other cattle scattered in every direction as he careened straight at Elon.

Her foot slipped in the stirrup as she tugged one rein to her knee. Possum executed a quick turnaround on the zigzagging trail. She held back a scream and anchored her butt in the saddle while they careened around a hairpin turn on the switchback.

Barks sounded from above. "Angel!" Elon yelled. The dog hadn't followed her, and stood ten feet uphill, teeth bared, in the path of the oncoming rustler.

"Angel come on!" she pleaded. Her heart thundered in her chest as the gap between her dog and the rustler's horse narrowed. "Don't you dare hurt her!" Elon turned Possum and charged straight up the bank to head off the bandit.

The rider skidded to a stop, a few feet to spare.

Those aren't man boobs! The female thief's blue eyes bore into Elon's before she turned her horse and galloped to her truck.

Elon neck-reined Possum back onto the path and twisted in the saddle, relieved to see Angel following. "Good dog."

Above them, the she-bandit dismounted and waved her cowboy hat to hustle her horse into the trailer. The other rider lifted the ramp and clamped it shut.

Mousy gray hair plastered against her skull exposed distinctively pointed ears. She ran to the passenger side of her truck, yanked open the door, and shouldered a rifle—aimed straight at Elon and Possum.

CHAPTER 5

Rane breathed in his favorite morning scent of fresh brewed coffee . . . and something else.

Homemade bread. He bounded downstairs, taking the last three in a single leap. Elon falling into his lap during the movie and his getting a full night's sleep topped his current success list. Toast from freshly baked bread rated third place —worth getting out of bed fifteen minutes early for. He'd have Elon all to himself before the crew arrived.

And he'd devised two snappy lines for a snappy woman. Maybe ask her what she was serving for "break fast." Or if she'd enjoyed the action at the end of the movie. He grinned. He certainly had caught a warm, cushy break.

No pans rattled in the empty kitchen. His eyes skimmed the cold cereal and loaves of bread on the table. He grinned. She'd return soon enough to clean up. And he'd be waiting. He sliced and toasted two pieces, spread jam, and made a swirl by flipping his knife.

The back door to the storeroom banged shut. Angel's toenails clattered on the linoleum floor. Rane twisted around, still grinning and ready to tease.

Had he heard a sob? Angel darted in, her sides heaving. The toast dropped to the table.

Elon stumbled through the doorway. Dirt smears covered her pasty white cheeks.

He bolted to the kitchen. "What happened?" His pulse spiked.

"Your thugs returned. I rode out and caught them stealing cattle. They, they . . ." she slunk onto a kitchen chair.

"Did they hurt you?" He kneeled at her side, lifting her chin. Terror gripped his chest.

"No. They only got three or four steers loaded into a huge trailer. But a woman bandit tried to run over Angel. And she's going to have puppies." Tears wet Elon's wide eyes.

They hadn't harmed her, thank God. He pulled her tight to his chest, clutching her shaking shoulders while she described the dangerous encounter.

Dark, cold fury rose with every tremble he absorbed from her. Damn cowards threatening her and stealing his cattle. Why now? When he was on the brink of success. He pushed anger away, his fingers stroking her back. He'd protect her at any cost. "It's okay, Elon. You and Angel aren't hurt. You're safe now."

Every fiber in his body demanded justice. "We'll catch them, don't worry." He lifted her chin, needing to see trust in her eyes.

"I was so mad, Rane, I aimed Possum to stop the rustler. I'm sorry."

Pride filled him. "I'd have done the same. Believe me." He patted the dog sitting next to his foot. "Angel wanted to protect you, Elon. You have a team in your corner."

Her body stilled. "The woman pointed a rifle at me, then shot into the nearby boulder. Possum stayed calm, even when a chunk of rock flew at us."

"Too close a call." He leaned in and held her tight against

his chest. "I won't let anything happen to you. I swear." In so short a time she'd gotten under his skin. Losing her would kill him.

She turned her head, and his lips brushed against hers.

The strength of Rane's arms and gentleness of the unintended, tender kiss sent ripples through her body, fading the horror at seeing the woman aim her gun. When he released his hold, his dark eyes held the look of a fiercely loyal protector. "Thank you." Outrage, fear, and an odd sense of hope bubbled in her chest at the idea of having found a safe place. She looked down at her hands, and her wedding band. Safe in Montana, she reminded herself. Contending with her swindler of a spouse remained an unsettling prospect.

Not if Rane joined the fray. "I know you'll protect me and Angel. I won't ride alone again beyond the pasture."

"Please don't, until we catch them." Rane instructed, as he handed her his white handkerchief. "Could you identify the shooter?"

"She wore a bandana. Had collar-length gray hair and blue eyes. Something else I can't quite recall." She wiped her cheeks and breathed in hints of orange, nutmeg, and star anise from Rane's aftershave. Old Spice used to remind her of baking, and now him.

He stood and slid a dusty bottle from the back of the cupboard, then poured a shot of amber liquid into a glass. "Here, drink this. You'll feel better."

"Just to warn you, I don't hold liquor well, so I usually avoid the stuff," she said, and tipped the glass to her lips. The bitter alcohol burned as it reached her throat.

"I'm not what you'd call a party animal, either," he shared in a deep, assuring tone. His eyes held kindness.

"And I'm drinking on an empty stomach." Warmth flushed her face. "Sorry for the scant breakfast. If you give me an hour, I'll make something decent."

"Big trailers hold a lot of cattle. You saved a dozen or more head. I'll cook for you. I need to call the sheriff first. We'll need you to take us to where you saw them. He'll take tire and footprints."

"We can show you." She rested her hand on Angel's back.

Controlled fury blasted from his voice during his call to the sheriff. He returned from his desk wearing a grim look. "I hope you eat eggs scrambled, it's my only specialty." He pulled a bowl from the cupboard, then opened the fridge door and removed a carton of eggs.

"Sounds perfect." Shells cracking against glass provided a welcome diversion.

"When do Angel's puppies arrive?" The casual question didn't match his jerky movement yanking a pan from the hook and slamming it on the burner.

"Not certain, but Ed thought in about three weeks." She rested her head in her hands and closed her eyes.

Familiar smells of melted butter and toast surrounded her. The eggs sputtered when he poured them into the pan. "We'll make Angel a quiet spot in the storeroom."

If she held the job until the puppies arrived. "Sounds perfect."

Rane presented her with a dinner plate full of enough fluffy eggs and jam-topped toast to feed several ravenous cowboys.

"Looks delicious, thank you." Even if her pants burst, she'd eat every solicitously prepared bite. "Rane, have they stolen cattle from any other ranches?"

"No. Just me. After we speak to the sheriff, take off the rest of the day and put your feet up."

"Work gets my mind off things."

"A practice I understand." A gleam lit his eyes. "Did you pack a swimsuit?"

"I think so."

"Good. Do you enjoy sitting in hot tubs?"

Rane didn't look like the spa type, so there must be a community pool nearby. "Ah, I haven't for years. I used to."

"Perfect. Be ready for a dip at three this afternoon, and I'll show you my private retreat near the creek."

Oh dear, he'd take it personally if she reneged. She nodded an uncomfortable agreement.

"Temps usually ninety-eight degrees."

An image of his muscled body in a speedo cranked her temperature considerably higher.

E lon punched her hand into a mound of sweet roll dough. Returning to the ridge where she'd encountered the gun-toting woman and viewing mug shots at the Hanlen County Sheriff's Office had upset her worse than she'd expected. A woman bandit must be driven by desperation.

Her palms formed the dough into a ball.

Sticky buns for tonight's dessert fit her mood. What had she done to deserve being threatened by a rifle in the morning and having to face a swimsuit episode in the afternoon? Agreeing to join him hot tubbing boded disaster.

Seeing Rane half-clothed was worth the sacrifice, she reminded herself and plodded to her room. The bottom dresser drawer held a mishmash of odd stuff. She dug out her swimsuit, a navy maillot from ten years ago, when the boys took swim lessons. Three brass fold-over clasps on the right looped into rings on the left, joining the sides from the V-neckline to end above her waist.

She wiggled into the stretchy material and stood, facing the mirror on the back of the bedroom door. Plenty of fabric covered her hips. She turned sideways and admired a flatter tummy. Physical labor and no late-night snacks made a difference.

She threw on a pair of jeans and a long-sleeved T-shirt, then removed her makeup. No raccoon eyes after this swim. Tucking a towel and hoodie under her arm, she left the bedroom.

Rane stood at the bottom of the stairs wearing cutoffs. His long legs fit the rest of his chiseled physique. His mouth dropped open. "Ah, gosh. You look different without makeup, younger and . . ." He cleared his throat. "I think we're having the final warm days of fall."

After his reaction, maybe her morning routine deserved revamping. She hated wearing multiple layers of foundation and blush. Tim's fat-shaming and snide comments had pushed her to try anything. "Autumn's my favorite season."

"Mine too. Fewer chores." He displayed the smooth, indented stone in his open palm. "Where'd you find this?"

"Angel brought it to me right before my first ride on Possum. What is it?"

"A paint pot used by braves. Probably from my family cemetery."

"Oh dear. I'm sorry."

"Not your fault Angel's a digger. I ride there once a month. No one's disturbed the place in years. We'll take a look after our dip in the warm pool. Ready?"

Disturbingly ready if he unclothed any further.

∼

Rane's eyes stayed riveted on Elon's swaying hips as they headed outside to visit the hot springs. He mentally fit her into his arms for a two-step. Her cheek would graze his shoulder.

The horses nickered at their approach. Elon fitted the saddle on Possum and ran her hands down each of the gelding's legs.

How I wish those fingers . . . Rane shook away the thought. He'd received no firm indication she bore any interest in an unschooled cowboy living in the middle of nowhere, except for his signature on her paycheck. They tacked their horses in companionable silence. Most women sent forth a constant stream of chatter, he recalled. Not Elon.

As he walked Keeper outside, a breeze rustled the leaves on the maple planted by his grandfather.

Elon exited the barn, tipped her head skyward, then ran her thumb over the muscle in Possum's neck and slowly under his chest.

Displaying those skillful moves to purposely torture him? Possum relaxed his head and began licking his lips. He bowed for her to put on the bridle. Smart gelding, Rane determined, and moved to her side. "We'll go through the side gate this time and head north." His fingers itched to touch her, even her boot. "Want a knee up?"

"Sure, anything to save Possum's back." She tilted her head his way, rosy kissable lips inches from his face.

Rane grasped her knee and shin, propelling her into the saddle. "Let me adjust your girth." His hand lingered, resting on her calf. He tightened the leather strap a quarter inch and patted her leg. "All set." Under her white T-shirt, the low-cut swimsuit created a dip in the fabric.

Quit ogling. Wobbly-kneed as a newborn calf, Rane stuck

his foot in the stirrup and hoisted himself onto Keeper's saddle, the leather seat harder than usual.

Fred approached from the bunkhouse, his hair mussed like he'd been napping. "Good day for a dip. Thought I'd take the steers a snack and give the old Farmall Cub a spin. Heard we might be in for some foul weather tomorrow."

"Yup. Thanks. There're enough bales on the trailer. You need help raising the hitch?"

Fred rolled his eyes. "Son, I've been attaching the trailer since before you were a mere notion." He strolled to his cherry red tractor, balanced on skinny front wheels.

"Cub?" she questioned.

"That's Fred's classic '48 International tractor. He's proud of how he restored the old girl."

"The equivalent of a T-Bird or Vette in Seattle. Certainly, more practical."

"She can still pull a light load, perfect for this kind of errand," Rane commented. Elon's smile of approval warmed his stomach better than hot coffee in January.

They travelled on a dusty path to the creek, cutting through scraggly paintbrush flowers, their pale orange blooms in stark contrast to dry grass. After half an hour, the trail meandered between shrubs and bushes.

Lazy summer afternoons when he'd been riding next to Shelly and her buckskin drifted into Rane's memory. Her friendship and then betrayal stained too many aspects of his adult life. His eyes glanced in the direction of her parents' spread. Brambles covered the trail to their house. Twenty years ago, there'd been a clear path.

"Angel, your nose hasn't risen from the ground once." Elon's laugh floated on the breeze.

Rane looked at his weathered, calloused hands. He loosened the reins to give Keeper his head, and let his body relax for the first time in months.

Bent grass snaked along the edge of the dirt path, its trail cutting into theirs from the direction of the highway.

"Hold on a second." He dismounted and crouched close to the ground.

"What's the matter?" Elon said.

Nothing worth ruining the day. "Odd track alongside the path." He scratched his chin and followed the unfamiliar indent running ahead of them. "Must've been a full-bellied gopher snake. They're harmless."

"Hopefully they don't swim," Elon said, and panned the horizon. "I assume the fall-colored trees winding into the foothills follow a creek."

"Bear Creek runs downhill into Sunrise Lake." He remounted Keeper. "It starts high enough on the mountain to flow year-round. You'll soon see why." Rane raised his hand as he moved through a sunshade of trees. "Watch your head."

Passing through the gold and russet canopy, they saw water rippling and gurgling between rocks. On the other bank, a gentle hill rose to a grove of towering pines. "Those are deer tracks to your left. We head away from the creek for a bit now."

He stopped beside a lopsided circle, twenty feet in diameter. Steam rose from the flat water, surrounded on the far side by boulders, and on the near side by tufts of grass ending at a sloping edge. "Okay, Elon. Here's our private pool at the Calderon spa." Both dismounted and the horses dove to munch the remnants of green grass growing beside the narrow rivulet, taking the overflow water of the hot springs to the creek. He undid Keeper's bridle and hung it on the saddle horn.

"It's enchanting." Elon's hushed voice held wonder. "Those smooth boulders are perfect for cool off benches. I expect to see a mermaid rise from the misty middle at any moment, slide onto one, and dip her fin in the pool."

The only mermaid in attendance removed Possum's bridle, and then struggled to pull her T-shirt over her chest. His pulse pounded. Three metal clips barely restrained her ample bosom. *Functional?*

"The water looks crystal clear." Elon threw a towel on the ground and slipped off her jeans. "Last one in's a stale croissant!" She skipped into the water, sending sparkling splashes around her trim legs. The navy-colored swimsuit hitched up on her round bottom.

Don't consider flipping one of those damn clasps on her swimsuit! his brain shouted. His body temperature rose ten degrees.

Angel dashed in after her. Concentrate on the dog, he coached himself and yanked off his shirt and sweatshirt. He loosened the girths on both horses.

"The water's deliciously warm, slowpoke." Elon tugged the suit to cover her butt, whipped around to face him, and bent over, showing a damn lot of cleavage. In a swift movement she swooped her arm, barely skimming her palm across the water and showering him with a glistening spray.

Add mind reading to her attributes. He blinked warm drips out of his eyes. "That's how you want to play, fine." In one leap, he landed next to her, cradling her warm, wet body in his arms. "Dry hair. Can't have that." He spun in a circle and let her go.

"Stop it." Elon giggled, arms flapping until she plopped into the deep end of the pool. She rose spluttering, pushed wet hair out of her eyes, and waggled dripping fingers at him. "Let's see if you're ticklish, cowboy." She closed in, ready to pounce.

Rane backed up; eyes open wide in mock fear. How perfectly she'd grant his wish to see if those buckles worked. Accidentally flipping open the top one wouldn't be difficult. He licked his lips, imagining the view after his thumb made short work of the clasp.

A gunshot blasted. A second shot pierced the air.

Fear ripped into him. "Came from the ridge," he declared. "Fred doesn't carry a rifle."

Tim jerked at the sound of distant gunfire, sending the bike frame against his calf and the binoculars onto his chest. He leaned out from the stand of ponderosa pines on the hillside.

"Who's shooting at what?" he muttered and lifted the field glasses. He panned out to the horizon. Near a ridge sat an old tractor hitched to a flatbed trailer. Black cows scattered in every direction. Farther out, an SUV raced along a side road.

His eyes scanned Calderon's ranch before returning to the swimming hole site of Elon's interrupted liaison with her cowboy. She'd not wasted time finding a new meal ticket—a man who got off on excess boobage, judging by his interest in her swimsuit choice.

Switching to the cell camera, he took more shots of Rane and Elon. Her hooking up could be used in his favor and photos provided concrete evidence. Carefully avoiding the gun, he slid the binoculars into his backpack, then lifted his Garmin handheld GPS and clicked on the location he'd pinned where his rented SUV sat.

He spun the bike and began peddling the quickest route. Dinner tonight merited a rare tenderloin. Maybe one from Calderon's fancy herd.

A smile came to his lips. Shots fired in daylight suggested the wild west remained untamed.

Stray bullets could hit anyone.

Rane reached the hot springs bank and strode to Keeper. The reality of the shot's location struck with the force of a jagged boulder. "I've gotta see if Fred's okay. He'd be throwing hay there by now." He tightened Keeper's girth and bridled the horse. "Head to the ranch, Elon. Call the sheriff. No one should be firing on my property." He jumped on Keeper.

"I'm coming along," she countered, and grabbed his T-shirt and hoodie from the ground, then tossed them onto her saddle. "I worked in a doctor's office."

Her tone implied she'd put up a fight. "Okay. Stay well behind me." He pivoted Keeper. "If I raise my rifle, you turn tail and run. Understood?"

"Understood. I can't believe anyone would shoot Fred," she said.

He couldn't answer. He brought up his energy, looked toward the upper pasture, and made a clucking sound. Keeper took the cues and charged through the shrubs, then broke into a gallop. Wind cooled his bare chest. Please not Fred, he prayed silently. Not the man who'd stepped in as a father figure when he'd needed him most.

Keeper topped the rise. In the distance, a dark SUV raced away like a bat outta hell, kicking up a cloud of dust and was already too far off for a shot. Steers ran past Keeper, nostrils flared.

"Fred!" No sign of him. Bales of hay remained piled on the trailer, blocking his view.

A smaller steer struggled to rise a few yards downhill, bearing a gash in its shoulder. "Whoa." Rane halted Keeper next to the trailer and jumped down.

Fred lay slumped behind a back wheel by the hitch. A dark pool of blood stained the dry grass under him.

"No!" Rane's heart thundered in his chest. He crouched

beside him. A dull shade of pale replaced the tan on Fred's wrinkled face. "Fred, I'm here." No answer.

"Ohmygod!" Elon shouted and scrambled off her horse to kneel beside them. She pressed her fingers to Fred's throat.

"He's got a pulse. A rapid one."

"Thank God," Rane said.

She took the T-shirt he'd left on the bank and ripped it apart. The first piece she wedged into Fred's thigh wound. "We've got to get him to a doctor. Thank goodness the bullet must not have hit an artery. I checked for phone bars when I spotted you. Found none." She scanned the ground, and her face went white. "He's lost a lot of blood."

"The closest access road is directly east," Rane said. "I'll lift him into the trailer. Ride ahead and check for a signal when you reach the next hill. Call Doc Kyle and send him to meet us at the old wooden stock gate off Bear Creek Road."

Elon nodded. "A veinous bleed needs immediate attention." She tore another thin strip from Rane's shirt and wrapped it around Fred's upper leg.

"And after you talk to Doc Kyle or 911, try to reach Ed to help the injured cow." Rane swiped moisture from his eyes. He couldn't lose Fred. "I'll lift him aboard. Gallop if you can."

"I'll find help," Elon shouted, and hopped onto Possum. "Come on, Angel."

He lifted the stoop-shouldered, lifeless frame into his arms. Tears blurred his eyesight. When had Fred become so light, so frail? Stepping onto the flatbed, he kicked off a bale of hay and settled him between two others.

"Stay awake, old buddy. I'm driving your Cub to Doc Kyle." No response. "It'll be okay." He patted Fred's shoulder, hopped down from the trailer, and settled himself into the high-pitched seat. The tractor rumbled downhill. He shifted into third gear and scanned the trail to avoid rocks and potholes.

Who'd do this to Fred? Heck, everyone in the county knew that he wouldn't hurt a fly. No, it wasn't directed at Fred. He'd appeared at the wrong time. Their intent must've been to kill his steers—a calculated move to destroy the Calderon Cattle Ranch.

The trek through the pasture seemed to take hours. He wiped sweat from his brow. How long did it take to bleed out?

CHAPTER 6

Elon reached higher ground. "Whoa, Possum." She yanked her phone from her pocket. Two bars appeared. She pressed Corrin's number and heard her blessed live voice. "Thank goodness you are home," she exclaimed. "This is an emergency call for help from the back of Rane's property."

Corrin gasped. "Okay, Elon. What can I do?"

"Someone ambushed and shot Fred. It's a thigh wound, and he's unconscious. Rane's bringing him to the wooden stock gate on Bear Creek Road. Can you ask Kyle to get there?"

"I believe he's in his office doing paperwork," Corrin responded. "I'll call you back to confirm. Stay put." The line went quiet.

"Good boy, Possum." She let out a long breath. "Graze for a minute." Loosening the reins, the horse dropped his head to the ground. Poor Fred, and poor Rane. Her hand jerked when the call came in.

"Kyle's aware of the spot," Corrin said. "He's heading there now and called for an ambulance."

"That's a relief."

"I'll notify the sheriff, too. Ride safe."

"If you can reach Ed, the vet, there's an injured cow. Thanks. Gotta run." Elon pocketed her phone, turned Possum, and galloped. The tractor came into view, steadily moving downhill.

A few yards away from it, she slowed to a trot. "Kyle's on his way. An ambulance, too."

Rane nodded, his knuckles white on the steering wheel, his face tense. "Good work."

"Keep following us, Angel" She moved Possum to the side of the flatbed, kicked out of the stirrup, slung her leg across his neck, and jumped to the trailer. Her body arched backward, arms flailing until she latched onto twine on a bale of hay and then righted herself.

Fred's eyes fluttered.

Kneeling beside him, she pushed the cloth into the wound. "Fred, stay awake, we're almost to Doc Kyle." She closed her eyes for a moment and prayed they'd get him help in time. "Fred, squeeze my hand." No response.

The waiting room outside ICU smelled of antiseptic and fear.

Rane shifted in the padded chair, set his elbows on his knees, and cradled his head. All his doing. He should've made Fred carry a gun, hell, they'd threatened Elon. Only the worst kind of vermin shot an unarmed old man.

A warm hand pressed into his back. "Hey," Elon whispered. "I believe the surgeon's approaching from the operating area. Probably news on Fred."

Rane turned to her and looked into the kindest eyes he'd ever seen. "Fred could've died alone out there."

She squeezed his hand. "I have faith he'll pull through."

"Mr. Calderon?" asked a female doctor wearing scrubs.

"Did Fred make it?" his voice cracked.

She offered a smile. "We stitched his thigh and gave him two units of blood. Staunching the wound saved him. He's also sporting a goose egg on the back of his head. Being dehydrated, it's no wonder he passed out."

The knot in his gut released. "Thank you, thank you," Rane said. "We'll make sure he drinks more. Fred hates hospitals. I donate blood, and I'll get my guys to go in with me next time. What's the discharge plan?"

"I want to see how he does this evening. At home he'll need to take antibiotics and painkillers. Crutches for a week, followed by a cane. His regular physician can adjust the schedule. Doctor Kyle Werner's territory?"

"Yes, indeed." Rane clasped her hand. "Thank you for stitching Fred." He wiped a tear from his eye. "I'm the closest to family he's got left. He treats me like his son." His knees felt softer than wet hay.

"We're all relieved." Elon moved to his side and put her arm around his waist.

"Dr. Werner's one of the finest," the surgeon said in a kindly tone. "Fred's heavily sedated. They wheeled him into recovery room number seventeen if you want to peek in." She motioned to the right. "I suggest you head home afterward. We should be able to release him sometime tomorrow."

"I'll stay by the phone. I think our heroine who bandaged Fred's wound and rode for help deserves a break." He tucked a stray curl behind Elon's ear. "Thank you again, doctor."

The woman nodded and headed toward the nurses' station.

"I need to see Fred." He let out a long breath.

Elon took his hand, her grip warm and steady. "Of course," she said.

When she left, he'd be alone again, even though instincts told him they shared much more than a growing attraction. Needing her scared the hell out of him.

~

Elon shut the door to the bunkhouse. Noon sun took the nip out of the air. She unbuttoned her sweater.

Angel ran to her leg, her tail wagging.

"Your buddy Fred returns home today." She patted Angel's rounded sides. "I've prepared clean digs for his recuperation."

In Seattle, she'd have carved pumpkins by now to greet trick or treaters on Friday night. Former life, former holiday traditions. She swung the pail holding cleaning supplies while she ascended the back stairs. Angel followed close behind. "Rane cut paychecks before he left. If we hurry, we should have time to cash mine before they get home." She stopped in front of the freezer. Her home?

The thought resurfaced as she opened the bank account in town using Rane's address and drove back to his spread.

His truck sat alongside the front porch. She passed it slowly and smiled, watching Rane tenderly assist Fred up the stairs and ease him onto the porch swing.

Everyone needed reminders as to who mattered in life. She fingered her locket and parked in front of the corral. "Come on, Angel, Fred will be glad to see you."

The dog bounded ahead of her, yipping at the sight of her buddy who snuck her meat scraps when he thought no one saw.

Rane swiveled his head, worry lines creasing his forehead. "Glad you're back. I need to borrow crutches from Doc Kyle.

He should've returned to his clinic by now. Ed sutured the steer they shot and has an antibiotic prescription for me. Can you stay beside Fred for an hour?"

"Son, the bullet she used wasn't tipped in poison." Fred scratched Angel on the head, then shooed Rane. "Quit your worryin'."

Elon climbed the steps. "I'd enjoy sharing the porch swing with my favorite silver-haired cowboy. I'm so happy you're okay." She patted Fred's hand and kissed his cheek; the weathered skin of a man who'd spent his life outside.

"Please sit beside me for a spell." Fred said. "Glad you two swam yesterday." His lips curled into a pained grin.

"You had us pretty scared." Elon settled onto the cushion beside him.

"Are you comfortable on the swing?" Rane asked.

"I'll be fine, son. Fresh air's what I need." Fred adjusted his leg and winced.

Rane flipped his key ring. "Okay. But you're taking another pain pill soon as I return." He laid his hand on Fred's shoulder. "Your old tractor moved right along through the pasture to get you to Doc Kyle. Monkeying around on her engine finally paid off." He shook his head. "I'm stunned it's a woman bandit."

"Me too. I can't believe she returned after I saw her," Elon said.

Fred held up a shaky finger. "Forgot to mention. She wore headphones." He rubbed his temple. "Must've been why she didn't hear me approach. Totin' one of those military-style guns." He turned to Elon. "Rane thinks after she bungled stealing the cattle the other morning, she planned to kill off the herd. When I spoke to Sheriff Riley in the hospital, he figured the same thing."

Instead, she'd left Fred to die. Fine hair rose on Elon's forearms. "What kind of woman, or man, is that cruel?"

"A nasty, determined one," Fred wheezed.

"Don't worry, old buddy. Sheriff Riley pulled footprints and tire tracks yesterday. We'll find her." Rane patted Fred's weathered hand. "My job's to keep you on the mend. The lady surgeon gave me a list of stuff for cleaning your wound. I'll grab the crutches and supplies and be back as soon as I can." The deep, tender tone melted her.

"Go to town," Fred urged, his warm smile showing unspoken love for Rane. A sentiment Tim never displayed toward his own boys.

She stared at her wedding ring. "I'll take good care of Fred while you're gone," she said.

"He might need a pain pill," Rane stammered.

"You remind me of some of the helicopter moms I've dealt with." She flicked her fingers to shoo him. "Your truck's calling. I can administer a pill."

"Yeah. And be one." Rane chuckled and walked to his truck. He reached in the bed of it and his jacket shifted, exposing a holster at his back. He climbed in and drove slowly up the hill.

"Rane's carrying a handgun. Is that normal?" she asked, quietly.

Fred stopped the swing. "When he took over the place, he carried it everywhere. He can shoot the slither off a snake."

Avoiding the question gave her the answer. "Hope he doesn't have to. I heated spiced cider, if you'd join me in a mug," Elon said. "I routinely made it a few days before Halloween to signal to my boys they'd better finalize trick or treating costumes." She sank against the back of the swinging chair.

Fred patted her knee. "You must miss your kids something fierce."

An understatement. "I've never been gone from them for this long since my parents died."

"Might do them good to stretch their wings. And cider sounds better than water to meet Rane's liquid intake."

"You're right. My guys are eighteen and responsible. She pushed off the swing. "I'll pour us each a mug. I've got your favorite stew simmering for dinner. Need a pillow?"

"That'd be nice for my back. You're a special lady, Elon. Rane told me how you jumped from Possum to the trailer to help me. You belong on the range." His smile lines crinkled around his kind eyes. "Thank you, again."

"You're very welcome." She brushed a tear, ducked in the house, and ladled two mugs of cider. On the way out, she tucked a sofa cushion under her arm.

Gravel crunched in the drive. Rane's back? She stepped into the open doorway, watching the black SUV with Washington plates park. Not a Beemer, thank goodness.

She handed Fred the mugs and prepared to wedge the pillow behind him. It dropped to the floor. Tim emerged from the SUV.

*M*anure. Tim wrinkled his nose.

The shock on Elon's pasty face justified the trip to the smelly bowels of Montana. He shifted the bundle of mail to one hand and placed Jasmine's tiny palm into the crook of his arm. Together, they approached the porch swing where his nemesis stood cowering behind an old geezer.

He stopped at the bottom step. "It took effort to find you, Elon. You've received mail, which needs your attention. Phone's dead, and the boys didn't share your address."

Elon's eyes narrowed. "Who's your friend, Tim? The one you bought the Beemer for?"

"It's none of your business, but yes." He kissed the woman's pale cheek. "Jasmine, this is Elon, my ex-wife."

"Technically, we're still married." She held up her left hand and glared. "In case you've forgotten. Oh wait, you forgot your vows of faithfulness after you left the altar. Guess your wedding ring came off shortly after."

Not his fault she'd never turned him on. He ignored her snide remark and glared back. Gone from her face was the hurt look she'd perfected, and upon closer inspection, she appeared trimmer than she'd been in years.

"No denial of your unfaithfulness?" Elon remarked. An unfamiliar contention gleamed in her eyes. "Circle that on the calendar."

Interesting personality changes, Tim concluded, and handed her the stack of bills—an amount certain to expedite her need of a settlement.

She flipped through the envelopes and postcards, her face growing tight, the skin stretching into a snarl. "You, you bastard! The address shows your name and a post office box. Ohmygod, you didn't pay any property taxes on the condo the last two years?" She took a step forward, her fists bunched.

The old man put his gnarled fingers around her wrist. "Seems to me, he's not worth the fight, Elon. We'll figure something out."

Tim felt his shoulders tighten. "With so many surgeries, getting mail closer to the hospital proved efficient. The moldy condo your folks gave to the boys is their problem now."

"You really are Dr. Deceitful, the nickname our neighbor coined years ago. I can't believe you'd let their inheritance be threatened by a tax sale." She faced Jasmine. "He's all yours, honey. And don't think he'll treat you any better."

Jasmine shrugged.

"I'll see you in court." Elon pointed her finger at Tim.

He smiled. "I'm still prepared to offer an amicable settlement. I did a little quick math, and I think you'll need around three thousand by Friday to keep the condo. I brought paperwork if you're interested in a loan from me."

Fred slapped the arm of the swing. "She doesn't need your money, you cradle-robbing shyster. She's got friends here. Friends who know how to treat a good person. Time for you and your mistress to get off our property."

"Well said." Elon patted the shoulder of the meddling old coot.

Heat rose from under Tim's collar. She'd made him angry for the last time. "We'll see how long your friends support you." He grabbed Jasmine's hand and took slow breaths to quell the fury roiling in his chest. Elon deserved a dose of nocturnal wild west action.

He opened the passenger door and assisted Jasmine in, then turned to Elon. "You hid behind your parents, you hid behind me, now you're hiding here. It's about time you faced your pathetic life."

~

Damn Tim and his conniving, manipulating ways. Elon slumped into the swing beside Fred, clutching the mail in her fist.

Her head fell to her chest. The only items of value she owned were her car and her grandmother's diamond engagement ring. She bit her lip. Neither were worth what she'd owe in back taxes and HOA dues.

Fred patted her knee. "I've got money stuck under the mattress. I'd be honored to give you a loan. In fact, I insist."

Fate sent her a man as honorable as her father, allowing her to break Tim's financial chokehold. She blew him a kiss. "You're a godsend. I thought I noticed a lumpy spot while I put clean sheets on your bed. I'll accept your offer on one condition."

"Name it, young lady."

She studied her right hand and the diamond solitaire she'd worn for the last sixteen years, after the police returned her parents' personal effects. "I'll give you my grandmother's wedding ring for collateral. More treasured than a treasure, though."

"Looks mighty special to me. And our transaction stays between you, me, and the porch swing. Deal?" Fred held out his hand, offering assistance and compassion.

Since her parents' death, she'd only felt solace once before, when Rane held her in his arms after the female bandit's threat. "Deal. Thank you." She matched his firm grip.

"There's a leather pouch between the mattress and the box spring. Feel around under where my pillow sits. Go grab it, and we'll figure out what you need."

"You're a lifesaver." Elon headed to the bunkhouse, located the pouch, and returned. She and Fred added the bills plus late fees.

Fred counted out hundreds. "Do you want extra if that varmint held a bill or two back?"

"No, Fred. You've done more than your share. I'll put the diamond in the pouch before I return it to your mattress." She tugged it off her finger and mustered a determined look. "Ahh. I don't want to chance losing your heirloom." He thumped his temple. "Memorized the combination to the wall safe Rane never uses. Help me inside, and we'll tuck it away before he returns."

"Bia bought this painting." He carefully lifted off the depiction of a proud hunter on horseback, gazing at a herd of buffalo. "Reminded her of her Blackfeet grandfather. You remind me of Bia—gentle, yet strong at the core."

"Kind of you to say. Rane implied my build's similar to hers." She sucked in her tummy.

"That's a compliment. Bia was a beautiful woman, inside and out. Not bony like the gal your ex-husband paraded to the porch. Heck, a good breeze would carry her away quicker than a paper napkin at a picnic."

"You're a treasure, Fred," Elon said, and in a few minutes, they'd stowed the ring and Fred's substantially lighter pouch inside the metal safe.

And none too soon. Rane's truck pulled alongside the porch. He jumped out of the cab and burst through the door. "Everything okay?" He studied Fred from head to toe.

"Thought I'd take a nap. Elon said she'd fix a spot on the couch."

"Good," Rane said. "You rest while I check out a survey balloon hovering the property for sale next door. Spotted it from the highway. Seems strange. They cashed my earnest money check, and I didn't request a survey. The parcel borders my land on two sides, the road on the third, and the owner who's selling on the fourth."

"Trust your intuition, son," Fred said. "I'd wager Elon and Angel could use a ride. Emmett's here if I need him."

Rane shifted from one foot to the other, then looked to the machine shop and back to Fred. "I'd prefer Elon staying by you."

"Not necessary." Fred raised his hand. "Trust me on this one, son."

"You're the one person I've always trusted." Rane straightened the pillow behind Fred. "You and Grandma Bia. You two believed me."

"That's old history." A sad smile rose to Fred's lips. "Get out on those horses. It'll do you both good."

Later she'd investigate why Rane couldn't trust his parents. For now, riding sounded divine. She turned to Rane. "May Angel and I join you?"

"I'd appreciate the company. Bring your phone and I'll

saddle the horses while you make our patient comfortable." He threw a mock salute to Fred and left.

Elon grabbed a crocheted afghan, placed a second pillow behind Fred, and kissed his cheek. "Rane's probably never expressed his love for you, but I see it in his eyes."

"Yup," Fred said. "We're both short on lovey-dovey words. Don't worry, the feeling's mutual between us." He shifted his shoulders into the pillows. "You keep him outta trouble, now." He winked. "Or not."

"I know your game," she teased, moved her phone to her pocket, and headed to the barn.

Rane handed her Possum's reins and took them a different direction on the ride, passing through several fenced pastures. Cattle of different sizes grazed in groups.

Calves trotted beside their mothers and a few nursed.

"What are those tags in their ears?" Elon asked.

"Expiration dates, of sorts."

Elon gasped. Of course. The frozen beef came from these cattle.

He glanced her way, must've caught her distressed expression, and rubbed his thigh. "Reminds me, the remaining calves need to be weaned. Should've done it last week."

Taking babies away from their mothers didn't warrant a response. She squeezed Possum's sides and trotted ahead of him.

"Elon, this is my life. My ancestors hunted buffalo on these lands. While they're on my ranch, my cattle roam free to graze or receive good feed. I don't hesitate to call Ed for veterinary care."

She slowed her horse. "Tomo could provide a testimonial."

"He's a permanent resident, helping me build the herd and my reputation for premium Wagyu. That's why I got so upset about the steaks you cooked by accident. I owe you an apology for my behavior. Will you forgive me?"

He'd ridden to her side, his head tilted and his demeanor almost shy as he waited for an answer. So handsome, so worried how she'd judge him.

No other man had ever looked at her that way. No other man caused the longing growing inside. She wove her fingers into Possum's mane, wondering how the hair brushing Rane's shirt collar felt. And being held in those arms . . .

Possum stumbled on a rock, jolting her out of a happy ever after daydream.

He'd sincerely asked forgiveness and she'd gone to la-la land. "I accept your apology." Warmth rose in her cheeks.

"Good. That's settled."

Unlike her pulse. "Ah. How long will you keep the machine shop running?"

"At least five years. My savings are tied to four-legged investments with a delayed payout." He pointed Keeper uphill. "We've reached where my property line runs."

Muscles bunched in Possum's shoulders while they climbed. She shifted her torso forward and gave him free rein to clamor to the top.

From the ridge, the highway stretched north and south.

A gold sedan cruised into sight and parked alongside the road. A portly man dressed in a suit opened the driver's door. Its magnetic *Dagger Realty* sign came into view for a moment. Another man, wearing a sheepskin coat and dark sunglasses, got out of the passenger side. His swagger reeked of an attitude she'd seen too often in Seattle—my money can buy whatever I want.

"There are plenty of parcels for sale in the next county over. I need to make it clear I'm buying this one." Rane turned his horse and took off.

His tone hadn't indicated friendly. Elon followed him at a canter, watching the scene unfold.

The driver greeted Rane with a cheesy smile and fidgeted when he spoke. His ruddy face darkened. He crossed and uncrossed his arms, tugged his ear, and changed his stance.

Elon stopped Possum a few yards away, recalling when she'd first caught Tim cheating. Based on what she'd witnessed, she attributed this type of body language to liars.

The reins dropped from her hands. She hunched over the grazing gelding's neck and grabbed them. That guy must be hiding something.

The passenger continued to throw glances her way, which she ignored. His look indicated interest.

She raised Possum's head. Stew juices needed thickening, and she'd promised biscuits for dinner. Neither would happen if she didn't hustle back to the kitchen.

"Elon, join us for a second." Irritation creased Rane's brow.

Mediating between men. Great. She smoothed her wind-blown hair and approached.

The pot-bellied driver lifted his hand. "I'm Don Underson, the local realtor, and this here's my client, Mr. Floten, a commercial property developer."

The smell of whiskey hit her nose. By the number of broken capillaries on Underson's face, they'd be heading to the tavern next. "Elon Hardy." She gave their outstretched hands cursory shakes.

Floten tipped his sunglasses onto his head. "Ms. Hardy, the new welder." He gave her a wide smile.

His tone mimicked the placating and irritating pharmaceutical salesmen trying to pitch to Tim at the clinic. Word of her untraditional skill set must've been broadcast in simulcast. "I've got work to attend to." She backed Possum away from the fray, not wanting any part of his game.

"The construction company I manage prides itself in diversity." Floten approached and handed her a card. He brushed his hand against her knee. "If this position doesn't work out, give me a call. I don't need more shoulder-to-the-holder types."

Rane moved his horse between her and Floten. "Ms. Hardy uses her brain. I employ men to supply the brawn."

Angering Rane wouldn't equal job security. Elon faked a smile. "I'm very happy at my current job." She jammed the card in her hip pocket.

"Sorry you boys weren't aware the land's sold." Rane shrugged. "Better vamoose before the squall hits." He nodded to the two men and flicked his hand toward his ranch. "After you, Elon."

The sooner they left, the better. She pressed one leg and Possum did a tight turnaround. At little urging, he cantered away from the cars.

Rane caught up, his face looking burned from an angry sun. They slowed to a walk.

"Not your friends, I gather," she offered.

"Nope." His voice held a steely edge. "They offered me twenty-five thousand to find fault with the purchase and sale agreement and release my interest on this land so they can do a building analysis. I didn't buy it to resell, and I don't budge easily."

Unless it concerned strays. "What are they proposing to build?"

"I've heard they want to build a prison. No confirmation or denial when I asked just now."

"Typical strategy of a land developer, I'd guess." She squeezed the saddle horn, recalling the realtor's body language. "Underson acted kind of odd. What do you think of them?"

"I think they're trying to horn in on my purchase and my

welder," he snapped. "Are you interested in his job offer or anything else he might suggest?" Cords stood out on his tight neck.

Whoa. Rane was jealous. Throwing out her opinion on the men lying might incite him further. "My job suits my needs," she stated as calmly as possible. "A prison. I've read Montana offers prime real estate for that growing, ah, business." The ugly topic ought to take his mind off Floten's offer.

"Not in Emma Springs if I can help it. Heard a rumor my neighbor considered selling. I committed to purchase his land before anyone else."

"The town should be grateful."

"Not my intent. The north side of this parcel adjoins the Blackfeet land I promised my grandmother I'd protect. Shame you didn't meet her. She baked out of frustration, too."

Elon jerked as if stung. "What do you mean?" she sputtered.

"Every time I make you mad, there's a delicious scent of something fresh-baked greeting me the next morning." His grin took five years off his face.

She'd do anything to keep those grins coming. Maybe she'd been wrong about the realtor lying. No sense giving Rane reason to think of her as a meddler.

Tonight, she'd bake as if she were competing to win the blue ribbon at the county fair.

E lon rubbed her eyes, unready for the shafts of morning light coming through thin drapes. Gun-toting rustlers, deceitful ex-husbands, and pushy land-grabbers made for unwelcome bedfellows. Last night, Rane had returned late after checking the herd and paced. Grandma must've worn earmuffs to sleep below his room.

She kicked off covers and pulled on a teal-colored blouse. The button on her tan cords gaped by inches. Hard work proved better than a gym membership. A smile formed while she recalled the cinnamon roll dough she'd mixed and left overnight in the refrigerator. She'd create a tiny one for herself.

Warm, orange-frosted beauties had greeted her boys every Halloween morning. Buttercream topped, warm pastries and hearty omelets might take Rane's mind off the cattle and land crisis for a few bites. Or not.

She stuck the coffee pot under running water and peered out the window. Rane approached from the foothills on horseback, silhouetted by pale sunlight threaded between mountains. *He must be tired.* An extra scoop of coffee went into the brew basket.

She turned the oven to a low temp and removed the mixing bowl from the fridge. The slightly risen sweet roll dough yielded to her touch. She flung flour, expertly dusting the counter in a single toss. In a few strokes, her wooden rolling pin created a rectangle of dough twice the normal size and perfectly even in thickness.

A concoction of cinnamon, sugar, a drizzle of honey, a tiny bit of coconut oil, and melted butter went onto the top before she rolled it into a log. She slid the panned slices of swirls in the oven to rise. Unease grew in her chest. She'd never been good at keeping secrets.

Precisely chopping onions for the omelets, she deliberated whether to tell Rane she'd noticed signs of dishonesty in the realtor's gestures. The land speculator wanted the adjoining land and Rane wouldn't budge. His words.

Her razor-sharp knife nicked a sliver of skin off her finger. She ran it under water and pulled a Band-Aid from her satchel. Superhero characters had placated kids in Tim's office. For her cut, she chose to unwrap the one with the figure wearing a red bustier and blue shorts. Wonder Woman might be considered an interfering broad in Montana.

A few minutes later, Rane's voice broke the somber mood of breakfast in the dining room. "I need you to continue keeping your eyes and ears open."

The workers nodded, their mouths quietly chewing.

"The calves and steers they stole may still be alive, and I'm depending on the money from selling them. It's no secret I've been building the cattle business by purchasing pricey animals."

What had been the date on Rane's giant tax bill? She gripped the handle on her coffee mug. Late November? If she didn't log enough overtime, she couldn't pay the remaining utility bills for the condo. If he didn't find the animals, could he pay her? She collected plates as the men finished eating, banging them into a tall pile.

The group filed out so silently one might think they'd traded slippers for steel-toed shoes and cowboy boots. The door swished shut.

All except one left. Rane frowned at her bandaged finger. "You have something you're not telling me, Elon." He leaned forward in his chair, hands clasped together.

Those keen eyes noticed far too much. She raised her chin. "Well, yes. I didn't want to mention it in front of the men. I noticed fishy behavior by the realtor yesterday."

"Please explain," he stated.

She'd witnessed the same flat tone from Tim just before a denial. Not the same. Rane believed in truth. "I think Underson lied."

"Your reasoning?" He tilted his chin to study her.

"His body language of fidgeting, arm crossing, ear tugging. I've seen it before."

"Where?"

Elon snatched an unused plate and held it against her

chest. "With my nearly ex-husband. He cheated and lied within a few days of our wedding." She turned and headed to the sink to let water help wash away memories.

Rane's warm palm settled on the back of her shoulder. "I'm sorry. Thank you for telling me." His hand dropped, removing the male comfort she'd craved for so many years. "Your observation provides a possible connection to the rustlers."

No way she'd meet his pitying eyes. She nodded.

"I need to check on Tomo." His deep, smooth voice soothed her, as if he sensed how close she was to cracking. "You okay?"

She nodded again. If he pushed, she'd divulge the pathetic story surrounding Tim's visit yesterday. He didn't need any more worries.

"Take your time cleaning up."

"I'll be done when you return and ready to melt iron."

"Good. In ten minutes, my wealthiest customer's dropping off an excavator bucket with a broken lip. Ready for a new challenge?"

Kids got split lips, not buckets. She'd find a tutorial video and memorize the blasted thing, weld by weld. "Absolutely."

"Find me when you're ready to start." His footsteps thudded in the hallway. The door banged shut.

Elon squeezed a sponge until it shredded apart in her hands. She'd managed simple welds so far. Her stomach tightened. Facing new challenges generally didn't bode well for her—like Tim's infidelity. Nineteen years ago, cradling a newborn babe in each arm, she'd found a receipt for a hotel bill from the previous night. "Needed a full night's sleep in a quiet room without crying babies," Tim told her. "Pediatric surgeons have demanding hours."

She shouldn't have been so naïve about excusing his absences. The decision to stay under his thumb cost too much, in confidence, in respect, and worse, in how he'd increasingly ignored their sons. She pitched the remains of the sponge in the waste can.

How stupid she'd been to drop out of Le Cordon Bleu to support the con artist, then rationalize it'd be better to raise twin sons in a two-parent home. Pride had kept up pretenses; her heart still bore the scars of his deceit.

Now, he'd do anything to further his image as a successful, dedicated pediatrician. Only she and the boys knew the real Tim. They needed the other copy of her parents' will, which left her the building and property where his medical practice sat, her only leverage in the divorce. Otherwise, he'd keep financial control until he immortalized his precious reputation.

If she continued fighting, he might do something worse than rigging the broken stairs and reporting her car as stolen. Would he sever all ties to their sons? Or, Lord forbid, would he threaten them? Hairs on the back of her neck stood on end.

Quit being melodramatic, she chided herself and stomped into her bedroom. She sat on the bed and flipped through videos of men in welding masks.

Halfway through the one featuring an excavator bucket repair, the phone signal cut out.

Tim stretched out in a chair supplied by the Three Falls version of a boutique. There wouldn't be a problem opening a sleeping pill and pouring the contents into Jasmine's piña colada during today's late lunch, he rationalized.

He stared at the dressing room door, waiting for Jasmine to appear in yet another dress that hugged her body. And she never disappointed him. A reason why he could count on her ordering the sweet drink with her meal.

"What do you think?" she asked, twirling for him.

What he thought wasn't acceptable to voice in mixed company. The saleswoman held a sparkly necklace. He barely scanned the strapless black mini. "We'll take both."

Montana stores cleared out summer stock this time of year and Jasmine had been excited to buy things for their Hawaii trip. The perfect excuse for them to spend another day in Three Falls, facilitating Elon's end to ruling his world. She'd balked at his settlement offer and now he'd act accordingly. A smile came to his lips. In a few hours, he'd be calling the shots.

Literally.

~

Banging metal sounds erupted from Elon's workspace. She peered out the window of the storeroom, then checked cell service again. Not one rotten bar, and she'd barely seen the opening of the tutorial on bucket welding.

Breaths came in shallow gulps while she crossed the drive.

Pounding stopped on the giant scoop sitting on the floor in front of Emmett. "Those broken pieces fought hard." He let a sledgehammer rest on his boot and wiped his brow.

Two dirty, flat hunks of metal lay on the floor at his feet.

"Thanks for dismembering those parts," Elon said.

"We're a team here," Rane snapped. He held a longer, flat piece against the outside of the teeth, then let it drop to the ground. "I cut this T1 hard plate to fit. They need this repaired ASAP. Have at it, Elon." He turned his back to her, and the two men left.

Something had riled him to Bull Boss again. Her fingers

pushed into her neck muscles. The first part of the video showed the narrow plate being welded to the inside of the bucket. Did she remember correctly?

Not the time to question Rane. He looked flat-out irritated at her, for whatever reason.

The large clamps for holding the metal piece in place nearly slipped from her hand. Welding alongside each tooth and in between should give the teeth plenty of strength to rip into earth.

She stood and stretched her back halfway through, proud of her work.

Rane strode by, glanced in, and glared. "The support lip belongs on the inside. This needs to be done by tonight." He grabbed the sledgehammer leaning against the wall.

"You placed it on the outside when you checked the fit," she said.

He fingered her welds, then raised the hammer and swung to dislodge her work. The bang struck an ear-splitting clang. "You should ask when you need help." He raised the sledge again.

"I thought it was the Montana way to push dirt." She covered her ears.

The next two bangs sounded twice as loud. The piece crashed to the cement floor.

Her chest tightened. She'd failed the real test. He'd fire her for certain.

Emmett appeared at the opening to the welding area, took one look at Rane's taunt stature, and left.

"Montana way?" Rane rolled his eyes. "Dirt's dirt. I measured the damn piece to see if the length fit." His voice rose. "Either you can weld, or not."

"I'm . . . I'm sorry." She gripped the edge of the welder's cart. "I'll finish it as quickly as possible. Lunch is in the

Crock Pot, ready to go. I'll ask the next time." Her voice threatened to crack.

She pressed her fingernails into her palms, willing herself not to cry. He deserved to be mad. She'd botched the job for his best customer.

"You should've told me your husband came here." Rane snarled, picked up the sledgehammer, and shoved it into the corner. He turned, glaring.

Wait, her welding mistake didn't fuel his anger? It was personal, as if she'd insulted him by not believing he'd be there for her. Was she ready for that? Ready to share how stupid she'd been trusting Tim? No, he wouldn't understand. "You have enough challenges. I didn't want to add to your burden by telling you Tim found me." She gulped. Bad word choice. The less he knew of her reasons for vanishing from Seattle the better. "I found the confrontation embarrassing, and you told me the first day we met that you didn't want details about my former life."

"That was a long time ago." His eyes softened. "You've endured a tough couple of days. Everyone makes mistakes."

Good, he hadn't caught her slip about running to Montana. "I'll weld the plate in the correct place pronto."

"If you can finish tonight, I'll deliver it at first light."

"Thank you, Rane. I appreciate your patience."

"You're a good person and a good worker." Rane's fist bunched. "The doctor and his fling arriving must've been worse for you than putting a dirty bandage on a festering wound."

She nodded. "It was, and I should've said something." A festering wound summed up Tim's impact on her life. Especially with him knowing where she lived. Her challenge was keeping things from going septic and deadly.

❧

Tim scanned the busy Three Falls restaurant from their corner booth. "Happy with your wardrobe for Hawaii, Jasmine?"

"Oh, yes." She patted the bag full of new clothes sitting beside her. "The sales lady mentioned there's a Halloween party at the VFW tomorrow night. Sounds fun. Is VFW a new car brand?" she asked innocently.

Her naïvety charmed him. "No, Jazz, and I need to head back to Seattle in the morning."

She threw him the pouty look he adored. He stroked her smooth hand. "The waiter's bringing you a piña colada. That'll make you feel better."

It didn't take alcohol to make him feel better. Opening the capsule and slipping the sleeping medication into her drink had transpired with a surgeon's precision. They'd made it back to the hotel room and enjoyed a little play time before she'd nodded off.

He covered her on the rumpled bed, tucked in his black shirt, and shouldered the backpack carrying the Honey Badger short-barreled rifle—appropriately named after the aggressive animal.

Soon enough, he'd be badgering someone's honey, alright.

Buying the lightweight gun had been worth every penny. He quietly shut the door to their room. No one appeared in the stairwell while he descended three flights to ground level.

Their rental SUV sat in the back corner of the parking lot, in the shadow of a brick building. No security cameras, and no one entered or exited the hotel. He slid behind the wheel and drove to the familiar side road, parked, and unloaded the bike.

Staying on the grassy area alongside the deer path wasn't easy. His hands wobbled on the handlebar. Leave no trace, his brain cautioned as he continued to the stand of trees within sight of Calderon's house.

He leaned the bike against a tree trunk, adjusted the telescoping stock, fitted on the silencer, and laid it atop his backpack. Subsonic 220 grain ammo filled the magazine, purported to make the shots quieter. Science in a practical application.

Tipping the binoculars to his eyes, he scoped the log house, machine shop, and attached open work area. Elon's rump protruded while she welded a huge bucket. The torch glowed blue in the fading dusk. Metal turned red where the nozzle touched.

He let the binoculars rest on his chest. The cowboy must work her twelve hours a day. Good, she'd finally earned her keep somewhere.

"Sorry to make it short-lived," he murmured. But he wasn't. If Elon got a say, there'd never be a hospital where his clinic sat. Even now he needed the space in the building's courtyard for something besides the flowers and benches she'd insisted memorialized her parents.

The community desperately required comprehensive medical services. Seattle hospitals routinely logged sixty people waiting for beds, lining the hallway on gurneys.

Dead parents didn't get a vote.

The SIG scope he'd removed from the pack and mounted atop the Honey Badger resembled a missile in shape. For the price, it had better provide the advertised accuracy at three hundred yards. He fitted his eye to the scope and adjusted the dial.

Hell, he could almost read the watts on the light over the barn. Another bulb above the shop flicked on. The old cowboy limped from the house, stopped to visit Elon, and then wandered into a low building.

Elon stood back, her hands on her hips. He centered the crosshairs on her back.

Flashing lights obscured his vision. *Damn! Not now!* He scrunched his eyes shut, willing the blind spot to recede.

By the time it did, she'd removed her gear and began jerkily stowing the heavy welding equipment. The silencer swung in a slow arc while he followed her motion. Too many obstacles for a clean shot. Patience paid off, he reminded himself and let out an angry breath.

In a few minutes Calderon appeared. A lanky younger guy joined them and pointed at the bucket. Elon grinned and Calderon patted her back in a friendly way. Didn't take a psychologist to ascertain they'd be sleeping together by now.

Enough already. You've planned well. Shooting from a quarter mile away from Calderon's house provides exit time. Biking to the SUV takes seven minutes max. By the time they saddle horses, or the cops show, you'll be long gone. He adjusted the gun butt into his shoulder.

The rancher's thick chest obscured a shot at Elon as they moved to the house. Two for one wouldn't be a bad deal. Could he hit moving targets from this distance?

The cowboy slipped inside while Elon stopped on the back porch and whistled.

A post shielded her torso. *Should've taken the shot.* His jaw clenched as a pathetic excuse of a dog ran inside ahead of her. She'd always wanted a flea-bitten mutt.

Should've hit her while she welded. He lowered the gun and ran his hands under his knit cap to release neck tension. After what seemed like hours, banging ceased in the machine shop and a group of men strolled into the house, then left after thirty minutes, rubbing their bellies. Everyone moved to the bunkhouse except Calderon and Elon.

He leaned against the trunk of the tree, watching, waiting. Should he chance it and move closer? He searched the terrain; no access without being in plain sight of any window facing the hillside.

A light beamed from the second floor and another on the lower level, at the back of the house. So, they weren't sleeping together? Which room held Elon?

If she adjusted a curtain, he'd take her out. He lifted the Honey Badger back into position. "Come on, pull the curtain," he whispered into darkening shadows, feeling the chilly night air settling around him.

His eyes darted between the windows. The upper light went out, then the one on the main floor. A tiny shaft glowed from the farthest wall at the back of the house.

Relief surged in his chest. Elon, a creature of habit, still read worthless paperbacks during her nightly ritual. Her reading light would sit above her scapula, so her heart would be five or six inches below. The gun's magazine held thirty bullets and thirty chances for a fatal hit.

No more hesitating. He steadied the rifle against his shoulder and took the calming breaths his brother taught him while they'd hunted rabbits as kids.

This target wasn't food on the table, the stakes were much, much higher. Countless people depended on him.

He wiped a bead of sweat from his brow and flicked off the safety. Blasting the hell out of the general area would take care of any uncertainties.

She'd be nearly settled in, he reasoned, while he pressed his finger against the trigger, aiming to kill.

CHAPTER 7

Elon wedged the pillow behind her back.

Tonight, every angle felt uncomfortable. The back-ache from redoing the welds didn't help.

Seeing Rane morph from angry to empathetic threw off her equilibrium. Tim never lost his cool, not even while confronting noisy neighbors.

Criminy. She'd forgotten to return a text to the friend next door who'd alerted her about Tim vacating the house the morning she'd left Seattle.

The week she'd been away from Seattle seemed like months. She adjusted the little reading light clipped to the headboard and tapped on the screen.

I'm out of town for a while. Appreciated your help. We'll catch up soon. She sent the text and leaned into the headboard inlaid in the shape of a four-leafed clover.

A bath took too much energy. If she fell asleep in her clothes, too bad. She stashed her phone in her pocket and grabbed the book from the nightstand.

Her phone pinged an incoming text from her neighbor. *Tim's skinny girlfriend has a malnourished brain. Over the fence she blabbed about his dream to construct a ten-story hospital where your folks' garden center sat. Thought you should know.*

Bastard! Fury burned in her chest. No civil reply to that bomb came to mind.

Angel shot to her feet, jumped to the floor, and growled at the window.

"Hey, you'll wake Rane. Not a good idea. He's got to deliver my do-over at dawn." She dropped her paperback.

The growl turned to snarls. She flopped off the bed and onto her knees, her hand corralling the barking dog against her chest. "Shhh. Is there a critter out—"

Glass shattered. Splinters hit her cheek.

"Ahh!"

The headboard shuddered as a volley of shots pummeled the wood. Chips hit her back. She pushed Angel to the floor and covered her.

The shots stopped. She inched them both away from the window, her heart pounding.

Glass shards covered her book. The curtain fluttered and a breeze hit the back of her neck.

"Elon!" Footsteps drummed on the hallway floor. "Are you okay?" Rane shouted.

The bedroom door flew open. "Gunfire. Get down," she choked out.

Angel dashed to the doorway, then stuck her head back in, whining.

"Stay!" Rane commanded the dog, then crouched low and moved beside Elon. "I've got you now," he whispered. He laid his arm across her back and while they both crept on their knees, he propelled her shaking body to the door. Pieces from the inlaid headboard lay scattered in all directions.

They reached the hallway. He rose and brought her to her feet.

The front door banged open. Angel lunged forward, but Elon caught her collar.

Rane stepped in front, squaring his shoulders in a protective stance.

"Rane?" Emmett called from the entry. "I heard glass breaking."

"Over here." A loud breath whooshed from Rane. "Call the police from my desk. Shots fired into the house. I'll grab my rifle."

Her knees went weak. She grabbed Rane's belt, and he threw his hand around her waist, guiding her to sit on a dining room chair. *So close.* She stroked Angel's head. "If those perky black ears hadn't heard something, I'd be—"

"Don't go there." Rane pulled two guns from a wall rack. "Stealing cattle and winging Fred is bad enough," he hissed. "But shooting my woman, inside our house," he jammed shells into a chamber of the longer barrel. His face turned a deeper shade of red.

His declaration stunned her. She lowered her eyes. "My bedtime ritual includes reading under a small, clip-on light. The tiny beam must've been visible through the window."

Emmett entered the dining room. "Sheriff Riley's on his way. I thought I heard gunshots. The rest of the guys kept snoring away."

"It wasn't loud," Rane said. "Creep must've used a silencer." He handed Emmett a gun.

"What was the target?" Emmett asked.

"Me," Elon whispered. "The bullets destroyed the headboard I'd been leaning against just a second earlier. Angel warned me. The cattle bandit knows I saw her."

"Keep covered and go warn the men. Not certain if the killer's gone." Rane pumped his shotgun. A spent round hit the floor, sending an ominous clatter into the deadly calm.

The long, horrible night ended after Sheriff Riley recorded Elon's account and did a final perimeter check. He'd issued an alert to stop any vehicles in the area and would send a team of officers at first light. Rane pulled her protectively to his side as they watched the patrol car's taillights fade.

"I'll double check on Fred and hit the sack," Emmett said, and left through the front door.

"Need anything, Elon?" Rane asked.

"Thanks. I'll fix myself tea." She located the clean tea kettle and set it on the stove. "Want one?"

"Nope. I'm sticking to water." Rane watched as she unscrewed the lid of the jar and filled the tea ball. "Grandma Bia steeped dried huckleberries and sage leaves."

"My mom had an herb garden renowned in the Seattle area. She schooled me on creating her calming recipe, and I keep a batch on hand. Tonight, I need a strong dose." She rubbed the front of her neck. "I don't remember when I screamed last. Made my throat scratchy."

Rane handed her the jar of honey. "Add this to your tea to soothe your throat."

They sat in silence at the old kitchen table, him sipping water while she dunked the tea ball. When the brew darkened, she added the honey and took a long swig of the sweet, warm liquid.

Her head fell back, her brain finally quiet, lasting until Angel bumped her leg. "You earned a gold star, pup." She lifted the dog's head and kissed between her eyes.

Rane scratched Angel's back. "I've missed having a dog around."

She smiled, then took another sip of the cooled tea.

"Tastes sharp again. Something's not right." She rotated the glass jar holding the dried leaves and flowers.

"Wait, that's not a lemon verbena leaf." She stood. "My mouth hurts, and I'm nauseous."

"What?" Rane asked.

Dizziness hit; her knees grew weak. "I think there's something poisonous in my tea. I don't know how, I was the one who prepared it using edible herbs and flowers from my garden."

Rane shot out of his chair. He grabbed the jar, lifted her off her feet and into his arms, and bolted outside. At his truck he set her feet on the ground, handed her the glass container, opened the passenger door, and slid her onto the seat. "We're heading to ER."

"Good idea," she mumbled.

The cool leather upholstery cushioned her weakening body as they barreled to the highway.

Scenery flew by.

Her heart thumped with the irregularity of a stand mixer fighting a lump of cold butter.

Rubbing her chest provided no relief.

"You okay?" Rane asked.

"Weird heartbeat," she managed.

He flicked on the overhead light and glanced into the jar.

"Is there foxglove in your garden?"

"Yes, but . . ." Words lost the struggle in her dry throat.

"Hold on." The truck sped faster. The jar dropped to the floorboard, and her chin dropped to her chest.

"We're here," Rane announced. "Stay awake, Elon."

A blue 'H' shone on a dark building. He careened around the corner into the parking lot and stopped by the glass sliding doors.

The seatbelt stuck when she fumbled the clasp. Finally, the belt came free.

Rane dashed around the truck, handed her the jar and cradled her in his arms, then jogged them into the building. "I think she's been poisoned by foxglove," he called to a woman seated behind a desk at the back of the room. People and voices shot to alert.

Elon felt his strong hold release after he laid her on a reclining bed. A nurse stood next to him. "You'll be okay, Elon. This time I knew what to do." He wiped a tear from his eye.

This time? She'd question him when her head quit spinning. The nurse lifted Elon's finger into a heart rate monitor and cuffed her arm for blood pressure.

A middle-aged woman wearing a white lab coat with a stethoscope draped around her neck entered the room. "I'm the ER doctor. What are the symptoms?"

"Headache," Elon sputtered.

"Pain in her mouth, queasy, and weird heart rate," Rane stated. "She spotted a different leaf in her homemade herbal tea. Looks like foxglove to me." He grabbed the jar from her lap.

Elon forced herself to concentrate. She swallowed hard. "Tea tasted bad lately. Thought the containers . . ."

Rane patted her arm. "It's okay." He turned to the doctor.

"She drank half a mug tonight, sweetened by honey."

The doctor glanced at the monitor. "Your heartbeat remains irregular, a typical indicator of foxglove poisoning." She put on gloves, opened the jar, and fingered the dried leaves. "Appears to be leaves from the toxic plant. I've seen this before. Begin administering the antidote, digoxin-Fab," she instructed the nurse, then placed the jar in a plastic bag. "I hope you only ingested enough for temporary sickness; more could be problematic. You should start recovering once the antidote enters your system." She left the room with the nurse.

A man in scrubs appeared, wheeling in a cart. "Foxglove's nasty stuff." He hooked up an IV. "You'll feel better shortly," he said, and rolled the empty cart out.

The phone in Elon's pocket rang. She struggled to pull it from her pocket, then swiped twice to answer the call. "Hallo?" Sheriff Riley's voice sounded tense. She shoved her cell to Rane. "For you."

Rane stepped into the hallway. When he returned, he'd gone pale. The doctor walked in behind him.

"More shoot . . . shooting, Rane?" Elon managed.

"No. They confirmed a different gun was used tonight to fire into your bedroom. It wasn't the same type that was used to shoot Fred. Could be two different shooters."

The doctor faced her. Worry lines creased her face. "You've been poisoned and shot at." She glanced at Rane, then met Elon's eyes. "I'm going to alert the police to the poisoning. Who wants to harm you, Ms. Hardy?"

"Cattle robber." *A stranger without access to her tea jar. Damn Tim.* "No, no, no," she mumbled, and turned to Rane. "Brought the jar from Tim's house." She rubbed her head, recalling a conversation in the back yard. "Years ago, he joked about it fixing my dad's heart."

"Who's Tim? The possible cattle robber?" the doctor asked.

"No," Rane stated. "He's a Seattle doctor who's almost her ex-husband. He confronted Elon yesterday at my ranch, where she works." He stepped to Elon's side and lifted her free hand, warming her fingers between his palms. "We'll nail the bastard. Don't you worry."

"I need to file the report," the doctor said quietly.

Elon closed her eyes and heard soft footsteps, then the door closed. The medical staff had gone. Horror seeped into her weary bones. Rane held her hand while she nodded off, letting the antidote work against Tim's poison.

She woke to the door whooshing open. The doctor stood by her side. She brushed brown hair away from her brow.

"Your vital signs are stable. Feeling better?"

"Yes. Thank you."

"Thanks go to your driver. I've notified the police this wasn't an accidental poisoning. They'll take a full statement," the doctor said.

Poisoned. Her body trembled. "I never thought Tim capable of murder."

"Nothing surprises me anymore." The doctor turned to Rane. "Your action got her here in time for a quick recovery." She smiled and opened the door. It slid closed behind her.

"Thank you, Rane." Elon clasped his hand. "How'd you learn about foxglove?"

"The worst way. When I was eight, I—" he pulled his hand away. "I showed my three-year-old sister how to suck sugar from blooming pink clover. I turned my back and didn't realize she'd eaten a damn foxglove blossom in a handful of clover blossoms she'd picked. Same color. Mom thought she had the flu."

"Oh, no. From what I've just experienced, the symptoms are very similar. And kids can be stoic."

He brushed another tear from his eye. "She was. By the time we figured it out, we'd waited too late to save her. Her weak heart hadn't been diagnosed and the stress from the poison killed her."

"How terrible. I can't imagine. And you were a little kid." She placed her hand on his forearm. "What a tragic accident."

"Mom never recovered. None of us did." He hung his head. "When grandma died and left me the spread, Dad moved them to Santa Fe. Too many memories, and he's a carver at heart, not a rancher."

She fingered her locket. "I can't fathom losing a child."

"Little Adele was the happiest baby—always gurgling or

cooing. Her smile made me do anything she wanted." He looked at his hands. "I found out the meaning of her name after she died. Adele means 'she knows.' Grandma Bia maintained an Old One told Adele she'd been granted limited time on earth, so she'd better use it to bring joy. And she did."

"I can't imagine the sorrow."

"Our family finally put a bit of the sadness behind us before the Shelly thing hit." His troubled eyes met hers, eyes filled with remorse, or guilt, or shame.

Hearing Rane's sad history helped her understand him. "I'm so sorry you lost your little sister in a terrible accident," Elon used her most soothing tone. "I understand tragedy, Rane. I blame myself for not noticing the loose drain plug in my parents' boat, even though I had a callous husband and toddlers to deal with. Maybe we can learn to let go of the past and start a new path together?"

He stroked her hand. "Grandma Bia embraced your type of wisdom, and so should I. A little spark flares here," he patted his chest, "when I talk to you."

"That brightened my day." She forced a weak smile. "You and Angel are my forever heroes."

"I've been called a lot of names." He touched her cheek. "Hero's one I'll take pride wearing." He gently kissed her. "You've now scared the crap out of me three times. Are we done?"

She'd never lie to him. "I'm afraid it's only the beginning if Tim's behind this. He's as determined as they come."

"Does the bastard shoot guns?"

Every nerve ending pinged, either from the antidote in her veins or fear. "I think he hunted for dinner as a kid. We never spent much time together. I'm more aware of your habits from the last week than I am of Tim's after two decades married to him."

He raised a brow. "Well," he stated. "You must've spent some time with him early on, you've got kids."

A jealous tone? "Not much time, and not in any . . . well . . ." She looked down, unable to meet his eyes. "My parents' property and money attracted him. Not me, in any physical way. Never gave me more than a couple chaste kisses. He had a string of model-thin mistresses to meet his sexual needs."

Rane's eyes widened. "Really? How'd he sire kids then? I mean, sorry."

"He figured I'd divorce him if we didn't have children, so he arranged for artificial insemination, and I birthed our wonderful sons. The only good things to come from him."

"Sorry, I jumped to the wrong conclusion. The guy's a total dirt bag. Glad you got the kids you wanted." He gave her a sheepish grin.

"Me, too. They've been worth every lonely hour. Countless nights I waited for him to come home, reading good books in bed." She closed her eyes. Tim had removed her light from the headboard once, when she'd taken the kids on an overnight with her mother. Her mouth went dry.

His name attached to a hospital equaled the pinnacle of success. He needed her to sign off or die.

Soft knocks on a wooden door woke Elon. Her eyes shot to the boarded-up lower part of the window. Midday sun shone through the upper pane of glass.

Right, she'd returned home after a late night at the hospital spent detailing to the police Tim's threatening behavior. "Yes?" she called from bed.

"I can run bathwater for you," Rane said from the hallway.

She lifted the covers, recalling a blurry vision of Corrin

helping her into her oldest pajamas. "That would be great. Come on in." She sat and hung her legs over the edge.

The door opened slowly.

Rane stepped to the bed, sat beside her, and took her hand in a warm, steady grip. "I'm so glad you're okay. Doc Kyle said I should check on you often. You'd gone out for the count. He wouldn't let me take you upstairs: he was worried you might get up in the middle of the night, be disoriented, and fall down the stairs. I slept on the couch and Angel stayed beside you."

"You both continue to be my heroes." She squeezed his hand. "No more shots fired?"

"Nope. The sheriff's department patrolled all night. One stood by your window." He gently touched her cheek. "Your safety is paramount. My brother, Chayton, is dating a woman who trained as a forensic investigator in Seattle. She moved here to be a Montana Fish, Wildlife & Parks warden. Sheriff Reilly saw Belle's skills and convinced her to be a reserve deputy sheriff. She'll help him identify clues to the shooter, or shooters."

"I hope so. You know, I longed for a brother, what's yours like?"

"He'll stop over soon. Chayton not only resembles me in looks, but in loyalty, and you're extended family now." He rubbed his thumb across her palm.

More than concern showed in his russet eyes. A warm sensation grew in Elon's chest. He'd treated her in a way she'd always dreamed of, a loving way, as part of his family. "Thank you for taking good care of me."

She cupped his chin and brought his face to hers, her lips finding his, proving to him he'd become more than her boss or her hero.

His eyes widened, then closed. He pulled her against his

muscled chest, his fingers pressing into her back, his strength seeping into her. Her mouth drew out his essence, hungrily finding every trace. She needed Rane to want her. Desperately.

Cravings for real love flamed in her chest. With each return kiss he branded his name on her soul, lit the darkness in her heart, and fulfilled desires she'd never known. She wrapped her arms around his neck and tilted her head, his eager lips promising the passion she longed for.

Not yet. She drew her head back and took a ragged breath. "I'm still legally married. If we continue Rane, I'll feel sleazy or guilty—something I don't want equated with you. I'm sorry. My entire being wants to continue as much as you. Do you believe me?"

A soft smile came to his lips. "After those kisses, I'd be a fool not to." He took her left hand and fingered the wedding band. "My brain respects your decision." He released a deep sigh. "Other parts of me don't. When will the split be final?"

"Not sure. Corrin originally thought around Thanksgiving we'd meet Tim and his lawyer in Seattle for settlement negotiations. Considering Tim tried to murder me, I'm not sure at this point. It could be much sooner."

All traces of the smile left his face. "I'll do whatever I can to protect you here." He rose from the edge of the bed and went in the bathroom.

"I know you will," she called to him. And Montana was where he belonged, where people depended on him, where he fit so perfectly into the rugged landscape.

Water splashed against the cast iron tub. She hadn't missed the tortured look on his face that pulled her in two directions. Was it a long shot to think she and Rane stood a chance at becoming a couple? Could the twins succeed on their own? Regardless, severing all ties to Tim came first.

She'd rather stay here, but the ugly door on her past didn't close until she faced Tim in Seattle. That was reality.

Her eyes darted to where the sheriff's team had chalked circles on the wall around fifteen or twenty shots. Empty gouges pockmarked the smooth, lavender-colored plaster. They'd swept the floor. She ran her hand against the brown vinyl headboard someone had swapped out for the destroyed one. Tim must've put the foxglove in her tea jar. But shooting her?

She glanced to the far wall and the beaded figure. Her furry angel had saved her first, then Rane. Elon pushed off the mattress and padded into the bathroom. Lavender perfumed the air. He leaned over the tub, pouring bath oil into steaming water cascading from the porcelain faucet.

That was the two of them. Scented oil and churning water becoming something better. Casting Rane aside would be a mistake. "My sons need me less and less," Elon began. "A man's guidance could help me sort out several aspects of my life."

He looked up from the rising water. "I have a bit of experience living alone at a young age. I'll share any other guidance, too." His smile turned wolfish as his eyes dropped.

She glanced down. The top button on her old pajamas had flopped open. "Your brain needs a bath, not that I'm complaining."

"Mm-hmm." He dipped his hand in the water, swirling a figure eight pattern. "Just the way I like it."

Her fingers fumbled to close her top. "The lavender smells wonderful. House specialty?"

"Corrin provided this bath oil. Don't undress, ahh, I mean wait a minute. I have a little Halloween surprise for you." He scooted past her and left the bedroom.

Bubbles rose in a mound at the end of the tub. Soothing

lavender filled her lungs. A false sense of serenity if there ever was one, she concluded. In the adjoining room, bullet holes in the plaster provided malevolent proof.

If Tim had been the shooter, giving him her parents' property might be her only chance to survive.

CHAPTER 8

Scared. Moments ago, he'd seen raw fear in Elon's eyes. Rane stood in his kitchen, his stomach tightening. Damn the cattle rustler and damn Tim.

He adjusted the holstered gun at the small of his back. Not much else he could do, besides ask for help from his brother and his girlfriend. On her first case as a game warden, Belle had enlisted Chayton's help, and they'd figured out the identity of the scumbag who'd plucked several eagles. If anyone could find clues to who'd pulled the trigger last night, it'd be them. Sheriff Riley had assured him Belle returned home today. A phone call to his brother to confirm her availability would be next on the agenda, right after he delivered the special treat to perk up Elon.

He dusted the bathtub tray caddy he'd found in the closet. The center section had an indent for the mug of cider he'd poured.

And catching Emmett in Three Falls by phone after his morning class had been perfect timing. Somehow the kid had managed to transport a dozen donuts safely on his motorcycle. Which one would be for Elon?

He loaded a cream-filled beauty with a frosted pumpkin face onto a plate, set it on the tray, and carried it down the hall.

The door to her room remained wide open. Elon stood with her back to him, her hands resting on the tub, shoulders drooping. Did she regret her earlier talk regarding their possible future? He cleared his throat.

"Oh. Didn't hear you." She straightened, and her eyes brightened at sight of the tray. "How did you know? How did you know what I always serve my kids for Halloween?"

"I hit redial and got ahold of both your sons this morning."

"Oh, thank you for thinking to call them. It completely slipped my mind." Her face paled. "I need to warn them Tim's dangerous."

"Taken care of. They've been worried. Both are glad his deadly plans are out in the open." He set the tray across the end of the tub.

She took a step toward him. "I should've heeded their warnings. My kids are sharp."

"You've had a full plate. They made another comment about being grateful you're living where you receive the respect and appreciation you deserve. Said in your last phone call you sounded happier than you had in a long time."

She slid her wedding band to her knuckle and back. "I tried to hide my unhappiness. It wasn't their fault."

How he'd like to yank the damn ring off and cram it down Tim's throat. He turned her to face him. "Your boys love you unconditionally, from what I heard."

Color rose in her cheeks. Her kissable lips parted. "I needed to hear that, Rane."

"If money's tight for you, I'll figure out a way to free up cash for their college educations."

She raised her eyes to his and put her palm on his chest,

then let it drop. Her body tensed. "To cover the condo bills and keep us solvent, I secured a loan."

From whom? His jaw clenched. Didn't matter. She didn't believe in him. The final letdown, that she'd decided to leave, would come next. He fiddled with the spigot, not wanting to show how badly her rejection stung. Not wanting her to return to Seattle before he'd won her over. If only he'd put less earnest money on the property. He tightened the hot water tap until it groaned.

She tugged his shirt sleeve. "I didn't mean to insult you, but you've mentioned stretched finances. An old friend with extra cash insisted on the loan. Please don't put that between us. Let's take things slowly and forge a bond, so to speak." Elon's voice held hope. "I believe things happen for a purpose."

Relief burst in his chest. "I can be as slow as the spring thaw." He took in a deep breath, "I never believed I'd find a woman patient enough to tolerate me."

"Give me a chance," she answered, in a husky voice.

"I will." He pulled her close, needing her to relax into him. And she did, each soft curve fitting perfectly. Her head tucked under his chin, and her steady breathing feathered onto his skin, precisely the kind of warmth he'd needed for so, so long.

She draped her arms around his waist. "I trust you Rane, but I've never had real affection from a man, so I may try your patience when I doubt myself. But there's no doubting the effect of your kisses or the way having you as my protector helps me sleep." She released her hold and looked into his eyes.

"Whatever you need to quell those doubts, I'll do or not do." He smiled and slid his hands down her arms and off her fingertips. "Right now, I should call my brother. I want him to look at any tracks the shooter left. He's a hoof trimmer and has an uncanny ability to identify soil imprints."

"You never mentioned your brother lived close by."

"On part of the family property." Rane moved to the doorway. "There's plenty you don't know." His attempt at being cavalier felt forced. Still, she grinned. "Didn't you have parents or siblings to recommend you divorce Tim years ago?" he asked.

"I'm an only child. My parents died in a boating accident when the twins were two. Mom was bolstering my courage to file a legal separation. I didn't have the energy to continue after their death." She dropped her head

Not having family would devastate a woman like Elon. "I'm sorry for your loss. Must've been tough on you to lose your parents while raising little kids." He met eyes filled by sorrow. "You've got my help now. Take a relaxing bath, and I'll introduce you to Chayton during dinner."

"I look forward to meeting him."

"Don't see him much, as he keeps busy working with horses and teaching Blackfeet kids the ceremonial dances. Matter of fact, the local kids also need job skills, such as baking or welding."

"I'd enjoy teaching them what I've learned." Her genuine kindness cut straight to his heart.

"Old cowboys like me should know basic cooking, too," he teased.

"Oh, dinner," she stammered. "I'll fix grilled cheese sandwiches or something. I goofed again and didn't thaw anything."

Her ex must've berated her. The ass deserved to be hung. "No need." He waved away the idea. "Emmett read the instructions on your fancy cook pot and promised pot roast by six. The other men acted nervous, so they're home tonight for trick or treating with their families."

"Very kind of you. Emmett gets bonus points for donuts and roast. You both do." She blew him a kiss and closed the bathroom door.

The woman didn't need a torch to melt steel, and he'd protect her at any cost. He jogged to the desk phone. His brother should've met Belle's plane by now.

Chayton answered on the first ring. "What?" he demanded.

He could picture his brother's purse-lipped scowl. His name meant falcon, and he'd worn the same intensely determined look of the namesake bird since he'd been a kid. "Hey, bro. Wouldn't interrupt your Belle reunion if I didn't need to ask for her help. Hope her mom's okay."

"Her mom's surgery went well. No homecoming for me and Belle. You're too late to catch her."

"What do you mean?" Rane thumped his fist on the desk.

"Chill. I briefed her on the way from the airport about the attacks to your ranch. Sheriff Riley picked up a horse trailer for Big Red and then retrieved Belle about ten minutes ago. They should be at your house any minute. I'll join you after I check an abscess on one of Kat's horses."

"You're still a little snot. Happy hoofing."

"Hey. Belle will catch the thug. Shooting harmless old Fred, then aiming at Elon, aka the Baking Queen. This has to end."

"It does. Who calls Elon the Baking Queen?"

"One of my clients offered me a tiny piece of an amazing cinnamon roll. Coveted the remainder like a kid unwilling to share a new toy."

Exactly how he felt after kissing Elon. Times a thousand.

"Stay for dinner if you can. Wagyu pot roast."

"Thought you'd never ask. Cause you don't. Can't wait to meet the woman who finally softened my older brother. Gotta run," he said, and the call ended.

Not softened. Elon forged new possibilities in his world. And Chayton should talk, he'd found a woman smart enough to put a smile on his little brother's somber face. And of all the females out there, a game warden people jumped to accommodate. Like trailering in Big Red, when she needed her favorite mount to investigate a crime.

Everyone in the county respected Officer Belle and knew she deserved unlimited access to the smart mule she'd confiscated from the eagle poacher—a once-abused animal who'd later shown trust and brains by saving Miranda while she fled from a Seattle hitman. Who'd have thought his cousin Grant's path to happiness included rescuing a city girl, then convincing her to marry him and live in Montana? The story he'd heard indicated the mule helped plead his case. The long-eared critter figured in Chayton's good fortune, too. Fairy tales may come true—for those lucky enough to appreciate the appearance of a smart mule or a rescued dog.

He rubbed his chin, focusing on the current challenge. Belle would use Big Red to backtrack the path the shooter took to his hillside. Chayton could ride Fred's horse, he decided, and headed to the barn to saddle Possum, Keeper, and Crystal.

Chains clanked as the sheriff's SUV rolled in, towing a horse trailer, then parked by the round pen. Belle and Officer Riley got out.

Rane tied his horses to the hitching post. "Glad you're home, Belle, and your Mom's okay."

"Thanks," Belle said. "I'll grab my crime scene kit. Riley told me he cordoned off the area where the shooter waited."

"Possum ready for another ride?" Riley asked.

"Yes, sir. And no one's touched the area," Rane stated, and turned to Belle. "I'll unload Red. Grant told me Miranda takes pride in Red helping you."

"After she heard my side of his story, she insisted he'd be

my mount of choice on field work." Belle bent her tall frame and wrestled the largest saddle bag he'd ever seen from the back seat of the SUV. "It mildly irritates Chayton when I don't use one of his horses. I think he's even cuter when he's riled."

Rane snorted. "You have to be the first woman to use 'Chayton' and 'cute' in the same sentence."

"Maybe there's a badge for knocking down the infamous Calderon prickly defense?"

"Possibly, but I'm no Boy Scout." He pointed to the shiny black duffle bag supporting pouches hanging from each end. "We shouldn't have to camp overnight."

"Shouldn't have to camp overnight? Ha. Not my experience dating a Calderon." She threw him a side eye and eased the bag to the ground. "Chayton fit my excavation kit, fingerprint kit, trace evidence kit, and other supplies in one fabulous pack. Sits securely behind Red's saddle."

Chayton must be serious about Belle to be so thoughtful. Well, heck, he'd do anything to make Elon's life easier in a heartbeat—given the chance. "I'll secure it on Red so we can head out before we lose the best daylight."

The three climbed onto saddles and rode side by side. "The cagey bastard used a silencer," Rane said.

Belle sat back in her saddle. "Here's what I find odd. The bullet they extracted from Fred's tractor isn't typically used in a hunting rifle. Neither is the subsonic 220 grain ammo pulled out of Elon's bedroom walls. It's commonly fired in indoor ranges from an AR-15 mini version, oddly enough called a Honey Badger. They cost around three grand new, not certain of the price on the black market."

"Thought I knew guns. Never heard of a Honey anything," Rane said.

"Some ranchers are using them to kill coyotes and bobcats," Sheriff Riley stated. "Using the silencer prevents scaring the herd animals into a stampede. For someone hiking or biking in from the highway, the minimal five-and-a-half-pound weight's an advantage."

"You two are scary with all the gun smarts." Rane looked at the dead grass alongside the trail. "I'd wager the shooter arrived by bike. I saw a strange, narrow track running beside the path to the creek the day Fred got hit."

"Makes sense. I'll note it on the report," Belle replied.

He looked north to the gradual slope holding a stand of hundred-year-old trees. Yellow crime tape rippled in the breeze. A flagged area like this didn't belong on his hillside.

"Took a lot of damn nerve to scout my property ahead of time," Rane growled.

The hair on the back of his neck rose. The cold-blooded killer who'd planned this attack wasn't finished. When would he strike next?

The Honey Badger tied to bricks hit the surging Columbia River, sending a two-foot splash into foggy morning air. Tim watched the drops hit the cold water.

One piece of evidence destroyed, from another botched attempt on Elon. Phoning the hospital and using the excuse about sending her flowers provided proof she'd already been released. The woman had survived three times: a damn cat with nine lives. He didn't have time for six more tries.

Tim yanked off his gloves, turned them inside out, and shoved them into a baggie. They'd be ditched in a dumpster at the next stop.

Inside the unzipped pack lay the black knitted cap he'd worn to cover his hair when he'd gotten close to Calderon's house. More wasted effort. No one saw him peddling that night in the godforsaken boondocks. He shouldered the pack and stomped to the SUV.

Jasmine stirred when he opened his door. She raised sleepy eyes to him. "How long have we been driving? My butt's sore."

"That's because you don't have much padding, my love." He turned the vehicle around on the one-lane road and steered onto I-90. "I made good time this morning while you slept, and we'll be home soon."

She nodded and sank back into her seat.

Another thing he appreciated. She never questioned, never did the math on point A to point B, and wasn't concerned about any other details that whiney Elon used to question.

"Can you find me a chai latte?" she purred.

"Use your cell and locate the next espresso stand. I loaded an app onto the phone I bought you."

"You are the best, Timmy." She twirled a strand of her long, glossy hair. "Maybe I should move out of my apartment."

The one he'd been bankrolling for the last sixteen months. "I'll help you pack during Thanksgiving weekend."

Elon would probably come home to cook a calorie laden turkey dinner for her spoiled brats. He'd suggest she meet him for mediation and document signing. An idea formed to get her alone, the thought blossoming brighter than a bouquet of her precious flowers.

Seattle's growing crimes included armed home invasions.

Elon adjusted her dangling skeleton earrings and smoothed a long orange sweater over her black leggings.

Voices came from the dining room. Her slippers made little noise on the wooden floor. She paused in the doorway and observed the couple seated at the table, deep in hushed conversation. The woman wrote on a notepad.

The young man's demeanor reminded her of the living room painting of the Blackfeet hunter. Pride and determination radiated from him. It changed when the slim-faced, ginger-haired woman nudged him. His chiseled features softened to resemble a younger version of Rane.

She cleared her throat and entered the room. "Excuse me. I'm Elon, Rane's new welder and cook. You must be Belle and Chayton?"

Belle stood. At close to six feet, her hand easily reached across the table. "Belle Mason. Glad to meet you, even though it's under less-than-perfect circumstances." She offered a firm shake. "I collected items from the crime scene that the lab in Washington may be able to pull prints from."

Chayton rose to a height a few inches taller than Belle.

He stuck out a calloused hand. "You're protected now by the Calderon family and our community."

"That means a great deal to me." Elon gave him a friendly shake and looked into dark brown eyes. She smiled, and his tense frame relaxed—tall, muscular, and slimmer compared to Rane.

Transparency offered the best results. "I appreciate everyone's help. I assume Rane's mentioned our suspicion this shooter may be the man who's divorcing me?"

"No. He explained the foxglove poisoning and implied we'd learn more tonight." Chayton combed long fingers through his smooth black hair. "Another suspect to place on the list."

Belle sat and jotted a note on her pad. "Please give me his full name and explain the reason he tried to poison and shoot you."

"Dr. Timothy Karl Hardy is determined to claim ownership of a block of prime commercial property in Seattle near the Space Needle. My parents willed it to me. I want the old brick building sitting on it to remain in memory of them. I heard a rumor he wants to use the site for a hospital. The copy of their will I possessed disappeared from its normal place sometime before I packed to leave."

"Buildable land sells for millions. Now we have motive," Belle stated. "Are you in possession of anything Dr. Hardy might've touched?" She twisted her torso and removed a clear plastic bag and gloves from a backpack slung on the empty chair beside her.

"No, I don't think so." Elon stared at the pack. "Wait. I have a luggage tag Tim filled out on a new bag of his."

"Good. I'll put a rush on the results," she replied. "The lab's always weeks behind unless it's a mur . . . an emergency."

Elon flinched. Her shoulder brushed the wall while they walked single file to her bedroom. Belle used gloves to remove the tag and placed it in an evidence bag.

Her body went on autopilot for the next few hours. Dinner proceeded in a blur. Did she thank Emmett for the donuts and cooking tonight?

Back in the bedroom, under the quilt, her brain kept returning to the image of her boys identifying her body. Murder—the ugliest word in the English language.

What the hell was Fred thinking today by outfitting his old tractor with a gun? Rane scraped his hand over his face. He must intend to throw hay to the cattle in the upper pasture. Should he stop the stubborn cowboy from setting out only a week after he'd been shot?

No. Pride in work kept Fred going.

The shotgun's barrel rattled against the top of the idling tractor's engine cover. Two green bungee cords held it in place. The stock poked out beside the steering wheel, within easy reach of where Fred would be sitting in a few moments—a capable marksman who'd taught Rane to shoot.

Straw beneath Rane's feet crunched as he moved to the side of Tomo's shelter for a better view. Pastel shades painted the horizon of the late November afternoon, a peaceful backdrop in an unsettling scene. He could insist on doing all the chores for a while.

Rane watched as Fred exited the barn with a hay hook and pushed against the cane. He hoisted himself onto the red metal seat, threw the tractor into first gear, and rumbled toward the pasture.

His old friend shouldn't be driving the Cub yet, shouldn't be checking on stock, and sure as hell shouldn't have to tote a firearm in case of two-legged vermin. He pressed his fist against a wooden support post, feeling the rough texture.

How his worries had changed in the last month.

Rane stepped back to Tomo and held his palm against the new patch of hair growth on the bull's broken leg— searching for any trace of heat and comparing it to the same area on the opposite leg. *No difference.*

He stood and stretched his back, then scratched the itchy spot between the bull's horns. "If BoneGlu works, you'll be trotting alongside Fred again when he's throwing out hay."

The old cowboy and the old bull were lucky. Damn frustrating that the snipers roamed free. Elon had seen the rustler's gray hair. Lots of older women resided in the county. He needed to recall the sharpshooting riders.

Elon and Angel approached. The dog waddled, carrying the weight of the pups. Her mistress was a different story.

Elon seemed more alluring by the hour, especially now that she walked toward him with affection in her eyes.

"Up for a short ride?" Elon asked. "Angel's super clingy. She needs exercise."

"Perfect solution to my problem. Fred headed out alone, and I don't think Doc Kyle's recommendation for him to start back gradually included cattle patrol so soon."

"Agreed," she stated.

Possum whinnied when Elon entered the barn. The gelding knew a good thing, too. She held a slice of carrot to him in her outstretched palm. The horse's lips gently lifted the treat. He chewed it, then brushed his muzzle against her cheek.

Elon sighed and scratched his coppery neck. "You're my good boy, aren't you?"

Rane removed grooming buckets from their hooks. Each day Elon smiled more frequently and seemed more relaxed. Extra grain to Possum tonight, Rane decided, and headed to the tack room. When the trial month ended, would she agree to work permanently for him before she headed to Seattle for the divorce mediation?

She'd secured both horses to tie-ups outside the stalls. He plastered on his brightest smile and handed her a rubber curry comb. The impulsive decision he'd made yesterday could backfire. Would she be thrilled, irritated, or worse, indifferent?

"Possum calms around you. He's a one-person horse fighting a pink complex. You prefer blue. I sent his registration paperwork to the AQHA and put in your name as his new owner."

No smart remark. No yelp of excitement. His heart pounded like a two-stroke engine.

～

Elon's hand continued making circular strokes on the sorrel's shoulder, while her brain flew to high gear. Rane assigning her as the legal owner of Possum showed he trusted her. Or he wanted her to stay. Or with any luck, both. A smile rose to her lips.

He'd continued brushing Keeper, keeping his back to her. A quarter would bounce off his tense shoulders. Nervous about her reply? Other women might fault him for not talking to her first. Whatever his past female issues, he'd taken a giant leap of faith in her.

Nonetheless, he deserved to squirm, just a bit. "Fully healed, he'd probably command a good price at auction. Being trained so well and all. How much do you think he'd bring?" She raised her hand holding the rubber curry comb.

Rane swung around, wild-eyed.

"Ahh, just kidding. Sound familiar?" She tossed the tool at his broad chest and watched as he scrambled to catch it. "Ballsy move, Mr. Calderon. And flattering."

A nervous grin stretched across his face. "Scared me for a minute there. Probably Possum, too."

Elon smiled. "He saw me cross my fingers." She blanketed and saddled her horse and whistled for Angel.

Ambling onto the path, the horses seemed happy to move slowly to accommodate the pregnant dog lumbering between them.

"This has been a pleasantly warm fall," Rane said, and urged Keeper up a slope.

"Pleasantly so, between gunshots." Elon adjusted her knees while Possum wove between boulders to follow them.

Angel's head went up, ears alert. She veered off the trail toward a flat rock and stopped.

Rattling came from in front of the dog.

Elon stood in her stirrups. A coiled rattlesnake hissed a foot from Angel's black nose.

"Come, Angel. Treat," Elon whispered, and snapped her fingers. Possum moved forward.

The dog stood on point, teeth bared. The rattling noise increased speed.

Possum pinned his ears, side-stepped, grabbed the dog's fluffy tail, and yanked her backward.

Elon gasped and grabbed the saddle horn to stay seated.

Angel yipped, but when the horse nudged her butt, she scooted onto the path.

The rattler slithered to the back side of the rock.

"Good boy, Possum." She hugged his neck.

"That's a trail horse," Rane called from a few yards away. "You stayed nice and calm, Elon. Good cowgirl."

"Possum's the hero. Snake venom could be deadly for unborn puppies." She scratched under his mane. "Extra carrots for you tonight."

Her heart beat double time. The friendly west didn't seem so friendly. Or maybe she was the crap magnet. Tonight, she'd planned to text the neighbor to see if Tim had reappeared in unfriendly Seattle.

The view out the kitchen window showed dwindling numbers of red, orange, and yellow leaves on branches preparing for winter snow. Elon returned to attacking cheese baked onto a grimy griddle pan, stewing about the latest text from her Seattle neighbor, which described Scrawny moving her crap into Tim's home.

Dangerous or not, Dad would've thrown the conniving louse out by his ear if he'd lived to see the injustice. But he hadn't. Knowing Tim remained seven hundred miles away brought a modicum of relief at a time when she had other worries.

Her focus shifted to the chart on the refrigerator which showed Angel's vitals. The last few readings indicated puppies arriving today or tomorrow. Malnourishment could cause problems.

A low whine came from the storeroom. Elon dropped the pan into warm dishwater and headed to the mother-to-be. Angel scratched at bedding in a shallow wood box Rane had built for her.

She knelt by her anxious dog, stroking soft fur. "It's going to be okay. I'll be right here if you need me." Half the bedding looked damp. "Let's find fresh towels, and then I'll get Rane," she assured the dog.

At the porch door, she flipped a sign she'd penned: 'QUIET-Enter by the front door. Puppies soon.'

Across the driveway, Rane bent over a tractor, his sexy butt straining against snug jeans. She approached quietly and put her hand on his shoulder, squeezing work-hardened muscles. "Angel's gone into labor."

"I'll boil water," he teased. "One more bolt to tighten, and I'll be right in to don my puppy-sized stethoscope."

She danced her fingers across his shoulders. "Silly, I've got Ed's phone number loaded into my cell phone."

"I bet you do." Rane pulled a rag from his pocket and wiped his hands. "She's a young dog. She'll do fine. You fix a fresh pot of coffee, and we'll go on standby."

With coffee brewing, Elon headed to the laundry room, grabbing another stack of clean washcloths and towels. She tiptoed to the doorway between the kitchen and storeroom.

Angel lay on her side, her tummy bulging.

Rane stepped quietly behind her. "I read that we should stay in the background and only assist if it appears she's in trouble," he calmly whispered into her ear.

"Yes, Ed told me something similar."

"Let's take a seat." Rane moved both kitchen chairs to have a view of the birth. "Look, the first pup." He grabbed Elon's hand and leaned forward.

Angel licked the coal black puppy.

"She's being a perfect mom," Elon whispered.

"That puppy seems large for a dog Angel's size. Resembles a Lab pup we had." His shoulder rubbed against her back as he maneuvered for a better view.

The black puppy began nursing.

An hour later, Elon thrummed the table. She rose halfway. "She's straining harder this time, Rane."

Angel whimpered.

"I've got to assist her." Elon jogged in and knelt on the floor. Two wet, white legs protruded at an odd angle. "This one's breech. Please hand me a pair of gloves."

She fitted them on and gently helped birth the last puppy. Angel pulled the black and white bundle toward her and began licking a tinier male pup.

"Good girl, Angel. You've got a son and daughter to enjoy." Elon rocked back and scratched between Angel's ears. "We're proud of you."

Rane supported Elon's elbow, lifting her from the floor. "You can breathe easier now, they're both nursing. The spot on the forehead of the coal black one reminds me of a crescent moon. The smaller one's the spitting image of Angel. Ought to name him Lucky. I've seen backwards calf births not have a happy ending."

"Tentatively we'll name him Lucky, until Miranda sees them. I promised her first choice. I'll call Ed to relay the good news."

"Well, Luna, at eight weeks you'll be moving to Miranda and Grant's." Elon gently returned the week-old coal black puppy to her mom and extracted the tiny, fluffy version of Angel. "May have to keep you, Lucky. I'm afraid by the way I've seen you wiggle when you nurse that you'll be the rambunctious one."

Angel jumped out of the box and ran to the storeroom door. She barked as ferociously as she had the night of the shooter.

Elon looked out the window. "Oh no."

A cherry red truck towing a trailer pulled alongside the welding area.

Did the pickup sport the offensive mud flaps she'd seen when the monsters tossed out Angel? She craned her neck. "Can't tell if it belongs to the creeps. It's okay. You're in a forever home now." She smoothed the raised hackles on Angel's neck, placed both puppies into their box and pointed. "Stay put, and I'll investigate."

Stuffing her arms into her warm coat, she took a deep breath. What if a good customer owned the truck? Rane needed the work, and she needed overtime on her paycheck.

Her feet slowed as she approached the trailer hitch. Mud splatters partially covered the words 'BABE TRADER' and the voluptuous chrome woman. She stared at the serene mountains, contemplating the moral dilemma roiling in her stomach.

The young driver of the truck, who wore a ball cap, stood at the door of the machine shop talking to Rane. They shared a laugh, then unhitched his trailer. It held a twenty-foot long, three-foot high contraption with wheels at each end, as well as a skinny support frame holding rows of bent, staggered tines aimed at the ground like clawing fingers. Many were broken.

Elon stood to her full height, arms crossed over her chest. Rane took one look at her, motioned for the driver to wait, and approached. His placating smile didn't faze her.

"I remember the description of the mud flaps and truck. Please hear me out," he whispered. "His folks own the biggest dairy farm in this half of Montana."

"His truck pitched out Angel. The scumbags probably guessed she'd gotten pregnant."

He rubbed the back of his neck. "I'll charge him triple for the repairs, and you can buy her several rawhide bones."

Elon shook her head and stuck her hands squarely on her hips. "I detest cruelty."

"Me, too." Worry lines creased his face. "I've got property taxes and a growing payroll. Without all the steers to sell, money's a bit tight."

Security for her boys or her values? "Find out if he threw her out or drove."

Rane nodded, then approached the driver. "Is this your rig?"

"Nope. Mine's in for a brake job." The young guy removed his cap and ran his hands through sandy brown hair. "Borrowed my cousin's pickup."

Elon faced him. "Is one of them bald?"

"That's a loser friend." The driver scowled. "What'd they do now?"

"Tossed a sweet, pregnant dog to the edge of the highway. I'd appreciate his number. We need to have a little chat," Elon said.

"I'll write out the douchebag's cell. How's the dog? Does she need a home?" he asked.

"I'm keeping her, and she's fine, as are the puppies. Thank you for asking. Appears some of those tines met their match. I assume you'd like them repaired?"

"Please. The old shank harrow's great for breaking up manure before a freeze."

From behind the kid, Rane raised his hands in prayer, then winked.

But what if the driver had admitted involvement? Her chest tightened. How well did she *really* know Rane Calderon?

Elon scowled. Cooking bacon and sausage patties at oh-dark-thirty rated hazard pay. Soft, raw pork felt disgusting and splattered on the clean range. And the men had hoovered every fatty scrap into their mouths each time she'd served some for breakfast over the past three weeks on the job.

Grabbing appliquéd potholders, she pulled the two loaded sheet pans from the oven.

"Mighty fine-looking breakfast, Ms. Hardy." Rane stood in the doorway, one hand behind his back.

Elon narrowed her eyes. She blew a wisp of hair out of her face and began to fork strips onto a heated platter. "What brings you into the far reaches of your domain?"

A bouquet of sorts appeared from behind his back. "I, ah, need a little favor." Leafy branches held reddish-orange berries.

She'd not be easily duped. "Complementing my cooking, clippings of mountain ash—it must be an enormous favor. Angel's abuser needs bail?"

"Thankfully, no. The . . . ahem . . . church committee called and asked if our ranch would donate some baked goods to the silent auction on Saturday. Seems everyone's heard tell of your pastry skills." His feet shuffled on the floor.

"That's two days away." Watching him squirm seemed

fair.

"Well, will you bake something for them? As a special favor to me." Same pleading tone he'd used on Tomo the bull —cowboy desperate and utterly compelling.

Several of her favorite recipes took little time. "Add fifty dollars to next month's meal budget, and I'll prepare mini carrot cakes and banana bread."

"There's a hard bargainer under your lovely exterior." He handed her the branches, his hand not releasing when her fingers overlapped his.

Elon felt prickles of pleasure. Heat radiated into her chest. She never needed to apply blush around this man.

A slow smile showed his perfect white teeth. He released her hand.

"I'll find a vase." She pulled open the doors beneath the sink. "I think I remember one under here."

She stuck her head into the cupboard, welcoming a moment to collect herself. Tingles radiated from her toes. If he only knew . . .

H e'd never made a girl blush. Ever. And to think when he hired Elon, he thought her name was E. Lon Hardy. Standing for Elspeth, or Ernest, or some other name a guy wouldn't broadcast. Nope, a fatal mistake, Rane determined, while staring at the most attractive fanny to ever grace this kitchen, bent in front of him while she rooted under the sink for a vase.

No vase. "Must've been seeing things," she muttered.

The urge to pull her close, kiss her, and more, crossed his mind daily. Not in the game plan yet. Patience paid off. "I have a pitcher in the dining room you can use." He offered her a hand up, wishing they'd met twenty years ago.

Maybe not. He'd sworn off women after disastrous results helping Shelly. And they'd only been friends. Long strides got him to the other room. He pulled the glass container from the sideboard, walked back to the kitchen, and set it on the table. "This should do." The crimson on her cheeks had faded, making her face lightly pink.

Maybe she'd stay longer if she got screwed in the divorce settlement. A dangerous thought. What if she never returned?

"How early do you need the baked goods?" she asked, and stuck the sprigs in the vase.

"Be great if they're ready by ten. The auction starts at noon. It's a good cause. The sanctuary needs a new roof." He turned on his heel and headed to where his men stood beside the machine shop.

He glanced at the Washington plates on her car. His stomach tightened.

Elon relaxed her fingers on her cell phone. "I accept your apology and your word that you won't abandon an animal again. Goodbye." She pressed the 'end call' button. The driver of the borrowed truck must've read the riot act to the creep who'd thrown Angel out. The loser whined for mercy when she'd threatened animal cruelty charges. Not a bad way to start the day. She took a swig of coffee and leaned against the kitchen counter.

Unfortunately, she couldn't caffeine away irritation at Rane's avoidance the better part of the last two days. Sweet words, a fall bouquet, handholding, and then poof, no more charm. The man changed his feelings faster than rainstorms moved over Seattle.

From the dining room came the familiar sounds of Rane

entering the house, sliding out his chair, and reeling off Saturday morning chores to the crew. She finished washing the frying pan and listened. His requested baked goods for the church sale sat on the sideboard, boxed and labeled. Not that he deserved them.

The room quieted while his troops ate, no doubt happy to head home in a few hours. On his way out, he grabbed the boxes and mumbled something resembling thanks.

She ignored him and collected dirty plates and mugs. A whine came from the storeroom doorway. Angel sat up, held tilted. One ear always creased perfectly, the other at a jaunty angle. The puppies yapped in agreement.

"You can't figure him out either, can you?" Elon ruffled the hair between Angel's ears and loaded the dishwasher. One more meal and she'd more than earned her day and a half off. "We'll go into town and check out the sights. Maybe bid on something at the church."

No need for her to attend the next meal if she provided paper plates. The pulled pork she'd fixed would stay warm in the crockpot, and beside it she placed buns, chips, and apples for lunch. The pastries the men ordered were boxed and labeled.

Fred entered the kitchen, wielding his intricately carved cane.

"Leg getting better?" she asked her favorite silver-haired cowboy.

"I'm certain all the good food you prepare helps. Came to check out the pups." Angel raised her paw to shake. He bent and stroked each dog. His gold-capped teeth showed when he grinned up at Elon. "Yup, you've brought a new source of light into this house. Hope you stay."

"Prior to the past few days, I'd considered the possibility." She dried her hands. "Rane's acting weird. Any idea why?"

"He got word yesterday they'll contract all his Wagyu

steaks. Problem is, rustlers may strike again, and the stolen calves and steers need to be found. My inkling's somethin' personal is bugging him, too. Gotta run into town and confirm the butcher can process fifty steers on short notice. Need anything?"

A little information proved better than none. "Not today."

"I'll do whatever I can to help. And thanks for breakfast." He patted her shoulder and shuffled through the dining room.

Personal issues of Rane's must mean her. "You're very welcome, Fred," she called to a dependable and polite man.

Cleanup completed, she stretched her back. "No welding on the docket, Angel. Time to head to town. Your pups will have their first car ride today to check out competition at the bake sale."

The three dogs settled into the cardboard box she'd secured in her back seat. The trip took longer at a puppy-on-board speed. She double checked each crossroad and slowly entered Emma Springs.

Rane's blue truck stood out, parked in front of a classic steepled church. Several patches dotted the roof.

Elon pulled into the last angled parking space adjacent to the main road through town.

"You stay here, Angel. I'll put in a couple of bids before we sightsee." She cracked the windows to catch the fall breeze.

A hand-lettered sign pointed the way to the sale in the church basement. Elon held the skinny metal handrail, intent on not tripping on the uneven cement stairs. At the bottom, overhead lights ringed the low ceiling, casting a bright glow over tables of baked goods. Platters and tiered cake plates bore showpiece items displayed on checked cloths, lining the perimeter of the rectangular area. The crowded room buzzed with chatter and laughter.

Rane stood in the far corner, holding a pigtailed toddler in his arms, a broad smile on his face while he bumped noses with the little girl.

Elon recognized one of his crew, Lefty, who extracted the child. A look of longing softened Rane's face. She clasped her locket, comprehending the change. Rane Calderon wanted a child of his own. A coat swished into her, and she stepped aside to let a woman pass through the tight space.

When she spotted Rane's head of black hair above the crowd five minutes later, he had his back to her, standing opposite an older couple, occupying a gap between tables.

His rigid posture implied he wasn't listening to small talk.

The woman swiped her hand across her eyes.

Crying? Elon forced herself to start at the nearest table and work her way around through the throng of townspeople. Two tables in, she felt a soft pinch on her elbow.

"I bet you're the new cook out at the Calderon Ranch. Ed's mentioned how pleased he was to meet you. I'm Ed's wife, Julia Bell. Thank you for the beautiful additions to our sale." The sweet-voiced lady wore a hairnet atop her wavy gray hair. Another woman slid by them. Julia grabbed her arm. "Elon, please meet the County Council President, Sharlene Underson."

The woman wearing a gray fedora kept her head low, shook hands, and left. Julia smiled broadly. "The sale brings everyone together."

Both friendly and unfriendly. Elon smiled back. "I'm honored to help raise money for your church. Rane doesn't ask many favors."

Rane's head twisted at the sound of his name. He shot a glance toward Elon, then turned back to the older woman.

"We're going to hold a live auction for your items. As the building fund treasurer, I can't wait to see how much they bring in. Please join us any Sunday for service."

"I will. Nice meeting you, Julia."

"Same here, dear." Julia patted Elon's arm before she moved through the crowd, laughing and chatting.

The tide of hopeful customers shuffled Elon past plates of brownies, cakes, and cookies. Each item sat on a bid sheet. She spotted a platter of flat, purplish-colored cupcakes, topped by a lumpy layer of frosting. She signed her name on the first line, bidding five dollars.

The surge of people brought her close to her target. The man ahead of her bumped Rane, who stepped on the edge of Elon's shoe. No words of apology or acknowledgement came from his tight lips. The awkward silence sliced into Elon. "Nice turnout, don't you think?" she said.

Rane's glazed eyes blinked. "Mr. and Mrs. Hopper, this here's Elon, she's a helper at my ranch."

Helper? Elon flinched. "Pleased to meet you." She waited for Rane to say more. Anything more.

The Hopper's nodded toward Elon and moved to the next table. Rane didn't budge an inch, standing like he faced a firing squad.

"Rane, you okay?" she whispered, and waited for an answer. His face remained devoid of emotion. "Guess I'm done here." Her voice cracked, matching the feeling in her chest.

Rane ignored her and stared at the Hoppers' backs.

He was either embarrassed she'd shown up or planning to hand her a pink slip, Elon speculated, and spotted the exit. She wove her way to the stairway, avoided Ed Bell, and scooted upstairs.

Her shaky fingers fumbled while fitting the key into her locked car. She yanked the door open. "We're getting out of here, Angel. The helper is off duty and insulted."

CHAPTER 9

Elon braked at the stop light, thrumming her fingers on the dash. Getting a hotel for two nights cost money she couldn't spare, and many didn't allow dogs. The light changed and she eased through the intersection.

Roy's stately Craftsman, built on the slight hill, commanded attention. In the driveway of the little cabin across the street, Corrin hosed suds off her Firebird.

Elon pulled in and leaned her head out the open window. "Need practice on another car?"

"Sure. Decent weather and I'm dressed to stay warm." Corrin smiled and sprayed the headlight of the grubby Mercedes. "I planned to call you for updates today. Glad you arrived in person."

Elon closed the window, let out Angel, and lifted the puppy box to the grass. "I heard a new twist to Tim's motivation, and I need a personal favor if your girl-time offer still stands." She grabbed the brush from the sudsy bucket and erased the layer of grime on her fender.

"Perfect timing." Corrin sprayed off muddy, soapy residue. "Sleepover?"

They continued to work in unison, Elon washing and Corrin rinsing. "If I can stay until early Monday morning, you have many pastries in your future." Elon scanned the street. "I'm fed up with Rane, and I need a break from him. Not that he'd notice."

Corrin tossed her a large beach towel. "From what I've heard, he'll notice alright." Those puppies are adorable. She leaned over the box. "Who wouldn't miss all of you?" She shut off the water spigot. "Temp's not supposed to dip tonight, but no sense taking chances. Kyle warned me the keyholes on the car can freeze. I'll lift the garage door, and you can drive on in. Let him wonder where you landed."

Elon dried the car, parked in the small garage, and took a deep breath. "Are you certain you don't mind me and Angel's family?"

"Nope, long as you provide the full version of both stories." Corrin shut the garage door.

Elon lifted the puppy box and followed her into the cottage. Angel stayed at her side. A hint of vinegar scented the air. "Been cleaning or pickling something?"

"Couldn't pickle anything if my life depended on it. I try to keep green and avoid cleaning chemicals. I brought a stash of MarketSpice cinnamon orange tea from Seattle. This might be a good time to break into it." She put a teakettle on the stove and turned on the gas burner.

"Sounds perfect. Bull Boss introduced me at the bake sale as a helper." She put the last two words in air quotes.

The blue flame jumped to action on Corrin's stove. "Oh my," Corrin sympathized. "Male minimalizing on parade."

"I figured you'd realize how deeply the snub hurt, and why I needed a testosterone reprieve."

"The male lawyers in my old Seattle office took marginalizing to a new level. Vent at will. Put the puppies wherever they will be comfortable."

"Thanks." She set them near the couch. "Besides repairing behemoth machines and feeding the crew of eight, I've been canning fruit and veggies for winter. I stop for produce at roadside stands. And I thought Rane and I were friends."

"The guy's daft not to appreciate Montana's version of a torch-wielding Martha Stewart, let alone a woman who'd consider being his friend. Before I forget, and on a positive note, Aunt Iris and Kyle's dad have been corresponding since Miranda's wedding."

Elon smiled. "That's wonderful. She and Mom were good friends. She's been lonely since her husband's passing."

"I guess there's no expiration date on love. Aunt Iris appears to be enamored enough to consider a future relocation to Emma Springs. It's likely I'll be in Seattle over Thanksgiving to help her purge. I can secure an appointment with Tim's lawyer to test the waters. What's your intel?"

"My former neighbor spoke to Tim's girlfriend. Seems he plans to sell my parents' property to a hospital for a multi-story medical facility. I think the gunshots and poisoned tea lead directly to him."

"Are the police aware of his motive?"

"Yes. I've alerted Sheriff Riley. He warned me to be careful on any trip to Seattle. They're checking for fingerprints to trace how the foxglove leaves got into the jar. He put a rush on the ballistics tests and will explore channels to confirm the potential hospital partnership. I plan to ask for Thanksgiving weekend off to visit my sons and locate my parents' copy of the will. I want to join you at the attorney's office."

"I'll call Tim's lawyer on Monday. For safety, I'll not mention your attendance."

"Thanks. My boys won't divulge my plans should their father make contact." She rubbed her forehead.

Spicy notes of cinnamon and orange perfumed the room

as Corrin poured steaming water into a teapot. "Fill me in on the exploits of Bull Boss."

Discussing the challenges and rewards of bringing men into their lives settled her. She took a break and let all the pups out for a nightly romp. Around midnight, she yawned, waved goodnight to Corrin, and let the soft cushions on the couch cradle her weary soul.

The negative emotion of the bake sale encounter took its toll. Her fingers hung off the couch, resting against Angel, who'd curled against her pups in the box on the floor. She closed her eyes, concentrating on the subdued and methodical ticking from a mantel clock and her faithful buddy's soft fur.

The peaceful solitude might give her a decent night's sleep, she reasoned, and burrowed her cheek into the pillow.

Pleasant clock chimes woke her. Morning sunlight shone through slits in the window blinds. She tipped one open. Mist rose off the beautiful lake. Swirls parted as a rowboat appeared holding a man and little boy.

Elon took the dogs outside, enjoying their peaceful morning routine before quietly returning inside.

"I can make you coffee." Corrin yawned, padded into the kitchen, and pulled a canister out of the cupboard. "You gave an interesting account of your ex, Rane, and facing the rustler. I thought my life seemed complicated."

Elon laughed. "Coffee sounds divine. Hearing last night about Miranda's challenges and your amoral law firm pushing your move to Emma Springs put things into perspective. Vindictive men forced us all to relocate recently. We've survived and prospered."

"And then some. Miranda and Grant are a perfect twosome." Corrin sighed.

"She deserves happiness after her ordeal." Elon adjusted the borrowed robe, which ended above her knees. "So do you. I don't want to impose further on your hospitality, if you have plans for today."

"I've put in long hours this week, so I planned to veg all day." She brought a mug to Elon.

"After beefville, I'm up for vegging in any capacity. Angel and the babies are content, too." She rubbed the soft mounds sleeping at the foot of the couch. Rane would surely welcome the dogs back.

Six chimes sounded from the mantle clock on Sunday morning. Rane thrummed his fingers on the table. He never waited for anyone. Never listened for tires on the driveway or watched for a door to open. Thankfully, Doc Kyle had stopped yesterday to check Fred's leg wound. When questioned, he'd thrown the hint Elon had holed up in town, not crashed her car in a ditch or much, much worse. Knowing she was safe hadn't made the hours go faster at 2:00 a.m., 3:00 a.m., or 4:00 a.m.

He rubbed his temples. Elon wouldn't return happy. Probably not ever. He needed fresh air.

When he entered the barn with carrots, the horses nickered friendly greetings. Even their welcome didn't help. He reentered the house to continue the worst day of his life, pacing the floor, picking up and plunking down the phone receiver in a pathetic need to pump Kyle for more information.

He opened the refrigerator door, then slammed it shut. Elon better be back Monday morning. Or what? He looked out at the sun setting behind the barn. Customers needed her, the crew needed her, and so did Possum.

Who the hell was he kidding? Life sucked without her. Good, bad, or frustrating.

By evening, he'd completed chores and read every line of the thick Sunday paper. Rane climbed the stairs to bed, the creaking wood the only sign of life in the house. Memories of Elon flashed through his brain quicker than a spring lightning storm—her slapping the bloody steak in front of him, growling to defend Possum, and he could almost smell the pastries she'd provided for the sale. The damn sale.

He crawled into bed and stared at the ceiling. His eyelids felt heavy, but his ears strained to identify night sounds drifting in through his open window until they turned to predawn noises.

Crunching gravel signaled a car. He checked the clock: just past four-thirty. Sleeping fully dressed paid off, he thought, as he stumbled downstairs and sat in the kitchen chair, ready and waiting.

Elon parked next to Rane's truck, its paint shining in the first glows of dawn light. She called Angel to her side, lifted the box holding the puppies, and used her hip to shut the car's door.

She nudged open the back door. "Stay beside me." Angel cocked her head and hugged her ankle, padding through the storeroom.

The light above the kitchen sink cast a soft glow on Rane, seated at the table. Rumpled clothing, red outlined eyes, and his chin covered with a stubbly beard. She almost felt sympathy. Almost.

"Where've you been?" He rotated the vase holding the wilted mountain ash.

"I have Saturday afternoon to Monday morning off, as stipulated in our contract, Mr. Calderon." She hung her keys on the hook. "Your terms."

"Where've you been?"

"None of your business, Mr. Calderon."

He pushed the plate holding the dark purple cupcakes from the bake sale across the table. "Paid five dollars for cupcakes that damn Sharlene Underson baked. I'll deduct it from your check."

"Fair enough. I didn't intend to burden you with a monetary inconvenience."

"Didn't intend, like hell." The veins popped at his temples. "Don't ever leave again without telling me where you're headed."

"Why? I'm the helper, Mr. Calderon. Your precise words to your friends." Two skillets clanked onto the cook stove.

"I was worried. I care about you, even if you don't think it's true."

"There's no reason to." She squeezed her eyes shut, willing the moisture to stay inside her lashes.

"The Hoppers are neighbors I hadn't spoken to in a long time. Caught me off guard seeing them." Rane rose and stopped.

The explanation didn't match his actions. Elon looked out the window to the hillside ablaze from tinted trees. "Your food will be served on time. I'll check the board in the machine shop for work as soon as I've cleared away breakfast."

By the sound of his boots, he'd left through the front door. In an hour the men filed in. Talk at the breakfast table centered on the fall roundup and bringing stock grazing from upper pastures closer to home. Rane would cull out heavier animals for the pending meat order and finish feeding the rest according to needed weight gain with some secret mix of corn, barley, and wheat bran.

Sounded like a chef with a mystery ingredient in a popular recipe. Elon chewed on her waffle. *Whatever.* Angel would enjoy camping out. She could chase endless prairie dogs, and they'd be sleeping in a tent. The pups were still at the crawling stage and easily corralled.

Roundup discussions continued at lunch and dinner. Elon listened carefully to the plans for the route, the creek crossing, and the preferred campsites. By the talk, her grandma's old campfire cookbook she'd brought might come in handy.

"Emmett, you're in charge of buying alfalfa pellets to feed the Percheron draft horses I'm borrowing to pull the chuckwagon." Rane detailed tasks for other men, his voice animated.

No orders to her about planning food seemed odd. She let the empty dinner dishes sit on the table and approached Rane, who'd just plucked his hat and coat from the hall tree. "So how many meals will I cook on an open fire?"

"No bean master on this trip. Pack simple grub for three days. There will be four of us. You're staying here. The rest of the men take vacation," he said as he walked through the doorway.

What! "But, but . . ." The door banged shut.

"I'm the cook, or bean master, Angel."

The dog continued eating her chow topped by scraps of ham.

"How dare he leave me behind and take the fun out of the job?" Elon slammed plates into the dishwasher.

Angel licked the bowl, hopped into the box holding her puppies, and squeezed her nose between her paws as if blocking angry noises.

In a few minutes, Elon gathered the two pups in her arms and motioned for Angel to follow her to their bedroom. She loaded them into the shallow wooden Pepsi crate she'd lined with a blanket and flipped through a magazine. At least it got dusky earlier.

Echoes of baled hay thumping onto the trailer in the barn

reached her open window. She pictured Rane's muscular form flinging each heavy bundle. She jumped off the bed and pounded the window shut.

A wicked smile crossed her lips as she drifted off to sleep, picturing a way for the Bull Boss to cave.

~

Thank goodness Rane didn't face the kitchen during meals. This morning, his shoulders remained ramrod straight, while he and his minions waited for grub.

Elon entered the dining room holding her head high.

Grit latched onto the heaping platter of round pancakes, all the while staring at her like a bear eyeing a huckleberry, located on her chest.

The guy gave her the creeps. Thankfully he'd passed the platter to Fred.

She slid the other plate holding the custom-shaped buttermilk creation in front of Rane. Stubby horns topped a bull's head with craisins for eyes and chocolate chip nostrils —a dead ringer for an angry Tomo.

Only one of the men noticed, bumping his neighbor and nodding toward Bull Boss.

Rane slathered on butter and half the pitcher of syrup, not disguising the shape quick enough to avert a couple snickers. His knife slashed the tender pancake, destroying her masterpiece.

She returned to the kitchen, smirking. Armed with the plate of pork patties, she stepped into the dining room. Round two. She forked the one shaped as a bull's hoof print onto Rane's empty plate, then handed off the platter.

All eyes focused on Rane's hand-crafted lumps of browned meat. "Oh, boy . . ." A booted foot whapped against a leg at the far end of the table. "Ouch," someone muttered.

She primly turned and receded to her domain. Next came the finale, the hind end of the bull, shaped in Danish, and decorated by a blackberry jam tail. Do or die, she bit her lip and set the plate in front of Rane.

Red crept past his shirt collar. She pivoted and rammed into a brick-like arm at her waist.

"We need to talk." Rane's chair tilted and nearly tipped backward as he pushed away from the table.

The room became dead silent. "There's a basket of Danish bear claws for the men," she squeaked.

"Leave it." Iron fingers cupped her elbow, propelling her upstairs into no-woman's land. They passed the unused bedrooms and bathroom, silently moving toward the master's lair at the end of the hallway.

His domain. "Whatever you have to say, you can do it right here. I'm not allowed in there." She planted her feet in front of his door.

He shoved it open. His palm pressed into her back to nudge her inside. "No more audiences, smart ass," he hissed.

No exit unless she jumped from the window. Blue-and silver-hued wooden furniture decorated the bedroom. Elon stopped at the bureau next to the door. The wood felt smooth and cool to her touch. "It's beautiful." The words tumbled out unexpectedly. She scanned the room to appreciate each piece.

Rane stood in the doorway, arms crossed at his chest. "Beetle Kill Pine. Something useable created by a pest. Sound familiar?" He stepped in and shut the door.

"That's rich. You're calling me the pest?" Her foot stomped. "You came on to me and then barely introduced me to your friends at the bake sale. Either embarrassed I showed up, or you are planning to fire me. Who knows! Now, you won't allow me to cook on the round up. You are the most bullish man I've ever met."

"I gathered you felt so. As do my men." His hands moved

to his hips. "Your presence never embarrasses me. However," he growled, "your opinion of how I run my ranch won't embarrass me in front of the crew. Do you understand?" His voice rumbled through the room.

"There are many things I don't understand, but embarrassment I get." Her voice dropped to a flat tone. "Sorry."

Rane's hand squeezed his hair, as if trying to extract the right words from his brain. He took a step toward her, his hands outstretched. "Honest, I really didn't mean to hurt you at the church. I'm sorry I did."

"Then share your story. Does this concern the girl from your past?" She looked away from him, not wanting to witness signs of a lie.

He rested one hand at her waist while turning her chin with his fingertip. "Yes. I can . . . try to explain." His low, halting voice begged her trust.

"That's all I ask," she promised. "I want to understand."

"Fred's the only one alive who knows." Pain-filled eyes looked deep within her, then he led her to his rocker and held it steady while she sat. "This may take a while."

"I've got all the time you need." Elon rocked slowly and methodically while he paced the floor.

"The older couple I introduced you to at church have a daughter, Shelly. We rode together from the time we took our ponies to grade school. Became best buddies, inseparable."

"Uh-huh," Elon murmured, sensing his awkwardness.

"I'm two years older, so after high school we didn't see much of each other." He moved to the window. "Driving home late at night from a party during my Christmas break from college, I saw Shelly walking along a snowy highway, so I gave her a ride to her house." He took a deep breath. "The next morning, Mr. Hopper pounded on our door. I woke to him cussing my name at eighty decibels."

"Oh dear." Elon stopped the rocker.

"I didn't notice the shiner on Shelly's right eye the night before. The dome light was out in my truck. Her father saw me drop her off, met her at the door, and jumped to the conclusion I'd attacked his daughter in a lover's fight. The next day, when he accused me, my folks took their side without hearing me out. I tried to tell them I'd only given her the damn ride."

"How horrible."

"Until then, I had no idea both families shared the notion we'd get hitched someday. They hadn't noticed the obvious, that Shelly and I treated one another more like a brother and sister. Nothing more ever occurred."

"Shelly didn't defend you?"

"She tried to, but her parents wouldn't listen to her. That night her dad accused her of being pregnant, which she wasn't. She left before dawn. All along I figured she blamed me to save her own hide." He slunk onto the edge of his bed.

"Oh, Rane. I am so sorry."

"I barely passed my college classes that term. Grandma Bia suffered a heart attack, and I made it home to see her two hours before she died. I blamed my parents siding with the Hoppers for her death."

"Oh dear."

"It gets worse. Dad's a craftsman at heart, not a rancher, I guess that's the reason Bia left the ranch to me in her will."

"That's a lot for someone, so young. You were twenty?"

"Nineteen. Dad and I had words about how I wanted to raise a specialty breed, like Wagyu. He thought I'd go bankrupt. When he realized I planned to use my saved-up college tuition for premium livestock, he yanked Chayton out of high school and moved them to Arizona."

Elon stopped rocking. Her heart ached for the family. Both families. "Oh, Rane. I'm so sorry."

"I hadn't spoken to the Hoppers since I got blamed for

hitting Shelly." Rane clutched the top of the dresser. "Just before you arrived at the bake sale, Mrs. Hopper told me Shelly's happily married with two kids. They're headed to visit her in California. Made amends a few years ago. They hadn't worked up the nerve to apologize to me. They grow 'em big and stubborn in Montana."

"In any state, that's inexcusable behavior in my book. Are your folks aware?"

"Why bother? Grandma Bia and Fred were the only adults who believed me. Chayton tried unsuccessfully to convince our old man." Rane sat on the edge of the bed.

"I won't defend your parents. However, I can't imagine the pain of losing two children." She reached her hand toward him. "It's not too late to reconcile."

"I can only take one thing at a time."

"You must've been totally shocked on Saturday." She sat back in the rocker, studying his slumped posture. "I'm sorry you felt betrayed by Shelly and your dad. Thank you for telling me."

"It's a relief to know the truth about that night." His body seemed to shrink.

To process his emotional wound, he'd need her companionship more than ever. "Take me on the round up. I want to learn more about you. Please, Rane."

"It's no place for a sweet, city woman."

"I'm tougher than you think. I raised two rambunctious boys."

"This isn't summer camp. We're talking unruly cattle, wild animals, and bad weather."

Her eyes searched the room and landed on a replica antique pistol hanging on the wall. "I'd be scared here all by myself. What if the shooter returns while you're gone?"

He rubbed a crease in his forehead. "Yeah. Fred made me consider that." He leaned toward her. "You'll need to do everything I say, when I say it, and no exceptions. Working the herd's dangerous."

"I understand your concern." She stroked his cheek, then rose from the rocker. "I follow instructions when I'm in unknown territory."

He stood and pulled her into his arms. "I won't let anything else happen to you. My draw to you is unknown territory. May I kiss you?"

Longing rose from her chest. "Please," she murmured.

Warmth and need from his troubled soul flowed into her. An honest need. She relaxed into his sensual kiss, feeling heat deep, deep down. Her arms circled his neck, pulling him close. The scent of hay, Old Spice, and Rane stirred her desires. She pulled her lips away for a second and moved her hand to his chest, then to the button on his flannel shirt. Her silver band caught the light.

Not now, not yet. And not when he's vulnerable. She kissed the edge of his mouth. "Your men must be placing bets downstairs."

"Yeah. Go on ahead. I'll follow in a couple minutes." Lingering passion brightened his eyes.

Someday, she'd fuel his flame. Warmth spread through her chest as she pulled the bedroom door closed behind her.

Rane skipped lunch. Luckily, she had welding projects to free her mind from his family problems and her new desires. He stayed quiet at dinner, listening to his men plan their part in the cattle drive and casting glances her way.

Tired and hopeful, she went to bed having a better understanding of Rane.

Seven showed for breakfast. No Rane. Did he regret his confession and their kiss? Elon drummed her fingers on the sideboard.

Lefty held his fork in midair when she grabbed his empty plate. "You seem in a hurry to end breakfast, Miss Hardy."

The machine shop guy irritated her. He insisted on drinking hot cocoa and seemed to brownnose Rane.

"Lists of supplies won't write themselves. I'm excited to see the wagon transporting my cooking implements." She gathered the remaining dirty plates.

Grit headed out after only one heaping portion of corned beef hash.

"You have a nice day, Miss Hardy." Lefty tipped his hat.

Suck-up or genuine? "You, too." She'd know the cowboys better by the end of next week, she concluded, and stacked plates. Their boss might drive her crazy in the meantime.

"Try this on." Rane stood at the kitchen doorway, holding a tan cowboy hat.

"Fits perfectly." Elon straightened the brim. "Your spare?"

"From when I was twelve. Hold out your hands." He laid a piece of paper on the table. "I need to find gloves to fit you."

Elon placed her hand on top of the paper, and Rane drew around it. "I think I'd be a woman's medium."

"No women's gloves here. I'll see what I can do. Never been so nervous about outfitting someone for a drive before." He folded the paper and tucked it in his breast pocket. "The wagon's ready for your inspection. See you later."

Nerves plagued Rane, a possibility she hadn't considered. "Do they make leather food handler's gloves?" He'd left before hearing her joke.

The kitchen got a lick and a promise, as her grandmother called a quick clean. "Okay Angel. I washed dishes and prepped lunch. Your pups are napping. Let's check out the chuckwagon."

Angel happily trotted after Elon. Outside was her favorite place to start an adventure. They headed into the side area of the barn. The chuckwagon sat in a corner.

The rear wheel topped her shoulder. "Wow, Angel. The

wagon's larger than I thought." She folded out the table at the back and sorted through cast iron pots and rough-looking ladles.

"There's a spot for the cook to sleep behind the seat." Grit's pompous voice echoed in the barn.

She glanced over her shoulder. "Not why I'm here."

He'd stepped inside the doors and stood with his hands folded across his chest.

"I'm busy figuring out what preparations to make." She picked up a large serving spoon.

Angel growled as his hand snaked around her waist. "Let's see if two fits in them sleepin' quarters." He grabbed the spoon and tossed it to the ground, then kicked at Angel.

"Go away, mutt."

A motor sputtered, then rumbled to life in the distance.

Damn bully. She shoved her fist into his side and broke his hold. "Leave Angel alone. And keep your hands off me! Rane wouldn't want you here. Go back to work," she yelled, and stepped toward the door.

He grabbed her belt. "The boss has his head under a tractor engine, he'll never hear." In one quick motion, he pulled her against his greasy bib overalls.

"Help!" Elon pushed against his chest.

He covered her mouth and pinned her against the wagon.

CHAPTER 10

Rane felt a tug on his pant leg. He gave it a good shake, figuring he'd caught his jeans on an exhaust clamp.

Angel barked, latched onto his pant leg, and yanked.

"Hey. Stop that." Rane stared at the dog, and she released, then ran ten feet and stopped, barking furiously.

"Got the message." He jumped from the rough-idling machine and ran after Angel, across the driveway and toward the barn.

"You bit my hand, bitch!" Grit's voice boomed through the cracked door. "I'll leave you alone when I'm good and ready."

The sickening sound of a flat-hand slap hit Rane's ears. He stormed in and grabbed Grit's neckband. "You're dead meat, asshole." Rane jerked him backwards and threw him against the door.

Grit rubbed his throat. "Much as you won't admit, you don't own me, and you don't own her. We were just having some fun."

"Like hell! I heard you hit her." Rane ran to Elon. "Do you need a doctor?"

Her face stood out pasty white in the dim interior, except for a red splotch on her cheek. She grabbed the front of his shirt. "No, you got here in time." Her body shook while she clung to him like a lifeline.

Red flashed in his field of vision. He gently pulled her hand away and leaned her against the fold down table. "He's done hurting you."

Elon nodded, and Rane cuffed his sleeves. "You're going to pay for this, Grit."

Grit spat on the ground and spread his legs wide. "Don't forget, I got friends working in the accessor's office and the grazing lease program."

"He's not worth the fight, Rane. Fire him." Elon clasped his wrist between her fingers. "Other mechanics want to work here. I'll tell Sheriff Riley what happened. Grit sets foot on the property again and I press charges."

A surly smirk rose on Grit's face. "Think you're pretty high and mighty cozying up to the boss. You'll have a reckoning one day."

Rane pushed Elon behind him. "Think you're tough, threatening a woman? You're lucky to only be fired. Take your toolbox and leave my property immediately." He pointed to the door. "Now! I'll send your final paycheck to your ex-wife and kids."

Grit rubbed his neck and left the barn, stomping to the machine shop.

Rane pulled Elon close, tucking her to his chest. Her breath still came in quick gasps. "I knew he'd been ogling you. I should've fired him sooner." He ran his hand down her back, slowly, calmly, hoping to stroke away the awful thoughts of what could've happened. "If I find any trace he's back on the property, I'll take action."

"He won't dare return." The voice of the brave, alluring woman he loved had returned. Adoration radiated in her eyes. She settled her head against his chest. "Thank you for defending me."

And damn if it didn't feel wonderful. "You can thank Angel for finding me." He cleared his throat. "And I'd be honored if you'd call it our ranch." He kissed the top of her head. "Marry me, Elon."

She tipped her face to him. "You know I can't accept a proposal."

"Your status is merely a detail. Marry me." He pressed his lips to hers.

She let the kiss linger, teasing him by not answering. "You're difficult to refuse," she sighed.

"Here's a compromise. An unofficial engagement. I want you by my side."

She fingered the collar of his shirt. "You can do better."

"What a crock of bull. There's no one better than you. You'll be getting a cowboy whose life has more twists than a lasso." He eased his arms from her waist.

Elon feathered circles onto his cheek. "I'm not on a straight course either. Give me time and we'll untangle together." A tear left her lashes. "My first husband wanted me for my parents' money. You want me for my job skills." She offered him a weak smile.

He wound a strand of her hair around his finger, then let it slip free. Any thoughts of living alone again puddled at his feet like spring mud. "No more kidding, Elon. I want you for the glow shining from your heart and the way your hair curls under your chin, and everything else." He thumbed away her stray tear. "I'll wait for you, however long it takes."

"I know, Rane Calderon."

"But what could you ever see in me?" he whispered.

~

Elon rested her cheek against Rane's chest again and listened to his steady heartbeat. Nothing stirred in the barn. Odors of polish and leather came from the nearby chuckwagon. "What do I see in you? A person I admire. I'm starting to glimpse the kind, gentle man who lives under the tough exterior. Your kisses feel like you really mean them. Not playing some game to get something, using me as a pawn."

"I'll never betray you," his deep voice held tenderness and raw honesty.

No, he wouldn't. She closed her eyes, capturing the moment. "I haven't felt protected since I lost my parents. Probably hard to understand."

"I kept this ranch functioning after my parents took off. I have a fair idea."

"Of course." She ran her fingers through his thick, shiny hair. "You also rescue women and horses."

"Only pretty ones." He kissed the tip of her nose.

"We're a strange pair; two middle agers experiencing things most teenagers are old pros at by sixteen." Elon stifled a giggle.

"Isn't forty the new twenty?" He pulled her to a bale of straw and sat her on his lap. "I want to hear about the good parts of your past. And I'll share mine. Tell me about your sons first. From what I heard on the phone, I already like them."

A perfect diversion from her evading his proposal. Elon snuggled against his shoulder. "Brandon's intuitive, or maybe sensitive's a better word. He's great on computers. Always has been, since he first sat at a keyboard. He can assist without making you cringe."

He nodded. "I'd appreciate that."

"Jeremy's the athletic, social one. He'll want to learn steer roping and where they hold Saturday night dances. He loves acting in plays."

"Great sounding kids. I can't wait to meet them."

Elon glanced at the floor and saw the big spoon. She took deep breaths, trying to quell her roller coaster of emotions. Rane's arms steadied her, and she needed the security after Grit's mauling. Later, she'd ask for Thanksgiving off.

Whoever the creepy Grit knew in high places, Rane's uphill battle threatened to be as steep as hers against Tim's wrath.

~

"Dr. Hardy, we're glad to meet you today." The Hospital Expansion Committee chairman shook Tim's hand and ushered him to an open seat. "Did your lawyer find anything amiss in our Letter of Intent to Purchase?"

Not with the seven-figure down payment they'd suggested. Tim smiled and sat up straight in the leather chair, seated beside a physician he'd admired since his residency program. "No, I'm certain the Hardy Hospital project will set a new standard for partnerships between individuals and healthcare providers concerned for the public welfare of Seattle."

"Exactly how we envision our future venture. We'll draft a contract for your approval and complete a feasibility study to see how many stories can be built. Ten may be a low estimate."

The study shouldn't take long. His visual acuity appeared unchanged, possibly indicating the stabilization stage of the retinal disease. He could relax on two fronts. "Onward and upward."

"Our legal team will prepare documents for you to sign to do a review of the title."

Tim cleared his throat. "Great." Tonight, he'd research how to delay the title search process until Elon no longer had a heartbeat.

❧

Sharlene Underson swung into the closest empty parking space to Dagger Realty. As council president, the town should give her an office, or at least a parking place, she concluded, as she lifted her packet of county council documents to be reviewed. Her eyes narrowed when two men exited McPherson's General Store, a few doors away.

One depended on a cane. Fred.

Her mouth pursed. Old fools shouldn't mess with rustlers.

"Really appreciate your help," Fred smiled warmly as McPherson himself loaded a box of supplies into the back of the pickup parked beside her.

"Hope it don't storm," he said to Fred, and ambled back inside.

Calderon's fall round up must be soon. She hoisted herself out of her new Corvette. "Party at the ranch? Didn't see an invite in the last Emma Springs Newsletter," she trilled and adjusted the brim on her newest cloche hat.

"Nope," Fred muttered.

The old geezer barely acknowledged her. "Hmmm." She touched her pointer finger to her chin. "Then I'd guess it's the time of year for bringing cattle from the higher ground."

"Not the boss." Fred's slumped shoulders rose in a weak shrug.

She sidled next to the truck and stood on tiptoe to scan the three boxes chocked full of waterproof matches, a new canteen, lantern fuel, and food. "Packages of dried beans and boxes of dried fruit. Seems odd. I heard you landed a gourmet cook at the ranch."

Fred slid the boxes together. "Yup," he said, and proceeded to hoist his injured leg into the cab. He slammed the door, pumped the gas pedal to coax his rusty beater to life, and backed out. He'd of clipped her new Bandolino boots if she hadn't jumped back.

It was time then. She'd need one more round of target practice. Despite the tight-lipped, ornery old codger, she'd wangled necessary information. Now to call in the troops. *Meet in the office ASAP,* she typed onto her phone screen. *Use the back door.* She hit send and pocketed her cell.

Thank goodness for low heels, Sharlene thought as she increased her pace on the sidewalk leading to the doorway of her husband's realty office. Overhead lights flicked on and illuminated her desk, Don's, and a worktable holding the printer and fax machine. A burnt smell hit her nose. Her stupid spouse had left the coffee pot on again.

She yanked the cord to unplug the coffee maker, jerked her desk drawer open, and snatched a topographical map. Unfolded, she studied the dotted line indicating a creek leading from leased property above Calderon's ranch to a lower pasture. Notes scribbled on the side and arrows denoted where she'd seen herds of cattle and which direction they'd run.

Calderon needed to get some processed for the beef contract. If her intel proved correct, those steers grazed near the north property line.

How convenient. At the last council meeting, the rancher leasing the adjacent government property on the hillside threatened to shoot the beavers damming the creek and flooding his grazing land. Council members had insisted he work through Montana Fish, Wildlife & Parks for a solution.

Nothing got done quickly through that worthless agency. She sat back in her chair, smiling at the irony.

A knock on the back door jolted her. Grit entered and Don followed, his unsteady gait a sign he'd been drinking again, another reason to leave him behind. "Good evening, boys. I texted you because an opportunity appeared." She scanned the alley before closing the door.

"With Calderon canning me, I need money, not opportunities," Grit grumbled.

Spoken like a true ignoramus. His philandering needn't ruin her plans. "Shut your pie hole. Your being fired put the entire operation in jeopardy. You're lucky to get a partial split."

"Partial! No way," Grit growled.

"My way or leave." She pointed to the door and watched him do a slow simmer. "Recapping, we have twenty-two calves being fattened for the Colorado stockyard and four steers. My contact assured me of a good price for prime veal.

The steers I plan to secure next necessitate we improve our game."

Grit cleared his throat. "Secure?" he snickered.

Losers. She tapped a spot on the paper. "There's a beaver dam at the top of a creek cutting through Calderon's property. He'll cross the dry ravine to move the animals. If we correctly time blasting the dam, part of the herd will be on one side of the wash and part on the other. In the confusion, it should be easy to run a larger group of steers to the trailer that Grit hauls in."

Don stuck his hands in his pockets. "Too risky to bash the beaver dam at exactly the right moment."

Sharlene rolled her eyes. "Grow a pair. Someone on the drive must need money. Campfires can be used to signal Calderon's movements. Grit's got time to camp on the ridge.

I'll loan him strong binoculars." And she'd drive there in her own getaway vehicle, just in case.

Grit stuck out his chest. "I've still got a contact in the shop who's whined about being strapped for cash. Lefty will tell me when they're leaving."

"Doesn't solve the problem of breaking the dam open," Don said.

"I'll supply Tannerite, that blows after you shoot it," Grit boasted. "If I load a couple milk jugs full of it and stash them in the right place, the dam will topple quicker than a popsicle house. We'll need a sharpshooter."

"My area of expertise," Sharlene declared. "Paint the milk jugs red, and I'll hit them." She eyed her worthless husband. "No drinking before, Don. Celebrate afterward."

Neither the vindictive oaf nor her tanked husband would be smart enough to wear gloves. Things were looking good. Four more Hanlen County properties on the agenda to be zoned commercial at the next county council meeting. Four more checks would be deposited in her account.

Soon enough she'd leave the backwater town in her dust, no matter who or what became collateral damage.

Elon woke a half hour before her alarm went off. Nerve endings pinged at the thought of accompanying Rane on real-life cattle round up.

The waterproof canvas bag he'd given her lay packed at the foot of the bed. Several pair of neatly rolled jeans and long-sleeved shirts fit in the bottom, tight as sardines. She'd handled cold weather watching kids' sports, but not wet and cold. A raincoat and gloves got stuffed in. She braided the back of her hair, pulled on the cowboy hat, and checked the mirror. Yup, not a bad look. Not that identity should be based on appearance, but she'd take cowgirl.

Walking the hallway, Luna ambled, Lucky bounced, and Angel strode proudly alongside her.

A similar bag to hers rested on the bottom stair. Elon dropped hers beside it and proceeded to the kitchen. Lingering scents of the stuffed brioche French toast she'd made last night perfumed the air.

Her yellow pad noting supplies lay on the counter. Yesterday, Fred had overseen the job of loading boxes of canned and dried food into the chuckwagon. She crossed out the task. Lastly, the cooler needed to be filled, topped with ice, and loaded. "Please let me not have left anything out," she whispered.

Lucky tugged the hem of her jeans. She patted three rounded, furry rumps. "Don't worry, pups, dog food's locked and loaded."

Angel's ears cocked. Food was her favorite word. She raised her front foot, trying to speed her breakfast delivery.

Elon shook the spotted paw. "We're going on a camping adventure. I've never slept in a tent, but I bet you've lived outside." She dropped kibbles in the metal bowl, then finished breakfast prep.

The cowboys sat in the dining room, drinking coffee and talking eagerly to each other. Grit's snarly face wasn't missed. Chocolate scents rose from Lefty's full mug.

"My first roundup, Fred," Elon said. "How many for you?"

Fred's posture relaxed. "Nearly thirty I reckon." He took a long swig of coffee and speared a chunk of sausage. "Enough to know I need to eat hearty before a long ride." He waved his fork and smiled.

Lefty pushed bites of food around on his plate. He stirred his hot cocoa.

"Were the biscuits and sausage gravy too rich for you, Lefty?" The young guy generally ate as if he had tapeworms.

"Nope." He folded his napkin, pushed in his chair, and headed out the door without his normal grin or thanks.

Elon glanced at Rane, who was scribbling last instructions for the neighbor feeding his remaining cows and calves. "Excitement must give some of the ranch hands butterflies in their stomachs."

Rane kept writing. "Guess so."

She carried a stack of dirty plates into the kitchen, then scraped Lefty's breakfast into the trash. Jeremy had struggled during his senior year in high school. Every time he'd bombed a quiz, she knew by how he'd pick at dinner. Weird that an experienced ranch hand like Lefty seemed to share her bad case of nerves.

Rane hefted the two gear bags from beside the stairs. One bag sufficed for Elon. He'd guessed correctly that she wasn't a high-maintenance type. He stepped through the front door, locking it for the first time he could recall.

Not everything had changed. The chuckwagon he'd bought at auction ten years back served them well. Refurbished by Fred's knowledgeable hands, the polished, light-brown poplar wood and black metal gleamed in the sun.

One of the gray Percherons hitched to it shook his cream-colored mane, jingling his harness and mirroring his own eagerness to start. The deep-chested, heavily muscled draft horses he'd borrowed had been bred for war, hopefully an unnecessary skill set for this trip.

He tipped his hat back to study the crew. The cook traditionally drove the rig, which was probably not going to happen on the outbound trip. Lefty, Emmett, and Fred chatted from atop their saddled horses. He'd assign the task to one of them.

Elon walked out of the barn leading Possum. "Hey, Rane. Emmett stowed the puppies in a box behind the seat, but Angel needs exercise, if that's okay." She patted her dog and mounted her horse, just as he stepped off the porch.

"Angel can follow us." His eyes never tired of watching her graceful limbs move. The heel of his boot missed the step, and he tripped, grabbing the rail to prevent a face plant.

No guffaws, so no one noticed. "Okay boys, I need a volunteer to do the first stretch driving the wagon. We'll take the reins after lunch." He winked at Elon, hoping she got the message he'd enjoy her sitting next to him.

She raised an eyebrow and stroked Possum's flank.

Lefty waved his hand. "I'll start." He tied his buckskin gelding to the back of the wagon, hopped aboard, and released the brake. His jacket caught, revealing a gun holster and signaling he'd honored the request to carry a firearm.

"Who says, 'Wagon's Ho'? The driver?" Elon watched as Rane and the others all shook their heads in mock disbelief.

"This isn't Hollywood, Ms. Hardy," Rane reminded her in his down-to-business voice. "No plug-ins, port-a-potties, or cell bars." He met her eyes. "Clear?"

"Very, Mr. Calderon. I'm fully aware of primitive conditions."

The wagon rumbled out the gate, cooking implements clanging. Rane followed and scanned the ridge, watching for any glint of steel.

The rifle butt brushed his knee, available at the first sign of danger.

~

Elon nudged Possum to keep step beside Rane. He had to be proud of what he owned. "This route's ruggedly beautiful. If I understood you correctly, you own part of this land and lease some from the government."

Rane tipped back his Stetson, his eyes trailing over rolling hills and flat pasture. "Yup. My parcel's a rectangle of nearly two thousand acres, and I rent an equal amount. Nearby ranches have the same deal on government land, fanning out from the back of my spread. The Blackfeet own a section butting up to both the eastern boundary of mine and the three-hundred-acre property for sale."

"That's an enormous amount of land."

"Not for Montana. But mine looks the best due to a grazing rotation schedule I devised. It won't take us a full day to hit the northern boundary of my spread, but it might take a while to gather the herd grazing there." He scratched his horse's neck. "Your Possum's a natural cow pony. If you ride close to the herd and he moves suddenly to avoid a steer, you must stay aboard."

"I'll try." Elon listened as he gave pointers and described his low stress way of bunching and moving cattle. Her initial job entailed cooking and keeping out of the way. "I think your method sounds smart. Natural anxiety and positioning instinct instead of fear, flight, and loss of weight."

"You're a good student. As the herd gets used to moving, I'll call on you to help."

Elon felt taller in the saddle. She rubbed Possum's neck. "You take care of me on the range, and I'll make certain you are never a cart horse." She looked at the two borrowed draft horses pulling the hefty chuckwagon up an unblemished hillside, then at Rane. "Do you ever feel alone riding across the vastness of untouched land?"

"When my folks first left, I'd camp out here for days at a

time. Fred stayed on site, giving me an opportunity to get a feel for my land." His eyes moved to the clear, cornflower blue sky. "I can't say I ever really felt alone. My elders, going back generations, are buried on this land, and I sense the connection to them."

"A heritage to be proud of."

"I should go to more powwows where Chayton's students dance." His brown eyes darkened. "I've felt alone in the house."

She'd finally heard the effect after his parents left him alone at such a young age. "I bet."

"For a couple of days last week."

She winced. "You know why I left."

"I do now. You've put life back into the ranch. And sometimes you frustrate the heck out of me."

"You've given me a reason to work my way out of my fake marriage. On the frustration scale I think we're even." Elon gave him a crooked smile, then turned around in her saddle. "Angel can't keep up. She chased every prairie dog this morning and now she's paying for it."

Angel lagged thirty feet behind, her tongue hanging out.

"I'll hold her in front of me." Rane dismounted Keeper, lifted Angel, and climbed back into the saddle. She settled on his lap, comfortably perched while he steadied her with one arm and held the reins in his other hand.

Elon smiled at Angel, who'd raised her head in a regal pose.

"Up through this draw, and we call it a morning." Rane scratched between the dog's ears.

The house and shop sat hours away from where the caravan stopped for lunch. Elon gazed at only hills and pastures for the first time in her life.

Lefty jumped off the wooden wagon seat. "Need a campfire going, ma'am?"

"No thanks." Lefty frowned.

"I packed sandwich supplies. There's nothing to heat."

He threw her a sheepish grin and patted his rear. "Sore bottom."

Elon studied him. He'd wanted a fire. "I may be sitting there next. Appears I should find something to cushion the seat."

He nodded and sauntered off.

In a few minutes the men gathered near the chuckwagon and chose sandwiches and sodas. Fred waved his drink. "I hope the herd isn't spread across hell's half acre." Red splotches appeared on his wrinkled cheeks. "Sorry, ma'am, for cussing."

"Apology accepted. I made snacks to stash in your saddle bags." She handed baggies of oatmeal cookies to each outstretched hand, recognizing their eagerness to see the herd.

"Let me help you pack." Fred stowed supplies and latched the drop-down tabletop that doubled as the rear tailgate.

"I'll tie Possum and Keeper to the back of the wagon." Rane said, and approached the grazing horses.

Elon moved to the front wheel and contemplated the seat above her head. The metal foot bar on the rim hit at chest level.

"Reach for the iron arm rest." Two hands grasped her waist and boosted her to the bar. "Our last cook stood taller than me. I'll nail another step into place for you tonight."

"Oh, I don't mind the friendly assistance." She climbed to the seat box and smiled at the face giving her stomach butterflies, the kind a teenager felt on a date with her first crush.

"Here's Angel." Rane handed her the dog, who jumped into the box confining her yipping pups.

"Doggies on board," she trilled, and settled into the seat, now padded by a sleeping bag.

He tossed her his hat. "I want to look at the wheels. It'll take me a second." Rane's hair glistened.

With a few long steps and a vault, he appeared at her side. He took the reins in hands calloused from honest work. His foot eased off the brake as he clucked to the horses. The two stocky, dappled-gray geldings moved out, effortlessly pulling the lumbering wagon.

A hawk made a shrill call overhead and black-tailed prairie dogs popped out their heads to whistle warnings. Clopping hooves on the hard ground matched the swaying rhythm of the seat. Elon's shoulder hit Rane's in a gentle ba-bump, ba-bump cadence.

Rane stroked Elon's wrist and brought her out of a blissful reprieve of letting her thoughts and worries slide away in the beauty of the moment.

"Sorry, pardner, we're nearing the spot difficult for even draft horses."

"Oh, my gosh, I'd lapsed into a peaceful daze."

"Whoa, there." The horses stopped at the edge of a ravine forty feet wide, dotted by large boulders. He put on a hand brake. "I heard beavers built a dam upstream. After the recent rains, this stream should be flowing to Sunrise Lake, more than the pathetic dribble at the bottom. If you look to your right, you can see the path on the mountainside.

Elon gripped Rane's shoulder and stood. Her breath caught in her throat. A curving, rocky path cut downhill through stratified rock.

"Uphill lies a road put in by a mining company a decade or so back. They thought the mountain hid easy-access coal." Ugly ruts cut through a stand of trees.

She lowered herself onto the seat so their hips and thighs touched. "Glad one of our recent presidents chose natural beauty over the good ol' boy club demanding fossil fuel money."

"Agreed. I'd install solar panels if I had the money." Rane let out a long sigh. "That rock sits atop my uppermost property boundary." He pointed to a giant gray boulder. "I'm relieved the exploration team didn't strike pay dirt and ruin the mountainside." Rane tugged the short braid hanging under her hat. "I've been mighty lucky more than once."

"Me, too." Elon kissed his cheek. "I'll hop off to lighten the load and make it easier for you to concentrate on getting us through this gully."

"Ride Possum and lead Keeper to the other side for me. I'll meet you in a jiffy." He kept hold of her wrist to steady her until her left foot hit grass.

Possum whickered at her approach. She looped Keeper's lead line over her saddle horn and rode down the rocky slope and up the other side. Fred, Lefty, and Emmett sat in prime position to watch the action and waved for her to join them.

Wood and iron grunted and groaned as Rane used the brake to descend the steeper and taller slope on his side of the gulley. The muscled horses slipped and whinnied but kept a steady pace. They chugged uphill, pulling her kitchen-on-wheels to safety. "Whoa, there, big boys," Rane called to the draft horses and eased them to stop on a flat, grassy spot.

"Strong Percherons," Fred said. "Come on cowboys, all is under control." The three trotted off together.

Elon dismounted and walked to the draft horses. "Good ponies. Extra carrots tonight for dinner." She patted each broad nose.

"They deserve a bucketful." Rane swiped his handkerchief across his brow. "Want to ride beside me again?" His deep, sexy voice made her quiver inside.

"I'd require a boost from the handsomest cowboy in Montana."

In one movement of long legs and broad shoulders, he stood beside her. Color tinted his cheeks. "Shucks, ma'am. Never been called handsome before."

Anticipation of Rane's strong touch made Elon's pulse pump. Tim never showed gallantry, at least not to her. "The local women must wear blinders."

She bit the inside of her cheek. With Rane's getting over being soured on women, would he still choose an insecure, inexperienced woman supporting two kids and battling a murderous ex?

~

"I need a minute to check the draft horses' hooves for stones." And time to chill, Rane determined, as he felt heat in his face from neck to hairline. If they'd heard Elon's blinder comment a few minutes earlier, he'd of caught hell from the cowboys. The dues owed for a woman's attention, he reckoned, and whistled while he moved to the team's front feet.

Every muscle thrummed with the energy he'd had as a twenty-year-old. "You big guys made me look good." He took a hoof pick out of his pocket and scraped away packed rocks and pebbles.

Elon waited a few steps away. His fingers itched at the thought of clasping her small waist to lift her up. He finished the second horse, scratched its rump, and moved to her side. "Maybe I won't add another step," he joked, and positioned her on the wrung, adding a light pat on her rear.

"You didn't hear me complain," she retorted.

An unfamiliar peace filled him after he joined her and took the reins. On schedule and seated beside the most charming, fun, and beautiful woman he'd ever met. The path in front of them wound onto hills. The sun rose in a crystal blue sky.

"What are you smiling at, cowboy?" Elon nudged his side, jokingly, but her voice held a serious edge. Her fingers tightened on the edge of the seat.

"Just thinking how fortunate I am to have met you. Few women are willing to meet new challenges head on. I admire that in you, amongst other things." He heard her let out a long breath. Her face relaxed into a soft smile. "Move out, horses." He clicked his tongue. "What about you?"

"I'm living a western story while my sons are managing college. This trip gives me the excitement of a kid during the first day of summer vacation. Anticipation kept me awake most of the night." She yawned, her brown lashes fluttering shut.

"If you're tired, you can lean against me and take another nap." Rane sat against the backrest, and she nestled into his side.

"Are we on a first date, Rane Calderon?" A sleepy grin graced her upturned, pretty face.

"If you say so. I got lucky and enlisted a fabulous chef for our dinner tonight." He kissed the top of her forehead.

She chuckled and rested against his shoulder.

Protecting her was cracking the defensive wall he'd formed against women after the Shelly mess. In mere minutes, her steady breathing told him she'd fallen asleep while the Percherons kept a steady, smooth pace.

Rane put his hand to his forehead to shield the sun, watching for anything out of place. Casper Ridge lay ahead. Below, his herd grazed in clumps scattered like buckshot across a wide swath of flat prairie grass and sculpted ravines. In half an hour, he danced his fingers on Elon's thigh. "Time to see the critters you'll be babysitting for the next two days." Rane moved his arm around her shoulder, holding her steady as she sat upright.

"I never imagined cows, or steers, to be picturesque." Elon dropped her sunglasses from the top of her head. "I take it those black splotches covering the hill are part of your retirement account?"

Pride coursed through Rane. He'd worked hard to build his herd. "Yup. Retirement and paying for insurance and lots of other expenses on the ranch. I do well fixing machinery, but I need an advance on the contracted cattle to stay solvent. I put a good chunk of earnest money on the other parcel of land. My hunch is Sheriff Riley's close to arresting the rustlers and finding my missing stock."

He noticed Elon's muscles tense. If Riley didn't come through, should she worry he couldn't meet payroll?

Rane's last words concerning finances bothered Elon. A delayed check would unravel her plans. Had he cleaned out his bank account, withdrawing the earnest money? If he tried to borrow from Fred, he'd get a rude awakening. She fidgeted on the wagon's seat, unable to find a comfortable position. "Where do we pitch our tents?" The bumpy ride increased in tempo as Rane neared camp.

He pointed to a flat area. "No tents needed under a clear night sky. We'll stop where there's smooth ground and grass for the horses."

She looked at his handsome profile. Worry lines remained etched deep in his cheek. "You have many families counting on you, Rane."

"I haven't mentioned this to anyone, but it seems the rustlers know when to steal my cattle. We've surprised them during unplanned rides off the normal ranch schedule."

"I figured Grit." She took a deep breath. "Do you think Lefty or Emmett are involved?"

"We'll find out soon enough. You stick close to me."

Elon edged tighter to his side. "There's no place I'd rather be." His white teeth flashed, making her insides hum. "You're grinning again." She poked his side.

"Am I?" He put his foot on top of the brake. "Whoa boys, you're done for the day."

The three cowboys trotted up. Fred's cane poked out of the rifle scabbard at his knee. "Percherons deserve some grain, I'd suspect," he said. "Emmett and Lefty can unhitch them while I dole out their grub."

Elon rubbed her hands together. Her first meal cooked on an open fire. She flipped open the back table and pulled out the cooler. Soon there'd be simmering chicken and chunks of potatoes in a cast iron pot, smothered in cream of mushroom soup gravy. Her stomach rumbled at the thought.

"I found some rocks to build a fire ring with, Ms. Hardy." Lefty brushed his hands on his worn jeans. "It's on the other side to keep smoke away. Coals ready in about twenty minutes for another one of your tasty meals."

"Thanks." He seemed considerate, so why did she doubt him? "Tell the guys it'll be an hour before dinner." She turned and bumped into Rane, who'd set the cooler on the ground. Beside it sat the empty puppy box. Angel lay on the grass, with Luna and Lucky contentedly nursing.

"Thought you might need more prep room. Anything else before I iron my tux?"

"You're taking good care of me. Lefty got the fire going."

"Good," he murmured.

A bird flapping a six-foot wingspan flew overhead. Elon squinted. "Golden eagle?"

"Turkey vulture." His eyes darted to his herd.

Elon shoved his shoulder. "Get out to your Wagyu babies."

"Need to be certain the buzzards didn't spot a carcass." Rane strode to Keeper, mounted, and trotted toward the herd.

The three cowboys fell in beside him.

Squeaks from prairie dogs sounded in the distance. "Let's get started, Angel. Your food's next, now that your pups are fed."

Her black tail wagged, and she gobbled her chow.

"On to the humans." Elon fished out the bagged poultry and vegetables she'd prepped before the trip. Unloading became the easy part—not burning the meal presented another challenge.

A pot outfitted by little legs caught her eye. She greased it and tossed in stew ingredients, letting it simmer for an hour.

Hearing no conversation at dinner equaled success in a cook's world. All five of them gorged on second or third helpings, using hunks of French bread to sop gravy.

"Emmett and Lefty, you're on dish duty tonight. I'm showing Elon herding techniques before dusk." Rane settled his hand at the small of her back, moving her to where the horses grazed.

"On a full stomach? A stroll on foot sounds challenging."

"Nothing too taxing. There's always a few renegade steers split off from the herd. I'll show you how to coax them back."

"I'll do my best, boss," she said, and pulled on her hat.

Rane eyed his men, and then leaned toward her. "If truth be told, I wanted to have you alone for a bit. Once we start moving the herd tomorrow, I'll be busy. Not much of a date." His warm breath tickled her ear.

"This is the best date I've ever been on."

Rane gave her knee a boost into the saddle. "Actually, I

haven't been on a date in twenty-some years." He untied Keeper and mounted.

"I'm closer to never. Tim's dating me equaled a con job." Elon felt the soft leather of the reins. "You've got my full attention, teacher."

"I don't expect you'll need to do too much. Possum's no youngster. Somewhere along the way, he learned to move cows. If in doubt, give him his head to take you away from danger."

"That's comforting. I'd appreciate a general idea how the stray shuffling works."

"I'll ride parallel to the straggler for a bit. Keeps prey animals calmer. A predator generally approaches from behind. If the steer returns willingly to the herd, I'm done. Otherwise, I use a cutting technique."

Rane and Keeper slowly sidled to within twenty feet from a young steer grazing well away from the herd. Immediately its head raised, and it trotted off.

Keeper moved in a wide arc, head to tail, until the animal returned to the group.

"Okay, my turn." Elon squeezed Possum's side and reined him to the outside of another loner. This steer glanced sideways and ambled to the herd. She smiled at Rane. His thumbs-up gesture made her ride taller.

A bark from Angel shifted her attention to the chuckwagon. The puppies hadn't moved, but smoke came from the campfire.

"Odd, I threw dirt on the coals I spread out, as you instructed." She pointed in the direction of two distinct puffs rising in the clear sky.

Rane scanned the surrounding hills. "Mighty odd. Lesson's over, let's head back."

CHAPTER 11

Damn smoke. Rane's heart pounded. From five hundred feet away, the wagon looked fine, and the horses grazed nearby, but only Fred and Emmett stood near the puppy box. "Hang back a little," he ordered Elon. He gritted his teeth and cantered Keeper straight for the campfire, now producing a thin, gray wisp from the back side of the chuckwagon. He rounded the end with the folded down table and reined in next to the cowboy squatting by the fire pit, holding a tin cup. An old burlap bag used for trash lay on the ground beside him. "I didn't think you drank coffee, Lefty."

"Uh, only when I'm out on a drive. Hope you don't mind —I poked the fire to warm a couple swigs left in the pot." He tipped his cup to his lips and then kicked dirt onto the hot embers.

Lying? Rane's gut tightened. "No, I guess I don't mind." He scanned the range. Dusk broke on the horizon behind glowing stubs of wood. Only grass and cattle as far as he could see. No sign of rustlers.

Elon trotted in, dismounted, and began undoing Keeper's girth straps.

"I'll stow your saddle." Rane pulled it off her horse, and watched Lefty walk past the tongue of the trailer. He headed to where Fred had laid out his sleeping bag, twenty feet farther away from them.

"Possum's a natural at managing strays." Elon removed his bridle. "Solve the smoke issue?" She stroked her horse's muscular legs.

"Seems Lefty needed some warmed-up coffee before hitting the hay."

Elon's fingers stopped. "There wasn't any coffee to warm up. Fred polished the last drops after dinner and cleaned out the pot."

Rane's jaw clenched. A cold foreboding settled deep in the pit of his stomach. "Lefty flat-out lied to me. I'm going to send Emmett at first light to bring a couple more men to help us. Something's up." He untacked Keeper and turned him out to graze. "Come on, Elon." The two of them walked to where Emmett rolled his sleeping bag. He tapped his shoulder. "We need to speak in private."

Emmett's young face went paler than normal. "Okay," he whispered.

"I trust you. That's why I'm asking a favor." Rane pressed his fingers through his hair.

He followed Rane and Elon. "Anything you need," he stated,

They faced north, Rane's eyes scanned acres of his leased land. "I think Lefty's in cahoots with the rustlers."

"He began actin' squirrelly the day after you fired Grit."

Elon wrung her hands. "Oh dear."

"I figured Grit might be involved." Rane pulled her to his side. "Emmett, lead your horse out of camp before dawn. Far enough so we can't hear you. Hightail it to the ranch, and call Grant or Tom Morley." He handed Emmett a slip of paper. "I brought their cell numbers. If they're home, they'll help us safely move the herd." He kicked a rock and watched it tumble downhill. "Ask them to call the sheriff and come armed."

Emmett raised his chin. "If I can't reach our cousins, I'll ask Mom and Dad. The Lazy K should be shuttered for overnight guests until spring. You can count on me to find help."

"Give a good look at the northern part of the big ravine," Rane said. "If I were a rustler, I'd bring trailers in using the old side road."

He turned to Elon. "Grant and Tom are former law officers. Emmett's parents, Kat and Trey Langley, defeated crooks in the past. We'll be covered. Meantime, can you put a poke together for Emmett and leave it in the cooler?"

"I assume you mean a sack lunch," she said. "My ham and cheese stuffed brioche should work."

"Yup." Rane nodded in the direction of Lefty, who'd moved to within earshot. He cleared his throat. "Appreciate your getting out early to assess the herd, Emmett. Tomorrow those cattle will all be wondering what we're doing. Fred's point man as usual."

His old friend staggered up, leaning on the cane. "Just 'cause my leg's a bit stiff, doesn't mean my eyes aren't sharp enough for point man. Rane and Lefty will be our swing riders. Sorry Emmett, you'll eat a little dust riding drag. Same rules, no shouting, whistling, or trotting. Just slow and easy, my stimulus and their response. I assume you all remember."

They nodded in agreement. Lefty shuffled his feet in the grass, nervous as hell.

∾

Elon studied the man she'd fallen in love with, whose lack of experience in real relationships equaled hers. He held the box holding the puppies in one hand and sleeping bags in the other. "I'd bet spotting the softest ground's a prerequisite to successful camping," she teased.

They'd walked out from one end of the chuckwagon, while the three cowboys headed in the opposite direction.

Rane offered her a genuine smile. Determined intensity hovered at the corners of his eyes. "I thought we might roll out our bags on the north side of the wagon. We'll be able to watch the sun set and stars rise. The cattle are scattered too far apart for the rustlers to strike tonight. I'll alert you at the first sign of trouble. Let's forget about them for a while."

His wrinkled brow told her he needed the break. "I'll watch for your signal tomorrow." She lifted out Luna and Lucky. "I love how they stumble on their wobbly legs. In my view, puppies, a sunset, and rising stars are a perfect end to a perfect date."

"I hoped you'd think so. You are one special treasure, Elon."

"I can't believe no other woman has pushed a battering ram through your armor before now. Must've been some who tried." An unfamiliar sensation tightened Elon's chest.

"Early on I caught an employee stealing tools. I fired him without pressing charges." Rane scratched each puppy under the chin. "Out of spite, the ingrate passed the rumor around town I preferred animals to women."

The same wisecrack she'd made to Corrin. "And people believed it?" Elon watched his face for a sign he'd been kidding. None came.

"Those who know me disputed the lie. Running the ranch took my full concentration."

"I bet." Elon thought of her parents and boys. She'd loved

working beside them as a team. Rane had lost everyone except Fred in a short time span. Poor guy, she thought, while they rolled out sleeping bags side by side. The valley they faced had no towns or cars and only infrequent sounds of mooing cattle. She sat cross legged on top of her bag, and watched the sky streaked by blues, purples, oranges, and gold. "It's the most gorgeous sunset I've witnessed."

Rane sat atop his dark green bag, his long legs bent at the knees. "There'll be many more," he promised in a smooth, sexy voice. "A lifetime of them, I hope. From the ridge by the ranch, we've a similar view of Mother Nature painting her finest."

Elon looked at her hands. Her future, for the moment, seemed assured due to their work capabilities. Should she profess what lay in her heart? "This job's been a lifesaver. My boys can stay in school, and I'm certain they're relieved we're no longer trampling each other in the condo."

"What about us?" Rane's words whispered on the breeze.

"You've asked the million-dollar question."

Rane stared at the sunset. "Hope I don't need that kind of cash to get your answer. I've never been clever at figuring out how women think." He grabbed a nearby stone and sent it flying.

"I thought I'd be alone the rest of my life. Here I am, nearly divorced and sitting next to a kind, handsome, reliable friend, who isn't *too* fond of animals—just enough." She poked him in the ribs. "Honestly, the feelings I have for you are frighteningly new."

"We make quite a pair, stumbling through the novelty of romance at forty."

"I think you're worth the wait."

"We'll see." He kissed her cheek.

Stars blinked in the dimming sky.

"I can identify some constellations for you," he offered.

"Impress me with your celestial knowledge. And for a few months, I'm still in my thirties." Elon sat back, propped on her elbows, head tilted skyward.

"Sorry. I figured you had kids after college, putting you near my age." He stretched out, hands under his head.

"I left culinary school to assist Tim in getting his practice functioning smoothly. Never took a paycheck or a camping trip. So, take me to the stars."

"Well, all kids can find the Big Dipper. There's Cassiopeia," his deep, relaxed voice began, then continued while zillions of stars appeared.

"Where'd you learn all of those?" Elon turned toward him.

"Shelly owned the dandiest glow-in-the-dark sky book. Night after night as kids, we rode out from the ranch and tested each other. Some of our best times together."

"I hope you speak to her again. Childhood friendships are very special. She never meant to hurt you." Elon squeezed his knee.

"I'll get her address, and you can help me write her a letter. Enough about my childhood." Rane put his hand over hers and slipped his other hand around her waist, pulling her close.

Elon curled her body against his side, then moved her lips to meet his, taking the lead, needing to cast the same spell tumbling her farther and farther out of control.

His return kisses didn't lie—he obviously wanted more. He lay back, pulling her upper body onto his muscled chest, his spicy masculine scent an aphrodisiac. His breaths came quicker, his arms tightened.

She must stop now, or not at all. Every desire shouted for more. More of Rane.

A coyote howled, and her brain did a reality check.

"Rane, sorry. I got carried away." She managed a nervous

laugh. "Sounds funny, the woman in a sexless marriage for twenty years, getting carried away." She rested her cheek against his soft flannel shirt, twining her fingers through strands of his thick, straight hair.

"Don't ever be sorry. We've got a lot of starry nights ahead of us." He sat up and gently lifted her to sit between his legs, with her back against his chest. He kneaded her shoulders. "You never ignored your wedding vows, knowing your husband cheated?" His hands stopped. "I'm sorry, none of my business."

She shifted her back against his fingers. "Odd as it seems in today's world, no hookups. The boys became my focus. Ironically, they were in a stroller when I saw Tim at a restaurant smooching a woman half his age and half my size. Seemed useless trying to please him. I covered the home front and monitored several aspects of the clinic. No energy to explore a divorce or find a love interest, not that I wanted to."

"Until now, I hope. We've got a good thing started."

Elon's body responded to the little circles Rane thumbed down her spine. Stress melted under his hands. "Yes, I see and feel the benefits of dating you." When he stopped, she slumped against his chest. "Professional massages are a wonderful perk."

"Normally it's the horses or Tomo getting a weekly session. Ed maintains my animals are the calmest he treats."

She bobbed her head. "Neigh, neigh. Can I get on the list?"

"You name the time, and my hands are yours." He kissed the base of her neck. "We have an early day tomorrow, so I'd better keep my hands in check."

"Felt marvelous. I'll be booking regular sessions, don't worry."

"My pleasure."

"I'm going to run to the privy." Rane steadied her arm as she rocked onto her feet and stood. She grabbed the flashlight and headed to the canvas shack erected for her benefit.

No sounds disturbed the peaceful campsite. Everyone must be asleep, she concluded, tiptoeing past the wagon.

These men treated her with the respect due an aunt or sister. Except Rane, thank goodness.

She spat out toothpaste and changed into sweats for sleeping. She'd bring the twins along on the next camping trip, she thought, as she passed the other cowboys.

Lefty rolled over. Maybe not.

Rane woke to dawn's first light breaking to their right, the glow spreading from the far hills to the green valley below. He stretched in the sleeping bag, cat-like, getting his joints ready for a full day in the saddle.

Nearing forty-one, his body issued a few creaks. Elon's steady breathing brought a sense of calm to his restless spirit. Last night he'd sensed the instant she'd fallen asleep after a full day on the range. No way had he ever imagined this moment when he'd seen her arrive on his ranch.

Rolling his sleeping bag, his eyes flicked to her. A dark auburn curl surrounded her left eye, giving her pretty face an exotic look. What a sick bastard Tim was. Using her for his goals and now threatening their sons' education. He'd wager Tim had fired into the house. If the shooter left clues from the ridge where he'd taken aim, Belle would find them.

Shouldering his gear, he quietly stepped to the wagon.

Lefty poked a burning fire. "Thought I'd put on coffee." He grabbed the nearby brew pot and set it on the grate. "Do you think the herd will move out easily, or are we in for a couple more days to return them to the ranch?"

Rane studied the man's back. "They looked calm last night when we rode near them. However, they'll scatter at a leaf falling sideways. Could be one day or four days to reach home."

Lefty's spine stiffened.

Not the answer he'd wanted. "The coffee pot's empty. Add water and grounds, and I'll go rouse Elon to start breakfast."

Made sense they planned to steal cattle on the return trip, hopefully after help arrived. Elon slept curled up like a baby. He stroked her shoulder. "Time to rise, cowgirl."

"Oh, sorry." She opened one eye and yawned. "Must be the fresh air, I slept through the whole night."

"I'm glad. After the Tim episode and the shootings, you've looked a bit worn most mornings." He squeezed her shoulder. "We all appreciate you coming along. Today you need to be extra careful. I know it's challenging."

Elon sat in her bag. "Less than you'd think. Better get the hobo hash started." She stretched her arms overhead. "Chef in sweats has a nice ring."

"The best food from the most beautiful chef on the planet, whatever she's wearing." He'd pressed close enough last night to know what lay beneath those sweats. If the beaver hadn't damned the creek, he'd ride back and take a cold plunge.

Elon's nose distinguished the scents of campfire and coffee when she approached the chuckwagon. Early light gave the setting serenity. The possibility of what lay ahead did not.

Lefty stood by the campfire, rubbing the back of his neck.

"Morning, ma'am. Hope you aren't sore from yesterday." Dark circles surrounded his eyes.

"Morning. I'm not sore. Hopefully Possum isn't."

"Rane's really picky about finding saddles to fit each horse for the animal's comfort."

"No surprise. Rane takes care of each of us and all his critters. I miss talking with my sons, Lefty. I'm always available for a chat."

"Ah, thanks. Gotta roll up my bag." He hesitated for a split second, then scooted away.

Should she have pressed him? "Breakfast in fifteen minutes," she called out, and dumped precooked sausage, bacon, and hash browns into a bowl. Beaten eggs completed the mixture before she dumped it into the fry pan.

She headed to the makeshift outhouse. Today would be a long day, in and out of the saddle. Thank goodness for loose, stretchy jeans. She pulled on her favorite pair and a blue flannel shirt and headed to find the hand sanitizer at the chuckwagon.

In a few minutes, clopping of equine feet came from behind her. She sprinkled cheddar cheese on the browned hash and turned her head.

Rane wore an ear-to-ear grin while sitting on Keeper. "I worked the herd a little, and they fell into position. I think we'll have a one-day drive instead of two," he said in a low tone, his eyes following Fred and Lefty's approach from the chuckwagon's tongue. He inhaled deeply and tipped his head back. "Breakfast smells wonderful," he declared, and rested his hands atop the saddle horn.

"I offer ride-up service, Mr. Calderon. Is this order for here or to go?" She pretended to write on a pad. The vision of him and Keeper by the campfire made a charming picture she'd memorize. Her cowboy, waiting for breakfast on horseback. An experience few women got in their lifetime.

"Rain check, please. Keeper earned a little snack before I can join you. I smelled eggs, rode by where the boys slept, and told them to hightail it over."

"Dang, I have a dinner bell and no reason to ring it." Elon pulled the frying pan off the coals. A plate of fresh fruit and toasted French bread completed the substantial breakfast.

"Where's Emmett?" Lefty picked at the small portion he'd taken.

"Met him earlier and he complained about a horrible toothache." Rane grabbed a canvas chair and sat next to Fred. "I sent him to town."

"Oh-kay." Fred tipped his hat back. "The wagon can follow behind at a slow pace, Elon can ride swing for a spell."

Rane undid his neckerchief and handed it to her. "Protection from dust, Elon. Don't want our gourmet cook uncomfortable." He raised his fork in a salute to her. "We never ate this good on a drive before. You're responsible for my having to let my belt out a couple notches. I usually tighten it by now." He speared the last egg off his plate. "Doubtful this trip."

Everyone laughed.

"Rane sporting a belly, that I want to see," Fred chuckled.

Elon packed garbage and leftovers while Rane and the men walked to the horses. Her mind moved to her next responsibilities. Possum knew cattle, and the fixings for lunch sat in the cooler. The possibility of rustlers shot an unwelcome chill up her spine.

She approached Rane. "I'm on alert today, and I promise I'll stay wherever you place me." She smoothed her jeans.

Rane waggled his eyebrows at her. She elbowed his side. "You know what I mean."

"Joking aside, you take off if anything doesn't look right." He moved to where the cowboys stood. "Elon will ride drag a little ahead of the wagon. Lefty's driving on the return trip."

A flicker of despair crossed Lefty's face, then he nodded. "Yes sir. We'll follow at a safe distance."

Being assigned to wagon duty bothered Lefty. Preference or another reason? Elon forced a smile. Boot in the stirrup, she pulled herself onto Possum, the creaking leather a welcome diversion.

Unblemished land stretched across scalloped hills. She breathed air perfumed by horsehide and fall grass. Mooing cattle created background music. All of this would stay filed away in her memory.

She'd send her sons a detailed email once they returned to the ranch. Brandon enjoyed her tales, but it'd be difficult to speculate Jeremy's reaction. He'd been most affected when Tim announced the divorce. She remembered the scene, sitting at the kitchen table, Brandon stony-faced and Jeremy suggesting a trial separation.

Brandon had felt the sting of Tim's indifference to his family early, evident in his eyes from about ten on.

Possum pawed the ground, probably happy to be headed back to the barn.

"Walk on." The chestnut responded to her as if she'd been riding him for years.

Lefty climbed into the wagon. He took the reins and stayed put until the herd moved ahead.

Fred veered his horse to the other side, watching the cattle and holding back.

"Doesn't resemble a noisy cattle drive in the movies," Elon called to Lefty. "Rane's method of herding keeps them calm."

"Yes, ma'am." Lefty kept his eyes on the northern ridge, so Elon glanced there often.

Rane headed Keeper into a wide crescent at the back of the herd, moving the cattle into a loose bunch. Fred found one stray, and his horse did the front-shoulder-to-back-end dance, sending the trotting steer to the herd.

By one o'clock, they'd reached the boulder above the forty-foot-wide ravine, marking the upper edge of Rane's property and the designated lunch stop. She raised her hand to her brow and scanned north. Nothing but a trickle of water flowing through a jagged cut in the earth.

Elon swung stiffly off Possum and landed with a thump to the ground. She unhooked Angel's bowl and tipped a canvas water bag to fill it. As she rounded the back of the wagon, Lefty threw twigs on another fire. "Snuff the fire, no cooking needed for this lunch."

He added the rest of the wood he'd collected to make it blaze. "Sure enough, ma'am." He dowsed the flames, first using a splash of water, then the whole cup. Two clouds of smoke puffed into the clear sky.

"I see some embers. I'll throw on more water." Elon moved Angel's full water bowl to the fire pit.

Lefty took her wrist, pulling the bowl back from over the fire.

"Don't want to waste any water, ma'am. I'll take care of it." He kicked dirt from the edge of the burnt stack of wood to the middle. "I can't wait to see what you fixed us for lunch."

Elon felt like she'd backed into a bull's horns. She spotted Rane removing Keeper's bridle. When she reached him, she tugged on his shirt sleeve. "Smoke signals again. I'm certain of it."

Elon verified his concern, Rane thought, as he chewed the hearty cheese- and ham-filled bun. He scanned the docile herd and relatively dry ravine they'd cross next. A perfect spot to be ambushed. No doubt Lefty had alerted someone of their moves. His fist bunched. Damn scoundrels needed their necks wrung. First, he needed to prevent a disaster.

Rane watched Elon offering more fruit. Emmet could've taken her home. Her hand wobbled as she closed the table-top. He never should've brought her. "Lefty, continue driving the rig, and Fred you lag behind in case we have steers refusing to cross. After the chuckwagon reaches the other side, I'll stay at the bottom to keep the herd flowing.

"Not a good plan, sir." Lefty kicked a rock.

"What's going on, Lefty? I need to know right now."

"Sorry, I haven't ever driven a wagon across a ravine, and I don't want to practice now." He turned his hat in his hands, circling the brim quickly through his fingers.

"Anything else?" Rane stared at the man he'd trusted for a year. "If there is, you need to tell me now."

"No, sir." His voice quavered.

"Okay then, reverse order. Fred drives across first, then Elon on horseback. I'll be point and Lefty pushes the steers forward."

Elon bent to retrieve a fallen napkin. When she rose, Rane leaned in close to her ear. "This is it. Whatever happens, you stay next to our chuckwagon and Fred. He'll protect you with his life."

Elon bunched the napkin in her fist. "You're the one I worry about, Rane."

Rane studied the unfolding scene, nerves tense. The nearly dry streambed with deep sides presented the perfect place to be attacked.

Fred handled the wagon like the pro he was. He topped

the far side of the ravine, waving his hat from his seat in the chuckwagon. Elon leaned back and let Possum pick his own way. Fred's Paint mare trailed behind her on a lead rope. She leaned over her horse's neck as they clamored to the top, then stopped near the chuckwagon. Fred had parked to the left of a patch of grass—the type certain to entice the first round of cattle to stop and eat. Elon stood in the stirrups and turned to give him a proud cowgirl thumbs up.

The most vulnerable two were safe. Rane waved back to her. If necessary, Possum could gallop Elon back to the ranch. Satisfied, he headed Keeper into the gulley, pushing cattle ahead. "Move out," Rane ordered. He side-stepped Keeper and felt heat radiating from the muscular animals as they passed. He stationed the horse in the base of the ravine.

In half an hour, a decent portion of the cattle grazed on the other side. Fred stood near the rim, downwind of the herd, holding a puppy. *One of them felt confident.*

Keeper stood his ground while a throng of steers continuously flowed around them, shuffled for position, and clamored up the slope. On the back ridge, arriving cattle mooed anxiously, milling near the ledge. Soon enough, Lefty would collect the last stragglers and shoo the bunch forward.

"Good job, Keeper." Rane patted his neck, then waved his hat to move the current horde of cattle.

The clanging dinner bell pierced the air. Rane spotted the bonnet of the parked chuckwagon, sitting to his left, atop the far bank of the ravine. On the slope below the wagon, the black and white puppy tumbled and scrambled, falling with each clumsy step.

"Damn," he hissed. Elon must've rung the bell to sound an alarm, possibly scaring the cattle. Rane steered that way.

Keeper did his best to dislodge steers, packed in seven or eight abreast. Black cow rumps rubbed against his boots.

From the corner of his eye he caught a glimpse of Fred, clamoring downhill after the puppy.

"Move!" he yelled at the string of cattle, now jammed together. He put two fingers to his lips and sent out a series of sharp blasts.

At the edge of the bank, Elon appeared on Possum. Aimed toward Fred, they dropped onto the slope.

Not good. If she fell, she'd be trampled. "Move out cows!"

Keeper flattened his ears and nipped a steer in the butt. The animal jumped out of the way.

A dull boom, and a piercing one, echoed off the rocks. The cattle panicked, circling him and churning dirt. Half the animals pivoted and ran toward the wrong bank.

A roaring noise came from Rane's right. He twisted his head. Water crashed over boulders, gushing into the chasm—a scant two hundred feet uphill.

"Flash flood! Outta there, Elon!" Rane turned Keeper to direct the steers away from her and Fred.

Satisfied the steers wouldn't trample Elon or Fred, Rane began zigzagging from left to right, pushing cattle up both sides of the ravine. Several of the group who'd reversed direction now danced between the drop off and the rim.

They'd likely drown if they didn't reach the bank.

He took the slope at an angle, waving his hat.

A steer broke from the group and did a U-turn. Its front feet slid, and it rammed Keeper's shoulder, throwing the horse off balance. Gravel and dirt flew as his gelding pawed to stay upright.

The steer twisted to rise, slipped, and slammed into Keeper's hip.

Rane's foot touched dirt as his horse fell to his knees, scrambling on loose rock. They slid backward, Keeper's front hooves clamoring for footing.

They'd both die if he didn't bail before they somersaulted

ass-over-teakettle into the gulley. He leaned forward and heaved himself off. His shoulder smacked into a boulder. Searing pain shot into his left arm.

Water crashing against rock boomed louder.

Keeper righted himself near the bottom of the ravine, shook, and bugled in fright.

Had Keeper been hurt? Rane shoved off the ground using his good hand.

The churning, muddy flood rushed downhill from eighty feet away. *What about Elon and Fred?* Dust clouds and the last cattle leaping to safety blocked his view. He whistled.

Keeper scrambled toward him, offering a last chance to escape. Rane grabbed the saddle horn and swung aboard. "Let's go!"

The horse lurched to the top. Churning water rushed through Keeper's powerful hind legs as he made the final leap onto the rim. Rane twisted his head around. The stupid steer that had U-turned scrambled to safety.

Thundering surges of the angry torrent blasted everything in its path. He swiped mud splatters from his eyes. "Elon!"

CHAPTER 12

I need to help Fred! Elon's heart thrummed in her ears. "Come on, Possum!" His swishing tail struck her knee.

Ten feet from them, the old cowboy cradled Lucky in one hand, struggling to climb while his other hand grabbed at uphill rocks. He'd never beat the water.

Crashing torrents barreled closer. Steers screamed in fright, jostling to jump onto the bank.

Fred's bad leg buckled. If he slipped trying to climb behind her, he'd fall into the surge. "Fred, grab Possum's tail. We'll tow you up." She reined the horse to turn uphill of Fred and held her breath.

"Got it!" Fred yelled. "If I fall, you keep going. Hear me?"

No way in hell. "Hold on! Attaboy, Possum. Up we go." The saddle horn punched her belly as she leaned forward.

Possum's shoulder muscles bunched when the gelding dug in and clambered to the top. The horse lumbered onto grass and stopped, his sides heaving.

She stroked his neck, "You did it, Possum," she said, and smiled at Fred, dusty but upright.

He squeezed her ankle. "Good riding." His body leaned against Possum's flank. "Good pony." He handed Elon the puppy and left his hand on the horse's rump while they walked to the tailgate of the chuckwagon. She placed the pup in the box beside his sister.

Instead of a doggy reunion, Angel jumped onto the ground and barked. Two riders who wore face covering bandanas wove their horses through the herd milling nearby. Elon gasped. "Stay here, Fred. I'll call Rane for help." She galloped Possum to the dinner bell and slammed the clapper, sending out another piercing ring.

One of the bandits veered to Fred.

"Fred, behind you. Look out!" The bandit whacked Fred on the head and pushed him to the ground.

She jumped off Possum and ran to Fred. "You okay?"

He blinked his eyes. "Yup. Just need to set a spell. Got the wind knocked outta me."

A mud-splattered horse and rider thundered in.

"Rane!" she shouted.

He slid off Keeper and lurched to her side. "Relieved to see you. Is Fred okay?" He dropped to one knee.

"Yes. A thug hit—" A shorter, teenaged version of Grit advanced on Rane from behind—same black hair, same stocky build, same feral look. He raised the bat he held. "Rane! Duck!"

Rane dropped his chin. The bat grazed his head, and he staggered.

A hand came from behind her, grabbed her wrist, reached around, and wrenched her other wrist to her back. She recognized the black hair growing out to the fingers. Bile rose in her throat.

"Now who's boss, Calderon?" Grit's greasy voice boomed. "I've got what I came for, her and a share of the steers." He spun Elon around and threw her over his shoulder. Bent at the waist, Elon hung like a rag doll, her face bouncing on his grimy back while she pushed off his shoulders and kicked her legs, trying to squirm free.

Grit's bulky forearm squeezed her thighs tight against his chest as he walked toward the chuckwagon. "You keep fighting me, Miss High and Mighty, and Junior will bash Calderon's head," he snarled.

Rane tried to stand upright. "Take the cattle. For God's sake, Grit, leave Elon alone. Your fight's with me."

Junior shoved the bat into Rane's limp shoulder, pushing him to his knees, then the kid lifted it high, ready to swing.

They'd hurt Rane regardless. Elon hammered Grit's back, aiming her knuckles into his kidneys. "You gutless thug!"

"Grit. Only a coward . . . asks his kid . . . to do his dirty work." Rane's voice came out in ragged grunts.

Grit faced Rane. He slowly lowered Elon the length of his chest, turned her, and clenched her wrists behind her back. "Heard you need a lesson giving a split tail what she deserves. Time to watch me now, boss."

Rane pushed from the ground with one arm, his face pale. Junior punched the bat into Rane's stomach, knocking him onto his butt.

Fury blazed in Elon's chest. "Stop!" She ground her heel into Grit's foot. His grip faltered, and she kneed him hard in the groin. As he folded at the waist, she shoved her elbow into his throat.

Grit stumbled to the ground, gagging and clutching his crotch.

Elon spun around. The kid had pinned Rane to the ground, straddling him and throwing punches—his young face pinched in rage.

Teenager or not, no one pummeled Rane. "Get off him!"

She charged over, kicked Junior's thigh, and shoved him to the ground. "No more!" She jumped on his back, keeping him down.

He rocked to shake her off. "You got my dad fired."

"Your father attacked me!"

The kid struggled to rise from the ground. She grabbed a wrist from each side and yanked until he fell onto his chest. Keeping both arms behind him, she gulped air.

Angel darted to Junior's face, her teeth bared. The kid quit squirming.

"Where'd you learn to fight?" Rane placed a shaky hand on her shoulder, blood dripping from the cut under his eye.

"My boys taught me a thing or two about self-defense. Never thought I'd use it."

A shadow loomed over them, large and bearlike.

A horse and rider clamored over the top edge of the ravine. A gunshot pierced the air.

"Help," Rane uttered and sank to the ground.

"No! Rane!" Elon screamed.

"I'm . . . not hit . . . Elon. My legs buckled." Pain shot into his shoulder.

Lefty swung off the horse, holding a pistol.

Grit grabbed his bleeding shoulder and stumbled to the side of the wagon. "You shot me, you idiot."

"I never should've let you talk me into this!" Lefty shouted.

Grit shook his bloody fist. "You're throwing away the money, and you'll put us all in jail."

"Rane's a fair man." Lefty kept the gun leveled at Grit's chest. "Ms. Hardy treated me kindly. And you're dangerous."

He turned to Elon, who continued holding the kid's wrists. "Ms. Hardy, I'll take over." He waved the end of his gun at Junior. "Go stand by Grit."

Angel growled deeper.

"Come here pup, good girl." Elon said, then moved her hand to steady Rane while he rose. "Don't pass out on me."

The last thing he wanted to do. "Don't want to," Rane groaned. "Jumped off Keeper and popped my shoulder out of the socket." He cradled the injured limb in his good hand.

"I assumed as much. Let's move you to the boulder near Fred." Elon's arm tightened around his waist. "Move your weight onto me. I won't break. One step at a time."

"Your knuckles are bleeding." The blood on Elon's pale skin made Rane's head thump.

"Rane, take a breath. It's not my blood," Elon scolded gently. "You saw the other guy."

"Let me help you, Ms. Hardy." Fred rubbed a red knot on his own forehead. "Rane, the two of us got bruised is all."

Rane struggled to focus. He pictured Elon, her fists punching. Bright flashes of light danced in front of him. "I'm kind of woozy."

"Hold on a bit longer." Elon eased him onto the flat spot on the boulder. "Fred, hold his good shoulder."

"Rane, this will hurt worse for a second." Elon's face blurred.

"Do it."

"I'm going to form an 'L' before I rotate your arm and shoulder," Elon spoke softly, supporting the wrist on his aching arm.

Rane squeezed his eyes shut and clenched his teeth. Her grip tightened for a second. Excruciating pain, then a pop brought instant relief. "Much better." He rubbed his shoulder socket. "Thanks."

He leaned his head against her hip and latched onto her belt with his good hand.

"Three riders just topped the hill." Lefty said, keeping his gun on Grit and the teenager.

"Emmett brought lawmen," Rane said. The inner strength he needed radiated from Elon. "They'll take Grit and the boy to the sheriff. What do I do about you, Lefty?"

"I screwed up bad. Send any pay to my wife. My little girl has a lung condition and needs to see an expensive specialist. Grit told me nobody would get hurt when we stole a few steers. I don't blame you for wanting me in jail."

He couldn't penalize Lefty's family. "You should have told me, but I'll consider not pressing charges." He tugged Elon's sleeve. "What do you say, cowgirl?"

"I agree. He saved us from Grit, and he was trying to help his daughter. In a very bad way," she scolded.

Lefty shuffled his feet in the dirt. "I'm really sorry."

"Help us find who's behind the rustling," Rane said.

"And if you need money, talk to me."

"I will."

Three horses trotted to the edge of camp. Emmett jumped off first. "Rane, are you okay?"

Rane pushed off the rock, then draped his good arm across Elon's shoulder. "We have it under control now. These two have been stealing my cattle." He pointed toward Grit.

"You took a fall bad enough to pop your shoulder out. Slow down." Elon planted her foot and grabbed his belt.

Rane smiled, watching his kinfolk dismount and approach. Both tall and broad-shouldered, they bore the confidence of former law enforcement officers. "We heard a gunshot," Grant said. "Anyone hit?"

"The bullet dinged one of the rustlers," Rane offered.

"I'll check him out in a minute." His cousin glanced at Grit.

"Elon, these two are part of the Morley clan—my Uncle Tom, and cousin, Grant. And boy am I glad to see them."

"It's a privilege to lend a hand." Uncle Tom smiled kindly at Elon. "Who's the lovely lady?"

She held so much more than beauty. "My heroine, Elon Hardy. I'm working my darndest to convince her to marry me someday." Rane squeezed her shoulder.

"It's about time, son. Grant finally got smart, I hoped you'd follow suit. Very nice to meet you, Elon." Tom pumped her hand.

"We, ah, caught a glimpse through the binoculars from the hill of Ms. Hardy in action a few minutes back." Grant offered his hand to her. "If you ever want a job in law enforcement, I can pull strings."

Elon blushed at the compliment. "Mess with one of my loved ones and you reckon with me." Her hand flew to her mouth, "I . . . I ahh brought a first aid kit if you need it for the brute." She pointed to Grit, slumped against the wagon wheel.

"I'm mighty thankful you're on my side." Rane brushed a kiss on Elon's cheek. "These relatives are retired from the Montana Highway Patrol and the FBI. They live a few miles from our ranch."

"Comforting thought that we have the good guys on our side." Elon smiled.

"I'd better assess the injuries." Grant walked to Grit. "If the gunshot isn't bad and he's able to travel, I'll bandage it so he can ride in the wagon to within cell phone range. Dad called the sheriff." He began probing Grit. "Similar to Miranda's flesh wound. Nasty, but not life threatening." He tore open an antiseptic wipe. "Besides Rane's shoulder, is anyone else hurt?"

"Fred took a hit to the head and a fall," Elon said.

"I'm okay, my head's gotten clobbered harder before." Fred patted the red bump on his temple.

Grant glanced at him. "Nice goose egg. Any dizziness?"

"Nah, had to catch my breath for a minute. Sorry I couldn't throw any punches." Fred unhitched his horse from the back of the wagon. "Follow me, Emmett. We need to check on the herd."

Tom stood at the edge of the gulley. "That was one heck of a wall of water. We heard it crashing from a long way off." He walked back to Rane. "Heard a couple of blasts prior. With all the debris, I'd surmise someone busted the beaver dam to send water rushing into the ravine on top of your herd. That takes a helluva lot of planning. Any idea who?"

"A drifter we met, right boys?" Grit scowled at Lefty.

"Grit mentioned a partner," Lefty said. "I didn't meet them."

"I paid him fifty bucks. He's long gone by now." Grit winced as Grant tightened the makeshift bandage on his shoulder. He narrowed his beady eyes, staring at Lefty.

Rane spoke so only Tom heard. "I figured out the partner. Can't do anything without proof or a confession."

Tom gave a slight nod and unclipped two pair of handcuffs from his belt. "You can lower your pistol, son."

"Thank you, sir." Lefty holstered his gun. "Grit was recently fired for attacking Elon."

Tom cuffed the teen and then looked at Lefty. "Aren't you the one who owned the Dodge Charger I caught speeding a few times back in 2010 on I-90?"

"Yes, sir, but I've changed my ways. I'm a family man now." Lefty cast a side-glance at Rane and Elon. "Rane's been more than fair to me, and I almost blew it." He scowled at Grit.

A look passed between the Morley's. Tom walked to Lefty and began a discussion.

Meanwhile, Grant spoke quietly to the teen. "The more you cooperate with the sheriff later, the easier it will be. We witnessed you assaulting Rane."

"Don't say nothin', son. You won't stay in jail. I've got connections." Grit's mouth became a tight, thin line.

Grant faced Grit. "Do you want me to tie you onto a horse or do you want to ride in the back of the wagon?"

Grit nodded toward the wagon.

"Then I'm going to take a couple photos of your injury." He pulled out his phone. "Your boy can join you."

The kid hung his head. "Thanks. And sorry. Not the first time the old man lied to me."

"Hopefully the last time you'll believe him without checking facts," Elon stated. "Rane needs to ride home on the seat. He dislocated his shoulder."

"I'm fine."

"Let me take a look," Grant said.

Rane pulled open his shirt. "I remember how you hated taking those advanced first aid classes before you joined the bureau." He flinched as Grant pressed on the muscles around the joint.

"Me, too. But it sure came in handy when I met my wife." He closed Rane's shirt. "The ball made it back to the socket. Who popped it?"

"Elon worked in a medical practice. Obviously, she's a good observer."

Grant leaned forward. "And I've seen the way she observes you, cousin," he said in a low voice. "Lucky man you are. I'll rig you a sling for the ride back." He untied a fleece pullover from the back of his saddle and laid Rane's bad arm in the torso part, then tied the sleeves around Rane's neck. "I'd suggest you stay off your horse. Dad and I can herd cattle."

Rane settled his forearm into the soft material, removing pressure off the sore shoulder. "This helps, and the wagon's fine by me if you'll assist Elon climbing to the seat. I'll give her a driving lesson, and we'll start back ahead of you."

"Sure thing. Dad handcuffed Grit and Junior in the rear, so they'll not bother you during your lesson." He winked at Rane.

Rane breathed easy for the first time since the flash flood. "We may be related through the Calderon gene pool on one side, but remember when you boost Elon aboard, I'm Blackfeet on my grandmother's side and inherited her keen eyesight."

"Using threats . . . you got it bad, too." Grant knuckled his cousin's good arm. "Glad to help you. We haven't seen much of you lately. Hope that changes."

"I got lucky when my life required changing." Rane's eyes followed Elon's movements as she tied Possum and Keeper to the back of the wagon. Every hour he spent with her, he loved her more. He knew little about charming a woman and his financial future hung by a thread. Could she ever love him?

"I thought you'd never ask." Elon rubbed her palms together as if she was excited to drive the wagon. Her mischievous eyes darted between Grant and him while he clamored to the seat of the wagon.

"The lady goes up next." Grant turned to Elon and waited until she grabbed the edge of the wheel, then put his hands at her waist and lifted her to the first wrung.

Elon stepped into a tiny space between Rane's leg and the wagon frame.

"I think I need you on my good side." Rane patted the seat to his right.

She wedged her legs between his thigh and the buckboard. "You're enjoying this."

Rane threw her an exaggerated pout. "I'm just a poor, injured cowboy."

"Yeah, right." Elon planted a quick kiss on his cheek. "I forgot Angel. The puppies are sleeping in their box behind our seat." She whistled and the dog loped to the wagon wheel, tail wagging. "Grant, can you lift my dog, too?"

"Sure thing." He stroked Angel's head before raising her to Elon. "She's sweet. Miranda can't wait to have a dog at the ranch. Very kind of you to offer her a puppy."

"She chose a perfect name: Luna. We've called the male Lucky. He earned it today, while escaping a thundering wall of water."

"Miranda would love to hear that story," Grant said.

"Deal." Elon threw up her thumb. "And I want to cook something special for all of you on a modern stove, if Rane approves."

"Miranda enjoys female company. You name the time, whether my cousin approves or not."

She wanted to cook his family dinner. Rane sighed. That signaled something else positive. "Hey, I'm sitting right here. I heartily approve of having you all for dinner. Despite Grit's plan, no one got seriously injured, and I didn't lose a single steer."

Grant untied his horse. "Ample reason to celebrate. You two head out, and we'll start the herd moving."

Rane leaned around Elon, brushing against her soft curves. "Grant, I owe you and Uncle Tom for helping me. I won't forget it."

"You'd do the same. It's in your blood." He tipped his hat and mounted his horse.

Elon lifted the medicine kit and tore open a pill packet. "Take these anti-inflammatories. At home, I'll apply ice."

Home, she'd called the ranch home. He popped the pills and swallowed. "Whatever you say, medicine woman."

Fred whistled and the last of the herd ambled from the gulch and followed behind the wagon.

"Ugh," Rane muttered. "Still feel like I'm being branded when I move.

"It will for a while. Your cousins are happy to help," Elon said.

Rane's eyes moved to Tom and Grant, who'd fanned out to be drag riders. "They're capable and willing. I'm a lucky man."

The wagon hit a dip in the trail, and Elon's knee bumped his leg. The connection, ever so subtle, sent surges through his body. For a moment, it numbed the pain in his shoulder. "And beyond lucky to have you."

"Mutual feeling." Elon pulled her leg back to rest against his thigh again. "I don't believe Grit's tale about a drifter breaking the levee. You didn't either." Her mouth set in a hard line. "It's the female thug who shot at Fred and aimed at me."

"Yup. We'll have to keep our eyes open and wait. The herd's safe closer to the ranch, and we took out three of the culprits."

Her hands tightened on the reins for an instant, then relaxed.

"Well done. Keep using a light, firm touch. This team reacts when you cue them."

"Thank you." She sat straighter. "Will Grit tell where they hid your calves?"

"Junior already described a foreclosed farm they're using to Tom. He'll call one of his Montana Stater friends as soon as he's in cell phone range. We need to locate my critters before their boss gets wind that we collared her henchmen."

"I'd put money the sheriff or highway patrol gets there first." Elon kept the draft horses at a steady pace, heading to the last rise visible on the horizon.

Rane placed his good arm on the ledge behind their seat, supporting Elon's back. Their bodies met in two places, a comfortable hum of current flowing between them.

Life played out routinely before Elon's arrival. Now, safeguarding her by keeping all his protective instincts on high alert put him in conflict with yielding to her care, akin to the gentle, innocent pressure from the nose of a curious calf.

Rane watched as Elon furrowed her brows, concentrating on proper rein tension to direct the horses. As large as they were, the Percherons responded to light guidance. Pride welled in his chest.

In a few months, she'd gone from a Seattle doctor's wife to an actual chuckwagon driver who'd fought off the thugs who were now trussed in the back like rump roasts.

If her kids got a long holiday break, he'd get them to the ranch. Kids enjoyed guns, horses, or tractors. He'd show them how jingling harnesses sounded better than any symphony.

She caught him studying her and smiled. "In Seattle, a neighbor might lend you their leaf blower. In Montana, you can borrow a pair of draft horses."

"It's a reciprocal loan," Rane admitted. "I plow snow for their owner."

Elon grinned. "I appreciated the old guy the moment he trotted the horses onto the ranch and expounded on your virtues, spitting out tobacco juice and truthful compliments."

"Aw, shucks," he muttered. Her words and the steady beats of clopping hooves smoothed leftover tension from rustlers and raging water.

He'd closed his eyes for a moment when he felt her body shoot to attention. "I see our draw." she chirped.

"You'll spot the ranch in a minute. Happy to be almost home?"

"Not so much as proving to myself that I'm not the incompetent wuss Tim pegged me for."

"You're amazing. If I ever meet the monster, he'd better not disrespect you in any way."

"Spoken like a true advocate, Rane Calderon. You've given me reasons to believe in myself."

"Let me know when you need more. In the meantime, I'll assist you driving downhill." Rane applied his foot to the brake, then craned his neck to look behind.

The steers crested the hill and pulsed into the pasture, stretched out like a black cat on a brown grassy couch, emitting low moos instead of purrs.

Daylight snuck past the edges of the machine shop as Elon pulled the team into the hazy security light glow.

"Welcome back." The elderly farmer who owned the Percherons stepped out the barn door, brushing hay off his bib overalls. "And look who's driving my gray beauties."

"Whoa." Elon released pressure as they halted, slackening the reins.

The taller horse nickered, pushing his nose into his owner's hand.

"Your gray beauties are gems." She stood and put her finger to her lips, calculating her dismount.

"I won't let you get hurt as long as I've got one good arm." Rane held Elon's hand, leaning over and not releasing until she'd landed.

"That's a gentleman." The old man smiled broadly and scratched his horse's neck.

"Hope Tomo behaved well," Rane said, and stood with his foot on the edge of the box.

"No problem from the bull, unlike your escapade. Tom called me. I'm glad the crook took the bullet." He spat a red streak into dirt.

"Gentleman or not, Rane Calderon," Elon declared, "don't you dare hop off and break something. Wait a minute. I have an idea." She hustled toward the machine shop.

He'd never tire of her rear view.

In a moment, Elon returned, carrying a ladder. She tipped it to the wagon's side and held it steady. "Okay, Rane. A dignified descent," she proclaimed, her natural beauty no longer hidden by female face paint.

"I bet you are a great mom." One rung at a time, he descended, not willing to scare her.

"No more accidents on my watch. I didn't put your shoulder back in place to have you fall again." She removed the ladder and propped it against the outside of the barn. "Next year, I hope the excitement level drops a hair."

Next year. Elon wanted to stay on his ranch. Pure joy rolled through him like water freed by the busted dam. "But we've got a great story to tell grandchildren."

Elon's eyes widened before she looked away.

"Rane!" Grant called.

He turned, still stunned at hearing she wanted to stay. By the reaction to his joke about grandkids, she seemed surprised he considered her kids part of the package. He'd straighten that out later.

"Got the cattle settled into the near pasture." Grant sat on his horse a few yards away.

"Emmett and Fred are throwing out bales of hay for

tonight and getting water tubs filled. I can't think of anything else."

"Nope. You've done great."

Elon returned and stood by his side. He snaked his hand around her slim waist.

"Yes sir, you'll be next." Grant tipped his hat. "Dad and I own stock trailers. We'll be in touch on timing to help transport the steers to the butcher. Take a deep breath and get a good night's sleep."

Tom rounded the corner. "All the steers are milling and chewing. Success."

"Hey, thanks again." Rane rubbed his aching shoulder. "I worried if they got stolen, I'd miss the deadline for beef aged a month. Yup, I can relax."

"We'll call you tomorrow to put a dinner date on the calendar," Elon said. "In the meantime, I'll take good care of your cousin. I'm calling Doc Kyle first thing to check out Rane and Fred."

She belonged by his side. Rane took a deep, deep breath, inhaling the sense of family.

He was afraid to exhale and lose the moment.

Her strong, handsome, and pale cowboy looked ready to drop. But Emma Springs residents jumped to action when needed and all was well now, Elon reminded herself.

Doc Kyle had driven over, confirming Rane and Fred's injuries weren't life threatening. Grit and his son had been taken into custody, and Officer Riley had written details regarding the flooding incident and violent attack. Finally, they'd all left, and she could make Rane comfortable.

"Come on, slugger." Elon supported his good arm to

move him from the dining room table to his recliner. "Doc Kyle suggested ice first, then a hot soak for your shoulder. Everything else waits until tomorrow."

Rane stopped in the entry, opposite the front door. "Please throw on the deadbolt." His deep, serious voice echoed what she knew all too well. Threats from the female cattle rustler hung over them.

The bolt slid into place with a resounding click. She returned to a solemn Rane. Moonlight from low in the night sky shone through the picture window, bathing his desk and the broken antler chair in a silvery glow.

"Skip the ice. I'll soak my shoulder in the tub if you'll scrub my back," even tired, the sound of Rane's sexy teasing got her blood pounding.

Tonight wasn't the time. "In your dreams. Relax in the recliner while I find ice packs. By the time I run your bath, you'll have chilled enough."

The thought of sponging his muscular body . . .

Angel danced at Elon's feet, ready for her late dinner. "You're next, my furry diversion." She poured dog kibbles, grabbed ice packs, and opened the first aid box shelved above the freezer. Someone had left an elastic band inside, which would work to secure the ice packs in place. She crossed into the living room, smiling as Rane's sleepy eyes opened expectantly.

"Hold this on your shoulder for me." Elon positioned the frozen pack. "I'll wrap it in place." She slid her hand between the chair and his back, untying Grant's makeshift sling. "You can let go now."

As she wound the band over his shoulder and across his chest, a longing stirred in her soul. Good sense told her to step back. Her arms wanted to cradle him while her traitorous lips kissed away pain. "Okay, that should hold you for now."

Rane's free hand reached out and clasped her waist, then settled her on his lap. "I'm sorry about Grit. I shouldn't have taken you along." He brushed a stray lock of hair from her cheek.

"My boots nailed to the floor wouldn't have stopped me from going with you on the cattle drive. If you'd left me, Grit would've assumed I'd be alone at the ranch."

"Well hell, I hadn't thought of that." Rane pressed his temple. "And the scumbag might've acted."

"The bad part's forgotten. Stars filling a night sky are what I'll remember." She kissed his forehead. "Permission to enter your bedroom?"

Rane's sleepy eyes sparked to aware. "Anytime. I forever cancel my earlier request."

"Request? More of a decree." She rose from Rane's solid thighs, her heart thumping double time. "Off I go to prepare the master's bath."

"In a tub that could hold two. Just saying."

"Quit daydreaming and rest." No sense kidding herself. Her body ached, and the thought of joining Rane in a warm, bubble-filled bathtub, propped against his broad chest, brought sensations she'd never experienced. She crossed the entry hall.

A nose bumped her ankle.

"Hey Angel, want to explore a new domain?" She grabbed a handrail and took one step at a time.

Dog nails tapped on wood planks as Elon led the way to his bedroom. A navy comforter accented the silvery blue frame on Rane's king-sized bed.

She pushed open the bathroom door, her hand hesitating before switching on lights, her body on edge over entering another private room of his.

An expanse of white tile glistened, highlighted by black accents in the open space. A deep, jetted tub took up one end of the room, an immense open shower the other. "One, two, three, four shower heads." Elon stepped to the edge of the stall, looking at chrome fixtures mounted high on the wall.

"This cowboy enjoys cleaning up." Elon patted Angel before stepping to the edge of the tub. She placed her hands on her hips, deciphering which knob controlled the drain.

"Care to join me?" Rane's husky voice echoed through the space.

CHAPTER 13

Elon sprang faster than a steer hitting an electric fence. Her butt thumped against the flat edge of the tub. Wide blue eyes stared at him.

"Rane Calderon, impaired or not, you're a blasted ghost, creeping the hallways without a sound." She ducked her head.

He'd worked hard at mastering silent steps in a creaky floored house. "Waking my folks wasn't popular when I'd head out on early morning rides. You didn't answer my question about joining me in the bathtub." He moved closer, wishing she'd slide into his arms instead of hiding her face.

"I married the only man I ever dated." her unsteady voice continued, barely audible above flowing water. "No one's flirted with me since his fake attempts in high school."

"Attraction fuels my attempts. My pulse jumped, imagining us in that tub."

She turned around, wiping wet hands on dusty jeans. "Mine too. But I can't move to another level yet." Her arms dropped to her sides, lifeless.

"Oh, my sweet Elon." He pulled her to him, gently

rubbing her back. "All those years I didn't want a woman complicating my life. Then I meet you, and my world flips from winter cold to bright sunshine." His fingers moved to her thick hair, touching her scalp, pulling through soft strands. "I can ratchet back a notch or several. Whatever you need."

"Not too much." Elon rested her head against his chest. "I've never felt desired before, and it's totally intoxicating."

"I'd say addictive." He nestled his face into her hair, now bearing the hint of a campfire. "We've shared so much, in so little time. I won't rush you."

"It shouldn't be long. Corrin has good ideas for speeding the process. I owe you an uncomplicated start."

"Us. We're in this together." Rane tipped her head, looking into deep, blue pools. "Thank you for taking care of me. I haven't spoken the words. There's thoughtfulness and concern in everything you do." He wanted to let go, to surrender to her loving heart, no matter what it cost.

Sunlight streamed through windowpanes and onto Elon. She snatched her watch off the nightstand. Good thing she'd forgotten to lower the shade. Getting up after 7 o'clock was not acceptable.

Thankfully, Rane had overestimated the time it would take to move the cattle, which gave her two days to rest and organize. The machine shop men wouldn't return until Monday. Five to cook for and hopefully they'd sleep in today, like the worn out puppies snoring in the box.

Angel lay curled at her feet. She nudged her speckled paw. "Wait until they start running. You're in for a wild ride." She scratched Angel's tummy and pulled on yoga pants to ready herself for a stretching session after breakfast.

No coffee scents greeted her from the hallway. Rane must've slept in.

Elon wrapped her arms around her trimmer midsection, then started a fire in the hearth to remove the chill. She hummed during breakfast prep and while she set out silverware.

The phone's loud ring startled her. She ran and answered before the second ring woke Rane. "Good morning, Calderon residence."

"Hi Elon, this is Tom. Good news for Rane. His calves and steers will arrive later today. They're a bit on the thin side, so warn him."

"Wonderful. He'll be relieved. Hey, can you all do dinner here tomorrow night?"

"Let me talk to our social directors. I think this weekend's open." He cleared his throat. "Elon, you can't believe how happy we are Rane met you."

"Very kind of you to say. My life's changed for the better. I'm looking forward to meeting your wife, Pat." She did a fist pump when the conversation ended and cradled the receiver.

Bare feet sliding on hardwood caught her attention. Rane veered from stair railing to doorframe, grasping each one for balance, his once tan face now a pain-filled gray.

"Hey, you need help." She grabbed his arm, pulling out a chair and steering him into it. "Appears you had a bad night."

"The latter part of it. I must have whacked my hip and knee when I landed against the boulder." He hitched the right leg of his sweatpants to his thigh to show her a purple knot.

"I'm going to get more ice. Do you have a lump on your hip or bruising?" She headed to find ice packs.

"Just bruising. You're welcome to check for yourself."

"I trust your judgement. Tom phoned a couple of minutes ago. Your calves come back today."

"Yes!" he shouted. "Those officers rock. I hear the calves' mamas mooing for their babies."

"I heard them, too. Tom said you may need to fatten them up."

"Not a problem."

"I hope dinner for our rescuers on Sunday isn't pushing your recovery. I offered the date before seeing you this morning." She adjusted ice packs.

"Twenty-four hours and I'll be a new man."

"If you explicitly follow Doc Kyle's instructions. You're not going to bounce back like a teen."

"Some things I bet I can do better as an adult." He raised a brow. "After a little practice."

"I've awakened a demon. I'll let the guys know the good news on the cattle." She ducked her head, bolted outside, and headed across the driveway. No way she'd let him see her burning cheeks.

They'd left the bunkhouse door cracked open. "Cattle come home today," she yelled in.

A truck pulling a stock trailer rumbled through the gap in the trees. Had to be the missing animals, she realized, and dashed back inside the house to alert Rane.

Too late. He'd pushed out of the chair. Apparently, jingling trailer chains affected Rane like sale signs call out to a shopper. Bleating moos came from the trailer and several cows in the field responded. "Our Wagyu babies are here." He took steps between chair and sofa, then sofa and hall tree. "Hey, take my arm and I'll help you," Elon commanded.

Sheriff Riley hopped out of the driver side. "We found them, Rane."

They'd made it through the front doorway. "Yes sir, and I'm mighty glad to hear mooing," Rane said, while leaning into her.

"No identifying necessary." Sheriff Riley grinned. "You raise the only local Wagyu beef."

Fred emerged from the bunkhouse and clapped the officer's shoulder. "I can't thank you enough for finding the calves before anything happened."

"You're welcome. The person we believe to be ringleader of the rustlers remains at large," the sheriff admitted. "Someone set fire to the barn right before we arrived, luckily in wet hay."

"Only a deranged or desperate person could be so cruel," Elon said, and steadied Rane.

He grabbed the porch rail. "They'd left my critters to burn?" Splinters of cracked paint dropped to the floor.

"We'll add charges of attempted arson as well as theft and cruelty to animals. A nationwide law recently passed we can use. Hey, what's that bull they tried to steal worth?"

Rane scratched his head. "Last year a breeder from Texas offered me five thousand for Tomo. His latest offspring are fifteen percent heavier than average, so he'd probably bring more at auction."

"I'll add the value to his attempted theft report. Where do you want them?"

Fred took off his hat. "Hold tight until I saddle my mare to ensure the calves return to their mothers." He cast a worried look at Rane. "Elon, I'd appreciate you and Angel helping me."

"You can watch from the porch swing, Rane." Elon snapped her fingers, and Angel moved to her side. "Angel has herding instincts."

"Let her lead the calves," Rane offered. "They'll follow her once they decide she's the alpha. Fred, from here on out, please carry your loaded Winchester in your scabbard."

～

On Sunday, Rane sat at his dining room table surrounded by family he'd come to know better. Pat, Miranda, and Elon occupied one end—three capable women. Pat's short hair framed intelligent, mischievous eyes. Miranda and Elon possessed inner and outer beauty. Tom and Grant flanked his sides, and from how they spoke, they realized how fortunate they were in finding the right women and working together as father and son.

Fred sat back, quietly studying the group.

For an instant, Rane thought of his folks sitting in an apartment. They'd made their decision. "Thank you, Elon, for another delicious meal," he said.

Tom patted his belly. "I'm adding spaghetti carbonara to a favorite food list."

"The French bread could've come from a Parisian bakery," Pat added.

Wait until she tasted the dessert he'd smelled earlier. Rane winked at Elon. "That's the word on the range. She began a cottage industry preparing baked goods in her off hours for the men to take to their families on the weekends. I worry sometimes she's burning too much midnight oil."

"Baking relaxes me." Satisfaction beamed from Elon, more than he'd seen when she'd completed a tough welding job.

Her true talents were wasted behind a torch, but he couldn't afford a full-time cook. Not yet. He shifted in his chair. "Maybe I can rearrange the storeroom to fit in a bakery case of sorts."

Tom folded his napkin and laid it at his place. "Great idea, and we'll help. In the meantime, you need cattle moved any time in exchange for dinner and it's a deal, nephew."

"This meal's not over," Elon announced. "For dessert, pain au chocolate—chocolate croissants. I've split them to hold a scoop of vanilla bean ice cream." She caught Rane's eye. "Do you prefer to stay here, or should we move to the living room?"

He'd never entertained before tonight. "Ah . . ., wherever you choose, chef."

Grant touched Miranda's shoulder "Are you warm enough?"

"I'm fine. Can't get used to the spoiled aspect of being married. When Grant found me alone in the woods, I'd nearly frozen to death." The eyes she raised to Grant were just short of mesmerized.

Rane felt a need deep in his gut, and it wasn't for pastry.

While they said goodbye to their dinner guests, Rane's fingertips pressed into Elon's shoulders, relaying his presence, and more importantly, his sincerity. She rested her back against his chest.

Miranda slipped into her jacket. "Now remember, come over any time for coffee." She squeezed Elon's hand. "You, too," she said to Rane. "Grant and Tom are dying to show you their newest wood creations. It's wonderful to see two generations working together in a business."

A father and son. Elon winced at a vivid memory of the father and son team who'd routinely serviced her parents' boat. Both men had solemnly attended her parents' funeral. No one knew for certain, but the police surmised one of them might have forgotten to check the drain plug after they'd done a hull repair prior to the accident, causing Dad's boat to take on water slowly and sink, far out in Puget Sound.

On that fatal day, she and Tim helped them launch it from the Alki Beach ramp. If she'd spotted the loose plug, they'd be alive. Pangs of remorse still plagued her. "We'll stop by soon," she murmured.

The group climbed into a Suburban, talking and laughing. Grant's mom pinched her son's cheek playfully.

Rane dropped his hands, pushing the door shut. "You okay?"

"I want what Grant has, two loving parents, waiting for a first grandchild. A woman never outgrows the need for her mother, in my case, my dad, too."

"Someday, maybe you'll be the grandma, and your kids will be counting on you for help."

Before the time came for grandbabies, getting him and his parents together presented a worthy challenge. Elon raised her chin. "You're right. Death can't be altered, whereas perspective can shift." She shut off the outside lights. He never replied. "I'm going to do dishes and turn in."

Rane blocked her path to the dining room. He lifted her hand, kissing her fingers. "Thank you for entertaining my family. It meant a lot to me." His eyes flicked to her empty ring finger on her right hand.

"I have an idea of what it meant, Rane. We may choose crappy friends, or in my case, a horrible husband, but our families have been there for us. We're lucky when we have them."

"Don't you always wear a diamond on this hand?"

Jeeze, he was a hawk. "My ring's tucked in a safe place. The diamond's a family heirloom." Now for more truth. "My mother died of hypothermia, wearing her life vest after a boating accident. The coroner said she'd wedged her hand into her bra—her last thoughts to protect the ring for me."

Rane bowed his head. "I'm really sorry you lost your folks." He squeezed her hand before releasing it. "I wondered if Tim gave the ring to you."

"Oh, gosh no. A cheap, silver band sufficed for our sham of a marriage." She stacked dirty dessert plates.

"Let me help clean up. I can lift using one good arm."

"Speaking of lift, I forgot to mention that since we've come back from cattle country, Possum lifts his feet for me to hoof pick and sticks his nose in the bridle."

"You're his human. And he trusts you." He grabbed a serving bowl and followed her into the kitchen. "All of us trust you."

Now it was time for her to trust him.

Elon studied her kitchen calendar. Today marked the Saturday prior to Thanksgiving. She'd called the airline and found open seats on a night flight out Wednesday and on the return trip to Three Falls next Saturday.

Rane's truck pulled into the driveway. She watched him park close to the back door, her brain weighing how to make her pitch to take a couple days off without pay. They'd nearly reached the trial month of welding, and she'd corrected her only mistake, the broken excavator lip. Should she mention she was caught up, or not?

He stepped in, carrying two overflowing grocery bags.

She grabbed one from his arms and smiled. "I'd like to see Jeremy and Brandon on Thanksgiving. I miss them. I'll prepare your dinner ahead of time, ready to be reheated. Dock my pay, but please let me take three days off."

"Sorry Elon, I told you the deal." He set his sack on the counter. "The ranch doesn't take holidays. I need you here." He turned and headed back out.

Her throat went dry. She'd waited too long. Metallic clangs reverberated in the kitchen as she unloaded the cans of pumpkin, green beans, and a canister of fried onions.

Rane returned, hands wrapped around a huge frozen turkey. "I need a place to put this thirty-pound bird, so it thaws slowly."

"You can put it . . ." Elon clenched her jaw. Words couldn't be withdrawn. Blast tuition, blast Tim, and blast Rane and his pterodactyl bird.

"I have the perfect spot, never mind." Rane backed out, bird in hand.

Metal baking pans flew out of the lower cupboard. Seven of them littered the floor when he returned.

Elon stood in the middle of the kitchen, hands on her hips. "You're in charge of the bird, I don't have anything wide enough to bake it in."

From behind his back, he produced a shiny new aluminum oil change pan.

She crossed her arms. "Too big to shut the oven door. Thirty pounds for a handful of us, you must be fond of turkey."

Rane avoided cake tins and baking sheets to reach the counter. He set the pan on its side, bending it into an oval. "Turkey's a nice switch, and here's your perfect pan. Thought leftovers might be appreciated." He opened the door and slid the pan on the lower rack. "Plenty of space." He grabbed pans, stacking them on the counter. "I'll leave the potatoes out in the storeroom to keep cool."

He'd solved the giant bird problem, not the empty space in her heart. If her boys had a car, she'd have them drive over. Two flights were too costly. "Rane, please reconsider my taking a couple days off."

"Heard in town the nearest machine shop will soon close. They did maintenance on county snow removal equipment. I'm drafting a letter today to the Montana Department of Transportation maintenance supervisor stating that we can handle equipment in this area needing repairs. Could be enough jobs to keep the crew running full time this winter. The reason I let the guys work overtime now is that farm machinery is mothballed December through March." He ran his fingers through his hair. "Maybe we can work out a couple days off for you near Christmas."

Elon spun on her heel and left the kitchen. This time she'd not let him see her pain.

Banging and humming from his shop's lathe and drill press didn't calm him. He should've spilled the news that he and Fred bought tickets for her sons to spend Thanksgiving at the ranch. To hell with surprises, if she'd returned to the kitchen, he'd tell her now. Rane glanced out the shop's window.

An unfamiliar SUV pulled in and parked near his front door. He bolted out of the machine shop, trotted across the drive, and pushed open the storeroom door.

Voices came from the entry—Elon's and a low-voiced male. He stopped beside the dining room table. Floten, the land developer, stood near the open doorway. At least Elon kept the scoundrel outside. He couldn't see her face, but her stiff spine showed she wasn't at ease.

He took a step toward her. No sign of Underson, the realtor.

"Here's my final offer," Floten said. "One-sixty to start and full benefits. I need the lead welder on site ASAP for the first overview by Seattle's planning department. I wrote HR's extension on the back." He shoved a card into her hand. "Do we have a deal?"

Rane froze, his heart thumping. Hourly or yearly, this offer beat what he paid Elon by a long shot.

She mumbled a response and closed the door. Her left

hand reached behind her head and grabbed the hair at her collar, twisting it into a tight mass.

Retreating two steps, he leaned against the sideboard. Her thirty-day trial ended this week. He straightened his shoulders and walked past the dining room table, where he'd begun his growing appreciation of her. "Saw the rig. Floten pushing the job offer?" he asked.

Elon turned. She faked a smile. "Yeah, he wants me to sign on for a project in Seattle."

Plenty of money to pay bills, and she'd be close to her kids for the holidays. "Can't look a gift horse in the mouth, I guess. Or ass in this case."

Letting her go—the hardest thing he'd ever do.

∽

Rane must've heard Floten's offer, and be teasing, judging by the same serious look he wore now, which usually came right before his grin and the habitual 'ahh, just kidding' line. Well this time, she'd be ready. She opened her mouth to give him a sharp retort about bulls.

Rane threw out his hand in the stop sign position. "Hey, no worries. Figured this wouldn't work out. I received a phone call from the old posting from a journeymen welder." He spoke faster than normal. "Men are more suited to throw around commercial snowplow equipment in subzero weather. Emmett can fill in until we bring him up to speed. You'll do fine bossing around a bunch of welders, you got my crew eating out of your hand," he said, and patted the plank table. "I'll finally be able to drop the pounds I packed on."

He wasn't kidding. Far from it. He'd made his decision, not giving her the chance to voice she preferred working here or say that she'd turned down Floten's offer. And he'd made no effort to convince her to stay.

Her body went numb. *He doesn't want you here.* How could she still be so clueless when it came to men? She'd fallen for another man playing her to get something. "Unless there's anything else, I'll head out Thursday morning, when my thirty days officially ends." She squared her shoulders and waited. This time she'd leave with a shred of dignity.

Rane avoided her eyes by looking first at the fireplace, then staring at the road.

The clock ticked in the background.

Say something, Rane, anything about our growing relationship or even why it failed. He never uttered a word, and she'd never plead with another man. *Damn Rane. Damn him to hell and back.* Her heart fell to her knees.

"There's a storm coming in." He crossed his arms, feet spread wide. "You're free to leave earlier for safer driving. I'll cut your paycheck. The skills you learned here will be invaluable."

Safe driving. Right. He'd probably hired the skilled-to-the-max welder to start Friday, after she'd packed the refrigerator full of turkey leftovers. "With an ego that size, it's invaluable that all your burly farm boys live in Montana." She'd worked hard to do every weld correctly. Tears formed in the corners of her eyes. She ducked into the hallway.

"Elon, it's for the best."

For him and his heavy lifting. "Precisely," she replied.

He mumbled something else. Didn't matter, she'd gotten her walking papers. The bedroom door banged shut behind her. She marched to the tissue box, extracted several, and blew her nose. No wonder his family departed, if he'd treated them the same way. And she thought she'd softened the Bull Boss. *Nope.*

Maybe she should go back and give him a piece of her mind about commitment. What good would it do? He'd needed to remove her from his payroll to make room for someone who'd excel at shoving around snowplows. Women and machine shops didn't mix in Rane Calderon's world.

That warning should be welded to his damn mailbox.

She dragged her suitcase from under the bed and stuffed in her pants from the drawers and the blouses off hangers. The empty closet gaped at her.

A tear fell unchecked from her cheek. The room looked exactly as when she'd come, minus the dust. She closed the door and put dirty linens in the clothes basket. Now came the tough part, leaving Possum.

Elon slipped on her boots, heading out the back door. Angel followed, keeping her nose next to her ankle. "Hope your puppies enjoy a long car trip. When Luna's old enough, we'll find someone to transport her to Miranda." Angel wagged her tail and spun a circle.

"Glad one of us is happy." Elon pushed the barn door open.

A familiar nicker greeted her as she spotted Fred working in the last stall, forking straw into a wheelbarrow.

She cleared her throat, to swallow the dryness away.

"Fred, I need a fa . . ." Her voice cracked, ". . . favor."

Fred leaned the muck rake against the stall door. He turned toward her, wiping his hands on his jeans. "Elon, what's wrong?"

She stood at Possum's stall, rubbing behind his ears. The simple words slammed her. She scrunched her eyes shut, burying her head in his russet neck. "I need you to walk Possum for me. Whatever you think will keep his leg in shape." She pulled back from the horse to face Fred and swiped her sleeve across her cheeks. "I'll add extra money for exercising Possum when I mail you loan payments."

Fred stood where he was, hands in his pockets. "Rane shot outta here on Keeper. I see a suitcase on the porch. What's going on?"

"I'm going back to Seattle."

"Rane will be fit to be tied." Fred scratched his head. "There were some plans." He shuffled his feet.

Yeah, Rane had plans alright. "He found someone better suited to his needs. This isn't the first time for me, so don't worry." Elon pressed her nose into Possum's soft cheek, breathing in the warm horsey smell.

"Gotta' be a mistake." He laid his hand on her shoulder for a moment. "I don't need money to walk your horse until things settle between you two." He stepped away, then closed the door as he left.

She wrapped her fingers in Possum's caramel-colored forelock, twisting it and letting it lie between his patient brown eyes. The gelding raised his head, nuzzling Elon's ear. "Fred will take good care of you until I find a place in Seattle to board you. We'll be trotting together again soon, I promise."

Tears wet her cheeks as she hugged her horse's neck. "It'll be okay, don't worry."

She closed Possum's stall door and crossed through the tack up area, her feet pushing strands of loose hay.

A low nicker broke the silence. She turned to see a copper-colored head aimed at her. "See you later, buddy."

Her breath came in gasps as she left the barn and stumbled to the house. So many changes since she'd first seen Rane sitting at the worn kitchen table, dirty dishes stacked behind him. The puppies stayed asleep while she loaded them in the car. Angel hopped in as copilot. The drive began under blustery clouds covering the eastern sky.

Maybe she'd beat the incoming storm. Not the one in her heart.

CHAPTER 14

Rane's stomach still felt as if someone sucker punched him. In the distance he recognized the outline of Grant and Miranda's log home.

Smoke curled from the chimney. He slowed Keeper to a trot, then a walk as he approached their house. Two hitching posts topped by iron horseheads flanked their porch. Rane tied Keeper to one of them, loosened the saddle, and stepped to the front door.

Miranda answered his knock. "What a nice surprise. Come on in." She smiled and opened the door wide. "Grant. Rane's here."

"I hope I'm not disturbing anything." Rane stayed on the edge of the porch. "Uh, may I put Keeper in where there's water?" He rubbed the ache in his sore shoulder. "It's a longer ride than I recalled."

"Sure, use the stall next to Big Red. Water spigot and a bucket to the left of the door. I'll have a cup of coffee waiting when you return. We're glad to see you."

Rane felt his insides tighten—like the panicked moment you realize you're being thrown from a bronco—flung in the air, out of control, and knowing the landing will be painful.

The horse went willingly into the stall, then turned. He stretched his neck and bumped noses with Big Red, the mule to his left.

Rane filled a water bucket and tossed a half flake of hay into the stall. He scratched Keeper's forehead, finger combing the little tuft of mane. "I need help sorting this out, old buddy. I may have messed things up bad." Keeper nickered softly. His feet felt heavier than a wet hay bale while he crossed the drive to their house.

Grant met Rane on the porch. "Just in the neighborhood, cousin?"

"Not exactly. I need some advice on women." Rane stepped inside, slipped his boots off, and set them on the mat next to two other pair. Their polished wood floors looked a darn sight better than his scratched ones. Elon must have to sweep three times a day. His chin dropped to his chest.

"Miranda's the expert. Whatever's bothering you, she'll help." Grant led him to a recliner in the living room. He hugged his wife as she slid onto the couch next to him. "Spill."

"Elon's leaving to take an offer to work in Seattle from the developer looking to build the prison. Close to twice what I'm paying her." He ran his thumb along the edge of the table. "Enough to pay her kids college expenses."

Miranda folded her hands. "Must've been hard for you to hear."

"She needs to gain confidence and earn more money." Rane sat back.

Grant crossed his arms. "Her words?"

"No. To battle her almost ex, money is the critical component. I gave her a thirty-day trial period, which ends in a couple days. Today, I overheard the developer offer her a high-paying job in Seattle, and I didn't give her an option to stay . . . due to any loyalty to me." He looked at Miranda, who'd narrowed her eyes. "It's in her best interest to leave me. I mean leave."

Grant shook his head. "But you didn't discuss options?"

"She looked ready to cry. Probably packing right now. Anyway, she wanted to spend Thanksgiving with her boys."

Grant tilted his head. "You told her how you felt about her?"

Rane froze, holding his cup in midair. "I'm not certain. I suggested a long-distance relationship, but she'd headed toward her bedroom and didn't respond."

Grant leaned toward Rane, eyes wide. "You canned Elon without explaining your reasoning or declaring you want her in your life? To her face?"

"I assume she's aware of how I feel about her." Rane's gut squeezed. He put his head in his hands.

Grant thumped the coffee table. "You can't assume anything after that debacle, you numbskull."

"Call her." Miranda reached behind her and pulled a phone from its cradle. "Right now. On her cell."

"Don't know that number by heart, it's written on a pad on my desk," Rane said.

Miranda twisted a strand of her long hair. "Do you have an answering machine in your house that she'd hear?"

"It's in the living room. She'd hear it from the kitchen."

"Talk loudly," Miranda said. "Beg."

Rane's trembling fingers dialed the number. Five rings and his recorded voice blared a message. He stepped toward the door. "Elon," he yelled. "Elon, if you're there, please wait for me. I'm sorry I didn't explain myself. I'll be there in twenty-five minutes, a half hour tops. Please, let's talk this through." He clicked off the phone.

"That should stall her." Miranda rose and moved to the

door. "You need to catch her before she changes her mind."

Rane grabbed his boots. "Thanks for the coffee. Wish me luck." He scooted outside and hopped down the porch steps pulling on one boot at a time.

"It'll work out, Rane." Grant caught up. "Miranda and I navigated a rough patch before we figured things out. Tell us how to help."

"No idea, and I'm scared as hell I lost her due to my stupidity." He headed into the barn, tightened the saddle, and mounted outside. "Come on Keeper, time to run home."

"Good luck, Rane." Grant's voice faded in the wind.

They cantered and galloped, finally approaching the last hill. Rane checked his watch. Eighteen minutes since the phone call. He crested the hill and stood in the stirrups.

Doesn't matter if she's mad as hell, if only she's there. He squinted and swung Keeper out to the far right. No car.

He walked his horse the rest of the way. She'd left. Sideways sleet pelted his cheek. Rane untacked Keeper, opened the front door, and flicked on a light. No tantalizing smells, no puppy yips, no greetings. He looked at the hall tree for her jacket and sweater. Gone.

He'd promised to buy her Montana winter gear a few days ago, even described the first ice of winter glazing onto Sunrise Lake—glassy shards beginning at the shoreline and spreading the frosty sheet as temps dipped, until only the lake's center stayed open. Now, he felt the same cold sensation creeping into his chest. He should've bought her a down parka as a gift weeks ago.

An envelope bearing his name in her handwriting hung from one of the hooks. *Please mail my last paycheck to the address below. Elon.*

He ran to the desk. The pad sat in its place, but someone must've ripped off the top sheet with her cell number. *Think, numbskull!*

Corrin knew how to contact her. He looked up her number and dialed. His fingers thrummed on the blotter. No answer.

Damn. He left her a message and one for Kyle.

Aimless wandering took him to the kitchen. Elon's domain. All the pots shone, and the counters held neatly labeled spices and canisters of baking ingredients.

Had he ever told her how organized everything looked and how lucky he felt? He walked into the storeroom, his feet scraping the floor, the hum of the freezer the only discernible noise. The wall of shelves held clear mason jars of canned fruits and vegetables of all colors. He identified apples, pears, tomatoes, beans, and beets.

Did I thank her for putting up produce, so we'd be set when snow hit? He leaned his forehead against the door. From outside, ice pellets plinked onto the window. The coolness of the glass cleared his brain for action. How to win her back?

Elon peered at her watch in the pre-dawn light. She flexed her fingers on the steering wheel. Fourteen hours, umpteen pit stops, a hundred bucks in gas, and she remained ten minutes out from the Seattle condo. Angel and the puppies slept peacefully.

Lucky dogs. Her thoughts raced while she tried to stay awake and make plans. She'd sneak in, then call Corrin to confirm meeting Tim's lawyer.

And accept Floten's job offer.

And forget Rane.

The last item would take herculean efforts. She glanced out the window at Lake Washington, where angry waves slapped against concrete bridge pilings. A yawn stretched her tired jaws. She'd not pulled an all-nighter since the twins struggled through baby colic. A bed, any bed, would be a welcome sight.

Her parking stall sat empty and dark. Like her spirit. She carried a puppy under each arm and led Angel upstairs and into the place her folks had purchased for a long retirement.

Another shattered dream.

Overstuffed chairs on carved legs brought sad memories as she entered the condo. The boys understood redecorating took money they didn't have, she thought, as she placed Luna and Lucky on the gold carpet.

Angel set out to smell each piece of furniture. Envisioning former occupants by sniffing?

After fifteen years, no scent of her mom's perfume lingered on the headrest of the padded rocker. She'd tried to find a hint of mom after she'd moved in. Tears wet her eyes. She stared at the teal chair and matching ottoman. Many days after their death, she'd rocked her boys in the special chair, watching the door for her folks to return home.

She stowed her bag near the couch that doubled as her bed. The three of them made the best of things—Brandon and Jeremy's old bunk beds now occupied the single bedroom.

Opening the drapes provided a view of Lake Washington. The water calmed as the sun rose. A curtain of fog lifted near the middle of the lake, exposing rippling water. She closed the drapes and located her earplugs and eye mask, needing sleep more than anything—excluding the man she'd left in Montana. Stretching out, she closed her eyes.

The scent of brewed coffee filled her nostrils. A hazy dream of riding double behind Rane on Possum lingered in her memory. Rubbing her eyes didn't erase it.

Jeremy sat at the kitchen counter. He poured a mug for her, handed it off, and sat on the edge of the couch. His tousled brown hair invited touching—but maybe he'd grown too old.

"Morning, Mom. Glad you arrived safely." He squeezed her hand. "Brandon's still sacked out. What's on your agenda today?"

"Calling an HR person about a job, then Corrin, my lawyer, who planned her trip to Seattle for Thanksgiving. And writing a grocery list for our holiday feast." She ruffled his hair, and he grinned.

"If you're tired, we can get takeouts on Thursday." He smiled kindly. "Look, we both think Rane sounded decent and hope we meet him some day. The phone quit ringing as I unlocked the condo yesterday. We don't get any calls on the landline number, but you called us from his house, so he'd have it."

"I'll contact him at some point. I kind of left in a huff, and I think he might've mumbled something to explain his viewpoint. I was in no shape to listen." She swung her feet to the floor and took a swig of coffee. "I hope you both understand that I may need to make a deal with your father to get him to pay for your winter quarter."

"A deal with the devil. Hope not. Brandon and I rummaged through two-thirds of the boxes in the storage area looking for the will. No luck. With three of us, it'll go faster."

"You bet." She took another sip from the mug, clenching tight to prevent her fingers from shaking. What if they never found a copy?

～

Not one blasted flight to Seattle. Rane slammed the phone receiver, his eyes shifting to the living room window and the thick onslaught of flurries. Fortunately, the kids' tickets they'd purchased to surprise Elon could be used at Christmas. By then she might be speaking to him.

A loud rap on the front door jolted him out of his perfect 'bring Elon home' scenario. He opened it to find Fred, rotating his hat slowly in his hand.

His old buddy wore an unfamiliar look of concern. "Is something wrong in the barn?"

Fred lifted his eyes. "Elon said yesterday you fired her. I'm not one to meddle, son. Way I see it though, one mighty fine woman drove out of here."

"I thought she wanted to leave and bungled things badly. I'll make us coffee and something to eat while I explain." He motioned to the kitchen table, put water in the pot, and dumped coffee into the hopper.

"Can't say I'm real hungry. She cried saying goodbye to the horses."

Rane stopped, picturing what he'd done to her. He told the story to Fred and let his head fall to his chest. "She never knew my reasoning, that the job Floten offered in Seattle would solve her money problems and I thought she'd be relieved to go. Seeing tears in her eyes unglued me." He lifted two mugs from the rack. "I'd do anything to make things right again. Problem is, I'm moving like a slipping clutch. I just can't get into gear."

The coffee pot spluttered behind him.

"I'm not the one you need to tell, she is," Fred said.

"I'll be on the next available flight to Seattle. The ice storm cancelled a bunch." He studied the man who'd been his anchor when his world exploded. Several times.

"Hasn't been easy for you, Rane. When your folks left, they told me to watch over you. You haven't done much that needed watchin' over, but this is different."

"I can't believe their nerve."

"They care. The gap between you and them got so wide, it

seemed no one could bridge it 'cept me. They're getting old, time marches on."

"Yeah, Elon said the same thing." He poured two mugs of coffee and offered one to Fred. "Thanks for being the bridge."

"Welcome. Elon brought a genuine smile to your face—missing for too many years." He sipped a little coffee and put the mug in the sink. "I got tack to clean. Someone must have her cell number."

"I'll try Corrin again. Thanks, Fred." He headed to his desk.

"Smile when you sweet-talk her, son," Fred offered. "She brought you to life."

And right now, he felt close to death.

⌇

Yes! Something had gone right. Elon wedged her cell phone between her shoulder and ear and grabbed a pad and pen from the condo's tiny kitchen counter.

"I received verification to hire you immediately," Floten's HR manager continued. "They hope you can start working tomorrow."

Two days' wages before Thanksgiving helped. "Certainly. I may need to clock out for a prescheduled meeting. I'll use lunch time."

"That request shouldn't be a problem."

Elon squeezed the pen. "Where and to whom do I check in with tomorrow?"

"I'll email you the address and name of the site manager. Thank you for your cooperation, you've made my job easier."

"Glad to hear." Unease rolled through Elon. Surely plenty of welders inhabited Seattle. And why so rushed? Quit second-guessing a great job offer, she scolded herself. Even a job located too many miles from Possum, Fred, and Rane.

An ambulance siren wailed in the distance, probably headed to a hospital. *Hope the doctors can save the victims.*

Doctor. Her jaw clenched. Damn Tim for taking the copy of the will from the house. The original must be in one of the dozen or so remaining boxes in the condo storage room. She'd go through the last stack today, but first she needed to share her employment news with Corrin.

"Hey Elon," Corrin's friendly voice answered. "Heard from Kyle you left Emma Springs. Was preparing to call you. We've got a one o'clock appointment with Tim's lawyer on Wednesday. Can you join me at Aunt Iris' place for planning tonight?"

The thought of seeing two friendly faces calmed her nerves. Long ago, her parents rented Iris and Charley space in their building. His death closed their jewelry store.

"Certainly. I enjoy Iris."

"Good. We'll polish our armor."

"Mom kept the documents that we compiled the first time I thought about divorcing the cheating louse. I found them in one of the kitchen drawers today."

"Wonderful. Bring them. Oh, Rane left a message to have you call him when you got a chance."

One emotional outlay at a time. She rubbed the nubby back of her cell. "Thanks. See you soon." She ended the call and pushed the records incriminating Tim into the tattered old envelope, then headed to the storage area.

After spending an unproductive six hours searching for a document that wasn't in storage, she had a productive meeting at Iris' later that evening. The strategy session proved Corrin's personality suited courtroom battles. Beyond a doubt, reasonable or otherwise.

Tim couldn't fight printed evidence. A nagging ache warned her he'd try.

~

On Wednesday, Elon pushed the elevator button for the fifty-second floor, the Seattle skyscraper perch of Tim's lawyer.

The higher one travelled in a building, the more money was spent—or lost, in her case. She studied her leather work boots, designed without a tongue and laces to avoid catching sparks. Nothing protected against verbal firestorms. No doubt, Tim would snicker at her attire, but she needed to log in every minute she could, with the hourly wage Floten paid. *Clothes didn't make the woman.*

The bell dinged and the steel door slid open to an expansive lobby featuring a view of the skyline. Her palms smoothed her Levi's, now fitting loosely over her hips after she tucked in a thick flannel shirt.

Corrin rose from a chair. "Here we go." She nodded toward the hallway.

A familiar, well-dressed man approached, wearing a black suit and dark red tie. "Surprised to see you, Ms. Hardy." Tim's lawyer held his beak-like nose tilted at an angle to scrutinize her. "Follow me, please." No handshake before he ushered them to a conference room.

Tim sat at a round table, floor-to-ceiling windows to his back. He remained seated, hands resting on russet mahogany, his gold cufflinks a contrast to the charcoal gray Armani suit. Thankfully, his lawyer sat next to him. Elon took the next chair and dropped her oversized purse to the floor. Corrin sat on the other side of Tim, her bag in her lap.

His lawyer cleared his throat. "I'll get to the point. The residence and medical clinic are legally owned by my client, Dr. Hardy. He acquired them both prior to marriage. He's willing to offer a cash settlement. I believe it to be a more than generous offer, under the circumstances. A picture equals a thousand words in court."

Tim smirked at Elon before removing a thick, square envelope from his pocket.

Elon smirked back. She'd done nothing wrong, and she'd made that clear to Corrin. Still, her leg bounced under the table.

"Before you show yours, so to speak, please close the blinds." Corrin stood up. "I won't talk into the sun." She opened her leather satchel and pulled out a file folder, two pens, and a yellow pad.

Tim's attorney lowered the shade.

"Thank you." Corrin straightened her stack and tapped a pen on the pad. "First of all, there are no circumstances, on our side of the table. No illicit affairs, or a recently-vanishing will naming Elon as the sole owner of the property the clinic sits on. Fingerprints are being validated from poisonous leaves added to Elon's tea, readily accessible to your client. My client never staged stairs to break or fired an assault rifle. All these issues will be brought forward, should this go to trial."

Tim withdrew the envelope and placed it in the chest pocket of his suit coat. His face paled.

The lawyer drew his lips together. "Please explain your accusations."

"Ask your client."

The lawyer cast a side eye at Tim. "Any other coincidental occurrences?"

"None are coincidental." Corrin flipped the page and continued. "Your client engaged in extramarital affairs throughout their marriage. We have photos, phone records, and credit card receipts dating back two decades. There are police reports from the recent attacks on Elon. My client never participated in any extramarital sexual encounters."

Elon sat straight in the chair, head high. While searching for the will, she'd found her parents' credit card receipts from the purchase of expensive medical equipment. Mom's organization never failed her. She removed a manila envelope from her purse and pushed copies toward the tight-lipped lawyer.

Tim grabbed the file. His face remained stony while he thumbed through documents. At times he held a paper off to the side, squinting. He found a blank page, ripped off the bottom, scribbled a few words, and folded the paper.

Notes to his lawyer? The entire meeting seemed off, especially his trouble reading. Vanity wouldn't prevent Tim from getting designer eyewear, just the opposite. At thirty he'd added gray streaks to his brown hair to look distinguished.

Corrin cleared her throat. "Preceding our next meeting, Tim Hardy needs to pay, in advance, for his two sons' winter quarter tuition at the University of Washington. He'll need to reimburse Elon for property taxes and HOA fees he failed to pay. And I suggest you rethink the cash settlement." She placed her notepads in her satchel.

The other lawyer stood and shook Corrin's outstretched hand. "We'll be in touch after reviewing your documents," he said in a formal tone.

Tim leaned over the empty chair and dropped the scribbled note into Elon's purse.

She zipped the bag shut and rose to leave.

Corrin smiled. "After you, Elon." The two women marched to the reception area and stood at the elevator. Corrin pressed the button. "Before I forget, Rane's left multiple additional messages wanting your cell number. He's desperate to speak to you. May I give it to him?"

A tiny sliver of hope rose in her chest. She did her best to squash it. "Sure. I'll hear the cowboy version of desperate. Probably needs to know how to boil water. We don't have a recorder on the condo's landline if he tried it."

"He's tried multiple times." The elevator opened to an empty car, and the women stepped inside. "I saw Tim deposit a slip of paper into your purse and his smirk at my tuition request," Corrin whispered.

"Can't wait to see what the louse wrote." The doors slid shut. Elon extracted the note and held it between them.

Run a paternity test on your brats. Her hand began to shake. "After all these years, he can't legally disown them, can he?"

"No." Corrin grabbed a corner of the paper. *Haven't you ever noticed the lack of resemblance to me—mentally or physically? Didn't get my money's worth from that sperm donor.*

"Parents are not legally responsible to pay for college. He's using emotional warfare prior to us hammering out his familial obligation to cover the costs," Corrin stated. "The twins share his last name, luckily not the blood of the monster."

E lon punched out on the makeshift time clock. Thank goodness this day was over. Had she expected better during the earlier meeting with the conniving, lying, perfectionist bastard, Tim? She fingered her locket, still shell-shocked from his note regarding paternity. The joke fell squarely on her.

Several in a row.

Two days spent near the project manager, and she'd easily concluded Floten hired her temporarily to meet equal opportunity laws for the role of managing an incoming crew of journeymen welders. How stupid of her not to realize she should've had to submit proof of the required credentials for a project of this size. Not like Rane's ranch, where her lack of skills could be augmented by You Tube.

They'd fire her as soon as the state reviewed her minimal

qualifications. Why hadn't Floten asked for her certification? "Criminy," she muttered. The jerk might've pulled her away from the ranch to jeopardize Rane's cash flow via the machine shop work. Had the new welder stepped in and kept Rane in the black? She locked the construction trailer and buttoned her wool coat, fighting more than the winter wind blasting through the open pit that was slated to house a government building. Had she been used again in a damn game benefitting an unscrupulous man?

Her work boots felt heavier on each step as she walked to the parking garage. Quit deliberating on returning Rane's calls, she told herself. His problems aren't your problems anymore, and he didn't need to know Floten's job would end shortly. The cold car seat didn't help legs tired from standing.

She removed the lanyard holding her ID tag and hung it on the rearview mirror, then rested her head on the steering wheel. Tomorrow morning she'd prep their Thanksgiving meal to be served late in the evening. No rule stated holiday dinners need to begin by two. Tonight, she could really use some girl time. The happy hour session suggested in an earlier message from her friend, Doreen, sounded perfect. She returned the text from her. *Off work. Name the place.*

A reply loaded. *Sorry, rain check. Here's the 'hood scoop from yesterday I wanted to share. Scrawny blabbed that Dr. Deceitful's finalizing negotiations to sell to the hospital and get a wing named after him. I'd like to wing him alright. Gotta run.*

No way! Conniving bastard! She pounded her fist on the wheel and backed out of the parking space. The steering wheel pulled slightly to the right. "What now?" After swinging into an open slot, she got out and circled the car.

"No!" An inch-long slash punctured the front right tire.

Twenty minutes later, after shooting in a can of Fix-A-Flat, she maneuvered the car to the condo in an angry fog, then took the dogs out for a brief walk.

While three furry friends watched, she baked a pecan and pumpkin pie. If the turkey wasn't frozen, she'd have jammed every crumb of bread stuffing into the cavity. She dunked the bird into a sink of cold water to thaw.

The boys were at a Friendsgiving party until late. Put your irritation into productive action, she scolded herself and headed to the storage unit. The puppies and Angel kept busy smelling assorted boxes and bins.

Rummaging through decorations and old books produced nothing resembling a will. She went to bed discouraged and woke to an overcast, windy day. Montana probably glistened in snow.

At two, she slid the fifteen-pound turkey into the tiny, condo-sized oven. The mitt slipped off her hand. She reached to retrieve it and noticed her mom's six-inch-wide hidey-hole behind the wooden toe kick.

Angel trotted beside her to watch.

"Deep enough for a will, pup?"

Brandon had replaced the board perfectly, she thought, as she slipped a butter knife between the two pieces of trim and removed one. Her fingers crept in, landing on the hard covers of her parents' old passports. She removed them and stuck her hand in up to her elbow. At the very back her fingers found smooth paper. Yes! She pulled a thick envelope out.

Last Will and Testament. Written in Mom's handwriting. She rocked back on her heels.

Tears came to her eyes while she held the faded ink on the tattered envelope to her heart.

Angel trotted to her and licked her cheek. "I think we found what we need, little pup." Elon stroked the dog's soft ears.

"Okay. Time to see." She unfolded the document, read through the beneficiary designation section, and carried it to the rocker.

Evicting Tim and selling the building equaled justice and financial security. She began rocking, to and fro, weighing the consequences of her decision at each up and down movement.

Selling meant no legacy to her parents, who'd scrimped to buy the old brick building featuring white masonry trim hanging like frosting below the roofline. They'd painstakingly gotten it refurbished. Few historic treasures like this remained, now that so many quiet neighborhoods were overshadowed by boxy high rises.

The rocker swung forward. Money equaled permanent freedom from Tim.

Honoring her parents meant a lot, but what she truly desired remained out of reach in Big Sky country. She tilted her head against the padded headrest and let the chair swing back. The absence of money moved her to Emma Springs, now the absence of love sliced into her with the jagged edge of a serrated bread knife.

Tomorrow she'd call Corrin with the news, then make copies of the will in the condo's management office and see if they'd store the original in their safe. She patted the paperwork. Two businesses leased a large section in the front of the building. Tim must've banked rent money in a separate account. If she booted him out and found another tenant, their combined rent would pay tuition and support them for the time being.

What came next? She sat and stared out at the water, her mind a blur.

The bedroom door opened. Jeremy and Brandon ambled out, yawning and tipping their noses to catch the faint turkey scent in the air. "Lovely smell of roasting turkey." Jeremy closed his eyes and waved his hands toward his nose.

"Glad you guys slept in a tiny bit," she teased. "We'll eat around five."

"What's up, Mom? You looked far, far away just now," Brandon said.

The sensitive one could be a counselor. "I found your grandparents' will, proving what I knew. They wanted me alone to inherit the land and building where the medical clinic now sits. Your father planned to demolish the entire block and sell it to the hospital. I left a message for Corrin to see when I can collect rents from the other two tenants in the building."

"Do what's best regarding your property, as long as you kick the asshole out first." Jeremy squared his broadening shoulders, emphasizing he wasn't an indecisive teen anymore. "Dr. Deceitful deserves a taste of his own medicine."

Exactly how she felt, and they deserved the entire truth about why he'd shunned them from day one. "I appreciate your loyalty to me. Tim's absences weren't your fault." She took a deep breath. "He may not be your biological dad."

Both boys' eyes grew wide. "Good," they blurted simultaneously.

Not what she'd expected. The knot in her stomach loosened. "He handed me a note in court stating my artificial insemination came from a donor, so your biological father is unknown. One more deceit, if he isn't lying. In a warped sense, it explains why he preferred treating strangers' kids rather than spending time raising you."

Brandon knelt by her side. "I try to act exactly the opposite of him and his obsession with designer logos and social status. Do what's best for you, Mom. We can get jobs or student loans until the finances are settled."

"Whatever happens, you're my boys, and we're a team."

"It's actually a relief not to be related to him," Jeremy said. "You've more than compensated for us not having a real dad." He lifted the two puppies and sat on the ottoman. "I'm still worried Dr. D's dangerous. Yesterday morning when I left for a jog, I thought I saw that new Beemer from his driveway jet out of the condo parking lot."

Elon flinched. "Before I left the parking garage last night, I noticed my tire had been slashed. If I'd gotten to I-5, it could've been dangerous." She thumped her head. "Tim could've been checking to see if I'd come home for Thanksgiving, and my ID with the building address is hanging from the mirror."

"That's scary, Mom," Jeremy said. "You may not be safe here."

She placed a hand on the shoulder of each son. "You've become astute, caring young men whom I love with all my heart."

"Back at you." Brandon took her hand from his shoulder and gave it a gentle squeeze. "Whatever transpires, we'll be fine here. You had a fight with Rane. Go make up and be safe and happy. I bet you didn't know that he and some guy named Fred bought us plane tickets to visit you over Thanksgiving."

Elon's mouth dropped open. Rane did care. She'd ignored his messages on her cell, the sting of his rejection too sharp.

Keeper's even walk should've been a healing balm. Rane let out a long breath and kept the reins loose. No balm could cure what ailed him. Elon hadn't returned either of the messages he'd left on her cell—probably blocked his number by now. Tonight, he'd try their landline again. Maybe one of the boys would pick up if they were having Thanksgiving dinner at the condo. And what if she wouldn't talk to him? He may have blasted to smithereens any future chance with her.

A rustling noise put Keeper on alert. Rane looked ahead. They'd travelled northwest and reached the edge of the Blackfeet burial site. *So much for paying attention.*

Mounds of freshly dug dirt stood out. Stakes with pink flags ran across the edge of the neighbor's property—his property in a few weeks.

What the hell? Rane tipped his head back and squinted at the survey balloon hovering over Blackfeet land. *Enough.* He wheeled Keeper toward the ranch. The steers seemed calm, and Thanksgiving or not, he'd stop by Don Underson's house to straighten out any confusion surrounding his earnest money on the adjoining property.

He cantered home and unsaddled Keeper. After turning him into his stall, he stopped to pet Possum. "I'll get her back old boy, don't you worry." He closed the barn doors behind him.

Pops and spits from laying a bead stopped from the welding area of the pole barn. Emmett stood beside a plow blade, the unlit torch in hand, shoulders tense. He tugged the helmet off his limp hair.

The kid tried hard, Rane acknowledged as he veered toward him. Wasn't his fault he'd only recently started welding classes. "Looks good, Emmett. I'll put the turkey TV dinners in the oven when I return from town."

"It looks crappy, Rane."

"I feel lucky to have you. No one else wants to work this far from Three Falls and no one works on a holiday."

"Nothing else to do." Emmett stepped back and shook his head. "Can't weld as good as Elon and I sure miss her cooking. No offense intended."

"None taken. Thought I'd call her tonight. See how the new job's going. Cross your fingers."

"If you want to build a little bakery off the storage room, I'm not the only one who'd help."

"I'll add that to my case for her return." He climbed in his truck and followed the rutted path to the road. No vehicles on the horizon in either direction.

Normal folks held a turkey drumstick in their fist right now, he thought as he accelerated on open highway to reach Emma Springs. His tires threw gravel when he shot into the Underson's empty driveway. Smoke rose from their chimney. He wiped his feet on their bristled mat and pounded the bell twice.

Sharlene cracked the door. The smell of spaghetti sauce wafted out. "Mr. Calderon, fancy seeing you here today." Her pink apron broadcast *Born to Shop but Forced to Cook* in black embroidery.

The apron didn't lie. From where he stood, he saw an empty spaghetti sauce jar on the counter. Fred had recently spotted her driving through town in a new Corvette chock-full of packages. "Mrs. Underson, I have an important real estate question for your husband."

"Oh, bother. Wait here." She opened the door and pointed to the inset tile on the entry floor, as if his boots dripped cow manure. "Make it quick, we're ready to eat our holiday meal." She walked through the living room and disappeared.

Framed photos covering half the wall showed Sharlene holding various trophies while standing next to a palomino. In several, she toted a rifle. She had to be the rustler. And what better reason for Elon to return than identifying her as the crook. Then, he'd be able to admit in person what a numbskull he'd been. He scanned the room, his world feeling much, much brighter.

A large flat screen TV occupied the remainder of the space, surrounded by pristine white leather sofas. Don Underson ambled toward him across a plush woven carpet, followed by stony-faced Sharlene. "Hi, Rane. Thinking of selling the ranch?" His smile radiated the warmth of a frozen water pipe. "Property's hot in your area."

The canned line set Rane's teeth on edge. "No can do. Our land's tied to a family trust. I'm here concerning a misplaced survey balloon shadowing my Blackfeet burial grounds. That land's protected by law and it's the reason I'm buying the parcel in front. My earnest money should've been logged into the real estate records."

"It was. Fact is, that's the third survey balloon and the company is irritated. The first two got shot by an arrow." His face hardened. "Illegal, in case you weren't aware."

Typical finger-pointing at the tribe. "Really?" Rane shrugged. "Any blindfolded kid with a Walmart bow and arrow could've hit it." He squared his shoulders. "If I downed one of the trespassing balloons, it'd be by a volley of buckshot, in case you weren't aware."

Sharlene stepped forward. "The county needs an infusion of new jobs. Graves can be moved, and tribal issues can be mitigated."

Mitigated like hell. His fist clenched. "My earnest money doesn't expire for a month. And historically, the so-called mitigation hasn't played out well for the Blackfeet. In case you aren't aware, Council President, there's this federal law called the NAGPRA—Native American Graves Protection and Repatriation Act. This isn't some minor issue."

"Never knew you took your heritage so seriously." Don sucked in his belly and crossed his arms over his chest. "Rumor has it you're having some financial issues, Rane. The seller accepted a backup offer for twenty percent more."

Sharlene pursed her thin lips. "You've always been a loner, Rane. Time to think of the welfare of the town. Mr. Floten and other investors have comprehensive plans for commercial development in this county. And they have money to invest." She narrowed her eyes, as if sighting in on him. "Don't screw it up," she threatened.

Jeremy and Brandon efficiently cleared the table and tidied the kitchen. Elon flipped through an old magazine and swiveled on the barstool, putting her back to the counter.

She scanned the room. A small TV sat in the corner, its screen black. Football never appealed to her or the kids. Light drizzle grayed out their view of Mercer Island. Waves chopped the lake.

"Want a cup of tea or anything, Mom?" Brandon asked, and headed in to join Jeremy, dishing up his third piece of pecan pie.

The old wall phone rang. Elon jumped. "No tea, thanks." Her heart raced.

Brandon answered it. "Sure, she's here." He fanned his face and stretched the long cord across the countertop, then tugged his brother's sleeve to remove him from the tiny space.

She let out her breath. "Hello?"

"Am I interrupting anything?" Rane asked politely. His voice lacked the deep, sexy vibe she remembered.

Her heart felt like it had shrunk a size. "Not a thing."

"I stopped at the Underson's today. Pretty certain Sharlene's the ringleader of the rustlers. If the police need you to identify her, how soon can you return to Emma Springs?"

Of course. Tim wasn't the only crazy in her life. "Ahh, I'd have to talk to the project manager to get time off."

"I'll cover a flight and lost wages," he countered. "In the meantime, I'll talk to Sheriff Riley. Glad you're doing okay. Bye."

"Bye," she muttered. She wasn't doing okay, far from it, had he bothered to ask. Rane sounded so different, so clipped. Could he be nervous?

Brandon touched her shoulder. "You don't look too happy."

"Rane needs me to identify a woman he suspects of being the person who shot Fred." She shrugged.

"Mom, it's a known fact, most guys hate talking on phones," Jeremy said from the living room. "Take time off and go to Montana. Give him another chance."

"Yeah. I left angry," she sighed. "For now, I'm going to leave Corrin a message about your possibly seeing Tim's Beemer, the slashed tire, and most importantly, the will I found. Then, I'll figure out when I can return to Emma Springs, if I have to."

Throughout the holiday, her mind kept returning to the fact that if Floten hadn't offered her the damn job, they'd all be in Montana right now, eating a thirty-pound turkey, and life would be grand. She imagined how Jeremy and Brandon would've enjoyed meeting the horses as she drifted off to sleep later that night.

An incoming text dinged on her phone. Elon sat up and shoved off the covers. *Who texts at 6 a.m.?* Floten's company. She squeezed the edge of the couch cushion and opened the attachment. How appropriate that on Black Friday she'd gotten their official and immediate letter of dismissal, due to her lack of welding certification. Well, it wasn't unexpected. She plodded into the kitchen and made a pot of coffee.

After two cups, Corrin's name appeared on the phone screen. "Morning," Elon said, then explained the progression of events.

Corrin repeated back notes while they talked, in her typical legal and pragmatic manner. "I've done some research," she said. "We've got leverage in the divorce. The bad news is a delay due to authenticating the will and sorting out rents and ownership parameters—possibly taking months. I'll keep you posted."

"Okay, bye." Elon ended the call.

In an hour, her cell phone showed a call coming in from an unfamiliar Montana number. "Hello," she began.

Sheriff Riley delivered brief pleasantries, then requested she return to Emma Springs at her earliest convenience to identify a potential suspect. Before he hung up, he asked to speak off the record. "I've known Rane my whole life, Ms. Hardy. He's been miserable since you left. Just thought you should know. Looking forward to seeing you, under the circumstances."

Was she looking forward to going back? "I'd like to nail the person who picked on Fred, too."

Rane's place in her life might be in question, but Tim's wasn't. She tugged off her tarnished wedding band once and for all, stepped onto the deck overlooking Lake Washington, and threw the silver ring into the cold, gray water. It sunk to the sludgy bottom, where it belonged.

Home on the range. Rane's turf. She'd bought new tires and made it in record time thanks to healthy energy bars, plenty of water, and dogs who slept in the car. Familiar bumps cradled the Mercedes while she drove the snow-packed lane leading to Rane. Would this welcome be similar to the first time?

Angel sat up, nose in the air. Elon opened the passenger window enough for the dog to stick out her head. The puppies shifted in their box.

The meadow, the barn, and the roof of the log house sparkled under a thin blanket of white. Rane dashed out the door of the shop, as if his nose had been glued to the window.

He opened her car door and smiled. "Damn, I'm happy to see you. Thank you for driving here again. I'm so, so sorry I forced you to leave. I needed to explain in person. To look in your eyes and tell you the truth."

Flutters of joy filled her chest. She swung out her legs and felt warmth in the hand he offered. "You go first, then it's my turn."

"I pushed you to take Floten's job, thinking you'd gain confidence and earn more than I could pay you. Will you accept my apology for being a fool?"

"Yes, if I can share part of the blame. I was hurt and should've laid out my feelings as a rational adult. Floten may have hired me to make you short-staffed right before applying for a loan."

"Yeah, you don't know the half of it."

"I've got plenty of time to listen. I got canned on Friday. Government jobs require certified workers."

"Thanks be to bureaucracy. I know a position open for an experienced welder and gourmet chef. Hope you're interested."

"I certainly am."

Strong arms pulled her to his chest. "The fringe benefits include a man who knows what it's like to lose the woman he loves. I love you, Elon. Those were the longest days I ever want to endure." He tilted her chin and searched her eyes.

"For me, too." She laced her fingers behind his neck and pulled his face close. "I love you, too."

His lips caressed hers, leaving no doubt he meant every word. Her body molded against him, where she wanted to stay.

Two puppies yipped, and Angel barked.

Rane nibbled her lip. "Enough to hold me for a minute, maybe two," he grinned.

Criminy sakes. The handsome factor surged off the chart when he smiled. "Agreed." She turned and folded the seat for the two puppies to jump out. Angel dashed after them. "We hit the last rest stop several hours ago."

He lifted her ringless left hand. "Glory be." His face radiated unfamiliar brightness. "It's final!"

"Mentally, I'm divorced from the deceitful louse." She squeezed his hand. "Technically, not quite. I pitched the ring into Lake Washington. Finding the will started the process of sorting out monies he owes me and when I can kick him out of the building I legally own."

He kissed her nose. "That's a jump start." Holding her at arm's length, he tilted his head, his brows furrowed. "What else happened? Did the bastard threaten you?"

His uncanny ability to read her again. "He slipped me a note stating my boys aren't biologically his, that he used a donor for my pregnancy. Both kids are relieved. Every part of my marriage was fake, forged, or part of his plan for stardom in the medical world via my parents' property. On Wednesday my tire was slashed. Jeremy spotted a car resembling his girl-friend's leaving the condo parking lot early that morning. Jeremy and Brandon think I'm safer with you."

Rane's jaw tightened. "That bastard's a piece of work. Regarding the paternity issue, your kids sounded too thoughtful to be his devil spawn." He lifted her chin. "You and I are real. Kyle recommended a counselor. If you'll accompany me, we can work through issues together."

"I'll go anywhere beside you, Rane Calderon. Maybe start at the front door of your house?"

He gave her a crooked grin. "My house that you've made into our home."

The days between Thanksgiving in Seattle and her first Christmas in Montana flew by. A steady stream of county equipment needing repair kept Elon sprinting between the kitchen stove and the welder. Emmett was a quick learner, and she shared what she knew.

After supper each evening, she got Rane all to herself. And the counseling sessions worked. By the third week, she'd expressed more fears, hopes, and desires than in her twenty-year marriage to Tim. Better yet, Rane reminisced about his little sister and his brother Chayton.

Elon's eyes shifted to a morning view his folks must miss. Early light cast the hills in a foggy haze, covering fruit trees at the edge of the pasture. She poured her first cup of coffee, breathing in the familiar freshly brewed scent and listened to the sounds of clanging metal and mooing cattle. The plan on exactly how to reunite his family kept bubbling into her thoughts. Fred proved to be a trusted ally, and he'd quelled her fears about Rane hating the reunion, or worse yet, hating her for making it happen. He'd phoned the senior Calderons, and now they expected a call from her with details.

Later this morning, she'd phone Rane's parents and then check flights. She glanced toward the barn. A snowstorm could throw a wrench into the idea, and the gray clouds to the north looked ominous.

No matter how cold it became, checking on Possum remained the second task of the day.

"Come on Angel, Luna, and Lucky. Time to hit the barn." The dogs bounded off the porch and waited at the barn door.

"Good morning, buddies." Elon announced her presence each day and smiled as Possum and the other horses nickered replies.

She handed her gelding an extra treat. "I'll do my best to

erase memories of that spoiled girl, using carrots and kindness." He finished chewing and put his nostrils close to her face. She gently sent him a puff of air and watched his eyes relax. "Okay, partner. Let's take Lucky and Luna out for their first short trail ride."

Sunlight brightened the yard, highlighting color patterns in the wood logs of Rane's home. The structure stood out against the barren field, strong and steady, like the man who inhabited it.

Rane and Fred stood in front of the machine shop, studying an odd-looking piece of equipment being unloaded.

"Hey guys, I'm going to let the puppies follow me across the lower pasture. I'll stay in sight of the house. Okay?"

Rane scanned the open hillside and flipped her a thumbs up.

Possum stood patiently while she saddled him. The five of them took off at a slow pace, with Angel darting between and behind the pups, keeping them moving forward. Pine scented air held the hint of snow.

Angel stopped. Her head turned toward a dark shadow moving in the tree line. The dog pivoted and herded her puppies to Possum's front feet and grabbed Lucky by the scruff of his neck. In the eyes she turned to her, Elon saw fright.

"Surprised you let Elon ride out alone, Rane." Fred scratched his chin. "I can write the work order on the irrigator, why don't you give my pony a chance to stretch her legs. Elon's gotta be a might jumpy knowing that female bandit's still on the loose. Darn shame she couldn't identify Sharlene as the shooter."

Rane nodded. "And now she knows we're watching. Elon

promised to stay in view of the ranch, but you're right to be concerned." He rushed into the barn and bridled the black and white mare. "Time for a quick ride, Crystal." He jumped on bareback, ducking under the barn door. *No one would harm Elon again. Not on his watch.*

He topped the hill at a canter. Elon trotted toward him, the puppies held against her chest. Angel dashed ahead. A dust cloud followed their trail.

What the hell had happened to drain the color from her face? "Hey, everything okay?" he called.

They stopped a few feet from one another. Possum bumped Crystal's nose.

"I saw movement inside the tree line," she said. "Possibly a bear?"

Rane moved to her side and grabbed Lucky. Elon's hands trembled on the reins.

He turned Crystal to head home. "Possibly a straggler. They forage before heading to a cave for winter. Should be done by now." He looked over his shoulder at the hillside.

"Angel barks at anything crawling, trotting, or flying. Instead, she moved the puppies to Possum and lifted one. I got the signal."

"Well, of course," Rane uttered. "She's a protective mom."

They both knew until the sheriff arrested someone, gun-wielding thugs still lurked in the shadows.

Tim drew a glass of water from the wobbly kitchen faucet. Every dilapidated fixture in the brick rambler bugged him, and now there'd be a delay on getting his payment. Why hadn't he gotten Elon's name off the commercial property title years ago?

Because she'd been putty in his palms since high school and he figured she'd remain that way. Well, she'd turned to concrete, and he'd blast her to bits if that became necessary to move forward on the much-needed hospital. He reread the building committee timeline.

They'd conducted an initial environmental assessment and now wanted him to sit in on interviews to hire an architectural firm. Thankfully, they'd delayed the title search and hadn't spotted Elon's maiden name.

Offering her a portion of the money might work. He rubbed his chin and stared out the kitchen window. Sharing wasn't his style. In front of the back fence, a scraggly brown seed head swayed when a bird landed and began to eat.

Elon cherished every damn plant in the yard from her parents' nursery. He glanced at the trash, where he'd shoved her folks' musty old wedding album that he'd found under the bed.

But what if . . . He located the neighborhood alert app on his phone. Two burglaries this week within ten blocks. Perfect timing. She'd jump at a chance to rescue precious photos of her parents, and he needed to strike before the divorce finalized.

Two weeks she'd kept quiet. Rane remained unaware of tonight's plan to bring his family together for Christmas Eve. A miracle, Elon thought, while straightening the couch pillows.

Since Jeremy and Brandon arrived yesterday, the house looked like a home. Large tennis shoes sat in a line by the entry and the extra coats Rane loaned the kids hung on the rack alongside his. A purple UW sweatshirt had been slung over the back of the couch.

All her favorite men in one place at last. She hugged herself, willing the surprise reunion tonight to go well. Willing Rane not to be angry. And willing his folks to arrive before she went batty.

Pacing in front of the window calmed her nerves. Her life rolled in an uphill swing and tonight she'd reach the pinnacle —if Rane accepted his parent's return. She threw another log onto the blazing fire.

Garlic and beef scents from the huge prime rib roasting in the oven signaled both her family's typical Christmas Eve and a Calderon reconciliation feast. She checked her cell. No word besides the earlier text from Brandon. *M/Ms. Calderon loaded successfully. Highway clear.* She looked out the window for the umpteenth time at lightly falling snow.

"Must've been a long list of supplies you gave your sons. They've been gone an hour." Rane descended the stairs and sighted in on her, as if he suspected something.

"Special ingredients I need to make our dinner perfect. My family always has prime rib on Christmas Eve, turkey on Christmas day, and leftovers for the next three days." She pulled her fingers through her hair. "My mom's goal was to stay in her pajamas all day on Christmas and I've tried to carry on her tradition."

"If pajamas equate to a cute little nighty, it gets my vote."

"It's winter in Montana, you do the math."

"I can crank on the furnace and build a roaring fire to warm up my chilly cowgirl." Rane pulled her close, popped a quick kiss on her lips, and released her. "Or I can think of other ways to turn up the heat."

Elon pushed on his chest, moving him back. "I need to check on the potatoes. Tell me if you see the boys arrive. And regarding your offer big guy—no ring, no fling."

"I always wanted an old-fashioned girl, and now I've got one. I'll watch for your car." Rane headed to his desk, and

Elon went into the kitchen, busying herself adding two extra table settings, then texting Brandon. *Close? Remember the ice.*

He replied immediately. *In the driveway.*

She took deep breaths. Counseling worked when you wanted change. Either Rane would show his parents forgiveness, or he'd never forgive her.

Angel barked, Luna and Lucky yipped, and Elon strained to identify that it was her car being parked near the house.

"They've arrived," Rane called out.

Elon wiped her hands on her apron, pulled it over her head, and smoothed her hair.

"The boys need help carrying things in." She hung her apron on the peg at the back of the door. "Can you meet me in the entry?"

"Sure, just a second." She watched him move her way—calm, happy, and unsuspecting. Different outcomes for the homecoming tortured her thoughts.

She jumped at the loud knock.

Rane pulled the door open and stiffened. His face turned to his granite mask. He stared at the older couple standing under the porch light, their faces weathered, their eyes expectant. The man resembled Rane, nearly as tall and broad-shouldered, with gray at the temples of his black hair. The woman looked longingly up at her son, her russet brown eyes glistening. Both were thin to almost frail. Red colored their cheeks.

"Rane, it's freezing out, let's bring everyone inside." She nudged Rane from guarding the entry.

His parents stepped in. Jeremy and Brandon followed, suitcases in hand.

"Set those at the foot of the stairs, boys." Elon looked back at the uncomfortably silent scene in the hall.

Rane's dad stuck out his hand. "Your gal sent us tickets, son."

Elon watched Rane do nothing. Absolutely nothing. She held her breath.

Rane turned to her, icy darkness in his accusing stare.

Could he be so hard-hearted? "I thought a good use of the first rent check from my parents' building was to bring your parents for a visit. I miss Mom and Dad so much." Tears moistened her eyes.

"Honey, please don't blame Elon," his mom said, and squeezed his forearm. "She told me how you've talked about Adele, how quickly you acted and how caring you were when she suffered the same foxglove poisoning symptoms that took our sweet baby girl." A tear rolled down her cheek. "Maybe we can all heal by talking about those we miss."

The fire crackled, breaking the stillness of the silent moments.

Rane's face softened. "You and Elon think alike, Mom. Family means everything, and it's time I realized what I've missed out on." He grasped his father's hand. "Elon and a counselor are trying to teach me, Dad."

"Son, sorry is an overused word, but we can't think of anything better to say." His father's gruff voice cracked. "Elon spelled out what happened to Shelly. What fools we've been. I'm so sorry for the time we lost."

Rane pulled Elon to his side, looking down at her. "She's a very special woman. Apology accepted. Welcome back to the ranch."

His mom stepped forward, brushing her fingertips on Rane's cheek. "I never thought we'd see you again." Tears flowed freely down her wrinkled cheeks. "I've missed you every hour of every day."

Elon placed her hand at Rane's lower back, pushing him to his mother. How well she could relate.

Rane pulled in his dad, hugging them both.

"I thought I'd have to kick Rane or something," Jeremy whispered in her ear.

"You did well, Mom, as usual," Brandon said.

Elon stood on tiptoe, first kissing one son and then the other. "Team effort, guys." She turned to Rane. "I'd appreciate an official introduction to your folks."

"Elon, please meet Mom and Dad, Mary and Harry Calderon. Mom and Dad, this is Elon Hardy." Pride filled his voice as he stepped back and slid his hand to her waist. "She and Grandma Bia are in a league of their own in spunk, quick thinking, and kindness."

"Rane Calderon, I never thought you'd find someone to match Bia," Mary said. "My mother-in-law treated me like her daughter. I'll never forget that." She patted Elon's arm. "Your boys told us a little about you. And I can't wait for the dinner they described, dear."

The door opened and Chayton, Belle, Fred, and Emmett entered. Mary, Harry, and Fred sat at the end of the table closest to the fireplace, sipping spiced cider while the rest of the group converged on the kitchen to get the glorious feast served.

The prime rib was fork tender and juicy, and Harry offered a toast midway through the meal. "Rane, Bia would be proud of how you're using her land. Chayton, she'd also be proud of how you're working with the Blackfeet youngsters. I wish she could see what you both have accomplished."

Rane and Chayton both beamed. Their childhood stories during three courses brought laughs and a picture of life on the ranch in earlier times. Elon basked in the glow of a family reunited.

The subjects casting a shadow on the festivities concerned

Tim and the rustlers. Try as she might, the only attributes of the female shooter she remembered clearly were gray hair and blue eyes.

But she'd noticed something else. She tapped her forehead, straining to recall a feature identifying the woman out there waiting, watching, and willing to kill.

Christmas morning arrived clear and bright. They'd assembled in the living room, beside a pine tree cut from the property.

"Here Elon, this present's for you." Rane dodged boxes precariously tipping in front of Brandon and Jeremy, his feet crunching wrapping paper strewn across the floor. Nerves rolled through his stomach like a fall thunderstorm.

He kneeled by Elon's chair, keeping one leg up and one flat on the rug.

Elon untied the bow, and slid her finger under each piece of tape, gently unwrapping the paper featuring a horse wearing a Santa hat.

Was she going to frame it? Heat rose from under his collar. Elon practiced her own brand of torture. Finally, she opened the box and pushed aside the tissue paper.

She extracted the smooth bridle. "It's beautiful, Rane, and it's bitless. Thank you." She turned it over, studying how the chin straps worked.

Rane held his breath, waiting.

Elon turned it to face her, admiring the soft leather. When her fingers moved to the U-shaped gold ring which dangled from the head buckle, she stopped. "A ring." Her eyes moved to his face.

"I have a jackknife to cut the string holding it." The room was quiet; no paper rustling, no excited words. He took her left hand. "Elon, I never thought I'd find love until you found me. Will you officially promise to marry me when you can?" He watched her face.

A flicker of regret crossed her features.

His heart sank. "Is it more than the legal issues?"

"I, I know you want children. I'm thirty-nine, I don't know if I can give them to you."

He pulled her to him, "I never considered kids. You are all I want, now and forever."

She put her hands against his chest, searching his face. "After the cattle drive, you joked we'd have stories to tell our grandchildren."

"Can't I be a grandpa to their children?" Rane pointed to Brandon and Jeremy.

Elon looked lovingly into his eyes. "Of course, and yes, I will marry you."

He raised her left hand and slipped the ring on her finger. "Don't get me wrong. I'm not opposed to more children," he offered quietly.

"Okay." She smiled and held her hand out to the group, showing chips of lime green stone outlining the 'U.'

"It's an odd shape for a reason," he said. "I wanted a symbol of my love to wrap around your mom's wedding ring." Hesitation clouded Elon's beautiful face.

"That's all been sorted out," Fred interjected.

Rane removed a ring from his pocket, lifted her right hand, and placed the treasured antique back on her finger. "When you're ready, the U shape fits perfectly around your family diamond. If you want to wear it that way. I asked a jeweler to use turquoise stones from a broken necklace Grandma Bia willed to me. The unusual green color is very rare and desirable. Just like the woman wearing it."

"Oh Rane. Thank you." Elon wrapped her arms around his neck and gave him a tender kiss, then spoke through tears. "Yes, I'll marry you and treasure both rings. I feel really loved by a man for the first time in my life."

Rane looked around his living room. Mom grinned from ear to ear. Brandon and Jeremy knuckle bumped each other. Dad stared at the top of the Christmas tree, his face solemn.

Sadness flickered across Elon's face after she turned the ring toward the tree lights.

She'd seen Dad's snub.

A dreary pall settled over Rane's house without the Christmas holiday sparkle and the twins' energy. They'd returned to the UW and the boxes of decorations resided in the attic until next year.

Elon balanced the stack of clean linens in her arms, every scent of her boys washed away. She headed to the guest bedroom the kids had used. Voices came from the room across the hall.

"She's a gold digger, Mary." Harry's gruff tone cut through her swifter than a warm knife through buttercream. "She needs a meal ticket for herself and those two boys. You watch, Rane will be stuck paying for their schooling."

"Harry, don't you remember, even as a teenager, Rane liked helping younger kids. If she can't bear him child . . ."

Elon dropped the sheets, turned, and teetered on the stop step. Her fingers found the handrail and she moved in a fog to the bottom.

Three dogs bounded from the kitchen. "Let's go for a ride, pups."

She shrugged into Rane's old parka and plucked her car keys off their hook.

The Mercedes crunched on snow as it travelled the endless highway. She turned at a mailbox painted with a flock of geese and proceeded through a stand of trees. Grant and Miranda's house sat at the foot of Mt. Hanlen, flanked by a pond on one side and barn on the other. A horse and a mule stretched their necks over fence rails as she parked near the log home.

"Come on Angel, bring your puppies onto the porch." Elon knocked on the carved door, smelling wood smoke drifting from a stone chimney.

"Elon, what a pleasant surprise. I'd gotten a bad case of post-Christmas blues." Miranda stood back from the open door. "Join me in a cup of cocoa?"

"Please."

Three dogs dashed into the hallway, looping around Miranda's legs. "The puppies have grown." She cuddled Luna. "You're going to live here soon."

"I don't want to impose if you're busy. I should have called."

"Not in the least."

"I thought you'd appreciate a puppy visit." She followed Miranda to a dining room facing a view of Mt. Hanlen and the peaceful pond. A wedding photo hung nearby. "You and Grant make a stunning and cunning couple."

Chocolate perfumed the air. Miranda set two cups on the table and motioned her to a chair. "It was a perfect wedding. I wish we'd known you then."

"I bet your family had a delightful time seeing Emma Springs."

"Grant's parents give me unconditional family love, which helps while I grieve the loss of my folks and my only brother, senselessly killed a few years back."

Elon turned her mug in circles on the table. "I'm sorry you lost your family. And I know the feeling. I lost my parents sixteen years ago. You're blessed to have Pat and Tom."

"Oh, I'm sorry. I didn't know. Experiencing death gives you a different appreciation for life. I didn't want to love again until I met Grant." Miranda straightened her wedding ring. "I thought it lovely that you surprised Rane and brought his folks for a Christmas visit." She took a sip, her steady eyes on Elon.

"Harry and Mary never told Grant they live in a camper. The money he sent each month paid for medical expenses, so I think they'll remain at the ranch."

"Oh. Is it easy having Rane's parents living in the house?"

"The three of them are catching up on lost years. When I look at Rane I see forgiveness for the first time."

"Not exactly my question."

She sat back. "You are perceptive. Mary helps me in the kitchen, and we enjoy un-man caving Rane's house. Harry presents another story. He inspired this visit when I over-heard him refer to me as a gold digger." Elon took a long swallow of rich, sweet cocoa.

"Oh, Elon, I'm so sorry. He obviously doesn't know you. Can I help?"

"Not sure. Every time I try to talk to him, he dodges me. I've explained my finances to Mary and tried to speak about it to Harry. No luck, the man doesn't trust what I say. Rane needs his parents again, but I can't handle his dad's shunning."

"Give Harry time, Elon. He'll see what a gem you are, and how much you and Rane love each other." Miranda reached her hand out and squeezed Elon's.

"Rane and his dad are a lot alike. And he went twenty years without compromising. It's hard. I want to be part of their family, except the invite seems lost in the mail."

"It hasn't been long, Elon. Have you and Rane discussed the problem?"

"No, and I won't. The look on his mom's face breaks my

heart. I catch her studying her son, as if she's trying to absorb all the years she missed. I'd leave rather than see them part ways again."

Luna, the black puppy, put broad paws on Miranda's lap. She snapped her fingers, and the smooth-haired pup flopped onto the floor. "Luna's frame seems a bit lanky for her brain to control. My younger brother bumped into tables like a gangly colt." A wistful look came to her face. She stroked the dog's back lovingly.

"I understand losing family," Elon offered.

Lucky nosed his sister out of the way to be petted. Luna swung around and rested her head against Miranda's leg. "They both inherited Angel's brains," she said. "I think Luna sensed I needed her just now."

"Luna's sensitive, she'll be a devoted buddy." Elon stretched her legs out under the table. "They're close to housebroken and ring a bell on the door when they want to go out."

"Perfect." Miranda lifted one of Luna's front legs. "She's going to be a sizable canine judging by those paws."

"If you want her today, I put chow in the car and a bunch of toys. They're both chew monsters."

"I'd welcome a distraction from all this snow, no worries on the chewing."

"Call me or Ed if you have questions. I've done hours of research on puppy rearing and Ed's been very patient. Their shots are done for the next three months. I'll go grab her belongings."

Elon walked to her car and fingered Luna's favorite toys as she put them in her padded sleeping basket alongside puppy chow. She used tiny steps to avoid sliding on the packed snow leading back to the porch.

Through the window, Miranda and the two puppies tugged on a knotted sock. Happiness radiated from her friend's face. Luna belonged in their home. She balanced the pile against the door frame and tapped using her boot.

A flush-faced Miranda opened the door. "My family dog lasted until I turned fifteen. I didn't realize how much I missed canine enthusiasm." She grabbed the dog food bag. "Here, let me help you."

Elon's phone chimed. "Oh, dear. My alarm for an appointment in town. Can you puppy sit for an hour or so?"

"Sure. It will help Luna acclimate better. Take your time."

Elon zipped the parka and slid onto her cold seat. Goosebumps rose on her arm as she entered Emma Springs.

'Kyle Werner, MD' hung on a sign from a post near a walkway. She parked in front of his white bungalow and sat for a moment. The question of her ability to bear another child had never surfaced after Tim delivered the twins by himself to save fees—and whispered in a threatening tone that she'd better be satisfied. And she'd obliged, even during countless sessions coddling stranger's babies in his office.

Then she'd witnessed Rane patiently and kindly guiding her boys at the ranch, like a caring father. She'd seen the delighted look on his face as he held Lefty's daughter.

Her chest thrummed at the idea that after they married, a baby might be possible. *Hold the excitement until tests verify your ability,* she reminded herself, and penguin-walked on the ice leading to the clinic door.

Dr. Kyle came around the side of the garage, slipping in heavy boots.

"Sorry, Elon. I intended to be here an hour ago. Needed to rework busted sewing on a ten-year-old I stitched last weekend." He opened a plastic bin on the back landing and flung a scoop of crystals onto the ice. "It should be somewhat melted by the time you leave."

"I'm getting used to imitating various animals as I

successfully hop through snow drifts and stay upright on ice. Maybe I should get waders for spring floods."

He flashed his surfer-boy grin, precisely as Corrin described. The blond doctor looked like he belonged in Malibu, but thankfully, he lived here. "Luckily, flooding's scarce. Come on in and let's get the ultrasound and blood work done to verify your fertility."

An hour later, Elon descended the last icy hill to their home, easing her Mercedes as far under the pole barn as space allowed. The world seemed brighter, even without confirmed test results.

Curling smoke rose from the chimney. Harry took pride in building fires in the stone fireplace. Elon shucked off her boots and slid off her jacket, eyeing her arm to be certain her sleeve covered the blood draw bandage. She stretched her hands to the warm glow. "You do a great job keeping us toasty. My chilly fingers are appreciative."

Harry rose from the rocker near the hearth. "Yup. Even old men have chores in the barn." He stomped outside.

A whine came from Lucky, who'd wandered in and nudged her leg. "Good idea. Let's see how Luna's doing." Miranda's exuberant voice during the phone call confirmed the pup had acclimated to her new home. Taking Angel and Lucky for a romp in the snow killed time, but all too soon she suffered through another dinner where Harry avoided talking to her. And he wasn't the silent type.

Rane spoke about successful treatments for Lefty's daughter and Harry commented plenty of times. Maybe he longed to be a grandfather, and her age bothered him. If she couldn't bear children, would it disappoint Rane? The question ran through her head about whether to tell him she'd asked Kyle for a fertility test.

The phone interrupted her quandary. Elon rose from the table and grabbed the receiver. "Calderon—"

"I got the part, Mom!" Jeremy announced. "I'm Romeo in the next play. Can you come to opening night?"

"Sure. Hold on." She covered the mouthpiece. "Sorry to interrupt. Jeremy's been into theater since he took the stage in preschool. Today, he landed the lead in a University of Washington play."

Heads turned her way. Rane began clapping and the rest followed, except Harry.

Elon held the receiver aloft for the round of cheers. "We're all excited for you. Text me details and I'll book a flight. Great job, Jeremy."

"Love you, Mom. Got to study the script. It's a quick turnaround time to the performance."

"You'll do fine, kiddo." She replaced the phone and stepped back into the conversation. In a couple minutes, Rane's folks headed upstairs.

Rane and Fred began clearing the table. "Put your feet up," Fred said. "Rane and I are on dish duty."

She glanced around the living room. A pile of haphazardly stacked old newspapers needing straightening caught her eye. Approaching them, she noticed that the top one showed Santa and two elves handing out gifts in an old Christmas advertisement. She grabbed the paper with trembling hands.

How could she have forgotten? "Rane," she called, waving the flyer. "I know what feature identified the female rustler." She ran to his desk computer, typed 'ear syndromes', and chose the correct one.

Fred and Rane peered at the photo she'd enlarged of the baby with thick cartilage and pointed ears. "I noticed her ears when she took her hat off to shoo in her horse. Apparently, her parents weren't aware of corrective surgery. Tim successfully treated an infant a few years ago." She raised her chin. "It's a rare condition. Any woman in town have similar ears?"

"Sharlene Underson," Fred said. "Her Pappi called her Santa's little present. The mother bought her all sorts of bonnets and hats to wear as a youngster."

"I never noticed," Rane said. "Her newly dyed brown hair covers her ears. I'll talk to Sheriff Riley and see how we can proceed with placing you close enough to identify her without a hat."

"They may need probable cause if they want to press charges," Elon stated.

Rane shook his head. "There's been plenty. She threatened me about the land sale when I stopped by their house at Thanksgiving. She displays shooting and riding awards in the living room."

Fred cleared his throat. "I try not to speak unkindly, but Sharlene grew from an ornery little girl to a bossy politician. I'd bet her and her realtor husband finagled getting money under the table for all those land deals she promoted. Don't trust her."

Elon pressed her fingers to her lips. A council chair would have connections.

Afternoon light melted snow on the tips of fir trees outside Elon's bedroom window. She grabbed the packet of papers Corrin had instructed her to study and secured them in her carry-on bag. All indications placed the divorce in the final phase.

Her cell phone rang while she wheeled her luggage to the kitchen.

"Elon, this is Sheriff Riley. You won't be needed to identify Sharlene as the rustler until her home's been searched. Security detained her at the airport wearing a wig and using a fake ID. Her carry-on contained an undisclosed amount of cash. Thought you and Rane could relax a bit. He's been worried she'd strike again."

"Thank you. I'm flying to Seattle today to see my son in a play. Rane still believes a different shooter tried to kill me in my bedroom. I hope she owns more than one style of rifle."

"That's my hope. Safe travels."

Through the window over the sink, she spotted a familiar figure wearing his perpetual frown. Harry Calderon presented another problem, more complicated than a delayed piece of legal paperwork, and one without a clear solution.

Facts were facts. Harry simply hated being around her. She wheeled her suitcase into the storeroom and propped it against the wall by the door. Some things never changed, others you could alter, and many didn't make sense. She'd be gone for a few days to Seattle, and Harry could jump for joy. Thank goodness the windstorm hadn't delayed flights.

The mantle clock chimed ten. In thirty minutes, Rane and his mom would return from church, and he'd transport her to the Three Falls Airport. Someday she'd attend the Sunday services. For now, mom and son needed to bond.

If Rane hoped she and Harry simply needed time alone to work things out, it appeared to be a lost cause. He never stayed in the same room as her unless forced to.

Like today. Barely a break in the blustery weather, and he'd headed outside. She stood on tiptoes to look through the small back door window. He'd moved the old grinding wheel out to the drive and begun sharpening garden tools. Seated on a wooden bench, bent over, he resembled Rane— same hair, same broad shoulders, same determination. The wheel sent out sparks as Harry beveled a shovel's cutting edge.

They both liked to garden, Elon realized. She put on a smile, ready to approach him and ask if he'd ordered seeds. Her fingers twisted the door handle.

Harry clutched his chest. His face turned pale. The shovel dropped to the ground and hit his coffee mug.

A shudder went through Elon. Chest pain? She jumped off the porch. "Harry, are you okay?"

Frightened eyes met hers. "I, I don't think so. My heart's being crushed in a vice."

Elon tugged out her phone. No bars. "Don't move. I'm going to call an aid car." She ran to Rane's desk and lifted the phone receiver. No dial tones. Her fingers trembled while she dashed off a quick note to him.

She rushed to her bedroom, grabbed her purse, and ran outside. "No phone reception. I'm taking you to the Three Falls Hospital," she said to Harry, and lifted him by the elbow.

"Probably a good idea," Beads of sweat glowed on his brow. "My doctor warned me I should carry nitro. Should've listened to him."

Stubborn men. "I carry baby aspirin due to my dad's heart trouble. It was a long time ago, but I've kept a fresh supply out of habit." She buckled him in and found the container in her purse, flopped four out, and handed the tiny pills to Harry. "Chew and swallow, please."

The engine revved as she accelerated and shifted quickly to fourth.

Every minute counted in a heart attack.

CHAPTER 15

Rane pulled onto his driveway, glad to be home. Today's message touched on looking deeper at people. "Dad could've benefitted from the sermon," he said to his mom. He fidgeted as his truck topped the rise, fighting uneasiness.

She nodded. "He'll come around. Elon's sweet."

No tan Mercedes. He checked his watch. He'd hustled Mom out of church to be ahead of schedule for Elon's trip to the airport, aware of her excitement to see Jeremy tonight.

The grinding wheel and a shovel sat in front of the welding shed. Dad's coffee mug lay on its side, a brown pool splattered on the white cement, ice crystals forming at the edges.

Angst rolled through his gut while he helped his mom out of the car and proceeded to the front door. "Elon," he called. Nothing. The kitchen and storeroom lights shone on empty rooms. Her suitcase propped against the wall didn't make sense. "Mom, do you see Dad?"

"No honey. You sound worried."

Rane strode to his desk and grabbed Elon's note. "Back in the truck, Mom. Elon thinks Dad's having heart trouble."

"Oh dear," she said, and hustled to the entry. "Harry's been in denial. His heart's not what it used to be."

"You should've told me. Luckily, Elon's the best in an emergency." He grabbed her suitcase. "I'll drop you at the hospital and take Elon to the airport. Jeremy's counting on her presence at his play."

The drive to Three Falls seemed to take twice as long, even at breakneck speeds. His mom gripped the seat, not saying a word. As they approached the hospital, a large medivac helicopter lifted off the rooftop pad. Rane followed its path toward Billings. Please let it not be Dad, he murmured.

Harry's eyes finally blinked open, and he surveyed the helicopter compartment occupied by Elon, a nurse, and a cardiology physician assistant. "You're supposed to be on a plane to Seattle, aren't you?" Harry mumbled to her, then his jaw tightened in pain.

"I won't leave you alone, Harry." Elon squeezed his work-roughened hand. "We're headed to Billings, where they have a team of specialists waiting to perform the surgery you need. I left a note at the ranch for Rane, and the Three Falls Hospital staff assured me they'd inform Rane and Mary when they arrive."

Tears wet his eyes. "I've been mean to you. Wouldn't believe you're as nice as you act. Will you accept my apology?"

"Sure." She kissed his cheek. "Now rest. You're in good hands."

"Because of you," he whispered, and closed his eyes.

The helicopter dipped and gently landed on top of a large white plus sign painted atop a brick building. As the rotors whirred to a standstill, two women rolled a gurney to the compartment door of the copter.

Elon let go of Harry's hand.

"He's stabilized." The PA announced before they transferred Harry to the wheeled bed.

Elon trailed behind, then slipped into the corner of the elevator. As promised, when the doors opened, a surgeon, the nurse, and PA conferred. The PA motioned, and they wheeled Harry through a set of double doors.

They'd made it. She sat in a lounge chair, propped her elbows on her lap, and let her head rest in her hands. Her phone timer dinged the warning to board her flight. Jeremy needed to be alerted. "How's my favorite thespian holding up," she began.

"Great," Jeremy exclaimed. "You caught me just before I headed out for the cast pre-party. I'm taking brownies to gorge on. Is your flight leaving on time?"

"I'm not sure. Harry's having emergency heart surgery, and I needed to transport him to the hospital. It involved a helicopter ride to Billings, so I missed my flight. I hope to be on one tonight or tomorrow to catch your next performance. I'm sorry, kiddo."

"Hey Mom, no worries. By then I'll be less nervous and more chill. Harry's going to be okay?"

"I hope so. I certainly appreciate your understanding."

"Harry's a crotchety old guy, but he showed us how to whittle at Christmas. Brandon and I both liked him. Give him a hug for us."

"Will do. And break a leg. Kind of an odd comment while I'm sitting outside the surgery doors."

"Love you, mom."

She clutched the phone to her chest. Despite Tim, she'd raised compassionate sons.

~

Tim reclined in his padded leather office chair, glad he'd declined invites for Friday evening socializing.

The strain of pretense made his sight worse. He tipped his head sideways to view emails on his monitor and opened the parental Husky Campus Newsletter from the University of Washington. Mom's Weekend should be soon. Luring Elon to Seattle was an imperative task.

A familiar face caught his eye. Jeremy wore a Renaissance costume and stood beside a pretty girl in a flowing gown. Elon would walk through fire to see her kid perform. Not precisely his plan, although the thought of watching her try made his heart drum.

~

Rane glanced at clouds on the horizon and let out a long breath. Elon's airplane rose in the sky, leaving Billings and headed for Seattle only one day late. He backed the truck out of the parking slot and turned onto the highway leading to the hospital. Today, they'd learn the timeline for Dad's recuperation. The doctor's prognosis sounded hopeful, thanks to Elon's quick actions.

Navigating the maze to the cardiac unit made him nervous, that or it gave him an unshakable sense of unease. He turned into his dad's room and spotted Kyle's blond head leaning over his father, speaking quietly, and calming everyone's nerves.

Kyle straightened and turned. "Rane, just in time for the

good prognosis. Your dad should be able to leave the hospital earlier than we thought."

"Great news. Thanks for stopping by, Doc."

"I'm glad I found you." Kyle's eyes held concern. "Can you join me in the hall for a moment?"

His mind raced while they stepped into a quiet corridor. "Something you're afraid to tell Mom?"

"No. Chayton tried to reach you on the room phone. He knew I planned to stop by today and called my cell a few minutes ago. It's about identifying the person who fired into Elon's bedroom. The leaves and dirt Belle bagged from where the shooter sat when they took aim, produced a hair. Same DNA as on Tim's luggage tag. Now they need to verify it's from her ex. Elon didn't answer when they tried to call her just now."

"Because I put her on a damn plane to Seattle thirty minutes ago." Rane checked his watch. "If I can make it to Three Falls in time, I can catch a flight going through Idaho."

Kyle stepped forward. "What can I do?"

"Tell Chayton to keep trying her cell. And alert Sheriff Riley she's on a plane to Seattle. Maybe he can have her paged at the airport," Rane said. "We've got to warn her there's proof that the murderous bastard's hunting her."

Brandon's smiling face in the crowd welcomed Elon as she stepped off the escalator at Sea-Tac. She pulled him into a hug. "How'd opening night go for Jeremy?"

"He did great maneuvering on stage when the lighting tech got sick at the end of the play. They're doing another rehearsal, and I need to head back to be an understudy technician. We got you a seat in the front row for tonight."

A woman ahead of them rolled a cart holding two dog

carriers. The overhead announcement crackled, and the dogs barked furiously.

Had they said Hardy? "Sounds perfect," she yelled over the din, and directed him to the car rental counter where an attendant handed her paperwork and keys in record time.

"Oh, Dr. Deceitful and Scrawny showed at last night's performance. He caught me on the way out and mentioned he found an album holding your parents' wedding photos at the back of a closet. He'll leave it outside the basement door. Probably too cheap to mail it."

Elon narrowed her eyes. "He knows I cherished those photos." She looked up to a sky filled with gray clouds. "No, he's hoping the rain ruins them, which would hurt me further." She squeezed Brandon's arm. "I'll drop you at the theater, stop at the house, and head back your way. I can beat the rain."

"Be careful. If his car's there, no photos are worth it."

Someday, Brandon might feel differently. "I'll run in and run out."

"Good. If we wrestle Jeremy away after practice, we could grab pizza." He tossed her overnight bag in the back seat and climbed into the silver car.

Brandon filled her in on classes en route to campus. Her body relaxed. The sons who'd struggled through grade school now used hard-won skills to succeed in a tougher environment at the UW.

"The stage door on the left of the building's unlocked. When you return, slip in there and head upstairs to the control room."

"Brilliant plan. Go learn to brighten the stage." She kissed his cheek and watched as he entered the building. He turned and waved, wearing a glorious, successful smile.

Satisfaction and relief filled her. She headed the car to the old house. SUVs and noisy buses crowded the highway, fighting for pole position. The old neighborhood looked less familiar and empty of activity. No cars, no one walking, no sign of her old life.

A *For Sale* sign hung on a freshly painted house on the corner. Once she'd considered these close neighbors to be her friends. Yet only one contacted her after word of the divorce hit the grapevine. Thank goodness Tim's girlfriend was dumb enough to confide in her. She'd text Doreen later about meeting for lunch tomorrow.

Nothing looked friendly anymore at Tim's house. No potted plants, no WELCOME mat, or bench by the front door. She rang the bell and stepped back, looking through sheer curtains into the formal living room.

No lights and no sounds. Her shoulders relaxed; she'd not have to deal with unwanted observers. The unkempt, fenced back yard bore no resemblance to what she'd left.

Leaves covered the path and drooping brown stems dotted the once-manicured beds. A garden hose looped across the lawn, no doubt creating dents in the grass as it wound its way to the sprinkler.

She avoided the hose and stopped beside the stairs leading to the basement. No album in sight. A yellow chrysanthemum rose out of the ground—planted in the exact spot where the pink foxglove bloomed for years. Her breath came in gasps.

"Figured out the problem tea component?" Tim's whispering voice chided.

She turned and clenched her fists. A ski mask covered his face. In his gloved hands he lifted Jeremy's old baseball bat, resting it on his shoulder, ready to swing.

Her eyes darted to the gate. She'd never get past him.

"Brandon and Jeremy know I'm here."

"Won't matter. There have been burglaries nearby. One more added to the list. No one's around to help you this time. And my doorbell camera has a wide angle. You haven't made this easy." Rage narrowed the eyes staring through the holes in the mask. He walked toward her, his arms tensed, elbows raised.

She glanced at the hose. One of his feet should be inside a loop after his next step. She waited until his foot entered the circle of hose, dropped her purse, and squatted.

"Still a klutz," he taunted.

She grabbed the end and yanked. The loop circled his ankles. "Burglar! Help!" she yelled. Another tug sent him tumbling to the ground.

She jumped up and dashed by him, her heart hammering in her chest.

Tim threw out the baseball bat and tripped her.

Twenty years of fury rose in her chest. She scrambled to her knees and grabbed the wide end of the bat, wrestling it from his hand while he loosened the hose at his ankles.

Shock widened his eyes as she whacked his shoulder. "You promised," she landed another swing to his ribs, "my dad that you'd take care of me. I heard your filthy lies over and over."

Tim lunged at her and knocked her onto her back, pinning her arms on either side of her body. His breath heated her neck. "Yeah, too bad my foot hit the drain plug in their boat."

She struggled to free her wrists, then swung her hips and knee.

His grip tightened.

"You're a monster!"

"Nope, a strategist. Easiest way to gain control of their building. Now it's game over." He put his hands at her throat, crushing her windpipe.

CHAPTER 16

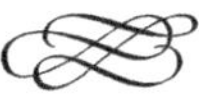

Rane swung his rental car into the driveway of the brick rambler. Nice-sized yard, nice neighborhood, not so nice occupant. A car identical to his sat parked in the drive.

Its hood felt warm to his touch. He might be in time to keep Elon from doing something she'd regret. Thumping noises came from the back yard. He spotted the sidewalk beside the garage and jogged through a gate.

Elon lay sprawled on the ground, being choked by a guy dressed in black. One punch from him sent the thug face first into a nearby shrub. "You gutless excuse of a man!" Rane grabbed him by the collar, pushed him to the ground, and used his belt to secure the man's hands behind his back.

Elon clutched her throat, "It's Tim," she rasped.

"Tried to warn you." Rane pulled Elon to his side. "They found one of his hairs on the hill at my ranch. Everyone's left messages on your cell."

"I must've left it on airplane mode in my excitement to see the boys."

"I'll nail you both for assault." Tim staggered and rose to his feet. "The bitch struck me twice."

Sirens cut the air, their blare rising by the second.

Elon rubbed her throat. "I'll plead self-defense for kicking your conniving, cold-blooded ass. And I'll have bruises and a witness."

A woman in a bathrobe stepped around the gate from the front yard. She waved a golf club in her hand. "Thought I might need this after hearing Tim's threats," she said in a loud whisper. "Stayed home today fighting laryngitis. Heard the commotion when I opened my window for some fresh air. I called the police and headed over in time to see your handsome man save your life."

"Doreen! You are a saint. I appreciate our friendship and your help." Elon said and brushed her fingers along Rane's jaw. "Tim nearly choked me to death. Thank you for being my hero, Rane."

"Just returning the favor. It took everything in me not to beat the creep to a pulp." He tenderly stroked the skin on her sore neck, then brushed his lips onto hers. "I love you, Elon. And I'll do anything to protect you and your boys."

A sensation of being cherished overwhelmed her. She melted into him, letting her body fully relax for the first time in months. "And I love you, Rane. Tonight, Tim will be in jail while we enjoy Jeremy's play. Tomorrow, we go home."

Three days later, Elon heard someone stomping snow off their feet at the front porch of her Montana home, the place where she belonged.

She glanced out the kitchen window, opened the door, and smiled at Corrin.

"The charges brought against Tim allowed me to expedite your divorce. I wanted to tell you in person." She shrugged off her down coat.

"I'm certainly relieved he's behind bars." Elon hung her coat and eased into a dining room chair. "Scares me to think of Tim bullying my kids if he'd managed to kill me."

Corrin took the seat opposite and slid papers from her briefcase. "Tim's lawyer overnighted these to me."

"I'm going to see if the hospital is agreeable to keeping part of Mom and Dad's building intact while designing a medical facility to serve the neighborhood. My parents believed in community." Elon signed in each of the spaces noted by Corrin's sticky notes. "I expect a thorough accounting of your time and an invoice showing Seattle rates."

"I've tracked my time. My sister's facing high medical bills, so I appreciate your support as a paying customer."

"I needed the virtual butt kicks from those stiletto heels you wore so well."

Corrin patted her snow boots. "I once told Miranda we're two Phoenix birds, rising from ashes. You've done the same, and I value your friendship. The three of us share more than a Seattle bond. Thugs don't turn us to pansies, they forge us to sharpened steel."

"Perfect analogy." Elon circled her pen in a stabbing motion. "Can you stay for tea?"

"Not today. Roy needs me back at ecology-central to research some legal findings. We're close to exposing an ugly group of developers. I'll take a rain check, or maybe snow or sleet check."

"So, am I divorced as of now?" Elon rotated the ring from Rane.

"You've passed the waiting period. I'll overnight these final documents to a friend of mine at my old office and they'll be filed in two days, three tops."

Elon held her chin in her hand, her elbow propped on the edge of the table. "I'm so, so ready to marry

Rane. I thought my shelf life for finding love had expired."

"Love has no 'Best Used by Date.' Kyle and I figured that out." Corrin grinned and snatched her coat off the hook. "I'll call you as soon as the ink dries on the filing, I promise." She squeezed Elon's hand. "You can't begin to imagine the vigilante attitude of folks in town after learning Tim shot at you here, then planned to murder you in Seattle. When this town falls for someone, they fall hard."

Elon rose from her chair. "I've heard those sentiments about you and Miranda. I'm going to use my new income to build a bakery. My plans include a teaching area in the back for teenagers. I'm hoping I'll get students from every part of the county."

"Great idea." She formed her fingers into a heart shape against her chest. "I'll provide free services on your project. I know the townsfolk will help. See you soon."

"Bye." Elon shut the door and stepped in front of the fireplace, where the glow from reddish embers added to the warmth thawing the final tinges of fear in her chest. She'd become a free woman.

From the machine shop, Rane caught a glimpse of the departing silver Firebird, piloted by the legal eagle he felt indebted to for his future happiness. He bounded to the house, sending splinters of thin ice under each excited step.

As he reached the porch, the front door opened wide. Elon ran into his arms. "Good news!"

Joy burst free in his chest. "Are you . . .?"

Round blue eyes met his, her face radiating delight. "By Thursday." She tugged him inside and shut the door.

Rane clasped her hands in his. "Will you marry me on Friday?"

"You know I will, Rane Calderon. Friday we'll start our life together as a married couple." She leaned in and nuzzled her lips against his, their sweetness promising the wait was well worth the torture.

A knock banged on the front door. "Guess we've got more company," Rane grumbled. "You won't have to cook for a month with all the casseroles in the freezer brought here after the town heard about Tim's last attack."

"Suits me. I've got other hobbies I want to start as a married woman." Elon raised a brow in a seductive manner.

"Be still my heart." He patted his chest and opened the door, eyeing a familiar young man about the same age as her sons. "Elon, please meet Grit's older son, Ray."

"On behalf of our family, I'm apologizing for what my father and my misinformed kid brother did to you." He handed her a vase holding carnations and smiled with kind eyes, unlike his father's.

Elon lifted a petal and smiled back. "I appreciate the flowers and your visit. I only judge a person by their actions, not by association."

"My dad wasn't always crazy ornery. He's a born hunter. Heck, he provided a lot of meat for many townsfolk who couldn't afford it in tough times. Five years ago, he took a bad fall out of his deer blind. He got brain scans and the like, but mom said his personality changed. They finally divorced."

"I'm sorry. Must've been hard on your family."

"Mom went back to school to become a teacher. My brother's getting counseling. I work for Grant Morley, in his wood shop."

Rane rubbed his chin. "Yup. The last time I visited there, you were building a swing set. We may need one of those and a cradle someday. I'll hire you."

"My pleasure, Mr. Calderon. Thank you for understanding." He shook both their hands and headed out the front door.

"What a sad story. He seems like such a nice young man. The world can be a strange place sometimes." Elon centered the vase on the well-used kitchen table. "If us having children doesn't work out, will you be very disappointed?"

"Never. If we're together, my world's perfect." Rane caressed her cheek. "I love you, Elon, and if the cradle is for grandchildren, I'll have him build us matching rockers for when we've grown old together."

E lon leaned toward Harry at the kitchen table. In the past week, they'd begun discussing secret plans for a real bakery, having heard Rane mention the possibility of a separate structure several times after she'd become his co-owner of the adjoining property. "Rane told me you're a natural at carving and drawing building plans. How about creating a set for a bakery and an addition on the house for you and Mary?"

Harry's coffee mug paused in midair, then he returned it to the kitchen table. "My mom, Bia, provided my creative genes and the property. Didn't inherit any money, though."

"I've come into my inheritance recently. Enough to cover the cost, if we're frugal."

"Well then, I'd be honored," Harry said. "Before I took over this ranch after dad died, I dreamed of using my skills to become an architect. Mary, Fred, and I need to consider our future mobility. How about we expand the bunk house into a larger rambler?"

"You don't want to live here?"

"Nope. You, Rane and the boys belong in the main house.

I'll draft initial blueprints and head to the planning department to research permits. Rane's a lucky man to have found you." He patted his chest. "Sorry it took my old ticker to drill home the realization that I got another chance to have a lovely and resourceful daughter in the house."

"You can't imagine what that means to me." Elon fought a tear and held out her hand. "By the way, your voice reminds me of my dad."

Gratitude warmed his dark eyes as he grasped her hand and squeezed. "He'd be mighty proud of you, just as we are to have you join our family. We'd never have come together again if it weren't for your efforts."

"After Rane shared his story, I understood why he buried the pain. Being part of a family is a cherished gift, Harry."

She looked at her baking tools wrapped in the handmade tan satchel and remembered her mom's nimble fingers making each stitch. A strong sense of her parents filled the room. "I want the building supplies to be my wedding present to Rane." Her fingers skimmed the worn edge of the scarred Formica table. "I'll need you to include an addition for classes on the back of the bakery. Several men who work here are worried about their kids getting job skills at the Blackfeet school. I can teach basic cooking and baking techniques."

"Bia was a strong woman and talented baker. She'd approve your idea to support the Niitsitapi, which means 'the real people.' My plans and labor can be our gift to you and Rane. This will delight Mary. Might've been a city girl when I swept her off her feet, but she fell in love with the mountainous countryside. Close to your story, I suspect."

Elon groaned. "Not hardly. Rane and I got off to a rocky start. He'd have sent me back to Seattle the first day if I hadn't helped Tomo. I guess I owe the friendly bull a bushel of apples."

"Rane helped a lot of families in this area. Tough to farm using broken equipment. Mary can organize a good old-fashioned barn raising. A few extra hands and a bit of prefab materials will enable us to frame in the bakery and house in a couple days." He rubbed his palms together. "I can't wait to tell Mary we won't be intruders for long."

"You'll never intrude in the family ranch. You go tell Mary."

"Thank you." Harry smiled straight at her and strode out the front door. In the driveway, he caught Mary mid-stride, then lifted her a few inches off her feet, and twirled her in a half circle, his face becoming a handsome, older version of Rane's. They headed to the bunkhouse holding hands.

Elon grinned into her coffee as she put the mug to her lips and sipped. Large flakes began to drift from the winter sky again. Even so, hearing Rane enter the house brought thoughts of sunshine, green shoots in the pasture, and new beginnings.

"Join me on the porch for a moment, please?" he asked. "Certainly."

He helped her into her coat and clasped her hand, leading her out the front door. His arm swept a wide arc across his land and toward the highway. "Your partnership owning the land protecting my Blackfeet heritage means more to me than I can express. If I didn't thank you properly before, I'd like to now."

Gently cradling her cheek, he lowered his mouth to hers, his kisses sending tiny, thrumming bolts of energy throughout her body. He folded her into his strong arms, protectively, lovingly. She pressed into his chest, wrapping her arms around his back, absorbing warmth and certainty. When he moved his lips to her cheeks, she fingered strands of his thick, black hair. "Whatever lays ahead, we'll support one another," she said, then met his loving russet eyes.

"Maybe someday we could build a little bakery on our property next door?" She held her breath.

"I like that idea. As long as you name the bull-shaped Danish creations after Tomo and not me."

"I'd never think of such a thing," she teased. "And speaking of creating something, I got good news from Kyle. Lord willing, we can have a baby."

Rane's jaw dropped, then he gave her the biggest smile she'd seen yet. "Really? Wow." He took her hands between his. "We've got the world at our feet," he promised in the deep, sexy voice she'd never tire of.

"You introduced me to that world, Rane Calderon." Fresh, crisp air surrounded them. A ray of sun bounced off a crevice on their side of Mt. Hanlen. Her journey of 747 miles had brought her to a welcoming family, and best of all, to Rane's honest love.

AFTERWORD

I hope you enjoyed Book 3, Elon and Rane's story, and that you'll take a moment to post a quick review on Amazon or Goodreads. If you'd like to read about Elon and Rane's wedding in the epilogue to *The Targeted Pawn*, please contact me at www.sallybrandle.com.

Happy trails,

Sally

For an exciting, sweet romance adventure from WWII, Sally wrote an enhanced memoir and provided an excerpt on the following pages:

Sapphire Promise.

Stroll back to 1930's Colonial Indonesian splendor where a teen rides her horse with her pet monkey. Delight in the blush of first love. Pull for the survival of a mom and daughter in the worst Japanese internment camp in the Pacific.

SAPPHIRE PROMISE EXCERPT

Chapter 1

APRIL 1939

- Hitler's Panzer tanks invade Czechoslovakia.
- Italy and Germany finalize a military alliance.
- Japanese Emperor Hirohito amasses a powerful Navy and Air Force. He uses poison gas against China.

BATAVIA, JAVA

When would Pappie get home to break up her quarantine exile with stories from the barn about her mare and her monkey? Annika Wolter paced another circuit between the Victrola record player that sat on her dresser and the armoire across the room. Two more days of seclusion upstairs and she'd be on horseback again instead of merely imagining rides on the hibiscus-filled trails. Thank the Lord her father's daily report through the closed bedroom door brightened the endless hours of reading and practicing her ballet performance for Mamma's fiftieth birthday. What if she wasn't over the mumps by her mother's party, like the doctor had promised?

Annika pressed her finger under her right ear and found the receding, yet tender, swollen gland. "Little kleuters needing highchairs get mumps, not young ladies of fifteen and a half," she mumbled to herself, and leaned onto the windowsill. Apricot-scents from oleander flowers drifted into her second-floor bedroom from the hedge below, planted along the circular driveway which led to Mansion Annika. She bit her lip. A grand house named in your honor mattered little when you were stuck in one of the seven bedrooms.

At any moment, Pappie and the chauffeur should be rounding the bend of the road that led onto Boxlaan. She looked past the rows of flowers which lined their driveway. Wait. Who was that crossing their grass?

A stranger approached from the far corner of the acre of lawn. Shades of copper shone in his dark brown hair.

She stood on tip toes and leaned close to the glass in the upper part of the window. His stride proclaimed athlete, not the stiff walk of an old zakenman who might be headed here to visit Pappie on business.

He marched into full view, dressed in the white Dutch uniform of an officer. The hip-length coat fitted perfectly across his broad shoulders. Freshly pressed trousers covered his long legs, and a small leather suitcase swung with each stride.

"Hmm." Annika tapped her cheek. Was this tall, mysterious guest a new boarder? If a herd of young soldiers preceded war, maybe war wouldn't be as horrible as Mamma and Pappie whispered. And no war had better start before she finished high school and completed nursing training, and certainly not before she had her first boyfriend. She moved to the side, lest the visitor catch her staring, and tucked her sleeveless blouse inside the waistband of her wide-legged trousers.

He continued toward their front door and for a moment tilted his head to study the lone wrought iron balcony which jutted out from the bedroom to Annika's right. Her pulse thrummed. No man should be so dashingly handsome as to compete with Errol Flynn. He swung his head to take in the tennis courts on the property next door, then looked over his shoulder at the cricket fields across the street, as if trying to determine a connection to the view from the balcony. The handsome stranger turned back toward Annika and rubbed his chin. His curiosity upped her admiration even further. "I'm going to marry him," she whispered.

At the veranda overhang, he disappeared. She groaned. His footsteps sounded on the flight of stairs.

Verdorie! Damn, she hated this blasted room! Annika thumped her hand against her dresser. The turntable shook on the Victrola. "My song for Saturday's performance!" she cried, and examined the brittle, 78 rpm shellac record. Whew, no scratched grooves. Her fingers relaxed and she slid the twelve-inch disc into its paper sleeve.

The mysterious stranger's suitcase suggested an overnight stay. Mamma hadn't mentioned him when she'd deposited today's lunch outside her door. She batted aside the billowing white mosquito netting which surrounded her bed, then opened her door, and leaned into the hallway. Two more days of exile would kill her! He might be gone by then!

In the distance, protective barks grew louder from Foxy, the family's wire fox terrier. If her furry little friend could talk, he'd quiz the stranger for details. A firm rap sounded from the wooden front door on the main level.

How unfair that her dog got to meet their visitor days before she would. Annika left the door open but retreated into the bedroom. Her future husband's hair shone like the russet brown Djati wood of her furniture.

In her room, a pink scarf fluttered, one filmy end tucked under the thin ribbon of spiraling teak wood that decorated the top of the mirror on her vanity. Annika caught sight of her reflection. Mamma said she had a heart-shaped face, and fashion magazines noted that as a plus. She laid her fingers alongside her chin. What demeanor would impress the dashing officer? Solemn and brooding, à la Greta Garbo? She posed. Or flirty like Janet Gaynor, her favorite American Hollywood star? She lifted one eyebrow and widened her hazel eyes, turned sideways, and looked over her shoulder into the mirror.

Posing was a useless waste of energy. She blew a wisp of light brown, wavy hair from her forehead. He'd never consider her. She was ugly. That's what Pappie's friend, Herman, had told her on his visits when she was a little girl. "Annika," he'd say in his soothing tone, "You're so smart. You're from such a good family. Tsk, tsk. Too bad you're so ugly." Many times, she'd heard him repeat that horrible observation.

Another knock sounded from below. Where were Luther and Ahmad, their servants who ushered guests into their home?

Mamma called out, "I'll greet our new lodger." Her pumps clicked on the white marble floor as she approached the entry from the living room. The heavy door creaked open.

Lodger. How exciting. Not a curmudgeon like the other paid boarders they sometimes hosted for extra money. Did she dare step out to peek? Her bare feet made no noise as she crept out of her bedroom and across the polished stone hallway. A few feet back from the row of carved staircase balusters, she crouched with her fingertips on the floor for balance. If she tipped her head, she could look between the wooden spindles to see the tall stranger who stood at attention in the open doorway. He towered above Annika's barely five-foot tall Mamma. When he smiled, his angular face lost any formality, making him impossibly handsome. Annika's breath hitched in her throat.

"Thank you for accommodating me on short notice, Mevrouw Wolter." The rich, deep timbre of his voice stirred unfamiliar feelings in Annika. He defined her vision of a Hollywood leading-man. A sigh escaped, piercing the quiet of the empty hall.

The stranger bent and stroked Foxy's head. "I hope a two-week stay isn't an inconvenience." His gaze flicked toward Annika's perch.

She jerked backward, tipped onto her heels, and thrust her hands to the floor to keep her butt from smacking the marble. That was close. Too close. Rising slowly, keeping her back to the wall, she slipped inside her bedroom. Warmth rose in her cheeks. Had he seen her? She continued to eavesdrop, her hand gripping the door frame.

"Foxy, you furry pest. Go visit Annika." Mamma ordered. "Sorry, he's really no bother."

"The pup's an unexpected bonus," his friendly voice assured her mother.

"Good. We're happy to accommodate you, Lieutenant Van Hoven," Mamma said. "I understood from Marta's phone call that the steamship carrying her relatives from Holland arrived early, putting you out of a guest room."

Annika blew out her breath. Close call. Marta's twin daughters were her friends, both of them cute, and both of them currently without a boyfriend.

"That's correct," the lieutenant replied. "I appreciate

staying next door to family friends. My quarters on base aren't quite ready. War preparations are slow and steady."

"So we've heard," Mamma agreed. "We feel fortunate to have Marta and her family as close neighbors. Please come inside. Tea is served at four and dinner at seven. In the meantime, I set out a pitcher of fresh lemonade on the shady veranda. I'll ask Emily to point out your room and give you a house tour."

Not Emily! Annika pushed her forehead into the wall. Her lips puckered as if she'd bitten into one of the blasted lemons. Mamma often voiced a saying: "Bitter in de mond maakt het hart gezond," *Bitter in the mouth makes the heart healthy*. Hers ached in pain. She clasped her hands in prayer and whispered, "Please don't let him meet Emily. Please let her be out on an errand." Her older cousin had glossy brown hair, alabaster skin, and elegant manners.

The distinctive clicks of doggy toenails sounded on the marble stairs. Foxy nosed open Annika's door. He'd been the runt of the litter and weighed under fifteen pounds, but his curiosity and energy were boundless.

Annika knelt and stroked down her dog's white neck, black shoulder, and tan back. Her own muscled forearms were brown as a bridle from hours spent riding her horse, Maggy. She hadn't paled a fraction in the five days since she'd come down with mumps, even though she had been sealed off to prevent the horrible virus she'd caught at school from infecting her family and servants. Foxy nudged her and she buried her head in his rough, wiry fur. The scent of freshly mown grass tugged at her restless soul. She should've been out on their lawn to meet their guest. She slumped against her dresser and pulled Foxy onto her lap.

"Emily," Mamma called from downstairs.

Demure footsteps pattered on the hallway floor outside

Annika's room. Her worst nightmare continued. She listened intently.

"Yes, ma'am?" Sweet, refined Emily replied from the top of the stairs.

"Please meet Lieutenant Van Hoven. He's the new boarder I mentioned. I'd appreciate you showing him around."

Mamma spoke often of finding a suitor for Emily, and the young lieutenant fit the bill. Annika clutched her blouse at heart level. How could any man not fall for nineteen-year-old Emily, a not-so-poor orphan, and the epitome of a fashionable young lady? "Verdorie," she hissed again, and set Foxy on the floor.

Why did she have the cousin who looked every bit as much like a movie star as he did? Annika rose and looked out the window. Tears wet her eyes. Why couldn't Emily have stayed in Holland with her uncle after her parents died a few years ago? Why had she decided, out of all her Dutch relatives, to join their family in Batavia? And why, for heaven sakes, had Emily been available today as tour guide for the handsome lieutenant? Annika Wolter's handsome lieutenant!

Why? Because life wasn't fair.

Annika tapped her foot on the floor. Where was her father? Shouldn't Pappie be the one showing the new boarder around and learning the important facts about him?

"Ladies. Please, call me Phillip," his smooth voice drifted to Annika, the deep tone sending longing into her chest, soothing her frustration.

Emily murmured something, then the clipped military footsteps faded as the pair must've entered the long hallway below, flanked at the far end by the two bedrooms reserved for boarders. They'd be halfway to the altar by the time Annika got released from her prison.

She crossed her arms over her chest. Movement caught her eye above a framed picture on the far wall. She dashed across the room and glimpsed the disappearing tip of a house gecko's tail. "If you're smart, you'll let me catch you," she advised the tiny intruder as she unhooked the watercolor painting of her horse. Cupping her hand, she gauged the spotted gecko's path and trapped it against the wall. "Gotcha." She gently carried it to the window, pushed her hand outside, and opened her fingers. The gecko stayed in her palm. She ran her finger over the gray body, spotted in black and white. "No hurry to leave? At least you have a choice." In an effortless leap, the gecko landed on the outside wall to her left. "The servants aren't as forgiving," she warned it before she pulled her arm in and drummed her fingers on the windowsill. Every other creature but Annika was headed somewhere today.

The gecko climbed up white stucco, past the small window of the storage room to her left, and then headed toward the red tile roof. Annika looked to the right. Only on the roof would the gecko have a better view than from her mother's private balcony. If the lieutenant asked, would Emily tell him how that balcony had been purposely positioned for Mamma to watch Pappie play tennis next door or cricket at The English Club fields on the other side of Boxlaan? Or that her parents had ordered the workers to chisel "Annika" into the cement floor of the balcony when they'd built here the year after her birth? That should be shared, too.

Pappie needed to get home to give out those details. She glanced at the English Sports Club on the corner a half block away. Overlooking the outdoor pool in the rear, a handful of businessmen in beige-colored suits sat at wicker patio tables. She frowned. If Pappie had stopped there first for his afternoon glass of whiskey, she wouldn't spot him without field glasses.

On the street outside the pool's fence, a horse pulled a two-wheeled buggy, or sado. Sunshine glinted off its metal roof. One passenger faced backward in the seat at the rear. The driver up front steered alongside a row of trees which kept the hot sun off the street vendors. Their tables would be loaded with fresh picked cucumbers, papaya, mango, and pineapple. Annika licked her lips and imagined the taste of ripe, sweet pineapple dipped in shaved coconut.

The sado stopped near the club's covered entry. A uniformed Indonesian doorman in a white turban assisted a stoop-shouldered man out of the rig. He shuffled inside and would probably spend the next few hours enjoying tea and pound cake while talking to his cronies in a cool corner and waiting for the dining room to open at seven. She'd often seen elderly men seated in rocking chairs on the veranda after she'd done laps in the club's swimming pool. Each time she'd passed them in the last few months they'd been arguing in Dutch about the Nazis.

Annika rubbed her temple. Could Hitler's plans of domination really stretch to peaceful Batavia, her home in the Dutch East Indies? No. Her fists clenched. She looked toward the horizon. Ninety miles to the west the peaceful Indian Ocean rippled onto their island's white sandy beaches, with Europe and Hitler thousands of miles beyond. Surely none of his tanks or planes could travel that far. She squinted. Right now, something was flying her way. Not a soaring falcon native to Java, but two biplanes that dipped and dodged one another high up in the blue sky. They circled and vanished, no doubt headed back to the military base before sunset at five-thirty. How did a soldier fill the twelve hours of daylight they received on Java year-round? Did they rise with the sun every morning between five and six, then get off duty at sunset between the same hours in the evening? She should ask Rudy, her oldest brother.

At this very moment, Rudy could be practicing in one of those biplanes. Annika pretended to be him by moving an imaginary center stick, adjusting goggles, and checking the gauges, exactly as Pappie and his friend had shown her when they'd taken her flying in a Piper Cub. Even by handling the controls for a few minutes, she'd felt the strange freedom Rudy often described he felt in a Koolhoven FK 51 aircraft, which the Royal Dutch Military had brought to Java for pilot training. If Rudy succeeded in joining the RAF out of England, where would he be sent to fight?

Her forearms blossomed with goosebumps. News clips at Batavia's movie theater warned of Hitler's threats. She closed her eyes and said a prayer for the German monster's swift defeat. Did she have the courage to confront an enemy, given the chance? She stared out the window again. Past the English Club's cricket fields sat The Batavia Civil Hospital for the poor. Since she'd been old enough to know what went on inside, she'd wanted to help sick people. That took plenty of courage, and medical knowledge helped in wartime.

In a metal case on her dresser sat the stethoscope Pappie had presented to her on her twelfth birthday. He'd known precisely what her dreams were, as always. Years of practice on tolerant pets and relatives had honed her skill in locating a heartbeat. Now she needed to practice patience. She wouldn't childishly pester any of the family with questions about Phillip. Instead, she'd show ladylike restraint. She straightened her spine and formed the slight suggestion of a reserved but approachable smile in the manner Oma Elodie had drummed into her.

What was she thinking? Pursuing someone so handsome was surely a lost cause. Annika dropped her chin to her chest. The boxy, stiff fronts of her pink ballet shoes caught her eye. She snatched them from beside her armoire, shoved in her feet, and tied the ribbons. The doctor had guaranteed that by Mamma's birthday celebration on Saturday night, her glands would be normal, and she wouldn't be contagious.

Only forty-eight hours remained for her to perfect the final pirouette of her Chopin piece and impress Phillip with her one talent. As she moved her body to balance en pointe, more than her toes ached.

ABOUT THE AUTHOR

Sally Brandle:

Sally Brandle is an award winning author of edgy, sweetly intimate love stories, providing a heartwarming, page-turning escape. Sally left a career as an industrial baking instructor to bring to life stories motivating readers to trust their instincts. Her rescue pets are her companions during long spells of writing. Afternoon thought sessions are spent riding on the wind with her thirty-four-year-old Quarter Horse.

Sign up for her newsletter at **www.sallybrandle.com**